THE SU
MIF

BY
CAROLINE ANDERSON

DR DI ANGELO'S BABY BOMBSHELL

BY
JANICE LYNN

ONE NIGHT, ONE BABY

Two bachelor doctors are in for a big surprise…

With their successful careers
and their hot-shot bachelor lifestyles, these doctors
have no idea what they're missing out on—
until two beautiful women rock their worlds
with a shock announcement!

These two men will need to risk everything
to prove they're fully committed to
becoming doting dads…and perfect husbands!

THE SURGEON'S MIRACLE
by Caroline Anderson

and

DR DI ANGELO'S BABY BOMBSHELL
by Janice Lynn

Bachelor Baby Surprise!

THE SURGEON'S MIRACLE

BY

CAROLINE ANDERSON

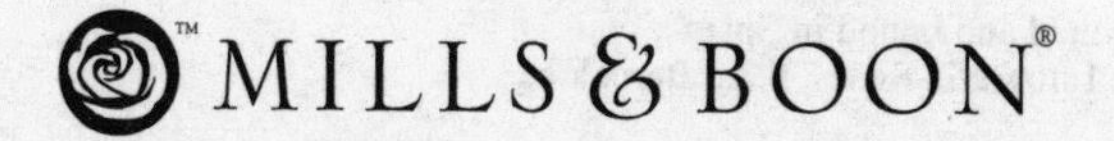

First published in Great Britain 2010
Harlequin Mills & Boon Limited,
Eton House, 18-24 Paradise Road, Richmond, Surrey TW9 1SR

ISBN: 978 0 263 87890 5

Harlequin Mills & Boon policy is to use papers that are natural, renewable and recyclable products and made from wood grown in sustainable forests. The logging and manufacturing process conform to the legal environmental regulations of the country of origin.

Printed and bound in Spain
by Litografia Rosés, S.A., Barcelona

Caroline Anderson has the mind of a butterfly. She's been a nurse, a secretary, a teacher, run her own soft-furnishing business, and now she's settled on writing. She says, 'I was looking for that elusive something. I finally realised it was variety, and now I have it in abundance. Every book brings new horizons and new friends, and in between books I have learned to be a juggler. My teacher husband John and I have two beautiful and talented daughters, Sarah and Hannah, umpteen pets, and several acres of Suffolk that nature tries to reclaim every time we turn our backs!' Caroline also writes for the Mills & Boon® Romance series.

Recent titles by the same author:

Mills & Boon® Medical™ Romance
THE REBEL OF PENHALLY BAY*
THE VALTIERI MARRIAGE DEAL†

Mills & Boon® Romance
THEIR CHRISTMAS FAMILY MIRACLE
TWO LITTLE MIRACLES

**Brides of Penhally Bay* mini-series
†*Billionaire Doctors*

Caroline Anderson has the [illegible] in Suffolk. She's [illegible]
[illegible]
[illegible]
She says, 'I [illegible]
[illegible]
[illegible]
[illegible]
[illegible]
[illegible]
[illegible]
[illegible]
[illegible]
[illegible]

Recent titles by the same author:

Mills & Boon® Medical™ Romance
THE [illegible]
[illegible]

Mills & Boon® Romance
THEIR CHRISTMAS [illegible]
TWO LITTLE MIRACLES

[illegible]

CHAPTER ONE

'GOT a minute, Libby?'

'Sure—' She looked up and flashed him a harassed smile, but it faded as soon as she caught sight of him. 'Wow, you look rough. I heard you were busy—sounds like a grim night.'

He grunted. If he looked half as rough as he felt, he must look like hell, because grim wasn't the word. 'It was pretty dire. There were three of us in there—someone removing a blood clot from his brain while I stabilised his fractures and someone else sorted out his spleen. It was pretty touch and go for a while,' he agreed. 'We were in Theatre for hours. The kid's only seven—it was a hit and run.'

Libby winced sympathetically. 'Poor little mite. How could anybody do that?'

'Search me. I have no idea.'

'How's he doing?'

He lifted his shoulders—in truth, there wasn't much he could add. 'He's stable—sort of.' That was enough. The bare bones—all he had the energy to explain.

Libby nodded, then bit her lip. 'Can you give me a sec, Andrew? I won't be long, I just need to finish this off.'

'That's fine, you carry on, I'm not in a hurry,' he murmured.

He wasn't. He'd given little Jacob the full focus of his energy and concentration, and it was time to step back and centre himself again. The neuro had got the clot out, the GS had glued the liver and removed the spleen and he'd restored the circulation to his feet and stabilised his legs and pelvis with external fixators, and somehow Jacob had turned the corner and was now in the paediatric intensive care unit, heavily sedated and hopefully on the road to recovery.

He'd just checked on the little boy again, and he was improving slightly, and although it was far too soon to be overconfident, for now, at least, Andrew could relax.

Goodness knows, he needed to. He was exhausted, in sore need of a break, and there was nothing more he could do anyway, for now, except watch Libby, and that was fine. He was more than happy to lounge against the doorjamb and watch the pretty young ward sister finish her task while his mind free-wheeled.

Ideally he'd be at home in bed after a night like that, but life wasn't ideal, and although it was only seven-thirty he'd already spent half an hour with Jacob's parents this morning, to fill them in on his part in the proceedings—and in thirty-six hours, after another full day at work, he'd have to go home and face the weekend from hell—another excuse for his mother to trot out a whole load of single girls in the vain hope that he'd find one to settle down with and secure the future of the family line.

It didn't make any difference that his brother's wife was pregnant. If anything it made it worse, because it just made his single status all the more obvious—and his mother, ever the fixer, wanted him to be as happy as Will. So the girls would all be there, and he'd have to deal with them all, from his hopelessly infatuated cousin Charlotte to the predatory gold-diggers, via the perfectly nice girls that he just wasn't interested in, and watching it all unfold would be his beloved mother with that hopeful look on her face.

Oh, hell. He was too tired for this, sick of warding them off, sick of making excuses to his mother, and the last thing—absolutely the *last* thing—he needed was this party. Correction—parties. Two of them.

With a muffled groan, he shifted his shoulders against the doorframe and watched Libby thoughtfully as she entered notes onto the computer at her desk. Nice girl, he thought. Really nice girl. If things were different, he might be tempted, but they weren't. More's the pity, because she really was lovely in every way.

Her lip was caught between even, perfect white teeth, her long lashes dark crescents against her creamy cheeks as she looked down at the keyboard. A lock of rich brown hair slid down out of her ponytail and she tucked it absently behind her ear. It looked soft, glossy, as if she'd just washed it this morning—in which case it would smell of apples. It always smelled of apples when she'd washed it…

How had he registered that? Goodness knows. Not deliberately, any more than he'd deliberately noticed the freckles scattered over her nose, or the curve of her bottom as she bent over a child, or the fact that even the hideously unflattering tunic couldn't disguise her perfectly proportioned breasts.

He wondered what she was doing this weekend. Something normal, he'd bet. The washing, or going to the cinema with friends. Curling up with a good book on the sofa next to her boyfriend.

He frowned. Scrub that last image. Although he'd never heard her talk about a boyfriend, he thought, his mind ticking over. And if all she *was* going to be doing was pottering about at home—

'Doing anything exciting this weekend?' he found himself saying before he could stop himself, and then held his breath for her reply.

Libby looked up from the notes she was finishing off and leant back in her chair, finally allowing herself the luxury of looking at him again. He looked exhausted—exhausted and rumpled and sexy, even more so than usual, so she took her time, enjoying the view.

'Now, then, let me think,' she said with a teasing smile. 'Flying to Paris, dinner in a fabulous restaurant, then going to the top of the Eiffel Tower to see the lights, strolling along the Seine by moonlight—or then again, maybe I'll just stay at home and tackle my laundry basket before it suffers a fatal rupture, and then get the duster out of retirement.'

He chuckled and shrugged away from the doorframe, with a lazy, economical gesture that did odd things to her pulse rate, and sauntered over, propping his taut, firm buttocks on the edge of her desk, folding his arms and staring down at her thoughtfully, long legs crossed at the ankle.

He'd had a hellish night, but he still managed to look drop-dead gorgeous. He was wearing theatre scrubs, drab and sexless and unrevealing, but on him they just looked amazing. He was so close she could feel his warmth, smell the subtle, masculine fragrance of his skin. If she moved her hand just a fraction to the right—

'Just your own laundry?'

'Well, I don't take in washing to supplement my income, if that's what you're implying!' she joked, convinced that it couldn't possibly be a corny chat-up line. Not from Andrew.

He grinned wearily. 'God forbid! Actually, I was trying in my rather clumsy and unsubtle way to find out if you live alone.'

Good heavens. So it *was* a chat-up line? Surely not. She didn't get that lucky—did she? She felt her mouth go dry and her heart hitch in her chest before she talked herself out of believing it, and then she couldn't resist the urge to poke a little fun at herself. 'Actually, no,' she said, pausing, then went on, 'but the cat doesn't generate a lot of washing—and before you say it,' she added quickly as he started to chuckle, 'I know that makes me a sad old spinster, but I love my cat and she's good company—even if she does shed all over my clothes and wake me up in the night for food. And—no, there's nobody else if that's what you were asking, either live-in or otherwise.'

One side of his mouth kicked up a fraction more. 'In which case, if the cat doesn't mind, I don't suppose I can persuade you to put the laundry on hold and come away with me to the country for the weekend? I can't promise you the Eiffel Tower, but we can certainly stroll by a river and I can guarantee the food will be good.'

Her heart lurched again and she sucked in a quiet breath and saved the file on the computer, then swivelled the chair round and made herself look calmly up at him, convinced she'd misheard. Either that or gone mad. But he'd wanted to talk to her, so maybe—

'Run that by me again? Did I imagine it, or did I just hear what sounded like an invitation for a dirty weekend?'

He gave another soft chuckle, then pulled a face and rubbed his jaw with his hand. Goodness knows when he'd shaved. Not that morning, anyway, and she heard the tantalising rasp of stubble against his fingers and nearly whimpered.

'Tempting thought,' he said, 'but no. I have—' He broke off and let out his breath on a gusty laugh that was half-sigh. 'It's my mother's sixtieth birthday party, and I can't get out of it. She's having a house party and a ball and the whole shebang, and I just know that all the single women she knows of childbearing age and the seventh cousin eight times removed will be dragged out of the woodwork and paraded in front of me—again. And there's nothing wrong with any of them, but—you know, if I wanted to have a relationship with any of them, I would have done it by now, but I don't, and I'm too tired for it, Libby,' he said with a sigh, scrubbing his hand round the back of his neck. 'I've been up all night, I'm going to have damn all time to take it easy before tomorrow night when it all kicks off and I really can't be bothered with making endless small talk and then because I haven't been downright rude, having to find excuses for not meeting up for coffee or going for drinks or having dinner or going to the races.'

'So,' she said slowly, torn between pity because he was so tired, wondering how big his ego really was, and trying not to drool too badly as he flexed his shoulders again, 'you want me as—let me get this right—some kind of deflector to shield you from this rampant horde of women that most men would give their eye teeth for a crack at?'

He chuckled softly, the sound rippling through her and turning her to jelly. 'Hardly a rampant horde, but, yes, if you like,' he said with a grin. 'But mostly I need someone to deflect my mother's attention from my single status—which incidentally I have no intention of changing in a hurry, much to her great disappointment.'

He was single? Amazing. How? And more to the point, why? What a tragic waste!

He tipped his head on one side, rolling his shoulders again as if he was easing out the kinks. 'So—will you?'

'Will I—?' she asked, distracted by those shoulders, her fingers itching to dig into the taut muscles and ease away the tension she knew she'd find there.

'Be my deflector? Let me drag you away from the laundry basket and the duster and take you away with me to the country for a strictly no-strings weekend?'

Her heart hiccuped at the thought, and she sat back and looked up into his eyes. His piercing, ice-blue eyes with the navy rims round the irises and the fetching, sexy little crinkles in the outer corners. Eyes that even bloodshot with exhaustion could turn her legs to spaghetti and her brains to mush with a single glance.

'So what's in it for me?' she asked bluntly, knowing in advance what her answer would be and how with the best will in the world she didn't have it in her to turn down an invitation from the most gorgeous man she'd ever met in her life—even if she didn't stand a chance, even if she was beating her head against a brick wall and getting that close to a work colleague ever again was top of her list of taboos.

He shrugged, wondering how he could sell it to her, suddenly desperate for her company, for her to say yes. 'A fabulous dinner tomorrow night, a lazy weekend in the beautiful Suffolk countryside, peaceful walks by the river with the dogs, a glittering formal ball on Saturday night.'

'Good food, you said?'

She was hooked. Andrew smiled and felt his heart thud with what had to be relief. 'Good food, good wine—good company…'

'Yours, I take it—not that you're vain or anything,' she said, her voice rich with mockery, and he chuckled and straightened up, refusing to be insulted. Actually he was refreshed by her blunt straightforwardness and teasing good-humour, and, oddly, incredibly fascinated by the tiny spangles of gold in the depths of her extraordinary sea-green eyes.

'Absolutely not. But I have it on good authority that I can be a charming companion, I can dance without treading on your toes—and unlike your cat, I won't moult on your clothes or demand food in the middle of the night. I'm even housetrained.'

She smiled, but her eyes were searching. 'No strings, you said?'

He felt a tug of disappointment and dismissed it. 'With the great and the good of Suffolk chaperoning us? Not a chance. Just you, me, and every single woman in a hundred miles.'

'And good food.'

'And good food. Excellent food. Mum uses a brilliant caterer for these functions.'

She nodded thoughtfully. 'So—this weekend. How dressy is it?'

He thought of the women who'd inevitably be there in their designer originals, and pulled a face. Libby probably didn't have anything like that, not on a nurse's salary. 'Dressy. Black tie tomorrow for dinner, white tie on Saturday for the ball.'

Libby's eyes widened. 'Wow. That's pretty formal. Tailcoats and floor-length gowns, isn't it?'

He nodded, studying her thoughtfully, hoping she wouldn't use it as an excuse to turn him down—or that she'd come and be embarrassed by the other women. He'd hate that for her.

'Right,' she said, after a short, considering pause.

Right, what? Right, she'd come, or right, it sounded like a nightmare and she wouldn't be seen dead near the place? 'Is that a problem? Do you have anything suitable?'

'I'm sure I can dredge up the odd rag,' she said drily, and he felt some of the tension ease out of him as she went on, 'So where will we stay?'

'At the house,' he said without hesitation. 'I'll tell my mother I'm bringing you. She'll be delighted.' Ridiculously delighted.

'Does she even know who I am?'

He felt his mouth twitch. 'No. I've never mentioned you. Or anyone else, come to that, so you're safe. You can be as inventive as you like, so long as you let me in on it.'

Libby sighed and rolled her eyes. 'Don't you go spinning your mother porkies, now, Andrew, or I won't come. We work together, you've asked me up for the weekend. End of. No inventiveness. I don't want to spend the entire weekend like a moonstruck teenager pretending to be in love with you.'

He was tempted to ask if it would be such a hardship, but thought better of it at the last second and smiled reassuringly. 'Of course not. I'll just tell her I'm bringing a plus one. I'll let her make any further leaps herself. Don't worry, you won't have to pretend to smile while I grope you for effect.'

Pity, she thought, but managed what she hoped was a normal smile. 'So—what time does this extravaganza start?'

'Seven for seven-thirty. I'd like to leave at six, but Murphy's Law says it's unlikely. Is that OK?'

'Fine,' she said, not sure if she'd lost her marbles or won the lottery.

'Great. I'll see you later.'

Lottery, she decided, watching him walk away. Good food, good wine—and definitely good company. And it might answer some of her abundant questions about the most enigmatic and attractive man she'd met in her entire twenty-seven years…

'You're doing *what*?'

'Going home with him for the weekend. It's his mother's sixtieth birthday party and there's a ball.'

'Good God,' Amy said weakly, and stared at her open-mouthed.

'What?'

'What? *What?* You stun me. You must be the only single woman in Suffolk who wouldn't kill for an invitation like that.'

She shook her head quickly, resisting the urge to tell Amy that according to Andrew all the single women in Suffolk had already been invited. 'No. It's not an invitation *like that*. It's strictly no strings.'

Amy laughed till the tears ran down her face. 'Yeah, right! You're going home for the weekend with *that man* and you're saying it's no strings? Are you both dead, or what? And what on earth are you going to wear?'

She felt a flicker of unease. 'I don't know. Clothes?' she said helpfully, and the physio rolled her eyes.

'Dear heaven. You do realise who'll be there, don't you? I mean, this isn't your ordinary, everyday birthday party for a little old lady.'

'She's only sixty!'

'She's only *Lady Ashenden*!' Amy said, imitating her voice, and Libby felt her own jaw drop. She snatched it back up and tried not to hyperventilate.

'Lady Ashenden—as in, Ashenden Place? The one that's open to the public? No! No, his name's not Ashenden, don't be silly!'

'No, he's the Hon. Andrew Langham-Jones, first son of Lord and Lady Ashenden, heir to the Ashenden estate, which as you rightly say is open to the public and only one of the most beautiful country piles in Suffolk—not to mention the family coffers and the flipping title! He's one of the most eligible bachelors around—good grief, Libby, I can't believe you didn't know about him!'

'Maybe because I don't gossip?' she suggested mildly, wondering if she ought to take it up if she was going to accept random invitations from gorgeous men without realising what she was letting herself in for. And of course, if he was the future Lord Ashenden, no wonder all the dowagers were trotting their daughters out! He wasn't being vain or egotistical at all, he was just being realistic, and she couldn't believe she'd been so stupid—but Amy could. Oh, yes. And Amy said so. Bluntly.

'You don't need to gossip, you just need to be alive! You just—you live in a cocoon, do you know that? You go home every night to your little house and your little cat and you snuggle down in front of the television and *you have no idea what's going on right under your nose!* No wonder you're still single!'

'I'm happy being single,' she lied, trying not to think about the lonely nights and the long weekends and the ridiculous farce of speed dating and internet dating and blind dates that she'd given up on ages ago.

'Rubbish,' Amy said briskly, and eyed her up and down. 'So—what are you wearing for this event?'

'Two events,' she corrected, wincing inwardly when she thought about it. *Lady Ashenden?* Oh, rats. 'A black-tie dinner tomorrow night and a white-tie formal ball the following night.'

Amy's eyes widened, then narrowed critically as she studied her friend, making Libby feel like an insect skewered on a pin. 'It's a pity your boobs are so lush,' Amy said candidly. 'I've got a fabulous ballgown—that smoky bluey-green one. But you'll probably fall out of it. Still, you can try it. It's the only long one I've got that's suitable and it's cut on the cross so it'll drape nicely and it'll be brilliant with your eyes. And you've got your classic LBD for tomorrow, haven't you?'

'If it doesn't need cleaning. I expect the cat's been sleeping on it—joke!' she added hastily, as Amy opened her mouth to tell her off again. 'It'll be fine. I had it cleaned after Christmas. And I've got a fairly decent pair of heels that do nice things to my legs.'

'They don't need to. You've got fabulous legs—well, you did have, the last time you let them out into the fresh air, which was ages ago, but I don't suppose they've changed. What time does your shift finish?'

'Three, but I've got to go home and feed the cat and put the washing on or I won't have anything at all to wear for the weekend.'

'Right, I'm off at five, so that gives you two hours and then I want you round at mine and we'll go through my wardrobe and see what I've got, because I know you haven't got anything unless you've got a secret life I don't know about. I can't remember the last time you told me about a date, and apart from this dreadful uniform the only other thing I ever see you in is jeans. Never mind, we'll find something even if I have to send you out shopping tomorrow. Actually, on second thoughts *I'll* go shopping. I can't trust you to buy anything sensible.'

Sensible? Libby nearly laughed out loud. She couldn't imagine that what Amy had in mind for her was in any way *sensible*, but she didn't have many options and she had even less time. 'I'm sure the bluey-green one will be fine,' she said with more confidence than she felt. 'I'll wear a minimiser bra.'

Amy laughed again as if she'd said something hysterically funny. 'Yeah, right. Just try the dress first and then we'll worry about the underwear. OK, I'm done here on the ward, I'm going back down to the gym to do my outpatients' list, and in between I'll be thinking about your outfits for the weekend. I might have another dress that would do if that one doesn't fit. I'll see you later—and don't forget to come round. I'll feed you. Half-five—and not a minute later. And bring your shoes and the LBD. Oh, and your jewellery and some bras.'

'Yeah, yeah—you are the most atrocious nag.'

'You'll love me this weekend when you don't look silly.'

'I hope so,' she muttered under her breath, and tugging her quote, dreadful, unquote uniform straight, she went to find Lucas, a fourteen-year-old who'd nearly lost his foot a week ago after a stupid stunt on his bike had gone horribly wrong. Andrew had re-aligned all the bones using an external fixator, but the surgery had been complicated, his recovery was going to be slow and Lucas was impatient.

He'd just gone for a walk with his mother, using his

crutches, and he'd been gone longer than she liked. It was his first excursion from the ward, the first time he'd been off without supervision from a member of staff; Amy had thought the exercise would do him good, but he'd missed his lunch now and Libby was getting concerned.

She found him in the corridor, propped up on a window sill and looking pale and shaky, and she smiled and perched next to him, wondering where his mother was. Poor woman. She was trying to juggle the family and be there for Lucas, but it wasn't easy for any of the mothers, and sometimes something had to give.

'Hi, Lucas. You've been gone a while—everything OK?'

The lanky teenager shrugged. 'S'pose. Mum had to take Kyle to the doctor. My nan rang—he's sick.'

'Oh, dear, that's a shame. Look, your lunch is waiting. Why don't I fetch a chair and you can ride back to the ward? You've probably done enough for the first time.'

'I can do it myself,' he insisted, shrugging up off the window sill and wobbling slightly on the crutches. Libby frowned. He had to learn how to use them, but the last thing he needed was to go over and damage the leg again, and he was strictly non-weight-bearing at the moment.

She fell into step beside him. 'OK, if you're sure. I'll walk back with you—it's a good excuse to have a break, and I could do with some time out. You guys are wearing me down!'

He grinned and took a few steps, but he had to pause again on the way, leaning over on the crutches and getting his breath, and Libby heard a quiet footfall behind her.

'How's it going, Lucas?'

She didn't need to turn to know who it was, and her pulse picked up as she turned to him with a smile. 'He's doing really well.'

Andrew grinned at him. 'Good man.'

Lucas straightened up again, Andrew's praise having a visible effect on his mood. He was tall—a good head taller than Libby, but for all his youth he could look Andrew in the eye already, and he had a way to go before he finished growing.

'I think this is the first time I've seen you standing up—you're going to be seriously tall, aren't you?' Andrew said, eyeing him thoughtfully, and Lucas shrugged.

'Always was. I'm going to be a basketball player.' His words tailed off, his face crumpling, but Andrew wouldn't let it go.

'Give it time,' he said softly. 'You can still do that. Your leg will heal.'

'Are you sure? 'Cos it doesn't feel any better yet. It's gonna take for *ever* and I feel like about a hundred.'

'Lucas, it's only been just over a week,' he said gently. 'It'll take a while, but I've fixed all the bones together, and once they've all knitted back into place and we can get the hardware off your ankle, you'll soon be up and running. Just be patient. You'll get there and you'll soon get your fitness back.' He looked around. 'So where's Mum today?'

'At the doctor's with my brother. He's got tonsillitis. He gets it all the time.'

'Poor kid. I used to get tonsillitis. It's nasty.'

'Better than smashing your leg up.'

Andrew grinned wryly. 'Yeah, it probably is.' His eyes flicked to Libby's. 'I'm on my way down to

A and E—lad with a classic fib fracture, apparently. I'm probably going to have to take him to Theatre, so you'll need to find room for him, but I'll be back up after I've seen him to check last night's admissions. And maybe we can find time for a coffee—I was hoping to get one earlier while we went through the notes together, but we got a little sidetracked,' he added softly, and she felt colour brush her cheeks.

So that was what he'd wanted. Not to ask her to go away for the weekend at all, but to talk through the notes. So why had he? 'I'll make you one when you get back,' she suggested, but he shook his head.

'Don't worry, I'll get them and grab some sandwiches and we can eat while we talk—unless you have plans for lunch?'

She shook her head, a wry smile tugging at her mouth. 'No. I hardly ever have time to eat, never mind plan it!'

He tutted. 'I'll get some for you, too, then, and I'll see you in a bit. It looks like you've got your hands pretty full with this young man for a minute.' He turned back to him and gave the boy's shoulder an encouraging squeeze. 'Chin up, Lucas. You'll get there.'

And with a smile at him and a slow, lazy wink at Libby, he strode off down the corridor, leaving her wondering how she was going to get through the weekend without melting into a puddle of mush.

'Right—let's get you back on the ward,' she said to Lucas, dragging her thoughts back in line, 'and you can start planning your return to basketball.'

He set off again, but by the time they got back to the ward he was exhausted, and once back at his bed she brought him his lunch and settled the rest of the boys in his bay down for a rest until the visitors arrived at three.

It took bribery and a little coercion, but finally by one-thirty they were all quiet and she headed back to the office where the endless paperwork was still waiting for her.

The paperwork, and Andrew, with sandwiches and coffee. 'I was about to start without you. Egg and cress or chicken salad?'

'Either,' she said, wondering why her office suddenly seemed so small and airless. Andrew was ripping open the packets, handing her one of each with a raised eyebrow, and she took them with a smile and tried to remember how to breathe. 'Thanks. So how's the kid with the fib fracture?'

'Sore and feeling a bit silly. Apparently the idea was to jump off his trampoline onto his skateboard, only he fell off the edge of the board when he landed.'

'Idiot! Of course he did! What *is* it with boys?'

Andrew winced. 'Don't. I can't tell you how many close shaves I had as a child. The kid's father was funny, though—reminded me of mine. He described it as an ill-conceived idea, poorly executed,' he said with a chuckle.

'Oh, dear. So no sympathy from that quarter, then,' she said, joining in his laughter while she studied the smudges under his eyes and wondered how he kept going.

'Not much. He's managed to snap the fibula but it's a nice clean break and it'll screw back easily—better than a ligament injury long term anyway. He'll be up on the ward in a minute, but he'd just had something to eat so I can't take him to Theatre till later. His name's Michael Warner,' he added, sinking his teeth into his sandwich and nearly making her whimper again.

Good grief, he was so physical! If watching him eat

was going to do this to her, how on earth was she going to get through two formal dinners without disgracing herself? She dragged her eyes away and tried to be practical. 'Right. Where do you want him? On the ward with the other boys?'

'Oh, yes, put him with the lads. He's twelve, he'll fit right in—and a bit more company might stop Lucas feeling sorry for himself.'

He attacked the sandwich again, and she gave a slightly strained laugh. 'I doubt it. He's sore and cross with himself and until he's running around again like before, he'll be wallowing in self-pity and grumpy as a grumpy thing.'

They shared a smile, and her lungs stopped working for a moment, a warm, fuzzy feeling spreading through her and leaving her weak. He'd shaved at some point, and changed into trousers with a cut to die for and a shirt so soft she just ached to touch it. Or was it the man inside?

'Damn—may I?' he asked, glancing at his squalling pager, and she nodded. He spoke briefly, then sighed and put the phone down.

'Right, I have to get on. Jacob needs a look,' he said, draining his coffee and putting the paper cup in the bin. 'I've checked my patients, they all seem fine unless you know different?' She shook her head and he nodded briskly. 'OK. I'll see you later. Tell young Michael I'll come. I'll stick him on the end of my afternoon list, but I'll be round before then to have a chat with him.'

'OK. Thanks for the lunch. What do I owe you?'

He gave her a lazy smile. 'Nothing. You can get them next time.'

Next time?

He headed off to PICU, and she followed him out

of the office, pulling herself together and trying not to think about next time. She was having enough trouble dealing with this time!

She went into the boys' bay to sort the bed out, and stood there for a moment considering the situation. There were six of them—Lucas, and Rajesh, another boy of the same age who'd had an open fracture of his right forearm which had been fixed and plated that morning. He wouldn't be there long. Then there was Joel, a boy of fifteen who'd fallen through the roof of the conservatory climbing out of the window above when he'd been grounded; he'd suffered multiple fractures and so was now well and truly grounded until the casts on both arms and the halo frame stabilising his neck could be removed.

Then there were Christopher and Jonathan, twin brothers who'd fallen out of a tree when a branch had snapped, and broken three legs and one arm between them. She'd like to keep them together for company. And Nico, with repaired ligaments in his ankle. He'd been cleared for discharge and was waiting to go, so she moved him into a chair to wait for his parents, and as she and the health care assistant finished remaking the bed, Michael arrived in a wheelchair with his long-suffering and patient father.

'Hi, there,' she said, going out and introducing herself with a smile. 'I'm Libby Tate, the ward sister, and you must be Michael. We're expecting you. Come on through, I'll show you to your bed.'

She'd put him between Lucas and Joel, the boy who'd fallen through the conservatory roof, and by the time he was settled against the pillows the banter had started. Good. He'd be fine, and a welcome distraction for Lucas and Joel.

She put the clipboard with his charts on the end of the bed and smiled at the boy and his father. 'Right, I'm off duty now, Michael, but the anaesthetist will be round to see you soon and Mr Langham-Jones is taking you down to Theatre in a while—he'll be up to see you afterwards to tell you how it went, and I'll be on in the morning so I'll catch up with you then. The others will look after you, won't you, boys?' she said to them all with a smile, and as soon as she'd handed over, she grabbed her coat and went out to her car, wondering if it was her imagination or if there was a spring in her step that hadn't been there earlier.

Yup. Definite spring, and she felt ridiculously lighthearted. Silly. It was a no-strings, pretend date. Not really a date at all. Her heart really shouldn't be getting excited.

But it was…

CHAPTER TWO

THE dress was gorgeous, shot with navy and olive green so it looked like the sea on a stormy day, the colours changing as the light caught it, and by the time Amy had poured her into the dress, hitched up the front a little for decency and scooped her hair into a knot and put a necklace round her throat, no amount of reasoning with her pulse was going to make a blind bit of difference.

Amy stood back and stared at her, and shook her head slowly. 'Wow.'

'D'you think?' Libby hitched the front up again and had her hand slapped for her pains.

'Leave it. You've got gorgeous boobs, be proud of them. Stick them out and hold your head up—that's better. Fabulous. You'll knock them all dead.'

'Knock them out, more like,' she said, shuffling her bra—clearly no room for a minimiser in there with that neckline!—and biting her lip. 'Are you sure it's all right?'

But Amy just rolled her eyes and draped an exquisite oyster-pink silk and cashmere pashmina around her shoulders. 'There. You can always cover your cleavage with this if it worries you. Don't lose it, it cost a fortune and it's my only real extravagance. And you can wear it tomorrow with the black. Let me see you in it?'

So Libby changed into her dearly loved and classic little black dress, the high scoop neck and on-the-knee hemline much more demure and discreet. The back dipped to a V just above her bra strap, and there was a tiny kick-pleat at the back to allow for movement, and she loved it. It was elegant, sophisticated and timeless—which was just as well because she'd had it for three years now and by her reckoning it still owed her a substantial amount of money. It was, however, a little more snug than it had been before Christmas, and she sucked in her stomach and sighed.

'You've given me too much to eat,' she said. 'Or I have, for weeks and weeks. It's too tight.'

'It's lovely,' Amy said, standing back and eyeing her critically. 'Very demure. Very sexy.'

'It's not meant to be sexy,' she said, her eyes widening. 'It's meant to be respectable!'

'It's perfectly respectable.'

She gave up, not entirely reassured, but her time and her options were dwindling by the minute. 'Good. Can I go now? I've got to get my jeans dry somehow so I can pack them in the morning. Apparently we're leaving at six and I don't finish work till five tomorrow, so I've got to wash my hair and pack tonight—all except for the things still in the washing machine. Oh, why aren't I better organised? I really wanted my nice cream jumper but it won't be dry, it takes ages.'

'I've got a jumper you can borrow,' Amy said, rummaging in her chest of drawers and pulling out a couple of clingy little scraps.

'It's only just April! I meant a *jumper*, Amy, not a second skin!'

'You'll be fine. Here. Take them anyway, they'll suit you. You can always wear your coat if you're cold.'

'In the house?'

'They're bound to have heating, you'll be fine. Go on, scoot. You've got things to do and you need a good night's sleep or you'll have bags under your eyes.'

Not a chance, she thought. There was no way she'd sleep. She was getting ridiculously excited, and when she walked onto the ward the next morning Andrew was there, lounging against the nursing station and chatting to Lucas's parents. He looked up and met her eyes and smiled, and her heart turned over in her chest.

Ridiculously excited, she told herself, trying not to grin like an idiot, and she went to find the staff nurse to do handover and made a futile attempt to ignore his presence.

Andrew watched her turn away and busy herself, and resisted the temptation to cut the conversation short. Despite their encouragement and constant support of Lucas, his parents were naturally worried about their son, and he took the time to reassure them yet again before he gave in to the need to speak to Libby.

She was at the nurses' station in the middle, talking to the staff nurse who'd been on since seven, and as he excused himself and crossed over to her she looked up, her smile lighting up her face and warming him like sunshine. He propped his arms on the counter and smiled back at her, glad it was between them because he was having trouble resisting the unexpected urge to drag her into his arms and kiss her.

Not a good move. He cleared his throat slightly.

'Hi, there.'

'Hi. How's things?' she asked, her voice music to his ears. 'I hear Jacob's improving. How did you get on with Michael?'

'OK. It was absolutely straightforward. He can go home today once the physio's got him up on crutches. I'll see him in the fracture clinic next week for follow-up, but he should be fine. He was lucky.'

'He was an idiot,' she reminded him drily, and he chuckled.

'True. And Jacob's looking good, considering, so I should be able to get away reasonably promptly tonight. Are you all set?' he added softly as the staff nurse turned away to answer the phone.

'I am. All packed and ready. I washed my hair last night so I should be OK for six. Well, except that I haven't got your mother a birthday present yet.'

'You don't have to do that! Just give her a card. She'll be overwhelmed with presents and it's the last thing she'd expect.'

'Sure?'

'I'm sure. Anyway, we need to head off as soon as we can. Will you have time to get ready?'

'I should. Do you want me to change before we go, then, or are we changing there?'

'Change before we go,' he advised, trying not to sniff for the scent of apples in her hair. 'The place'll be in chaos and it'll be easier. Tell me your address and I'll pick you up as soon after six as I can get to you.'

'Fourteen Elm Grove,' she said. 'It's off Wood Farm Drive, but it's sort of buried. I can give you directions.'

'No, I'll find it. Postcode?' he asked, keying the information into his BlackBerry, and she gave him the code. 'OK. The sat-nav should do it, but you'd better give me your phone number in case it fails. It has been known.'

'Surely not,' she said with a teasing smile, and he felt a kick in his gut.

No strings? Who was he kidding?

It was going to be an interesting weekend…

The day was chaos.

After she'd seen Michael and his parents to discuss his discharge, there were several other post-op patients who needed her attention, and of course there was Lucas. He was desperate to show off his new-found skills with the crutches, and as Amy had been up to the ward to equip Michael with his own set and show him how to use them, they were busy competing, the accident clearly not having slowed Michael down at all.

She stopped them before there was another accident, threatened to confiscate the crutches from Lucas, saw Michael off with his paperwork, then had to deal with an IV crisis in a tearful, wriggling three-year-old, and by the time she'd handed over and got away, it was nearly five-thirty. So much for her plans to slip off early!

She raced home, ripped off her uniform and had the quickest shower on record, skimmed the lightest of make-up onto her face, brushed her hair and pulled on her dress as the doorbell rang just after six. She wriggled the zip up and then, grabbing her shoes and evening bag, she ran downstairs and threw open the door, hardly pausing to greet him as she ran back into the living room, hopping on one foot as she put her shoes on on the move.

'Sorry, I'm on the drag, I couldn't get away,' she said breathlessly over her shoulder, then turned and stopped talking, because he was standing there behind her, looking utterly, devastatingly gorgeous in his DJ, the dress shirt with its immaculate black bow-tie blinding white against his skin, his jaw freshly shaved, his hair—damp?

'Either you have far too much gel in your hair or it's still wet,' she pointed out unnecessarily, and he gave a soft grunt of laughter.

'I showered and changed at the hospital or I wouldn't be here now,' he said wryly. 'I was hoping to get away early, but you know what it's like. Are you all packed and ready?'

She laughed with him. 'Sort of. Hang on.' She rummaged in her case, came up with the perfume and spritzed herself lightly, then threw it back into the case and zipped the lid. 'Now I'm ready,' she said with a slightly nervous grin. 'Will I do, or will I disgrace you?'

She gave a self-conscious twirl, and he ran his eyes over her. 'No, you won't disgrace me,' he said softly with an odd note in his voice. 'Turn around, your zip's not quite up.' And she felt his fingers cool against her heated skin as he pulled the zip up the last half-inch and fastened the hook, then smoothed it with his hand and stepped back.

'All done,' he said, and she tugged it straight and turned to pick up her coat.

'Oh, Kitty!' she wailed. 'You rascal—you can see why I wear black,' she added drily to Andrew, and he chuckled, eased the black cat off her coat, gave it a shake to remove the hair and held it out for her, settling it solicitously on her shoulders, and she wondered if she'd imagined his hands lingering for the tiniest moment.

Her shoulders tingling, she reached for her case, but he was there first, leaving her to scoop up her handbag and keys, then she followed him out of the door.

'So who feeds the cat while you're away?' he asked, opening the car door for her and tucking her coat in.

'Oh, I've got an automatic thingie. I've set it.'

'In which minute?' he asked with a chuckle, then slid behind the wheel and threw her a smile. 'You look lovely, by the way,' he added softly, making her heart hiccup and her insides tighten with anticipation. 'Much better than the uniform.'

'Well, that wouldn't be hard. It's a bit tight, though. I haven't worn it since before Christmas—I must have been staving off the cold a bit too enthusiastically,' she said with a rueful smile, but he shook his head.

'It's perfect. You look very convincing.'

Convincing. Of course. That was what this was all about, and she'd better not forget it. He'd only invited her as an afterthought, and she needed to keep that in mind. This was not, repeat not, a date. She was there to be convincing, and so convincing she'd be. End of. She flashed him a bright smile. 'Well, that's a relief! I won't be pitched out on my ear as a fraud, at least.'

They shared the smile as he started the engine and headed out into the countryside. She had no idea where they were going. Somewhere near Southwold? She'd meant to look it up on the internet to see if she could find the address of the Ashenden pile, as Amy called it, but she simply hadn't had time. She hadn't had time to draw breath, really, since yesterday morning, and as she sank back into the soft but supportive leather seat, she realised just how tired she was.

'All right?'

'Yes—it's just been a busy day. Well, busy week, really. I'm glad it's a sit-down formal dinner, because I don't think my feet would cope with standing up all evening in these ridiculous heels after a day like today.'

He peered across at the footwell in the dark. 'Are they ridiculous? I thought they looked rather good.'

He did? 'Thank you—but looking good and feeling good aren't the same thing,' she explained ruefully, and his lips twitched.

'No, I can imagine. I've only worn high heels once, and it was excruciating.'

She shifted in the seat, turning to face him, struggling to hold down her incredulous laughter. 'You've worn high heels?'

He grinned. 'And a dress. It's amazing what my brother can persuade me to do for charity,' he said drily.

That piqued her interest—that and the thought of Andrew in a dress and heels. 'Any particular one?'

'Meningococcal disease. He had it as a teenager and could have lost his limbs, but he was lucky and he's very aware of that, so now he fundraises for research—well, the whole family do, he makes sure of it. The house and gardens are open to the public alternate weekends during the summer and they hold events in the park and split the proceeds between the charities and the estate.'

'Gosh, that sounds like a lot of hard work.'

'It is. Will's the estate manager, so he just incorporates it into his workload, and Mum oversees the garden and the house, but it's pretty much a full-time job for them keeping the place ticking over. And one day it'll be my job.'

She detected a note of resignation in his voice and tipped her head on one side enquiringly. 'You don't sound thrilled.'

He laughed. 'I'm not. I have a job, in case you haven't noticed, but I'm the oldest, so I get the short straw. Not for a while, though. Dad's only sixty-three and he's as fit as a flea, so between them hopefully they'll struggle on for a good few years yet.'

'I take it your brother will be there this weekend?'

'Will? Oh, yes. And his wife Sally. She's their events manager at the moment, but she'll be off for the summer on maternity leave, which should make life interesting.'

'I'm sure. Will they cope without her?'

He chuckled. 'I have no idea, but I'm not volunteering, I can assure you. I have quite enough to do.'

'I imagine you do. Does your brother know you're bringing me, by the way?'

He turned towards her, and in the dim light she could see his eyebrow twitch. 'As in, did I tell him I'm bringing a girl? Yes. Did I mention why? No.'

She smiled at that. 'Won't he think it's odd?'

'That I have a social life? No. Should he?'

'No, of course not, but I didn't mean that.' She shrugged. 'I meant—I don't know—that none of them have ever heard of me. Won't there be a lot of speculation? Most people wouldn't turn up for their mother's sixtieth birthday with a total stranger in tow.'

'They would if they had my mother,' he said drily, making her laugh. 'And anyway, speculation is the general idea, isn't it?'

'Probably.' She rested her head back and looked across at him. 'Tell me about your mother, I'm sure she can't be that bad,' she said, and listened to him talking about his parents and his childhood with great affection. They were obviously a close-knit and loving family, and she envied them that. Her father was dead, her mother was remarried and lived in blissful penury in Ireland with her artist husband, and she and her married elder sister hardly ever spoke. It wasn't that they didn't like each other, but with seven years and several hundred miles between them, they had little in common, and the last time she'd seen her had been at a great-aunt's funeral a few months ago—a gathering that had opened a potentially devastating can of worms.

'So that's us. My father, my mother, me, my brother and his wife and a whole horde of cats and dogs and horses and cattle and deer—I take it you're all right with dogs, by the way? We have quite a few.'

She pulled herself back to the present and put the troubling thoughts aside. 'I'm fine with dogs. I'd have one if I wasn't at work all day.'

'Ditto. Not to mention half the night.'

'Mmm. So tell me about Jacob. I know you're happier with him now but did you get last night off?'

He laughed and scrubbed his hand around the back of his neck. 'Sort of. His left leg was swelling a bit yesterday—that was why they paged me. They thought he might be getting compartment syndrome, but nothing came of it, and I popped in before I went home last night and I went in again early this morning and it seems to have settled. He's OK—well, orthopaedic-wise, anyway, for the moment. The head injury's still a bit of a worry and he might need further surgery later on his legs and pelvis if he makes it, but at least that's looking increasingly likely, thank goodness.'

'So will you have to go back over the weekend?' she asked, wondering whether he would abandon her to the mercy of his mother and the dowagers, or take her back to Audley with him, but he was shaking his head.

'No, I hope not. This leg is the only critical issue I can see that might involve me, so I might take a quick run back tomorrow to check him, but the team are pretty good and he was looking stable when I left.'

He turned his head and she caught the flash of teeth as he smiled. 'Don't worry, I won't abandon you. I'll leave you with Will, if I have to dash off. He'll look after you.'

'I'll look forward to meeting him. He sounds interesting.'

'He is, but I hope you're tough. He's got a wicked sense of humour and he's a bit of a tease, and I don't suppose for a moment he'll be subtle. Stand by to be quizzed.'

'I'm sure I'll cope,' she said drily. 'I manage the boys on the ward.'

That made him laugh, and as they turned off the road and rattled over a cattle grid, he threw her a grin. 'Ready for this?'

'As I'll ever be,' she said, although she wasn't really sure. Not now she knew a little more about them and the scale of the estate. It was sounding grander by the minute. 'What do I call your mother?' she asked as an afterthought.

'Jane—and my father's Tony.'

Or Lord Ashenden. Or should it be Sir Tony? Sir Anthony? She had no idea. Was he a lord? An earl? A baron? A marquis?

The titles were confusing, the whole aristocratic hierarchy a mystery to her, and she resolved to find out more about it. Not that it would be necessary to know, after this weekend, of course, because it would never affect her again. She reminded herself of that as they pulled up in what looked like the courtyard of an old stable block and he cut the engine. So far, so good, she thought, looking around in the gloom. It didn't look too outrageously grand—except of course this was the back. The front was probably altogether different.

By the time she'd fumbled with the catch on her seat belt, the door was open and he was helping her out. 'Watch where you walk, it can be a bit uneven on the cobbles and you don't want to fall off your stilts and wring your ankle.'

'What about our cases?'

'I'll get them later, unless you want anything from yours now?' he said, and when she shook her head, he ushered her towards a well-lit doorway with a firm, steadying hand on her back.

'We'll see if Will and Sally are still here—they've got the east wing,' he said, and she just about stopped her jaw dropping. The east wing? Good grief! Well, she'd known it was big, but for some reason it was only just starting to sink in *how* big, and she realised her whole house would probably fit into one of the stables!

'Shop!' he yelled, banging on the door, and it swung in to reveal a younger version of him, slightly taller, identical ice-blue eyes mocking as he scanned his brother's face.

'You're cutting it a bit fine, aren't you?'

'Yeah, well, some of us have to go to work. And it's not as if you're in there already.'

'I have been. I came back to check the dog and ring you. Ma was starting to panic. Hi, you must be Libby,' he said, turning the full force of his charm on her. 'Come on in. I'm Will,' he said, and shook her hand firmly. He was looking intrigued and curious and welcoming all at once, and she smiled back, relishing the strength of his grip and utterly charmed by his smile and frank, assessing eyes—eyes just like his brother's.

'Hello, Will. It's good to meet you. Andrew's just been telling me a bit about you.'

'It'll all be lies,' he said with a grin. 'So—how come my brother's failed to mention you? Is he keeping you a deep, dark secret from Ma?'

She chuckled. 'I couldn't possibly comment,' she said lightly, and he laughed.

'You don't need to. Discreet isn't the word—getting information out of him is like getting blood out of a stone,' he said with a grin, and then stepped aside to let a great, shaggy grey dog through. 'This is Lara. Are you all right with dogs?'

'I'm fine with dogs. Hello, Lara. Aren't you gorgeous?'

'No, she's a pain,' Will said affectionately as the lurcher thrashed her long, skinny tail against his leg and slurped Libby's hand. 'She's a terrible thief, so I've cleverly trained her to steal my father's newspapers every morning, but the downside is if we leave anything on the worktop, she eats it.'

Libby laughed and rubbed the dog's head. 'Oh, darling, are you a naughty girl?' she murmured, and Lara slurped her again with her tongue.

'You'd better believe it,' Andrew said drily, then sighed. 'Come on, then, I suppose we ought to go and get this over with. Where's Sally?'

'In the kitchen trying to stop Ma interfering with the caterers. Come on, let's go and find them and then the birthday girl can make her grand entrance.'

Leaving the mournful Lara on the other side of a door, Will ushered them down a corridor into what was obviously the main part of the house, and then Andrew took her coat, putting it on a hook beside his as they went through into a huge and beautifully equipped kitchen and a scene of organised pandemonium.

'Andrew, darling! At last—I thought you were going to make some weak excuse about work like you usually do!'

'I don't know what you mean,' he teased. He bent his head and kissed his mother's cheek, hugging her gently, and then turned and drew Libby forward.

'Mum, this is Libby Tate. Libby, my mother, Jane.'

Lady Ashenden was elegant, beautifully groomed and she looked a little flustered. Her dark hair was threaded with silver, swept up into a smooth pleat—unlike Libby's own which was twisted up and skewered more or less in place with faux-ivory pins—and she realised that Andrew and Will both had her eyes.

Piercing eyes, searching, which turned on her and seemed, to Libby's relief, to like what they saw, because she embraced her warmly and kissed her cheeks. 'Libby, welcome to Ashenden. This is Sally, my daughter-in-law.'

Sally was small, obviously pregnant and had the same friendly openness as Will. She buzzed Libby's cheek and grinned. 'Hi, there. Welcome to the madhouse. I'll look forward to catching up with you later, but in the meantime, Jane, isn't it time we went up?'

'I'm sure it is. They don't need us in here fussing and you've done enough, darling. Let's leave them to it, I'm sure they can cope without us.'

And Jane turned away from her, missing the eye-rolling and laughter that passed between her and Will, and the intimate smile which followed as Will drew the pregnant woman up against his side and hugged her tenderly. They were obviously very much in love, Libby thought, and felt a wash of restless longing. If only there was someone in her life who felt like that about her, but even if there was, there would be no guarantee they'd have Will and Sally's happy ending.

The question-mark hanging over her future loomed again, but there wasn't time to dwell on it, and as they left the kitchen and walked along a magnificent curved hallway with tall, elegant windows overlooking the floodlit front of the house, she was brought firmly back to the here and now as the scale of the house began to register.

Amy hadn't been exaggerating, Libby thought. It really was a stately home—a vast, magnificent, Palladian country house, the centre part built in a crescent around a carriage-sweep at the front of the house, and as they reached the entrance hall, bracketed by broad, sweeping stairs that led up towards an ornate domed ceiling soaring far above them, Jane led them across a rug that would no doubt have been priceless if it hadn't been worn thin by the passage of generations, and through an open doorway.

As soon as they entered the drawing room—jaw-dropping in its proportions and dripping with antiques and old masters—they were swept into a round of introductions and fleeting, meaningless conversations. They lost Sally and Will somewhere along the way, and then Andrew grabbed two glasses of champagne from a passing waiter, steered her into a quiet corner and gave her a rueful smile.

'Sorry, it's a bit full on if you're not used to it.'

Full on? She was utterly out of her depth! 'I thought it was just dinner?' she murmured, and he laughed.

'It is dinner, but there's nothing just about it. Dinner will be about forty people, and tomorrow will be a couple of hundred, I expect. Possibly more. And she'll know every last one of them and the names of all their children and dogs and horses—she's a legend.'

'And she wants to see you married.'

'Mmm. All ready to take over this crumbling old heap of dry rot.'

'Are you whingeing about the ancestral home again, bro'?' Will murmured from behind them, and he gave a soft snort and turned to him.

'Would I? Thankfully they're both looking well, so I don't have to worry about it for donkey's years. Have you got a drink?'

'No, but I'll have champagne, if you're offering, and I expect Sally'll have some elderflower cordial. Don't worry about Libby, I'll entertain her while you're gone.'

Libby met Will's twinkling eyes as Andrew walked away to get the drinks. 'So, tell me about this crumbling old heap of dry rot. Does he really hate it?' she said to him, and he chuckled.

'Oh, he loves it to bits, really, but he thinks it should be mine, since I run it. The law of primogeniture offends his sense of right and wrong.'

'And yours?'

He shrugged casually. 'It's just one of those things, isn't it? If you split the estate with every generation, you end up with nothing left—and if you ask him about it, he'll tell you we're just caretakers, which is right. Glorified janitors. But he's welcome to the title—and frankly he's welcome to the house. The east wing is much nicer—I still get to enjoy the grounds, but it's cosier than the house, and the heating bills aren't quite as stratospheric, and I can walk to work. And whatever he's told you, I only run the estate because I'm too lazy to do anything else!'

They were laughing as Andrew returned, a ripple of interest following him as the single girls monitored his progress. Or was it Will they were interested in? She couldn't blame them. Both men were strikingly good-looking and she felt completely overshadowed in the glittering crowd of slender, elegant women with their bright, witty banter and designer dresses.

Until Sally came over a moment later, short and round and utterly charming, and smiled at her and gave her a hug.

'Finally I get to meet you properly! This is such fun, I didn't know my brother-in-law had a deep, dark secret.'

Andrew rolled his eyes. 'Just because I don't gossip.'

'Yeah, yeah,' Sally said, and took her by the arm mischievously. 'So—tell all. I gather you're colleagues. That must be tricky. What's he like to work with, because his brother's a nightmare—'

'I am not!'

'You are. You're hopelessly disorganised.'

Will grinned. 'That's why I employed you.'

'No, it's why you married me. You were terrified I'd leg it and you wouldn't find anyone else who could cope with your filing system.'

'It's a good system!'

'It's a collection of piles on the floor, William!' she corrected with a grin, and Libby laughed.

'Sounds rather like my desk,' she said with a smile at

Will, then turned back to Sally. 'So what do you actually do? Andrew said something about being events manager.'

'Oh, that's just a fancy title for doing anything and everything. I'm just a dogsbody,' she grumbled cheerfully, but Will shook his head.

'She's actually my PA as well, and she helps me run the charity side of things, too,' Will said. 'We'd be lost without her—will be lost when she has the baby, but it's not why I married her. I married her because I struggle to boil water and she's a darned good cook.'

And rather more than that, Libby wouldn't mind guessing, hearing the pride in his voice and seeing the warmth in his eyes as he smiled at Sally, and yet again, she felt a twinge of envy.

If only Andrew would look at her like that—would ever, in the future, look at her like that—but he wouldn't. Why would he? Their worlds were light-years apart. He'd only invited her here this weekend as an afterthought. He'd never noticed her before, never singled her out, never been anything but the perfect colleague. She was only here because he needed a shield, and he'd made that perfectly clear.

Not that she needed to worry. She wasn't in the market for a relationship either at the moment, with him or with anybody else, and she'd do well to remember that fact.

CHAPTER THREE

HER thoughts were interrupted as they all filed through to the dining room, and she found herself seated at a long table between a jovial, middle-aged man who looked like a farmer, and Will.

Andrew was opposite her, and as she looked up and caught his eye he sent her a slow wink and she felt his foot slide against hers.

Playing footsie? Playing 'let's pretend'? Or giving her moral support?

The latter, she realised as he withdrew his foot and started talking to Sally, and she suppressed a little pang of disappointment as she turned to the man on her right with a smile. 'Hello, I'm Libby Tate,' she said.

'Ah, yes, Andrew's girl. You're breaking hearts all round this table, I hope you realise?' he said softly, and held out his hand. 'Chris Turner. We're neighbours and old friends of the family. It's nice to meet you, Libby—very nice. I always knew he'd settle down in his own time, and it's good to see him looking happy.'

Oh, good grief. What on earth was she supposed to say to that? Nothing, apparently. Chris just winked and sat back with a kindly smile. 'So, tell me, what do you do?'

'I'm a ward sister on Paediatrics. I work alongside Andrew at the Audley Memorial Hospital.'

'Ah. A *real* person. That explains it all.'

She frowned in confusion, and Chris chuckled.

'My wife Louise and I have watched the boys grow up, and we always knew they'd go their own way. Why Andrew's taken so long I can't imagine, but I expect he was just waiting for the right woman.'

'Are you stirring, Turner?' Andrew said from across the table where he'd clearly been watching and lip-reading, and Chris chuckled again.

'Of course not. Would I?'

'Probably. It's all lies, Libby. You don't want to listen to anything he says.'

She did, though, because he was telling her all sorts of fascinating things about Andrew, and she was hanging on his every word. It emerged that far from being a farmer, Chris was a GP, the Ashendens' family doctor, his wife the local vicar, and he told her hilarious stories of Andrew's childhood, the humour fading at one point as he talked about Will's illness, and how much it had affected Andrew, who'd been at medical school at the time.

'He changed then. He used to be a bit of a wild child, but then suddenly, it was as if the joy went out of him.'

'Because of Will?' she asked, her voice hushed.

Chris shrugged. 'Who knows? But he's a good man,' he said softly. 'If Will hadn't recovered so well I'm sure he would have chucked in his career to come home and help care for him if it had been necessary. It's the sort of thing he'd do without a second thought, but he never talks about it. He just gets on with it, no matter what it costs him in terms of time and effort, and when

Will recovered so well, he threw himself back into medicine and he's been focussed on it ever since, to the exclusion of everything else. He's a fantastically dedicated doctor—but you already know that. I'm preaching to the converted.'

'Oh, you are. He's amazing,' she agreed thoughtfully. She'd seen him at work, seen how dedicated he was, and it made sense now—the close way he followed up his young patients, the passionate zeal with which he directed their treatment, the dedicated focus on his career. No wonder he didn't have a wife and family. He simply didn't have time.

But Chris was right, she'd seen him smile more in the last day or two than she had in all the previous months she'd known him. Was that down to her? No, surely not. He was just showing her another side of himself, a side that Chris had maybe not seen recently.

She glanced up at Andrew and caught his eye, and he winked at her, then turned back to Will. That he had a very close bond with his younger brother was blindingly obvious from the banter that was taking place between them now across the table. The teasing affection between them brought a lump to her throat and she wanted to talk to Will, to hear more from him about Andrew, and when Chris's attention was taken by the lady on his other side, Will turned towards her and gave her a rueful grin.

'Sorry, I've been neglecting you,' he said.

'Don't worry,' she said, smiling back. 'Chris has been looking after me. You can pay me back in a minute, though, I'm struggling to work out which knife and fork I need next,' she added in an undertone, and he laughed out loud, making Andrew frown curiously at them.

'Frightful, isn't it?' he said with a playful wince. 'Starting at the outside and working inwards is usually a good plan, but if you want to be sure, watch Andrew, not me. He's pretty good on the old protocol, but I don't care. Frankly I don't have a lot of time for it. I'm much more interested in the people.' His eyes flicked over her, the curiosity in them undisguised. 'On the subject of which, how long have you known my brother?' he murmured, and she felt her heart lurch a little.

Here we go, she thought, determined not to lie and hoping he wouldn't put her in the position where she had to. 'Six months,' she told him, 'since he started at the hospital.'

'Good grief, the dark horse,' he said slowly, shooting a glance in Andrew's direction. 'Still, I can see why he'd want to keep you to himself, but it's too late now, he's rumbled. You can save me a dance tomorrow night. Rumour has it I'm better than him.'

'I wonder who started that rumour?' she teased, but then confessed, 'I wouldn't know what he's like. We haven't danced together yet.' Or anything else apart from work, come to that, she thought with another hitch in her pulse, but Will didn't need to know that.

'Well, here's your chance. You can dance with us both and judge for yourself. Not that you'd be disloyal and unkind enough to tell either of us the truth,' he said with gentle mockery. 'So—tell me about yourself, Libby Tate. What makes you tick?'

'Oh, there's nothing to tell,' she said lightly, wondering what Andrew would have told him and how much of it she was going to contradict if she said anything, but Will just smiled.

'I'll just bet there is,' he said, his voice still low. 'I

think you're probably a complex and fascinating woman, but I get the feeling he doesn't know much about you, either. Curious.'

Suddenly she couldn't do this—couldn't lie to his brother, pretend they were together when they weren't. Not like that, anyway—and not when he'd already worked it out.

'We haven't been going out together long,' she admitted, for Andrew's sake not revealing just how brief their non-relationship was, but Will just nodded and smiled slightly.

'No. I thought not. Correct me if I'm wrong, but I've got a sneaking suspicion you're only here as a smoke-screen to disguise the fact that he doesn't have a social life—or am I mistaken?'

She felt her cheeks heat, and he chuckled softly. 'Don't worry, your secret's safe with me, and maybe that is why he's invited you, but I get the feeling there's more to it—or at least, maybe you'd like there to be, and I can see Andrew would.'

She opened her mouth to protest, but he just arched a brow slightly and murmured, 'Just so you know, I probably ought to warn you Ma's put you together in his room.'

Her fork slipped through her fingers, and he caught it between his hand and the edge of the table, meeting her shocked eyes with a grin. 'Steady, now,' he murmured, then his smile softened. 'Don't worry, there's a hideously uncomfortable divan in the dressing room. He'll sleep on that, he's nothing if not a gentle-man.'

Did she want that? She met Andrew's watchful eyes across the table, and suddenly she wasn't so sure. She wondered if he'd known about their sleeping arrangements before, and decided probably not. He was too straightforward to be devious, that much she did know about him, and he'd promised her no strings.

So would he take the divan? Or break his promise?

Divan, she realised, and felt a flicker of something that could easily have been disappointment.

Andrew thought the dinner would never end.

Libby was sandwiched between his brother and Chris Turner, and one after the other they were telling tales about him. He knew this from the mocking glances he kept getting from Will, and the active curiosity of Chris's steady, unruffled gaze.

He had no idea what Will was asking her. She'd blushed at one point and shot him a slightly desperate glance, but there was nothing he could do about it in the way of damage limitation from the other side of the table. He'd just have to talk to her later and find out what he'd said. Of course, if he'd been sitting next to her…

At last, when his nerves were stretched to breaking point, the meal came to and end and they all headed for the drawing room, and as soon as he could he reached Libby's side and slid a possessive arm around her waist, giving her a reassuring squeeze.

'Hi. Have you survived?' he murmured.

She laughed brightly, but a soft blush touched her cheeks and sent his blood pressure rocketing. 'Of course. Your brother and Chris have been fascinating dinner companions.'

'I'm sure,' he said drily. 'I should have got to the seating plan.'

'No, that was me,' Will said with a grin that made

Libby feel distinctly nervous. 'I wanted to get to know your new woman.'

'Did you. Well, what a surprise. More coffee, Libby, or another drink?'

She shook her head. 'No, I don't need any more alcohol and the coffee'll keep me awake and I'm wilting on my feet, I'm afraid. Would it be dreadfully rude to turn in?'

'Not at all, I think it sounds an excellent idea. I'll get our cases in from the car and we can make ourselves scarce. Will, do you have any idea where Mum's put us?'

'Your room.'

Just that. Nothing more, except for the knowing look in Will's eyes, and Andrew stifled a groan, nodded curtly and turned to Libby. 'I'll get the luggage and come back for you,' he said, and left her there with Will and Sally while he headed for the back stairs and the way out to the car.

Damn. He couldn't believe his mother would have done that, but maybe she'd thought she was being broad-minded. After all, he was thirty-four. It wouldn't be unlikely that he'd be sharing a room with his girlfriend.

Only she wasn't his girlfriend, more's the pity, and he had rather expected his mother to be more old-fashioned about it.

Damn, damn, damn!

He hauled their cases out of the boot of his car, plipped the remote and took them up to his room.

Flowers. Flowers on the chest of drawers. He'd *never* had flowers in his room—but come to that, he'd never stayed here with a woman. He realised in shock that it was the first time he'd ever brought a woman home—

well, if you didn't count innocent teenage flings and friends from college, which he didn't—and he'd had no idea how his mother would react.

Or overreact.

He stuck his head round the corner into the dressing room and saw the small divan neatly made up, and he heaved a sigh of relief. She'd left his options open, bless her heart, and he was sure they'd cope. Except, of course, that the little bed was a heap of springs and far too small for his adult frame, but there was no way he'd ask Libby to sleep on it. It was out of the Spanish Inquisition.

He'd manage. There probably wasn't another option, anyway. The house would be bursting at the seams, even Will and Sally's spare rooms would have been pressed into service, and at least in this room they had the choice of sleeping arrangements. Not that it was much of a choice. He put his case on the hateful little daybed, hers on the big, comfortable half-tester in the main room, switched on the bedside lights and went back down to retrieve her, because he was running out of steam. Two sleepless nights on the trot were getting to him, and he had no idea if he'd be called back to the hospital tonight for little Jacob.

He hoped not. He'd only had one glass of champagne all evening just in case, and he'd left half of that, but if he didn't get his head down soon he'd be no good in an emergency anyway.

She was standing where he'd left her, engaged in conversation with his cousin Charlotte, and his heart sank. Charlotte was a nightmare. She'd had a crush on him for years, and she wouldn't be wasting any time laying her claim.

'Hi, Charlie,' he said, just to annoy her, and buzzed her cheek briefly before turning to Libby and sliding his arm around her waist and easing her closer. 'I'm sorry, you're going to have to excuse us, we're both bushed and we need an early night, don't we, darling?'

She tilted her face up to his and smiled, and only he could see the mockery in her eyes. 'Oh, yes, absolutely. Sorry. It's been lovely to meet you, Charlotte. Night, Will, night, Sally. See you tomorrow.'

And slipping her arm around his waist, she wriggled closer and let him steer her towards the stairs.

'Darling?' she murmured under her breath, shooting him a sideways look as they went together up the first step, and he chuckled.

'Sorry. That was for Cousin Charlotte's benefit.'

'Ahh. Would that be zillionth cousin Charlotte umpteen times removed, by any chance?' she said lightly, and he laughed again.

'That would be the one. I thought Will would have the sense to lose her for you.'

'I think Will imagined I could take care of myself,' she replied, easing out of his hold as soon as they'd turned the corner and were out of view. 'He also tells me you're a gentleman.'

He turned the knob and pushed the bedroom door open. 'Sadly, he's right,' he said, closing the door behind them and stifling a sigh of regret. 'I'll be sleeping round the corner. The bathroom's through there; I'll let you go first.'

She woke on Saturday morning to the sound of water running, and lay and listened as Andrew showered in the en suite bathroom which had been stolen from part of the adjoining dressing room where he'd spent the night, as she'd realised he would. It was still early—only half past seven, and they'd been up until after midnight, so she wondered if he'd had a call to go to the hospital.

No. He wouldn't be showering if that was the case, he'd just dress and run. A sunbeam slanted through a chink in the curtains, and she crept out of bed and opened them. It was a beautiful day—gloriously sunny, the sky a brilliant blue with scudding white clouds and the promise of spring.

But only the promise. She shivered a little, realising that the sunshine was deceptive. The heating was on—she could hear the pipes creaking, but the old house must be as leaky as a sieve and trying to heat it was inevitably to fight a losing battle. She could feel the draught around the window frame as she stood looking out across the rolling parkland towards the river in the distance. The willows by the river were bursting into leaf, and she could hear birds singing.

Beautiful, she thought, and smiled. Much better than Paris, and she'd still get her riverside walk. Pity about her cream jumper…

The bathroom door opened and Andrew walked out, naked except for a towel wrapped round his waist and looking bright-eyed and bushy-tailed and full of the joys of spring. And mouthwateringly gorgeous.

He grinned at her. 'Morning. I didn't expect that you'd be up yet. I hope I didn't wake you.'

She shook her head. 'Not really. I never sleep late, and to be honest it's so quiet here it's a little eerie. There isn't a soul about, only the birds.'

'Will's sure to be up. He always rides first thing, and he's bound to be out today—it's a gorgeous day.'

She dragged her eyes off his chest. 'So I see,' she replied, turning back to the window and trying not to think too much about that broad, muscular expanse under the scatter of dark hair glistening with water droplets. 'Can we go for that walk you were talking about?'

'Sure. I'll throw my clothes on and leave you to get ready. I'll be in the kitchen. I take it you can find your way?'

'I'm sure I'll manage. I'll ring you on your mobile if I get lost,' she joked. 'Down the stairs and along the corridor?'

'Go the easy way—turn left, straight to the end of the landing, down the back stairs and the kitchen's at the bottom,' he told her. 'I'll go and get the kettle on—do you want breakfast now or do you want to wait for the whole full English shindig with kippers and scrambled egg and Cousin Charlotte?'

She laughed and turned away from the window. 'I think we can avoid Cousin Charlotte. You do realise she's in love with you, do you?'

He gave a wry smile. 'Oh, yes. She tells me every time she gets me alone, which is as infrequently as I can manage it. She's been in love with me for years. So—fancy a cooked breakfast? I can probably rustle something up.'

Libby shook her head. 'No, I'm still full from last night. I'll have a quick shower and join you in a minute, then could we have tea and toast?'

'Sure. I'll give you ten minutes.' He went into the dressing room, pulling on a pair of well-worn jeans and his weary old loafers to the sound of running water in the shower, dragging a jumper over his head as he headed for the door and tried not to think of what she was doing behind the bathroom door.

He needed to get out of there, to suck some air into

his lungs and forget about how she'd looked when he'd woken, her hair trailed across her pillow, the soft, silky strands fanned out against the white Egyptian cotton, her lashes lying like crescents against her pale cheeks—and then just a few minutes later, standing in front of the window with the early morning sun behind her, outlining her body perfectly through the fine fabric of her nightdress. Her long and perfectly respectable nightdress—if you didn't count the effect of the sunlight streaming through it…

He went down to the kitchen and let the dogs out, then put the kettle on the Aga and hummed softly as it boiled. There was a mountain of bread of every description in the larder, and he chose a lovely nutty wholemeal, sliced it and sandwiched it in the wire toasting gadget and clamped it under the hob cover, flipping it after a minute to toast the other side, and as he pulled it out the door opened and Libby came in, looking fresh as a daisy and squeaky-clean, and he just wanted to hug her.

Instead, he smiled, poured boiling water on the tea bags and stacked the toast on a plate in the middle of the battered old table. 'Just shove the dogs out of the way and sit down. Jam, marmalade, honey or Marmite?'

'Oh, marmalade, please. Thanks. That smells fantastic. Hello, dogs, aren't you lovely? Oh, tea—bless you!'

And she buried her nose in the mug and breathed deeply, her fingers wrapped round it, the steam drifting around her like a wraith, and he wanted her as he hadn't wanted a woman in years.

Or maybe for ever…

It really was the most gorgeous day. The wind was chilly, but she was well wrapped up. Andrew had kitted her out in borrowed wellies and a thick, warm jacket, and he took her down to the river, as he'd promised.

'This is lovely,' she sighed, leaning against a fence and staring out over the lightly ruffled water. The sunlight was sparkling on it, and she could see birds bobbing about near the shore.

He propped his elbows on the rail beside her and gave her a wry smile. 'I'm sorry it's not the Seine.'

'Oh, no, don't be sorry, it's beautiful,' she murmured, watching a swan circling lazily in the water. 'So peaceful—it's bliss. I can't think of anything better.'

He smiled, and they strolled on, the dogs milling around and sniffing, and Lara appeared out of nowhere and joined them, the three of them racing off into the undergrowth after a rabbit.

'Will can't be far away,' Andrew said, and a few moments later they heard the drum of approaching hoofbeats. Will pulled up alongside them, grinning down at them as the bay mare caught her breath, sides heaving, chest wet and flecked with foam.

'Morning!'

Libby smiled up at him. 'Good morning. What a lovely day.'

'Been somewhere in a hurry?' Andrew asked mildly, eyeing the sweaty horse, but Will just laughed.

'We went round the new cross-country course again. She's brilliant, I love her.'

'I thought she was a temperamental cow?'

He laughed again. 'She was—last week. That's women for you, but she's the bravest horse I've ever had. You ought to take her for a ride, you'll love her.'

'I'll take your word for it, she's a bit feisty for me,' Andrew said, patting the mare's wet, steaming neck and rubbing her nose. 'I'm getting too old to break things, and so are you.'

'Rubbish, you're just a coward and, anyway, she's a schoolmistress, safe as houses. I'd put a child on her.'

'I shouldn't tell Sally that,' he muttered drily, but Will just laughed.

'Seen Lara, by the way? She's messed off again.'

'Oh, she's around somewhere. She got distracted by a rabbit and went off with the others. We'll bring her back.'

'No, she'll come, she won't want to miss breakfast. We're having bacon and she's already clocked it, the thief. Sally only just got there first. Never trust a lurcher, Libby,' he advised with a grin, then he turned in the saddle and let out a piercing whistle, and Lara came bounding up, tongue lolling, grinning cheerfully. She'd obviously had a lovely run, and with a wave Will turned his mare towards the house and made his way back at a much more sedate pace, Lara trotting at the horse's heels.

'Is your brother a bit of a daredevil?' Libby asked thoughtfully, watching him ride away, and Andrew gave a grunt of laughter.

'Just a bit. Fortunately, he's got the most natural seat I've ever seen, and he just stays stuck—which is a good job, because he's got more courage than sense and he gives Mum and Sally fits. I thought with the baby coming, maybe he'd settle down, become a bit more responsible, but he's just crazy. That's how he got into the charity thing—he was doing sky-dives and bungee-jumps and marathons, stuff like that, and it occurred to him he could raise money doing it, so it sort of legitimises his lunacy.'

'So what does Sally think of it?'

He shrugged. 'She just grits her teeth, but I know she's getting more worried. I mean, it's not just her now, is it, and sometimes I think he hasn't got a shred of responsibility.'

'Is it just a reaction to his illness?' she asked, thinking about what Chris had said the night before, and Andrew nodded.

'Yes. Well, I think so, in a way. He didn't die, he got away with it, so he thinks he can get away with anything. Only one day he'll find out he can't, and then Sally will be left picking up the pieces.'

They strolled on for a while, but the wind off the water was chilly, even with a thick jacket on, so they turned away from the river, heading back across the park to the house by a different route. And as they walked, she got her first real appreciation of the scale of the house and its grounds—his heritage, his destiny and, extraordinarily, his home. It was just another world and, beautiful though it was, she didn't envy him any of it for an instant. Except maybe the peace and quiet and the sense of space. That was really special.

They went through a little wood, and startled a small herd of deer. They lifted their heads, stood motionless for a second and then bounded away, leaving her entranced. 'Oh—how lovely,' she murmured. 'They're beautiful!'

'Yes, they are. They're a bit destructive, though. Mum constantly wages war on them. They get into the garden and cause havoc. So do the rabbits, which we're overrun with. One of the drawbacks of the sandy soil, I'm afraid, but the garden's walled, so it's not as bad as it could be.'

They emerged from the wood and he stopped her with his hand on her arm. 'Look—can you see the folly?'

She looked where he was pointing, but she couldn't see anything. Not until he came right up beside her. 'There—look along my arm,' he murmured, leaning closer so she could do that, the warmth of his body surrounding her. She breathed deeply, drawing in the scent of his skin, and then she opened her eyes and there it was, a little circular building sheltering on the edge of another small wood some distance away.

'Oh, it's pretty!'

'It is—it's delightful. Completely useless, but delightful. My great-grandfather's idea, apparently. He built it for his wife, but she hated it. Called it lewd and uncivilised and refused to go there.'

'Strange woman. I think it's lovely.'

'So do I, but she had a point. I'll show you later, if we've got time.'

They joined a track cutting across the park, and as they approached the house, she saw it from the front for the first time, with the huge green copper dome that must be above that beautiful ceiling in the entrance hall, and it took her breath away. It was glorious. Magnificent—and a terrifying responsibility. No wonder he was daunted by it—or at least, if not daunted, fighting against the inevitability of it.

She could see people milling about, vans being unloaded, others arriving, and here and there a group of people strolling on the grass. She recognised some of them from the night before, and realised they were the guests. The others were much more businesslike, engaged, she imagined, on preparing the house for the ball.

'So what happens for the rest of the day?' she asked, wondering how she'd cope if they had to go shooting, for example, but his words reassured her.

'Oh, I'm sure there'll be a packed programme of activities for anyone who can be bothered. We can join in, if you want, or keep our heads down and chill. Up to you.'

'Chill?' she suggested tentatively, horribly aware of how grand it all was and how out of her depth she'd felt last night amongst all the socialite butterflies, and he flashed her a smile.

'That would be my preference,' he said honestly, 'but I don't want you to be bored.'

'Oh, I won't be bored,' she assured him instantly. 'How could I be bored? Look at it! It's so beautiful here, all this stunning countryside.'

His mouth lifted in a wry smile. 'All I see is a pile of responsibilities stretching away into the hereafter. It should go to Will, really. He's the one who loves it, the one with the vision. He knows every inch of it far better than I ever will. You ought to ask him to give you a guided tour.'

'I'd rather you showed me.'

His smile softened. 'So would I. We'll take a drive this afternoon, go for a walk in the woods—we could have lunch out, if you like, rather than stay here. There's a pub in the village down on the river, it's rather nice. Or we can take a picnic and eat it in the folly. I'm sure there's something in one of the fridges we can steal.'

'Shouldn't we be here for lunch? The dutiful son and all that?' she asked, but he shook his head, his eyes glinting with mischief.

'Only if you want to brave Charlie again.'

'Oh, poor Charlotte. I think I'll pass,' she said with a contrite smile. 'I feel so guilty when she tells me you're virtually engaged.'

'Don't. It's just her wishful thinking, she'll get over it one day.'

'In which case, a picnic in the folly sounds perfect. Won't the caterers mind if you raid the fridge, though?'

His smile widened. 'No,' he said confidently. 'We'll steal it from the family kitchen. The caterers for tonight's extravaganza will be working in the visitors' centre—they've got a big catering kitchen over there and it's perfect for such a large function, but the cooks who work in the visitors' centre restaurant will be doing lunch in the house, and they won't mind if we steal something from the buffet stash. They love me.'

His grin was cocky and boyish and endearing, and she could easily see how they might indeed love him. It wouldn't be hard at all, she thought wistfully, and felt sorry for Charlotte all over again.

They went in through the back door, into the family kitchen where they'd had breakfast with the dogs, and found breakfast cleared away and the team of cooks in full swing preparing lunch for the house guests; they greeted him with smiles and told him to help himself, so Andrew swiped a few slices of asparagus and mushroom quiche still warm from the oven, a bowl of salad and a handful of crusty rolls, put them in a basket with a bottle of spring water and some plastic cups and a bunch of grapes and some cheese, and they headed off in the car. She took her borrowed boots and jacket, and they drove to the edge of a wood, parked the car and walked to the folly.

'Oh, it's beautiful! The walls are all painted!' she exclaimed, her eyes wide as she stepped inside and stared around.

He saw the moment she registered the content, the

soft colour that swept her cheeks, the muffled laugh through fingers pressed lightly against her lips. 'I understand now why she thought it was lewd and uncivilised, but really they're lovely,' she said, turning to him with a smile, and he smiled back, watching her as she looked again at the paintings of naked lovers frolicking in the woods; her eyes were entranced, and he was pleased he'd brought her here—pleased he'd had the idea of the picnic and that she hadn't wanted to do all the tedious and organised things that the others would be doing. This way he had her to himself, but the downside was they were alone in a room designed for lovers, a room filled with images that heated his imagination and made his thoughts run riot.

Thoughts filled with images of him and Libby.

And that was worrying. It wasn't supposed to be like this; she was there for show, not for him to sneak away with alone and have more fun than he'd had in years, frolicking in the folly surrounded by nymphs in gauzy gowns flitting through the fading scenery. The memory of her this morning with the sun streaming through her fine cotton nightdress hit him in the solar plexus, and his breath jammed in his throat.

'It'll be warmer outside,' he said, suddenly desperate to get away from the paintings, so they went back out into the sunshine and sat down on the steps, looking out over a bend in the river in the distance, and they ate the picnic slowly, savouring the view, somehow not needing to talk. So refreshing, he thought, to sit with her and not have to fill the silence.

A squirrel came up to them, head tilted slightly on one side, and she threw it a tiny crumb of quiche.

'Feeding the wildlife?' he murmured, and the

squirrel grabbed it and fled, darting up a tree and disappearing.

'It's probably got young,' she said.

'Probably. Are you all done?'

'Mmm. That was lovely, thank you. Much nicer than being polite to poor little Charlotte. So what now?'

'I can show you the bits we didn't get to this morning, if you like?'

'Sounds good.'

'Let's go, then,' he said, packing up the things and getting to his feet. They walked and drove and walked again, and despite everything he'd said about the place, she could see that he loved it.

It was in his blood, in his bones. How could he not love it? And yet he was right, it was an awesome responsibility, and as he talked about it, about how they were merely caretakers for the future generations, about the struggle to make ends meet, the difficulties of opening the house and gardens to the public, the rules and regulations, the health and safety implications, she could see how it could be a love-hate relationship.

'It must be a nightmare opening to the public,' she mused as they stood and looked at the house across the wide expanse of the park. 'I can't imagine anything more stressful than having people wandering through my home touching everything. Do you use all the rooms and have to clear them up the night before?'

He laughed softly and shook his head. 'No. The ones we open are the big rooms that we don't use that much, and now Will's in the east wing and I don't live here any more it's much easier. Visitors don't have access to all the house, by any means, and the walkways are all roped off to corral them a bit, but there's always the odd one who tries to escape from the guides. There's a bedroom Queen Victoria stayed in and the old nursery, and the drawing room and dining room we used last night, and of course the ballroom, which you'll see later. That's gorgeous. And the old Victorian kitchen. That's next to the family kitchen and it's lovely, but it's never used. It's just a museum piece now, like one of the bathrooms and some of the other bits like part of the stable block and the old coach house, but it's all pretty strung out so they feel they've seen more than they have, really.'

Another kitchen? That made three—four if she counted Will and Sally's. 'Don't you ever get lost?' she asked, slightly dazed, but he just smiled and shook his head.

'No. I grew up here, don't forget, and Will and I had the run of the place.'

'I bet you were a nightmare.'

'Who, me? No way,' he said, eyes alight with mischief, and she could just imagine him as an eight-year-old, all skinned knees and sparkling eyes and wicked little grin, ricocheting from one scrape to another.

And just the thought was enough to make her heart ache. If she was lucky, then one day she might have a son, a little boy like Andrew must have been—but that all depended on which way the dice had fallen, and until she knew…

She shivered as the wind picked up and the temperature dropped, and he realised he'd rambled on and kept her out in the wind for ages. 'I'm sorry, you're cold—have you seen enough?' he asked, and she nodded, so they headed back towards the car. She snuggled down inside the jacket and turned the collar up, and he looked at the glow in her cheeks and the sparkle in her eyes, and felt a surge of regret that this wasn't a real relationship, that they were in his room together under false pretences and that once they returned to Audley tomorrow it would all come to an end and they'd go back to normal, him the overworked, harassed consultant, her the overworked but always cheerful ward sister.

Hell, it was going to be hard to do that. He'd forgotten what they were supposed to be doing, had let himself get carried away by the moment and spent the day having fun with her—good, clean, healthy fun, free of ties and responsibilities and obligations, and it had been wonderful.

He wanted to pull her into his arms and kiss her, to fold her against his chest and hold her tight, just stand there with her in his arms while time stood still and the world moved on without them. But he couldn't. He had responsibilities that day, and he'd shirked them long enough. The ball was taken care of, but he had a duty to the other guests, and his mother was probably going to hang him out to dry if he didn't get back there soon.

Either that or she'd be planning the wedding.

He unlocked the car, opened the door for her and as she slid in and reached for the seat belt their eyes met and she smiled.

'Thank you, Andrew. I've had the best day,' she said, and he just couldn't help himself. He leant in and kissed her—the lightest, slightest brush of his lips against hers, but his heart kicked hard against his ribs and blood surged through him.

He stepped back and shut the door a little more firmly than was necessary, went round and slid behind the wheel and drove home in silence, regret for what could never be wedged like a ball in his throat.

If the dinner party had been a glittering occasion, the ball that night promised to be a firework display. The place had been a hive of activity from dawn onwards, and the pace had only picked up as the day went on. Now, though, was the lull before the storm. The cars and vans were gone or parked out of sight, the stage was set, and she felt a tingle of excitement. She'd never been to a white-tie ball before, and she was assailed by doubts about Amy's dress.

Oh, well, nothing she could do about it now. It was all she had with her and it would have to do.

Andrew changed first. He disappeared into his dressing room and emerged in trousers and a shirt hanging open down the front. The wing collar was attached, but the stiffly starched front was meant to close with studs. The studs he had in his hand.

'Can you put these in for me? This shirt is an instrument of torture and I just can't do it. There's a pocket here you can put your hand in to make it easier to reach,' he demonstrated, and so she found herself nose to nose with his warm, solid, muscular chest, breathing in the scent of cologne and soap and, underlying it all, the drugging, masculine scent of his body.

Following his instructions, she put the first stud through from the back and her fingers brushed against the soft scatter of dark hair, sending heat coursing through her.

Darn it, how could he do this to her? She was almost whimpering by the time she'd fastened the last one, her fingers against the shirt front picking up the steady, even beat of his heart, the warmth of his body, the solidity, while the subtle spicy tones of his aftershave curled around her nostrils and teased her.

Andrew was struggling, too, the feel of her fingers tormenting him unbearably. 'All done,' she said at last, and he thanked her, stepping back the moment her hands fell away, and wheeled round and disappeared to assemble the rest of his elaborate and formal dress.

He wondered if she had any idea of the effect she had on him. Watching her, her soft, full bottom lip caught between her even white teeth, feeling her slender fingers brush against his chest, inhaling the scent of apples that drifted from her hair—it had been enough to kill him. And he was going to have to dance with her tonight. It would be expected, by her, by his mother, and most particularly by all the women who'd like to be in her place.

Maybe she'd hate dancing and they could sit it out, he thought, clutching at straws, but he had a feeling Libby didn't hate anything. She wasn't a wild party girl by any means, but she'd enjoyed herself last night, mixed easily with his friends and family, and he just knew she'd want to dance. Not that he didn't want to. Rather the opposite, but he just didn't trust himself to hold her in his arms without disgracing himself.

By the time he emerged in the long black tailcoat and white waistcoat over the satin-stripe trousers, his white bow-tie finally tied to his satisfaction, he'd managed to get himself back under control to a certain extent. 'Right, are you OK to get ready on your own or will you need help with anything?' he asked, hoping she'd say she could cope, and to his relief she nodded.

'I'll be fine.'

'Right. I'm going to help Will. He doesn't stand a

prayer of getting into this lot on his own, and Sally will be up to her eyes. She's organising the ball. Come down and find us—if you go down the back stairs by the kitchen, then turn left, you'll see the door to their wing in front of you. Just bang on the door and come in when you're done.'

Libby nodded, and he went out and shut the door, pausing for a moment to suck in a deep breath before striding along the corridor and down to the communicating door.

He rapped sharply and went in, to find his brother upstairs in the bedroom struggling to attach the starched shirt collar.

'Here, let me,' he said, taking over. 'They're an utter pain in the butt. I just got Libby to dress me. Damn Mum and her grand ideas.'

Will laughed and relinquished the task, lounging against the wall and watching thoughtfully. 'So—had a good day with Libby?'

'Lovely,' he said tightly, trying not to think about it. 'Right, put this on and let's try and do the front studs,' he said, holding out the shirt, and Will shrugged into it and stood while he struggled with the fastenings. 'Cock-eyed, antiquated arrangement,' he grumbled, then stood back. 'Bow-tie?'

'I can do that. Have a drink—there's a nice malt in the kitchen.'

'No. I might have to shoot off.'

'You can't!'

'There's a boy in PICU—'

'When isn't there? Ring and find out how he's doing. Then you can relax.'

'Never that straightforward, though, is it?' he

murmured, keying in the number and checking on his little patient.

'Well?'

'He's stable. No change—which is good. I'm hopeful.'

'Excellent. So get yourself a drink and tell me all about Libby while I do this blasted tie up.'

CHAPTER FOUR

SHE stared at herself in the mirror.

It was a fabulous dress, she had to agree with Amy, but the cleavage worried her and she was concerned about the formality of the occasion. Was flesh allowed? Because there was plenty of it.

She groaned and gave the top another little tug. If only Andrew was here and she could show it to him before she walked through the house and made an utter fool of herself, but of course he wasn't, and he wasn't going to be, so she shrugged, draped the oyster pink pashmina around her shoulders and flipped the end back over her left shoulder so it covered her chest, and then studied her reflection again.

Better. More—well, less, really. She wriggled into the shoes, turned sideways for one last check for VPL, then took a deep breath and opened the door, to find Andrew on the other side, his hand poised to knock.

'Ah—you're ready,' he said, his eyes scanning her. 'I was just coming to check you were OK.'

'Yes—well, I think so. Will I do? Formal enough?'

He opened his mouth, shut it as if he'd thought better of whatever he was going to say and nodded. 'Perfect,' he said, but she wasn't convinced. What had he been going to say?

'Is there a subtext—like, no flesh showing or anything?' she asked, still unsure because of course he couldn't see the neckline with the pashmina in the way, but he just gave a slightly strained laugh and shook his head.

'No, flesh is fine. I've just seen Charlie in the hall, with a dress slit up virtually to the waist, so unless there really isn't a front to that dress under the shawl thing, I don't think you've got a problem. You'll have to go a long way to show more than her.'

She felt her shoulders drop with relief, and the pashmina slid down and his eyes tracked its path, stopping at her cleavage, and they both froze.

She swallowed hard. 'Still think it's all right?' she asked, her nerves on edge for some reason, and after an endless moment he reached for the pashmina and tucked it back over her left shoulder again with gentle fingers.

'On second thoughts, perhaps a little decorum. I don't want my father having a heart attack,' he said gruffly, and then offered her his arm. 'Shall we?'

Damn. She'd known it was too much. Oh, well, it was too late now, but at least she could keep the dress covered. They reached the hall, and Sally came quickly over to them. 'Libby—I've got a corsage for you,' she said, handing her a delicate creamy-white orchid spray, and then she smiled brightly and hurried off.

'I could pin the pashmina with it,' she suggested, and he nodded, looking relieved.

'Good idea. Here, let me.' And he pinned it in place, giving her a fleeting, enigmatic smile, then tucked her hand back in his arm and led her into the fray.

'Oh, my goodness, there are so many people,' she murmured, and he squeezed her hand.

'Don't worry, I won't abandon you,' he promised, and he didn't. He kept her close all evening, and she was astonished to discover that she was seated next to him at the top table.

If she was supposed to be some kind of deflector for the single girls, she couldn't have been given a more high-profile position, she realised, feeling Charlotte's eyes on her, and she felt the most appalling fraud. The cutlery conundrum came back to haunt her, and if she'd thought that last night's dinner was formal, this was even more so.

But she coped, somehow, managing the endless selection of knives and forks and spoons by following Andrew's lead, making polite conversation to his uncle on her other side and hoping that she wouldn't knock over her wine glass or drop something down the pashmina so she had to take it off and reveal all.

But she got through the meal without a disaster, and then his father tapped a glass and stood up.

'Friends, family, may I have your attention? As you all know, we're here to celebrate Jane's birthday, and I just wanted to say a very few words in praise of a woman who's been a remarkable wife and companion to me for nearly thirty-five years—forty, if you count the time I spent chasing after her before she let me catch her,' he said to a ripple of laughter. 'And I'd be lying if I said she didn't look a day older than on her twenty-first birthday, but she's certainly no less beautiful, at least to me, and I would just like to thank her, in front of you all, for the many years of happiness she's brought me, for the laughter and tears, the companionship, the challenge, and most particularly for the precious gift of our two sons. I know they would like a chance to thank her publicly for all she's done, so if you could bear with us—Andrew? Would you like to start?'

He'd known it was coming, but he'd managed to ignore it, so preoccupied by the earlier glimpse of Libby's cleavage that his brain had been all but wiped clean. He got to his feet and smiled at everyone, then looked up the table to his mother, ignoring the hastily scribbled notes in his pocket and deciding to wing it. This was his mother, after all. If he couldn't tell her what he thought of her without notes, it was a pretty poor thing.

'You had no idea what you started thirty-four years ago, did you, Mum?' he teased. 'Well, let me tell you. You made me curious. You made me want to know the answers, to persevere until I got them, to change the way it was if I didn't like what I learned, and to live with what I couldn't change. You taught me never to give up, never to give in, never to walk away from anything except a fight. You taught me the difference between right and wrong, the difference between pride and arrogance. You taught me to walk, to ride, to swim, to laugh at myself and not others, to read all sorts of fascinating and amazing things—and to love. You taught me not only to work, but also to play, the value of family, the importance of caring.

'You're a remarkable woman, and you've made me what I am; I owe it all to you, so thank you for that, from the bottom of my heart.'

He sat down again, a lump in his throat, and felt Libby's hand squeeze his under the table before she turned towards Will. He was on his feet, and as they all waited for him to speak, the applause died away until the silence in the room was deafening.

Libby swallowed and bit her lip, her hand still in Andrew's, her eyes fixed on his brother. For the first time, Will wasn't smiling, and she felt her heart miss a beat.

'Well, what can I say?' he began eventually. 'I do public speaking all the time as part of my fundraising work, but this isn't public, this is my mother, the woman who gave birth to me, who taught me all the things she taught Andrew—and, technically, she's entitled to her pension now, but there's no way I'm going to let her retire from the fray without a fight,' he said, smiling briefly at the ripple of laughter through the room. But then his smile faded and he carried on.

'She had no idea when she had us, as Andrew said, what she was letting herself in for. I'm sure we were vile to bring up. Two healthy young boys, hell bent on living as fast and as hard as possible, but then it all got a little more serious, and without Ma's quick thinking I know I wouldn't be here today, so I cannot—*cannot*—underestimate what she means to me, and to the charities for which she works so tirelessly.

'It's because of her,' he concluded, 'that I'm able to stand here in front of you today on my own two feet, to thank her, and to ask you to join with me in raising a glass to her and wishing her a very happy birthday. Happy birthday, Ma. And thank you.'

Everyone got to their feet, the applause thunderous as Will turned to his mother and hugged her hard, then sat down, his eyes over-bright.

She glanced up at Andrew and realised he wasn't doing much better as he turned to her and held the chair for her to sit down again.

'You OK?' she murmured, and he smiled wryly and nodded.

'Yeah, I'm fine. It's just—he never talks about it like that. Not so openly, not to her. And it's—'

'Ladies and gentlemen, could I have your attention, please?'

Sally was on her feet now, standing beside Will with an envelope in her hand, and she looked round at everyone, then continued as silence fell, 'Her sons don't know this, but Lady Ashenden asked not to receive any presents for her birthday. As she put it, "What on earth could a woman of my age possibly need that I haven't already got?" And so, at her suggestion, anyone who felt that they would like to commemorate her birthday in this way was invited to make a donation to the charities they support for meningitis research and meningococcal disease, and I have to say you've been amazingly generous, because the total at the moment, not counting several last-minute donations, stands at twenty-seven thousand, six hundred and forty-five pounds.'

Will's jaw sagged, and beside Libby, Andrew sucked in his breath.

He looked across at Will, realised he was beyond saying anything and got to his feet again, holding his hands up for silence. 'I don't know what to say,' he began when the cheers and clapping had died away. 'Thank you, obviously. Thank you all so very, very much. The difference your generosity and the generosity of others like you all over the country makes to the children reached by these charities is immeasurable, and for them, for all the children who through donations like this one achieve a greater measure of independence and self-belief, we would all like to give you our heartfelt thanks. And, Mum, I guess we owe you lunch.'

That brought laughter to a room filled with too much

emotion, and moments later a huge birthday cake was wheeled in, blazing with candles, and they all—him, his brother, his father—had to go with her to blow the candles out.

Lady Ashenden, near to tears but quietly dignified, thanked all her guests—for coming, for their enormous generosity—and then put her arms around both of her sons and hugged them hard.

For Libby, sitting alone now on the top table, the whole event was deeply moving, and she felt incredibly privileged to have been invited. Will's story had had a happy ending, but it wasn't always like that. She'd seen it happen, seen the devastation caused by the disease. Not many. It wasn't that common, but you never forgot the children you'd worked with in that situation, and even one was too many.

Surreptitiously she wiped away her tears, sniffed hard and drained her wine glass.

'Bit of a tear-jerker, isn't it?'

She looked at Sally, who'd perched on Andrew's chair beside her, and dredged up a smile. 'Yes. How did you manage to speak to everyone after that? I would have been in bits. I *was* in bits.'

She shrugged. 'I've heard him speak before, and it's always very powerful. That's how he's so effective at fundraising. He does it every time—but this time, it was about his mother, and, well, to be honest I nearly didn't make it! Still, it's over now. They'll bring the cake round, and she's going to circulate while we all have coffee and eat the cake, then it's dancing! And Will says you've promised him a dance, so don't forget.'

Libby laughed. 'Yes—he says he's a better dancer than Andrew, and I have to check it out.'

'Does he, indeed? We'll see about that,' Andrew murmured from behind her, and she felt his hands settle warmly on her shoulders and pull her back against him. She tilted her head back to smile at him, and he dropped a kiss lightly on her forehead. She'd been about to reply, but the words dried up instantly and she forgot her own name as he scooped her up and sat down, settling her back on his lap with his arms looped round her waist.

Instinctively she put her arm around his shoulders to steady herself, her hand splayed over his shoulder, feeling the play of muscle beneath her fingertips through the fine wool of his tailcoat. She could feel the warmth from his muscular legs seeping through her dress, the solid bulk of his chest against her side, and the fact that they were doing it all for Cousin Charlotte's benefit seemed neither here nor there.

Her heart skittering in her chest, she ate her cake perched on his lap, sipped her coffee, laughed with them all when Will came over and cracked an endless succession of dreadful jokes, and then finally it was time to dance. The doors through to the ballroom were rolled aside, the music started and Andrew patted her on the bottom.

'Up you get, it's time to go and check out Will's theory,' he said, his eyes challenging his brother's, and her heart, which had only just settled, lurched against her ribs. She realised she'd been waiting for this since Will had issued the challenge the night before, and at last she was going to know what it was like to be held in Andrew's arms.

There was no question in her mind who would win. Will was fabulous—funny, sexy, outrageous—but he did nothing for her. Andrew, on the other hand…

The four of them headed to the dance floor in time to see Lord and Lady Ashenden have the first dance, and when Libby saw the string quartet, she felt a bubble of delighted laughter rise in her throat.

'Oh, proper dancing!' she said softly, enchanted.

He grinned. 'Well, we can make it improper if you like, but it's a little public.'

She punched his arm lightly and laughed, trying to ignore the little shiver of anticipation. 'You know what I mean. I just haven't ever done it except at dance classes. I didn't think people still did except on television.'

'Only sometimes. And one of the advantages of a stuffy, classical education is that I'm unlikely to step on your toes too often,' he said with a wry smile, and held out his hand to her, sketching a mocking bow as his eyes sparkled with challenge. 'So, shall we show my brother what we're made of?'

He'd been aching to hold her in his arms all night, longing for the moment to come, and he discovered to his delight that she was a beautiful, natural dancer. She followed his lead without a hitch, her hand light on his shoulder, her body just a fraction too far away for his liking—but that was probably just as well, given the total lack of privacy.

And when the time came he was reluctant in the extreme to hand her over to Will.

'She's lovely,' Sally said, smiling up at him as he led her to the side of the dance floor and settled her into a chair so that she could rest. 'A real sweetheart. I'm so glad you've found her.'

'Don't jump the gun,' he warned. 'She's just a friend.'

'Of course she is,' Sally said calmly. 'She's pretty, though. Delightful. And very intelligent. Will likes her a lot.'

'I can see that,' he growled, watching his laughing brother and the woman who was supposed to be his girlfriend twirling past in a flutter of shimmering silk and coat tails. Damn him, if he held her any closer…

'It's about time you found somebody nice,' Sally murmured, and he grunted. If only, he thought.

If only…

'So who's better?'

Torn by loyalty and honesty and a dislike of conflict of any sort, Libby looked from one brother to the other, and shook her head. 'Technically, I don't have the expertise to choose between you, so I would say you're quits. Andrew's very easy to follow, and Will might have the edge when it comes to fancy moves. You're both extremely good, and neither of you trod on my toes, which rates an A star in my book.'

'Very prettily put, but you didn't answer the question,' Will said, grinning. 'I knew you wouldn't.'

'Equal first?' she offered. 'I can't choose between you.'

'Or won't.'

'Oh, Libby, just tell him he's better,' Andrew groaned. 'Let him win. He won't give up until you do. It's not worth it.'

'OK, he's better. Is that what you want to hear?'

'Yes!' Will said smugly, and punched the air.

Andrew rolled his eyes and sighed. 'He's going to be insufferable. Take him away, Sally.'

'Good idea,' Sally said, hoisting herself out of the

chair and rubbing her back. 'It's past my bedtime and it's certainly past his.'

'Oh, promises,' Will murmured with a grin, and he slung his arm round Sally's shoulders, winked at them and steered her towards the door, looking slightly the worse for wear.

'So, who *is* better?' Andrew asked softly, wondering what she'd say now they were alone, and she turned and met his eyes.

'I don't know. I think I need to check a few things out again,' she said deadpan.

His mouth quirked in a fleeting smile, and he held out his hand. 'Check away,' he murmured, drawing her into his arms and easing her closer.

The tempo had slowed, and he rested his cheek against her hair and breathed in the curiously intoxicating scent of apples. Her body settled gently against his, so he felt the soft press of her breasts against his chest, the light brush of her thighs, the curve of her waist under his hand.

He could feel himself responding, felt her breath catch, then ease out again as she settled yet closer, and suddenly he couldn't take it any more. He was too tired to control his reaction, too tired to fight the need to hold her; the lack of sleep was beginning to catch up with him, and he didn't count the few hours he'd spent trying not to fall off the miserable excuse for a bed in the dressing room, so he forced himself to ease away and meet her eyes. 'To be honest, I could call it a night, Libby, unless you want to stay up? I'm bushed.'

'I'm more than happy to give up. These shoes are killing me,' she murmured. Her eyes were soft, luminous, and he wasn't sure if she'd misunderstood his intentions. He hoped not. He really had meant it when he had said no strings.

They made their way upstairs, and at the bedroom door he hesitated. He couldn't go in there with her—not now. Not yet. He couldn't trust himself while his arms still held the memory of her body swaying against him for dance after dance after dance. 'I just want to say goodnight to my parents,' he said a little desperately. 'I need to head off in the morning early and we probably won't see them before we go. Don't wait up for me.'

And turning on his heel he left her there, walking swiftly away before he gave in to the temptation to usher her through the door, strip off that dress that only he had seen the top of, and make love to her until neither of them could move another muscle.

So that was her told.

Don't wait up for me, indeed. Of course not. Why would she? After all, she wasn't really his girlfriend, and she'd done her job now, fended off the girls all evening, smiled and laughed through one dance after another in his arms so he didn't have to dance with them.

Show only, just a smokescreen, a deflector for the poor, love-lorn Charlotte and her cohorts, Libby thought wearily, and unpinning the orchid from her shoulder and removing the shawl, she peeled off the dress, pulled on her nightdress and took off her make-up, cleaned her teeth and slid into the chilly bed.

It would have been nice if he'd been in it with her, she thought, and then laughed softly to herself. Nice? There would have been nothing nice about it, it would have been amazing. Incredible. And utterly not going to happen.

She turned over so her back was to the door, and waited for him. She'd turned out the light in her room, leaving on the dressing-room light so he could see, and lay there in the semi-darkness waiting for his return, knowing that when he came back to the room he'd expect to find her sleeping, but she couldn't sleep, for some reason. Not until he was back.

Eventually she heard him moving quietly around, heard the click of the switch as the light went out and the room settled into darkness, and then at last, exhausted, she drifted off to sleep…

It was pitch-dark when she woke.

She could hear him moving around, and she sat up and peered towards the noise.

'Andrew?'

'Oh, Libby, I'm sorry, I didn't mean to wake you. I was going to get a drink from the kitchen.'

'I could do with one, too. Can I come with you?'

'Sure. We can make a cup of tea, if you like.'

She turned on her bedside light and then regretted it instantly, because he was wearing a pair of loose cotton scrub trousers and nothing else. They hung low on his hips, showing the taut, firm abdomen, the broad, deep chest and wide shoulders she'd found so fascinating the previous morning when he'd emerged from the shower in his towel, but that had been before she'd danced with him, before she'd felt that solid, muscular body against hers, felt his masculine response, and she felt her tongue dry up and stick to the roof of her mouth.

'Did you steal them from the hospital?' she asked, raising a brow at the impromptu PJs and trying to remember how to breathe, and he chuckled.

'No, they're from college. I found them in the drawer. I don't—ah…'

He trailed off, and she felt warmth brush her cheeks. He didn't—what? Wear anything usually? She closed her eyes for a second and turned back the bedclothes, tugging her nightdress down over her legs even though it was more than respectable, and trying very hard not to think about him wearing nothing.

'Do you have a dressing gown?' he asked, and when she shook her head, he handed her the one off the back of the door and pulled on the jumper he'd been wearing the previous day. Better, but not much, she thought, the image of him burned on her retinas.

She shrugged into the dressing gown and realised instantly it was his. His scent was on it, her warmth releasing a heady mixture of his signature cologne and that subtle masculine essence that was his alone. It was like having him wrapped around her, holding her close, she thought, and her heart picked up speed.

She followed him through the house, along the dark corridor and down the stairs to the warm, cosy kitchen where they'd had breakfast the previous morning. The dogs greeted them sleepily, and Andrew sat her down at the table and put the kettle on the Aga, then pulled out another chair and stretched out his legs towards the warmth, tipping his head back and closing his eyes.

'Bliss. I love the house when everyone's asleep,' he murmured.

'I get the feeling that being awake at night is a habit for you, or am I wrong?'

He shrugged. 'No, you're not wrong. I don't tend to sleep well. Too busy, I suppose. I just felt thirsty, and my mind was working.'

'Jacob?'

He opened his eyes and levered himself upright again. 'No. Well, a bit, but mostly family stuff. I was thinking about Mum, about all she's done over the years.'

About how she'd put him in the same room as Libby and left him to die of frustration…

The kettle boiled and he got to his feet and made them tea—green tea for him, chamomile for Libby, so they weren't awake for the rest of the night—then leant over Libby to put her cup down and got another drift of apples from her hair.

Damn, he was going to embarrass himself at this rate, he thought, and turning the chair so he was facing the table, he sat down and propped his elbows on the scrubbed pine surface and sipped his tea until he was back under control.

They didn't talk, just sat in a comfortable silence as they had over their picnic, and drank their tea until it was finished. And then the tension, suddenly, was back.

'I suppose we ought to get some more sleep,' she said eventually, and he nodded.

'Yes, we probably should.'

They went back up to his room, the tension somehow ratcheting up with every step, and as they reached the door Libby's heart was in her mouth. Would he kiss her? No. Why would he?

But he hesitated, closing the door and standing there, his eyes locked with hers, and she could see the need in them.

'Andrew?' she said softly, his name an invitation, should he choose to accept it, but he closed his eyes fleetingly.

'Libby, no,' he murmured. 'I promised you—'

'I won't hold you to it.'

He shook his head. 'I can't—Libby, there are all sorts of reasons.'

'Such as? Are you married and I don't know?'

He laughed at that, the sound soft, a little raw. 'No, I'm not married.'

'Then stay with me. Please?'

'Libby, I—' Oh, God, she didn't know what she was asking of him. He saw the uncertainty in her eyes, knew how much it had taken for her to ask him, and he couldn't do it, couldn't leave her, couldn't turn away from her in that moment no matter how stupid it was to stay. How dangerous.

He held out his arms to her, and she went into them, warm and soft and yielding, and he felt heat sear through him. 'Libby—'

Her lips found his, gentle at first, tentative, but then when he gave up fighting it and started to kiss her back she gave a little sob and arched against him, and he cradled her face in his hands and deepened the kiss, ravaging her mouth, tasting the sweetness, the satin softness, searching out the hot, honeyed depths, their tongues tangling as they duelled. Her legs parted to the pressure of his thigh, and he rocked against her, aching for her, needing her, needing to bury himself inside her and take the treasure she was offering.

His hand left her face, feathering down over her throat, tracing the pulse that hammered beneath his fingertips, down over her collar bone, over the satin-soft skin of her chest until it reached the warm, enticing swell of her breast. The nightdress was in the way, tangled round her legs, hampering his hand at her breast, and he pushed himself away, stripping back the bedclothes, peeling off his sweater and reaching for her, easing the dressing gown aside so it slid down her arms and puddled on the floor behind her.

She held up her arms, her eyes locked with his, and with a tiny hiss of breath he reached for the hem of her nightdress and stripped it off her.

He heard it rip, but he didn't care. He was beyond caring, beyond anything except making the woman standing there beside him his. He tugged at the cord on his scrubs, the knot releasing so they fell to the floor with his dressing gown and the torn nightdress as he stood there drinking her in with his gaze. Her eyes were wide and liquid, her mouth softly swollen, her breasts full and yet yielding, perfect, the dusky rose nipples tightly pebbled and so, so tempting. He lowered his head, taking one in his mouth, drawing it in, suckling on her deeply as she arched against him, crying out.

'Andrew, please!'

His hand moved on, down over the smooth plane of her flank, across her hip, over the bowl of her pelvis, on again.

She bucked against him, her legs jerking as his hand found her, found the secret, hidden depths, the moist heat of her most intimate places. His thumb grazed her and her eyes flew wide, her breath catching, and suddenly he couldn't wait another moment.

Scooping her up in his arms, he laid her gently on the bed, his eyes still fixed on hers, their breath mingling as he moved over her and entered her with one long, slow stroke, driving her over the edge, her body convulsing around him, her cries dragging him after her to join her in the wild tumult of their release…

* * *

She woke for the second morning in a row to the sound of running water, and she lay and pictured him in the shower. She could do it better today, could see his body, knew it, every inch.

Beautiful. Magnificent. Solidly powerful, lean and graceful, potent.

Oh, lord.

She heard the water stop, then gave him a moment and tapped on the door, tugging her ripped nightdress into place. 'Are you decent? Can I come in?'

'Yeah, sure.'

She opened the door and sucked in her breath. 'Oh! Sorry—I thought—'

His mouth twisted into a wry, teasing smile and he lowered the towel from his hair. 'I've just made love to you, Libby,' he murmured softly. 'Exactly which bit of me do you want covered up?'

She felt the heat in her cheeks, but she held her ground and dragged her eyes from his body. 'Actually, that was the thing I wanted to talk to you about. Last night, when we—you didn't use—I'm not on the Pill,' she muttered, floundering to an embarrassed halt.

He put the towel he was holding in one hand back on the towel rail and let out a long, thoughtful sigh. 'Well, I don't think it's an issue—not for you, at any rate. I—ah…' He hesitated, gave a low laugh and met her eyes, his own carefully blank. 'I can't get you pregnant.'

'What—? Why not?'

'Because I'm infertile,' he said quietly.

She felt her mouth drop open with shock, and shut it with a little snap. 'How do you know?'

He gave a little grunt of laughter. 'Oh, we were

messing about at college,' he said with forced lightness. 'You know what it's like—well, no, to be fair, you probably don't, you're not a boy, but we had one of these stupid ideas that we'd become sperm donors. Loads of medical students do it, and we decided it was no hardship—and there we were, in the lab without a lecturer, all these microscopes lying about, and someone decided while we were on the subject that it would be funny to see who'd got the highest sperm count. And I didn't have any. Well, a few, swimming in circles, whereas they had millions all thrashing away and swimming like hell.'

She sagged against the wall, hugging her arms around her torn nightdress, staring at him blankly, trying to imagine what it had been like for this young man in the prime of his life to find out something so devastating. 'So—what did they say? Your friends?'

'Nothing. They didn't know. I accidentally contaminated my sample from someone else's Petri dish—not very honest, but I was reeling, really. I needed time to take it in, and I certainly wasn't ready to go public with that lot.'

'Oh, Andrew,' she said softly, her heart aching for him. 'That must have been awful.'

His mouth tugged down at one side. 'It was. But then I thought, later that day when I'd calmed down a bit and it had sunk in, I'd had glandular fever after I started uni, I'd had mumps really badly at seventeen, and Will had only just been discharged from hospital. It had been a comprehensively bloody four years, what with one thing and another, and I thought, well, it's just temporary. It'll recover. But it didn't.'

'You got it tested properly?'

He shook his head. 'What's to test? Either they're there, swimming, or they're not. I managed to wangle my way out of the sperm donor thing and checked again, a few weeks later. Then periodically until eventually I gave up. It seemed pointless, going on, there's a limit to how often you want to remind yourself of something like that.'

'And you've never got anybody pregnant?'

'I've never had unprotected sex before last night,' he said softly, then breaking eye contact at last, he turned back to the basin and started to shave, and she watched him for a moment, let his words play through her head, and she felt warmth flood her body—warmth, at his gentle admission of this new intimacy, and then, perversely, regret that it could have no consequences. And relief, because there was no way she could afford to get accidentally pregnant.

Not yet, at least. Not until she knew…

CHAPTER FIVE

SHE left him to it, going back to the bedroom and sitting on the bed, staring at the rumpled sheets where she'd lain in his arms all night.

Infertile.

She shook her head, struggling to take it in, and then lifted her case and put it on the bed and started to pack. She found clean underwear, packed all the things she didn't need, then when he was out of the bathroom she showered quickly, wrapped her hair in a towel and packed her wash things.

She knew he wanted to get away promptly this morning, the condition of the child in PICU worrying away at him even though he hadn't admitted it last night, and anyway she had to get back to feed the cat.

She was glad they were leaving early before anyone else would be about. She was still feeling the shock of his revelation all the way down to her toes, and she was sure it would show in her eyes—quite apart from the whisker burn on her top lip and the softness around her eyes, a dead giveaway of how they'd spent the night. And sitting with his family over breakfast while they sized her up as potential material for a daughter-in-law and mother of the future Lord Ashenden would be too much. His poor parents were so desperate for him to give them grandchildren, and the fact that Sally was pregnant didn't alter that.

His parents, Jane especially, wanted him settled with a wife and children; she'd gathered that much from the odd hint and joke over the course of the weekend, and now she knew the truth, her heart ached for him. No wonder he hadn't wanted to come home for the house party! It was a miracle he ever came home at all.

'Leave your case on the bed, I'll come up and get it in a minute. I'm going to make tea,' he called through the door.

'Don't worry, take it now,' she said, coming out of the bathroom in a towel and throwing her wash bag and nightdress into the top of the case and zipping it shut. 'I've got everything I need.'

Everything except him, but that was never going to happen. She reached for his arm, meeting his eyes, seeing the pain still echoed there, dragged back to life by their conversation.

'Andrew, I'm so sorry.'

'Don't be. It doesn't matter.'

'You don't want children?'

His smile was sad. 'I'm a paediatrician, Libby. What do you think? But we don't always get what we want, and I have a fulfilling and very rewarding life. Besides, I'm still single. And I don't need children to make me happy.'

'But your mother does. She's desperate for you to settle down—and it's why you're still single, isn't it? Does she even know?'

He shook his head. 'No. And she doesn't need to know. Nobody knows.'

'Not even Will?'

He gave a short laugh. 'Especially not Will.'

So he didn't even have his brother's comfort or support.

'Ah, Libby, no, don't cry for me,' he said softly, and drew her into his arms. 'Hush now, come on. It's all right, truly. I'm OK. And I'll marry one day, someone who's already got children so she doesn't feel tempted to leave me because there's something missing in her life.'

'Do you really think all women are that shallow?' she demanded, but he just laughed softly.

'No. Not shallow, not at all. But the drive to procreate is a strong one, and I wouldn't ask any woman to give up her right to be a mother. It wouldn't be fair.'

'And what about you, Andrew? What about what's fair to you?'

He didn't answer, just turned away after a moment, picked up her case and left the room.

They were gone half an hour later, without disturbing anyone. He'd already said goodbye to his parents the night before, and he'd ring Will later. He'd understand—and, anyway, he was probably still in bed with Sally, sleeping off his excesses, or else he'd be out riding.

'I need to go straight to the hospital. Is it OK if I just drop you off and shoot away?' he asked, and she nodded.

'Of course it is. Anyway, I've got things to do.'

'Laundry?' he suggested, his smile wry.

She laughed. 'You guessed it. And dusting. And vacuuming up the drifts of cat hair.'

He pulled up outside her little modern terraced house and cut the engine, then lifted her case out of the boot and put it down in her hall. 'Thank you for coming with me,' he said softly. 'And I'm sorry—it really wasn't meant to end up the way it did. I shouldn't have taken advantage of you last night.'

'Excuse me?' Her mouth kicked up in a smile that unravelled something deep in his gut. 'I don't remember you taking advantage—if anyone did, it was me. I seem to remember I kissed you first.'

'OK,' he said at last, giving her a fleeting smile. 'I'll give you that. But—Libby, I meant what I said. I'm not in the market for a serious relationship. I don't want to hurt you, and I don't want to get hurt myself, and I think it might be all too easy to fall into a relationship that hurts us both in the end.'

Her eyes clouded, and she gave a slight nod and stepped back. 'That's OK. I understand. We're just friends. Not even that, really. Colleagues. We'll just pretend it never happened.'

He nodded, kissed her cheek and left her there, getting back into the car and driving away, his eyes on the rear-view mirror until he couldn't see her house any longer.

Colleagues. What a curiously unpalatable thought.

'Oh, Kitty, how could I be so stupid? I've gone and fallen in love with him,' she told the cat. Scooping her up, she sat down on the sofa and tried to cuddle her, but the cat was hungry and not having any of it, so she fed her, unpacked her suitcase and hung up Amy's dress.

The pashmina was crumpled, but she put it on a hanger and sorted out her washing, started the first load off and then emptied the dishwasher, cleaned the kitchen and got the vacuum cleaner out. She'd be fine if she kept busy, she told herself, but then she realised she couldn't see, so she gave up, had a howl, blew her nose and made a cup of tea and went to phone Amy.

She'd be gagging to know how it had gone, but she'd only get a very edited version of the truth, and she could always talk about Will. Amy would be fascinated.

Except Amy wasn't there. Amy was obviously out having some fun of her own, and so Libby put the phone back in the cradle and flicked through the television channels.

Nothing. There was never anything on, and in the middle of a Sunday there was hardly going to be anything riveting. A film she'd seen dozens of times, some sheepdog trials—she threw the remote control down in disgust and went out to the kitchen, dragged the washing out of the machine, loaded it with the next lot and carried the pile of wet clothes upstairs to hang in her bathroom—because, of course, today it was raining.

April showers, torrents of rain falling like stair-rods, hammering on the windows and bouncing off the roof of her little conservatory. Nothing would dry outside today, and precious little would dry inside. And she'd let it drift for too long.

Oh, damn, she thought, and decided to have a bath. A nice long, hot soak, a cup of tea and a book. And who cared if it was the middle of the day?

'How's he been?'

'Good.' The PICU charge nurse talked him through the charts, and he went and spoke to the parents—exhausted, drained, but still fighting—and bent over the bed with a smile.

'Hi, Jacob. How are you doing?' he asked, although

the boy was unconscious and on a ventilator. 'I'm just going to have a look at you, see what's going on here.'

He scanned the monitors, examined the damaged limbs for swelling, checked the pulse in his feet and nodded. 'His legs and pelvis are looking good,' he said to the parents.

'Do you think so?' Jacob's mother Tracy said, hope in her voice. 'We can't really tell, but his toes are nice and pink and he's been—I don't know, quieter, somehow. More as if he's resting, more comfortable.'

He felt the tension ease a fraction. Not completely, he would never become complacent, but Jacob seemed more stable.

'He's making progress. I'm happier with him than I was before the weekend, and I think we'll get a good result.'

Then he headed to the ward and had a chat to the boys, checked with the nursing staff that they had no problems or queries and then left the ward, hurrying to get back out into the fresh air again, restless and uncertain about how to fill the rest of the day.

Which was absurd, because he had a mountain of paperwork to deal with on his desk at home, his laundry was in no better a situation than Libby's—although to be fair that was because he hadn't got round to dropping it into the dry cleaner's for them to deal with—and he ought to go to the supermarket before it shut at four.

He'd do that first.

He must be crazy.

Andrew sat at the end of Libby's little cul-de-sac and stared at her house pensively. He'd told her the situation, told her he didn't want a relationship, and he didn't, he really didn't, so why the hell was he here, hovering outside like some kind of bloody stalker?

But he wanted her. Wanted to see her, wanted to talk to her, wanted to hold her. He could take her out to dinner, bring her back, leave her at the door. He didn't have to make love to her—

Who was he kidding? His body was getting hard just thinking about her. And she knew the score. And she, as she'd pointed out, had been the one who'd made the first move. She'd reached for him.

And even if it had only been a split second before he would have reached for her, nevertheless, she *had* made the first move.

But she hadn't known the truth then. If she had, would it have made a difference? He'd never know. And he had bags full of food that needed to go in the fridge. He'd taken enough of her time.

And then her front door opened and she came out, dressed in jeans and a thick cream jumper with a binbag in her hand, and she looked up and saw him and stopped in her tracks.

He got out of the car and walked over to her slowly, and her eyes searched his face.

'What? What is it? Not the kid in PICU?'

He shook his head. 'No. He's looking better—well, slightly. I just—I've been to the supermarket, and I was virtually passing, and—'

He scrubbed a hand round the back of his neck, then smiled at her, and Libby felt her heart turn over. 'I know I said a load of stuff this morning about not having relationships, but—are you busy?'

She felt herself smile before she could control it, and shook her head. 'No, Andrew, I'm not busy. Come in. Have you got anything that needs to be in the fridge?'

He shook his head. 'It'll keep. It's not exactly hot out here, and the temperature's starting to drop already. It'll be fine—ah. Except for the ice cream.'

'You bought ice cream? What sort?'

'Belgian chocolate. Is there any other sort?'

She laughed. 'You'd better bring it in, but don't blame me if you don't get to take it home.' And dumping the binbag in her wheelie bin, she went back into the house and left him to follow.

'Oh. You've brought a bag. Does that all need the freezer?'

He shook his head. 'No. It's the bag with the ice cream in it, but I've got other things in here—things I was going to cook tonight. I just wondered, if you really aren't busy, if you'd let me cook for you. But if you are, just tell me to take a hike.'

'I'm not busy,' she said, taking the bag out of his hand, extracting the ice cream and putting it in the freezer, then putting the bag in the fridge. 'Tea?'

'Lovely. I haven't had a drink for hours.'

'Neither have I. I've been in the bath and I fell asleep.'

Oh, hell, he thought. Why had she told him that? Now all he could see was her beautiful, curvy body lapped by warm water, and desire, hot, hard and far from slaked by last night's all too brief interlude, came screaming back to life.

This was such a profoundly lousy idea, he thought, but then she put the kettle on and turned towards him, propped herself against the worktop and smiled a rueful smile and he thought, She feels the same. She wasn't going to do this, but she wants to just as much as I do.

And there was no way he could walk away.

Libby studied him for a long moment. There was a muscle working in his jaw, and she could see the throb of his pulse just above the unbuttoned collar of his shirt. She reached into the cupboard above the kettle, took out two glasses and filled them with water, handing him one.

He tilted his head in puzzlement, taking it from her and lifting it to his lips.

'You didn't really want to wait for tea, did you?' she murmured, and he choked on the water.

Laughing helplessly, she took the glass out of his hand and slapped him on the back, then as he straightened, eyes streaming, his mouth curved with self-deprecating humour, she slipped her hand into his and led him out of the kitchen, through the living room and up the stairs. By the time she turned to face him, they were standing by her bed and all trace of the smile was gone, replaced by a burning urgency in his eyes that stole her breath away.

'I think you're trying to kill me,' he said softly as she peeled off the white sweater and dropped it on the floor. She'd kicked off her shoes, unfastened her jeans and started to slide them down her hips before he moved, then he tore his shirt off over his head, buttons pinging in all directions, kicked off his shoes, shucked his trousers, boxers and socks in one movement and eased her slowly up against him.

'Oh, that feels so good,' he muttered, then his mouth found hers and she sighed with relief.

She'd really thought it was over, that they'd go back to being colleagues, that the weekend would be put aside as if it had never happened—but no. He kissed her as if he'd die without her, slanting his head to get a better angle, one hand threaded into her hair, his fingers splayed, cradling her head, the other hand sliding round behind her and cupping her bottom, groaning as he hauled her closer, so she felt the hard jut of his erection against her abdomen.

Then he lifted his head and stared down into her eyes, easing away fractionally, his chest heaving. 'Libby, I—I bought condoms,' he said gruffly. 'I didn't know if you were worried about it—you know, for other reasons.'

She shook her head. 'No. I trust you, and I've always been really careful, so if you don't think it's necessary I don't want anything between us.'

He sucked in his breath and closed his eyes then, still holding her with one arm, he dragged the quilt out of the way with the other hand and tipped her back onto the mattress and followed her down, one solid, hair-strewn leg wedged between hers, his hand finding her breast, cupping it tenderly as he brushed his lips across it with a groan.

'You're gorgeous, do you know that? So much woman…'

She felt the deep, slow tug of his mouth on her nipple, the ache low down intensifying, and she tunnelled her fingers through his hair and held him close, giving herself up to the slow, painstaking and very thorough appraisal he was making of her body with his hands and lips.

Her own hands and lips were busy, too, exploring the fascinating textures of his body, the smooth satin skin over corded muscle and sinew, the ripple of reaction as she stroked teasingly over his abdomen, the coarse silk of his body hair, the taste of salt, the warm, rich scent of musk.

There was no hurry now. No urgency. They both knew where this was going to end, and they were taking their time, savouring every second, every last caress.

But then he lifted his head, staring down into her eyes, his own strangely intense.

'I need you, Libby,' he said softly. 'You have no idea how much I need you.'

She reached up, her hand gentle on his cheek, cradling his jaw, relishing the harsh rasp of his beard against her palm.

Her touch was sweet to him, her smile enough to break his heart.

'I'm here,' she murmured, and for a crazy instant, he thought it sounded like a vow…

Libby went into work the following morning walking on air and with a smile she could do nothing to hide.

At least, not from Amy, who promptly grabbed her arm and dragged her into the office when she came up to the ward just before eight, as Libby finished the drugs round.

'Well? I nearly went crazy yesterday! Why didn't you ring me?'

'I tried—you were engaged, then you were out.'

'I wasn't out—oh, rats, you must have rung when I was in the shower. You should have left a message, I've been on edge all night! So, tell all—was it fantastic?'

'Absolutely,' she said, the smile winning hands down. 'It was amazing. Fabulous. Such a beautiful place, and the food was incredible.'

Amy smiled. 'Great. And Andrew?'

Her brows went up, her head tilted, and Libby sighed

inwardly. She might have known she wouldn't get away with it! 'We had a lovely weekend; it was a fabulous party, the dress was perfect, so thank you very much for lending it to me, and I didn't fall out of it, which was a relief! I'll get it cleaned.'

'And Andrew?' she prompted again, and Libby shrugged and tried hard not to look away.

'He was lovely—a perfect gentleman. We had a great time, talked a lot, and I've got to know him a bit better, to understand what motivates him. It'll be very useful for working with him.'

Amy's jaw sagged. 'That's it?'

'That's it,' she lied, determined to keep their private moments just that, but Amy looked sceptical and slightly disgusted.

'You're hopeless! "It'll be very useful for working with him,"' she mimicked, making little quote marks in the air and rolling her eyes. 'I despair of you! You go away with that *hunk* and that's the best you can come up with—good grief, Libby, opportunities like that are wasted on you,' she said, and, turning round, she almost fell over Andrew in the office doorway.

Over her head their eyes met, Libby's bubbling over with laughter, Andrew's slightly stunned. Lifting his hands, he stepped back, smiled and said, 'Morning!' and Amy went scarlet, mumbled something unintelligible and fled.

'What was that about?' he asked softly, frowning after her, and Libby chuckled.

'She was getting a bit too close to the nitty-gritty. I thought—well, I didn't know, but I imagined you didn't want to go public,' she said in a quiet undertone, and he nodded.

'No. Thanks for that. I owe you.'

'No, you don't. I don't want it spread all round the hospital either, and I love Amy to bits but it's so easy to let things slip out and then someone else'll get hold of it and it'll be pinned on the notice-board before we know it.'

'Sounds about right. So she thinks I'm a hunk, does she?' he mused thoughtfully, and then Libby caught the twinkle in his eye and laughed.

'Don't get carried away. She's been trying to fix me up with someone for over a year. Any single half-eligible male in the hospital is a hunk under those circumstances.'

'So who's she been trying to fix you up with?' he asked, and for a moment she wondered if that really had been a flash of jealousy in his eyes.

'Nobody. Anybody,' she said honestly. 'I don't date.'

'Why?'

Her heart thumped. Trust Andrew to get straight to the heart of it, but she wasn't ready to talk about it, and this wasn't the time.

'Oh—this and that,' she said flippantly, but she gave a twisted little smile that tugged at his heartstrings.

'Sounds messy,' he murmured, searching her eyes for clues.

She shrugged, the simple gesture hiding a world of hurt. 'A little bit. Whatever,' she said, injecting artificial brightness into her voice. 'What can I do for you?'

'Nothing. I was just passing, on my way back from clinics, and I thought I'd pop in, say hi.'

'Well, hi,' she said, smiling again with her eyes, the demons apparently banished, put back in their box. 'Not busy today?'

'Oh, I'm always busy, but somehow the lure was irresistible.' Something warm and gentle flickered in his expressive eyes, unravelling her a little. 'In fact, how about lunch?'

'Lunch? That would be lovely, if you've got time. Where? The canteen?'

He pulled a face. 'That doesn't really square with keeping things quiet, does it? I've got a better idea. Why don't I pick up some sandwiches and you come to my office for lunch? I've got a coffee machine in there—you know where it is, don't you?'

She nodded. 'What time?'

'What time can you do? Is one any good?'

'Should be fine.'

'Good. We can always pretend it's work.' And glancing over his shoulder, he pushed the door shut and eased her into his arms, dropping a lingering, tender kiss on her lips. 'Just to keep you going,' he murmured, and then with a mischievous wink, he opened the door and strolled out, hands in his pockets, leaving her heart fluttering and a smile on her face she could do nothing about.

She sucked in a deep breath, gave him a minute to get off the ward and then went out. There was lots she should be doing. Joel needed turning, Lucas probably needed stringing up and the twins were getting bored and needed a change of scenery. A little concentration on something other than Andrew would be good for her, she decided, and finding a nurse to help her, she started work.

CHAPTER SIX

SHE tapped on Andrew's door and went in at his crisp, decisive 'Yes!'

He looked up and blinked, as if he'd been miles away. 'Is it really one already? Sorry, I've been up to my eyes, I had no idea it was so late.'

He closed the folder, got to his feet and came over to her, pushed the door shut and hugged her. 'Sorry, it's been a bit mad round here. I'll make us coffee—have a look through the sandwiches and choose what you want. I wasn't sure what you'd like.'

While he fiddled with the coffee maker, she stared at the pile of plastic containers on his desk and chuckled, poking them around with her finger so she could read the labels. 'Is that why there are four different sorts?'

'Oh, don't worry, I'll eat them later if we don't finish them.'

She picked out the prawn salad on wholemeal and waggled them at him. 'Can I have these?'

'You can have whatever you want. I like them all. Here, coffee.'

He handed her a mug, pulled up another chair to his

desk and sat down beside her, ripping the lid off the chicken tikka sandwich and sinking his teeth into it. 'Ah, that's better. I'm starving. The bread was off, I haven't had breakfast.'

'How can bread be off?'

'You know, blue hairy bits.'

She winced. 'Sounds worse than my fridge.'

'It is. I forgot to buy bread yesterday at the supermarket—something to do with a certain ward sister I couldn't get out of my mind,' he said mildly, but his eyes were teasing and she couldn't help smiling back.

'Is that right?'

'It's right.' He chomped down on the sandwich again, demolishing it in another two bites and starting on the next packet. 'So—good day so far?'

She dusted off her hands and picked up her mug. 'I'd like to say yes, but actually, now you come to mention it, not really. There's someone I'd like to talk to you about. Joel. His spirits are down.'

'I'm not surprised. He's going to be a long time in that halo, and having both arms in plaster isn't good either.'

'No. And he hates having to ask for help with all the personal stuff. I was wondering when we could get him up.'

'Oh, probably soon. I'd like him home in a week or two. He'll need looking after, of course, but it's a case of time now and his fracture's stable. I'll get him X-rayed again and see if we think he's ready to start mobilising. And Lucas, too—we need to think about discharging him soon. He must be driving you mad.'

'He is, bless his heart, but I'll miss him.'

He chuckled. 'Liar. He's a pain.'

'No, he's a good kid. Just a little reckless.'

'Talking of which,' he added slowly, 'are you busy this evening? Will and Sally are staying at mine tonight. She's got an antenatal appointment tomorrow, and they're coming in time for supper. We were going to get a takeaway. Would you like to join us?'

'I wouldn't dream of gatecrashing your evening,' she protested, but he just laughed and leant over and kissed her softly.

'Don't be silly. You won't be gatecrashing. I've been wondering how I could slide off later and come round to your house. You'll just save me the effort of sneaking around.'

She searched his eyes, looking for doubts, and found none. 'He'll know, if he sees us together,' she murmured, and he nodded.

'I know. But I trust him, and while I don't want the entire hospital talking about us, I'm quite happy for my brother to know. And, anyway, I'm pretty sure he already does.'

She smiled. 'Then, thank you, that would be lovely. You'd better give me your address—and directions, because I don't have a sat-nav.'

He laughed softly. 'I'll come and get you. Six-thirty, OK?'

'Fine. I'll look forward to it. What should I wear?'

'Oh, nothing smart. Jeans?'

'Jeans it is,' she said with a relieved smile, and sipped her coffee. 'How's Jacob, by the way? I take it he's no worse, since you haven't mentioned him. Or was it him you were running around after all morning?'

'No, fortunately not, that was just following up after the weekend and doing my clinic. He's doing well.

We're really hopeful. I've just come from a multi-disciplinary team meeting in PICU, and they're talking about cutting back on the sedation, see how he does. The swelling on his brain's subsiding and he's looking good.'

'Fantastic. I'll keep my fingers crossed. You'll have to let me know how it goes.' She smiled wryly and got to her feet. 'I'd better get on. I've promised Lucas he can go down to the coffee shop with his mum for lunch, and he's talked about nothing but basketball since you mentioned it, apparently! I feel sorry for Amy. She's going to have to get him up and running again double-quick!'

He chuckled, threw their sandwich wrappers in the bin and dropped another of those teasing, lingering kisses on her lips. 'Talking of which, I have to get on, too. I'll see you later,' he murmured, then with a slow, lazy wink, he opened the door for her, waggled his fingers in farewell and went the other way towards the clinics, whistling softly and leaving her to head back to the ward, her heart singing.

She was seeing him tonight, at his home, with his brother. Going public, albeit in a private sort of way. That had to be good—didn't it? Progress?

She was shocked at how much she hoped so.

He picked her up at six thirty-two, by which time she'd showered, changed and changed again. Twice.

Still just jeans, but different jeans, and the cream jumper she'd had on the night before, but then she went back to the original top, not as warm but prettier. And then changed back again into the jumper, just as the doorbell rang. Pretty be damned. She wasn't going to be cold, and there was a bitter nip to the air this evening, to remind them all that it was only April and frosts were not yet a thing of the past.

'We could always skip supper,' he said, sliding his arms round her and nuzzling her neck. 'You smell gorgeous. Apples and cinnamon—like apple pie.'

She laughed a little breathlessly. 'That's apple shampoo and a spicy scent Amy gave me for Christmas.'

'Good for Amy—nice choice,' he said, releasing her reluctantly and standing back. 'Ready to go? Where's your overnight bag?'

She hesitated. 'Is that a good idea? Then I'll have to rely on you for transport tomorrow. That's going to be a bit obvious when we arrive for work.'

He nodded. 'You're right.'

'You could always stay here, though,' she suggested tentatively.

'Or you could follow me in your car, with your things. That way we can all see more of each other and I'll have time to talk to Will in the morning. I've got some things I need to discuss with him before I go to work, and I don't need to start tomorrow until eight-thirty, but you can shoot off when you're ready.'

'Oh.' She felt a flicker of doubt. The weekend at his parents' house was one thing. This, inviting her round to join him for the night while Will and Sally were there, was quite another, for a man who'd said he didn't want a relationship. 'Are you sure you want me to come?'

'Absolutely sure. I told you that earlier. Get your things. I'll draw you a map in case you lose me.'

'Don't lose me,' she said, and he smiled as if he understood.

'I won't,' he promised.

* * *

She stuck to him like glue.

His first stop was to the Indian takeaway on the corner near the hospital, and then he headed out into the country.

Not far, just a couple of miles, but far enough that they left the lights behind them and turned onto a narrow, winding little lane. He swept onto a gently shelving drive, triggering security lights, and came to a halt in front of a sprawling single-storey barn conversion, and she parked beside him and looked around.

It was impressive, but not overly so—not outrageously ostentatious like Ashenden, just tasteful and well groomed, the gravel free of weeds, the low beds of ground cover neatly tended, the house itself welcoming, with big, heavy pots of clipped bay each side of the entrance, formal and yet understated. She couldn't wait to see the inside.

There was a 4 x 4 on the drive—Will's? Probably.

'Slow enough?' he asked, resting his arm on the top of her door and smiling down at her as she cut the engine.

'Perfect. Is that Will's car?'

He nodded. 'They've been here a while. Come on in.'

He opened the door, and Lara bounded out, grinning and licking and checking out the bag of takeaway in Andrew's hand. 'Get off, you rude dog,' he said affectionately, pushing her away, and ushered Libby in. 'Welcome to my home,' he said, and she knew he meant it, knew this and not the 'crumbling pile of dry rot' that he loved in spite of himself was where he came to recharge his batteries.

She looked around, at the heavily beamed walls and ceilings, the simple furnishings, the clean, unfussy lines.

It was him, through and through, and she could see

him here so easily, so absolutely. 'I love it,' she said, unable to hold back her smile. 'Oh, I love it. It's beautiful. How did you find it?'

He laughed. 'Easy. It was falling down. I bought it five years ago, and I've been working on it ever since.'

'You have?' she said, surprised, and he shrugged.

'Not all of it, of course, but I've done a lot of the sand-blasting of the beams and decorating and stuff like that, and I've done all the garden landscaping. It's how I relax. I'll show you round later, but we ought to eat this now or it'll be cold.'

He led her through to a huge open room, with a kitchen at one end, a dining area in the middle and comfortable, welcoming seating at the other end, where Will and Sally had made themselves at home.

'Grub's up,' Andrew said, waving the bag, and they got up and came over, kissing her on the cheek, greeting her like an old friend, and she felt a flicker of guilt that she'd deceived them at the weekend. Not now, though. Now, it seemed, they did have a relationship of sorts, although she wasn't quite sure what sort. Time would no doubt tell.

Andrew put the bag down in the middle of the table, ripped the tops off the containers, stuck spoons in them and they all helped themselves, piling their plates with the delicious, fragrant food. There were bottles of beer standing on the table, condensation running down the outsides, and even though it was cool outside she was beginning to think her cream jumper might be over the top. The house was gorgeously warm, and she could feel the glow coming off the wood-burner behind her.

'So, what time's your appointment tomorrow, Sally?' Andrew asked.

'Ten. And then I think I might go and do a little light shopping.'

Will groaned. 'Not more baby stuff. How much is that going to cost me?'

She laughed and patted his cheek. 'Less than you think. I might even get you a new pair of jeans. Those are dreadful.'

'They're nicely broken in. Leave me alone, you sound like my mother. If you want to do something useful, you can pass me a chunk of Peshwari naan.'

Andrew chuckled. 'You won't get him out of those jeans, Sally, unless you cut them up,' he advised softly, passing the basket of naan breads. 'He's welded to them.'

Her eyes sparkled. 'Now, there's a thought. Got any scissors, Andrew?'

'Forget it. They're my jeans,' Will said, looking as if he didn't quite trust her not to do it.

'They don't look any worse than the ones you were wearing on Saturday,' Libby told Andrew, and he grinned.

'Family trait. We like knackered old jeans.'

'Rebellion?'

'Nah. Antiques. You saw the rug in the hall.'

She laughed and helped herself to another scoop of butter chicken, resigned to eating lettuce the following day if necessary, and allowed herself to relax into the affectionate banter. It was lovely to see them off duty, to see the interaction between Andrew and Will, to see him as a brother as well as a doctor.

They talked about anything and everything, comfortable, relaxed, and after they'd finished eating they cleared the table and hid the leftovers from Lara, then migrated to the sofas that bracketed the wood-burner and Andrew put his arm round her and tucked her against his side. She wondered what Will would make of that, and the wisdom of it, of leaving herself wide open to hurt when she knew this was going nowhere.

But Andrew was just as wide open, and maybe he was beginning to rethink his stand on staying single.

Not that he'd be thinking of her in all that, of course not. They were poles apart. But lying there on the sofa with his arm around her, somehow they didn't seem so far apart, just a man and a woman, relaxing with family and being normal. He was probably just lonely, and enjoying her company. She'd do the same, take it at face value, enjoy it while it lasted and be grateful.

'Thank you for inviting me,' she said later, as they lay entangled in the huge bed that sat squarely opposite the curtainless window of his bedroom. 'I didn't like to muscle in, but they didn't seem to mind at all.'

He trailed a finger idly over her shoulder. 'They don't. They really like you.'

'I like them, too. Sally's gorgeous. She'll be a lovely mother. When's the baby due?'

'Six weeks, I think. She's having it in the Audley, so no doubt I'll get a call from Will all panic-stricken when she goes into labour.'

'Do you think he'll panic?'

'Will? Definitely. He doesn't care what he does to himself, but he's incredibly protective of Sally. It's just a pity he can't see that it cuts both ways.'

She snuggled closer. 'He is a bit of an idiot, isn't he? But he's fun.'

'Oh, yes. He's lots of fun. He's the face of the family now, really, the high-profile one. He loves all the publicity and drama—I just hate it. I'm happy to let him get on with it. I just wish I wasn't going to inherit it all at the end. He'd be much better at it—look at the way he handles all the charity stuff.'

She shifted so they were face to face and she could see his eyes. 'Does it worry you, living in his shadow?' she asked softly, and for a moment he said nothing, a thousand expressions flitting over his face in the moonlight, and finally he gave a low laugh.

'That's a strange remark.'

'Is it? It's how I see you both. He's like a tumbling, cascading waterfall, hurtling through life sparkling with sunlight and sweeping everyone along with him, whereas you're the smooth water, the still, quiet river, the surface unruffled but underneath teeming with life, sustaining it all without fuss.'

His brow creased. 'Is that a bad thing?'

'No! Absolutely not. It's just the way you both are. I wondered if it was always like that, if he was always the brash, colourful one that everyone noticed. Chris said you used to be a bit of a wild child.'

He frowned slightly. 'That was a long time ago. And as for Will, they certainly noticed him when he went off the rails. I was constantly hauling his backside out of trouble—but I'm quite happy to let him overshadow me now. Frankly he's welcome to the limelight. I'm just surprised you picked up on it.'

'Why?'

He shrugged. 'It's just that most people don't see it like that,' he murmured, his voice quietly resigned. 'They think I'm the dull one, and Will's the interesting one—but I guess it's OK. I'm used to it now. And it suits me, really. Leaves me free to do what I want to do without an audience. My life hasn't really changed because of his illness, but his has. I'm still a doctor, still doing what I would have done before, although the emphasis might have changed slightly, but essentially I'm still doing what I set out to do in the first place.'

'And Will? He said he was only estate manager because he was too lazy to do anything else. Is that true?'

Andrew shook his head. 'No. He didn't do well at school after he was ill—his life was thrown into chaos, and when he recovered he lost the plot a bit and turned into a party animal. He's settled down a bit, of course, but he threw away his chance of going to uni, which was a shame, because he wanted to be an architect. I don't think he minds, though. As I said, he loves the estate and he's brilliant at running it.'

'Chris Turner said you would have given up medicine to come home and look after him if necessary.'

His smile was wry. 'Did he? Who knows? Luckily I didn't have to, but the whole business might have changed my focus, though.'

'In what way?'

'I would always have gone into orthopaedics, but probably not paediatrics,' he admitted honestly. 'Especially after finding out I can't have kids. It's a bit like rubbing salt into the wound on a daily basis, but at least I get to spend time with children. It's bitter-sweet, really, and it can be stressful. Losing little patients is much harder than losing older ones. They've got so much ahead of them, so much to live for, and telling their parents they've lost their fight, or that their lives are going to be changed for ever—that's hard. I get down sometimes, doing that. If I'd known what I know now, I might not have done it, but I did, and I wouldn't change it now. I couldn't walk away from them, even if I spend every day being reminded that I'll never have any of my own.'

'You might. There are all sorts of things they can do with IVF these days.'

'I know, but not if there isn't anything there to work with.'

'You could find out.'

He shook his head. 'Libby, I know. There's no point beating myself up about it. I've accepted it. Just let it go.'

He met her eyes, lifted a hand and stroked away the tear that had dribbled down from the corner of her eye and puddled against her nose, and the tender gesture unravelled her.

She sniffed, and he pulled her back into his arms and kissed away the tears, then made love to her again, slowly, tenderly, until she thought her heart would burst with love for him, this gentle, dedicated man who had so much to offer and did it so quietly, without fuss or fanfare or arrogance.

She would love him for ever, she realised, even though this relationship would inevitably have to end, because he didn't do relationships, wouldn't marry, held himself back from commitment because of a fear that later he alone might not be enough for the woman he married—that he could imagine he wouldn't be enough for anyone horrified her. He had so much to offer, so much to love—if only he would give her a chance.

And, in fact, it might not even be an issue. She needed to talk to her sister, to find out how she was getting on and take that first step towards finding out if she herself was affected by the genetic blight that had afflicted her family, because at the moment, with such massive unresolved issues in her own life, Libby wasn't in a position herself to make a commitment to Andrew anyway.

Not until she had answers of her own…

CHAPTER SEVEN

THE week flew by, and she saw Andrew every day.

Sometimes it was just to snatch coffee, sometimes they managed lunch too, but he rang her on Tuesday evening, and he spent Wednesday night with her.

On Thursday, Joel was allowed out of bed to sit in a chair for the first time, and although his parents were anxious about it, his neck fracture was stable, the halo was holding his head steady and although he was a little shaky, he was pleased to be able to see things from the right angle again.

He was sad to see Lucas go, though, and so was Libby. She'd grown fond of the sullen, stroppy teenager, and she saw him off that morning with mixed feelings.

'Promise you'll pop up and see us when you come in to the fracture clinic,' she said, and he nodded.

'Yeah, I'll come,' he agreed, and then to her surprise, he leant over and hugged her awkwardly. 'You're OK, Sister, d'you know that, man? You're a nag and all that, but you're OK.'

She laughed a little unsteadily and let him go. 'You take care of yourself. We'll see you soon,' she said, and watched him swing down the corridor on his crutches, his skill with them hugely improved after all the zooming around the ward he'd been doing while he'd driven them mad for the last week or so.

She went back onto the ward and found Andrew there, checking on a little girl who'd been brought in for surgery the previous day on her Achilles tendons. They were too short to allow her to stand except on tiptoe, and Andrew had lengthened them with a Z-plasty to enable her to stand and walk properly at last.

But now she was sore and unhappy, and he was trying to examine her without success while the mother held her new baby in her arms and tried to soothe little Chloe and keep her older son out of mischief at the same time. So where was the nurse who should have been with Andrew?

It looked like a situation that was rapidly heading out of control, and as she went over to them he looked up and gave her a relieved smile.

She didn't wait for him to ask for help, just scooped up the little girl she'd already cuddled several times that morning, and sat down on the bed with her cradled firmly in her arms so Andrew could look at her feet, which were taped up now into a normal position following her surgery.

'Hello, sweetheart! Goodness me, you're looking pretty now! Did Mummy bring you in a new T-shirt?'

She sniffed and nodded, and Libby duly admired the duck on her tummy. 'That's such a pretty duck. What colour is it? Is it green?'

She giggled round her thumb. 'No.'

'Is it blue?'

Another giggle. 'No!'

'I know! It's red!'

The thumb came out. 'No, it's not! It's yellow!'

Libby blinked and laughed. 'So it is—silly me. Fancy me getting it wrong. I'll have to go back to school!'

Andrew was straightening up, his examination complete, and he gave her a thoughtful look before turning to the mother. 'OK. That's lovely. Her feet are looking much better.'

'They look normal now. I can't believe it. I really didn't think they'd ever look like that,' the mother said, her eyes filling.

He squeezed her shoulder gently. 'I told you they would. The position's everything I could have hoped for and, given a few days for it to settle, I'm sure you'll find she'll be able to start standing soon and before you know it, she'll be running around with her brother, won't you, Chloe?'

'Will she be able to walk like me?' the brother asked, and Andrew smiled.

'I'm sure she will, very soon.'

'I'll have to hide my toys.'

'Or you could share them,' their mother suggested gently, making him pull a mulish face.

'Hey, it's good to share. You can have twice as much fun with two of you,' Libby offered, and with a smile at the family they left them to consider the ramifications of a little girl soon to be mobile for the first time.

'Thanks for that,' Andrew murmured as they walked away. 'Sam had to bail on me—she had a vomiting child to clean up. I thought I'd be OK but then the baby kicked off and Chloe started to cry.'

'She's going to be great, though. You've done a good job,' she said, and he shot her a grin.

'It was easy. So straightforward for something that

makes so much difference. Who would have thought that a little zig-zag cut in a tendon could make the difference between being crippled and being normal?'

'Who, indeed. Lucas has gone, by the way.'

'I know. I saw him earlier and wished him luck. I'll see him in Outpatients.'

'Mmm. Remind him to come in and see us. I think the boys'll miss him.'

'I think you will,' he teased, and she smiled.

'You know, I think you might be right?'

Andrew opened his mouth, but then his pager went off and he gave her a wry grin. 'That'll teach me to think about coffee,' he said with a groan. 'I'll see you later.'

He did, but only fleetingly. He came onto the ward to check Chloe and found Libby cuddling her again, because mum had gone home to feed and change the baby, taking her big brother, and wouldn't be back for a while. And even though Libby's shift was over, she couldn't leave the little one sobbing her heart out alone.

'I thought you'd finished?' he said softly, crouching down beside them and grinning at Chloe. 'Hi, sweets. Are you OK?'

'Want Mummy,' she said, and cuddled into Libby's chest, her heart-rending sobs tugging at him.

'I think her pain relief needs looking at,' Libby murmured, and he nodded and checked the chart, upping the dose to give her a little extra cover to help her settle for the evening. 'While you're at it, Joel's been a bit uncomfortable. I think he might have a pin-track infection in one of his halo screws. I've sent a swab off to the lab.'

'I'll check him and write him up for something if necessary. When did you do the swab?'

'Twelve?'

'So it won't be back till lunchtime tomorrow. I'll have a look now.'

He straightened up. 'I'm on duty tonight—I'm covering for Patrick Corrigan, and it looks like it'll be busy, so I probably won't see you later.'

'OK,' she said, stifling the disappointment. 'I've got lots to do tonight anyway.'

'It's the weekend tomorrow,' he said softly. 'We could—oh, rats, I'd better go,' he sighed, glancing at his pager. 'Look, I'll call you later. We'll arrange something.'

He strode away, his long legs eating up the ward, and she saw him turn into the bay containing the older boys—checking on Joel, as he'd promised. She rocked Chloe, torn between getting her the extra dose of pain relief and settling her to sleep, and wondered what he'd suggest they did this weekend.

Nothing like the previous one, she was sure, but she felt a flutter of nervous anticipation. A quiet dinner in? Taking her out to a restaurant? A walk in the park?

Maybe nothing much at all. Maybe he'd just want to spend the time alone, and maybe the something he'd said they'd arrange would turn out to be a very small something indeed.

'You're being ridiculous,' she muttered, and Chloe stirred slightly, silencing her. She *was* being ridiculous. She wasn't supposed to be letting her heart get involved.

Too late, of course. It had been too late for that the moment he'd kissed her in the park, after they'd had lunch in the folly and walked through the woods just six days ago.

Certainly too late by the time he'd made love to her on Saturday night, and by Sunday evening any hope of remaining detached had been firmly blown out of the water.

But she still wondered what they'd be doing this weekend...

Andrew was desperate to get Libby to himself. They'd been so busy at work that he'd hardly seen her.

Well, that wasn't true. Considering they weren't supposed to be having a relationship, he was seeing a crazy amount of her, but it still wasn't enough, and he wanted her to himself. And he wanted to do nothing. Go nowhere, do nothing, just chill. He wondered if she'd be horribly disappointed if he suggested that, but it had been a busy couple of weeks and he just needed some down-time.

They'd do the garden, he decided. He didn't know if she liked gardening, but his needed attention whether she liked it or not, so if she didn't he'd just have to cut the grass and leave the rest for another time, he decided.

Always assuming Jacob was doing all right. They'd lightened the sedation that morning and he'd become restless, so they'd increased the pain relief and he'd settled. The fixators on his legs and pelvis were doing a good job and Andrew had no intention of interfering with them. The bones were well aligned and he was healing fast, so it was best left, and because he wasn't on call and little Jacob was still stable by the evening, his weekend was his own. They would split it between the two houses, because of Kitty, but tonight he wanted to be in his own home, with Libby.

He picked her up when he'd finished work at seven and took her back to his house, filling her in on the way about Jacob's progress, and she thought he was more relaxed than she'd ever seen him.

Relaxed and open and—happy.

Chris Turner would be impressed, she thought, remembering his comments a week ago at dinner.

Exactly a week, in fact, since the dinner party for his mother's birthday. Only a week. Heavens. It seemed much more. They seemed to have done so much in that time, gone so far, and yet they'd gone nowhere. They were still skirting around the question of their relationship, still taking every moment as it came, and to expect anything else would be greedy, she told herself as Andrew disappeared for a shower.

He came back a few minutes later in his favourite worn old jeans and a heavy cotton shirt, rolled up his sleeves and cooked for her, while she perched on a stool at the breakfast bar and watched him, his hands quick and precise, the surgeon at work. He sliced and shredded and chopped, threw everything into a wok and stir-fried it, poured in a jar of sauce and served it up on a bed of rice.

'Wow,' she said, savouring the first mouthful. 'This is gorgeous.'

'It's my speciality—fork food in bottled sauce. I only cook things that can be eaten with one hand because I'm usually eating while I check my email or write a report, and I have a very limited repertoire, so enjoy it while you can, because you'll very quickly get sick of it.'

She chuckled, but his words made her think. Was he intending her to be around for long enough to grow tired of his choice of menu? Or was it, indeed, a very short list?

Whatever, she'd savour every moment.

'Do you like gardening?' he asked suddenly, and she glanced up and saw a frown pleating his forehead.

'Yes—well, I think so, but I don't really know. It all depends on what you call gardening. I've only got a tiny garden, but I love pottering in it and I'd like to do more. Why?'

'Because I need to cut the grass tomorrow and the hedge could do with trimming and some of the borders need a tweak, but I don't want to bore you to death.'

'You won't bore me to death. It sounds fun.'

His frown disappeared. 'Good,' he said softly, and she realised he'd been troubled about it.

Why? Because he didn't know her, of course. They'd hurtled into this relationship by accident, really, without thought or planning, and she was pretty sure Andrew didn't do that. She was also pretty sure that the only reason they were still seeing each other was because it was easy. She hadn't expected anything, hadn't demanded anything, and so long as they both kept it light and just enjoyed each other's company, it was harmless.

In theory.

And for now, at least, she could keep it that way. Her appointment with the genetic counsellor hadn't come through yet, so she could stall the decision she had to make that could have a lasting and devastating impact on her future, and live solely for the present.

She put it out of her mind, ate the food he'd cooked for her, drank a couple of glasses of wine and went to bed with him, falling asleep in his arms. And on Saturday morning, because it had rained overnight and the grass was too wet to cut, they had a lie-in and then drove to Ashenden.

'We'll see if my parents are around, maybe have a coffee, then we could have lunch in the pub and go for a walk, if you like.'

Will and Sally were just unloading shopping out of

the boot of their car when they pulled up, and they all went into the main family kitchen and found Jane and Tony in front of the Aga, drinking coffee with the dogs snoring at their feet.

'Have you got a pot on the go there, Ma?' Will asked, and she nodded and filled four mugs and slid them across the table, throwing Libby a welcoming smile.

'It's lovely to see you again, Libby. Did you enjoy last weekend?'

'Oh, I did. It was wonderful. Thank you so much for including me.'

'Oh, it's a pleasure,' she said, and Libby could almost hear the wedding bells ringing. Oh, Andrew, she thought, and stifled a sigh. They'd be so disappointed if they knew the truth.

She sat and listened to them talking, Will and his father discussing estate business, Andrew chipping in and offering his opinion, and then Will glanced at his watch and drained his mug. 'We ought to be getting on. Sally's decided to decorate the nursery and I've been given the job. Why don't you two drop by on your way home after your walk and have tea?'

'OK. We won't be with you long, though, I've got things to do in the garden this afternoon.'

'Me, too,' Jane added, getting to her feet. 'I've got a major programme of replanting going on in the rose garden this season, and there are some old ones to come out and lots of perennials that need lifting, and I still haven't drawn up a plan. Tony, I could do with a hand with that, if you've got time.'

She bent over and dropped a kiss on Andrew's cheek, then smiled at Libby. 'I'm sorry we've got to rush off. I hope we'll see you again soon—perhaps Andrew will bring you over for supper one night.'

'Of course I will,' Andrew said easily, getting to his feet as they left, and then he scooped up the mugs, put them in the dishwasher and turned to Libby. 'Shall we make a move?'

Lunch in the pub was lovely.

She started by looking at the pudding menu, chose the end of her meal and then planned the beginning, while Andrew rolled his eyes and chuckled.

'What? *What*? Why waste a good pudding by getting too full first?'

'Women. So what are you having?'

'Raspberry crème brûlée, preceded by crayfish and scallop risotto—or maybe I want the rice pudding, in which case the risotto is silly,' she said, making him laugh again.

'The risotto's gorgeous, and so's the crème brûlée. Have the rice pudding another time.'

'Or you could have it and we could share.'

He chuckled. 'We could. I was going to have apple crumble.'

'Oh! That's nice, too—stop laughing at me!'

She had the risotto in the end, and stole some of his pan-fried chicken liver and bacon salad, and they shared the puddings over coffee, which meant they were running out of time.

'Do you still want a walk, or tea with Will and Sally? We haven't really got time for both if I'm going to cut the grass.'

'Will and Sally?' she suggested, and he nodded.

'Good idea. We can see this nursery and admire their handiwork.'

She'd only been in the hall of the east wing, and she

was looking forward to seeing the rest of it. She was busy thinking that the entrance was a bit of a disappointment, however, when it dawned on her that it was actually the back door.

There was a bell push, but Andrew just knocked and walked in, to find Sally in the kitchen in Will's arms. 'Put her down,' he said drily, and Will grunted, dropped a tender, lingering kiss on Sally's lips and let her go.

'Spoilsport. I'm just taking advantage of the last few weeks of having my wife to myself before it all comes to a grinding halt. How was lunch?'

'Lovely. I ate too much,' Libby confessed, and Sally laughed.

'Oh, you wait till you're pregnant. You can't eat a darned thing without feeling full, and then ten seconds later you're starving again! I've turned into a herbivore—I graze constantly. Tea or coffee?'

'Coffee,' Andrew said, and Libby said nothing, because Sally's words were echoing in her head. If she stayed with Andrew, managed to convince him that they'd be happy together, she'd never be pregnant, never know what Sally was talking about, never have to decorate a nursery or walk the landing all night with a grizzly baby or go to a parents' evening and get roped into the PTA.

'We've just had coffee,' she said, coming to at last, but Will just grinned.

'Ah, but this is good coffee, not Ma's decaf rubbish or the stuff they serve in the pub. And we've got serious chocolate biscuits.'

She opened her mouth to say no, caught sight of the packet Will was waggling and buckled. 'Oh, well, then, that's different,' she said with a laugh, and after they'd admired Will's handiwork in the nursery, they ended up sitting around the table in the kitchen—a huge room with high ceilings and glorious views over the river—and drinking coffee and eating biscuits for over an hour before Andrew stood up and pulled her to her feet.

'Come on, or it'll be dark before we get home and get that grass cut,' he said, and something about the word 'home' just took her breath away.

No, she told herself, getting to her feet and saying goodbye to the others. It was just a figure of speech, a casual remark. It wasn't home—not hers, not *theirs*, no matter how ludicrously tempting it sounded. Home was her little house, with Kitty and her redundant duster and vacuum cleaner and the washing machine that thought it had been pensioned off, not Andrew's beautiful barn with its spectacular views and rustic charm.

And she'd better not forget it.

The next week was busy, as ever, and they fell into the pattern of the previous week. They met for coffee whenever they could, snatching a few minutes here and there, and if they could they'd have lunch, but more often they'd meet up after work and spend the night together in one house or the other. And for people who weren't supposed to be having a relationship, Libby thought, they were actually doing a fine job of it!

They went over for supper with Will and Sally on Tuesday night, and because he'd got away early and it was a beautiful evening, they went out into the park and walked around the Great Wood before supper, the dogs milling around their feet and sending a small herd of deer fleeing into the cover, vanishing like mist.

The sun was setting over the fields in the distance, the sky shot with red and gold, and as she strolled along with Andrew, she thought she'd never been so happy.

They went back to the house for supper, eaten in the kitchen, and because Sally was tired and they had to work in the morning, they left early and went back—to Andrew's house, yet again, for the night, and she lay in his arms and listened to the sound of his heart as she fell asleep.

'Are you going on holiday this year?' he asked casually the next morning as they were lying together contemplating the unwelcome thought of getting out of bed.

'Maybe, later on when my bank account's recovered from last year's extravagance. Why?'

'Make sure your passport's valid. I had to look at mine yesterday because I've got a conference coming up and I'll need it, and I've had it so long I couldn't remember when it expires. It's just so easy to overlook and then you check just before you go and all hell breaks loose. It's happened to me before and it was a nightmare. I only just got it back in time.'

She ran a fingertip over his chin and down his throat, relishing the rough rasp of his morning beard. 'So you aren't about to whisk me away anywhere exotic, then?' she teased, hoping he'd say yes, but he just chuckled.

'Sadly not, but it's an idea. I suppose you could come to this conference with me, if you aren't doing anything else, but it might be rather dull, though. They tend to be a bit hectic and it's only in Brussels, not very exotic at all.'

'Oh, you make it sound so exciting,' she said drily. 'I think I'll pass.'

'They don't run all night,' he murmured, and she snuggled back down with her head on his chest, listening to the steady, even beat of his heart under her ear.

'No, I suppose they don't. You'd have to make it irresistible, though, to tempt me.'

His laugh rumbled under her ear. 'Well, you'd better check your passport when you get home, hadn't you? It would be a shame if you talk me into taking you and then you end up not being able to come after all.'

She felt a little twinge of disappointment that it was only an afterthought and he didn't sound over-enthusiastic, but that was silly. Why on earth should he be thinking of taking her away? Not that they needed to go away, anyway, because just to be here with him was all that she asked.

She loved waking up in his house, with the uncurtained window overlooking open countryside just there at the foot of the bed, so they could lie there and stare out across the fields and not see a soul. And despite all her attempts to hold herself in check, it was beginning to feel more and more like home, and staying there was getting to be a habit.

'It's so lovely here,' she murmured. 'Really peaceful.'

'It is. I love it. I could stay here all day.'

'Sadly not,' she said drily, and sighed. 'Poor Kitty. I'm beginning to feel so guilty about her. She must think I don't love her any more.'

'We'll stay there tonight,' he said. 'And all weekend. Will and Sally are tied up with a charity event on Sunday at Ashenden, and I'm keeping well out of it. We can get pizza and a DVD and lie in front of the telly with the cat and feed her cheese.'

'You do realise she's just a cupboard lover, don't you?' Libby said drily, prising herself off his chest and getting out of bed. 'I'm going to shower or I'll be late for work.'

'I need to get in early, too. I'll shower with you.'

'So, tell me, how is this going to speed things up?' she asked, as he took her into his arms under the pounding spray and kissed her thoroughly.

'Multi-tasking,' he said, and muffled her laughter with his kiss.

She'd wondered, as he'd made love to her in the shower, how long it would be before the bubble burst, and later that morning something happened that brought reality home with a vengeance.

Andrew appeared on the ward holding a set of notes, and paused at the nurses' station. 'Could we have a word?' he murmured, and she smiled.

'Could we have a word,' was code for 'come into the office, I want to hug you,' but once they were in there, his first words drove all such thoughts out of her head.

'I've got a patient coming in later today that I wanted to talk to you about. Briefly, he had a fall from his wheelchair two weeks ago and broke his arm, but he's getting pins and needles now. I reviewed it yesterday in the fracture clinic and it needs surgery, so I'm admitting him. The problem is he's got DMD.'

DMD. Duchenne muscular dystrophy. She felt the blood drain out of her face, and she had to remind herself to breathe.

'His heart isn't great and his pCO2 is high—his lungs are very compromised because of pronounced scoliosis, so he's not a good surgical risk, but the cardiologist and physicians are going to review him tomorrow and we'll see if we think we can go ahead with the arm under general anaesthetic. Otherwise I'll have to do it with a nerve block and mild sedation, but that's a bit grim for a kid, and for his parents.'

She nodded, still reeling. Why? Why now, of all the times, when she'd just discovered how much it mattered that she wasn't—?

'OK, this is the picture show,' he said, snapping plates up onto the box light in the office. 'Here's the arm—you can see how it's displaced now, compared to straight after the fracture. And this is his spine. You can see the curvature here—and this was two years ago. It's worse now. His lung capacity is becoming more compromised, and he's finding it all more uncomfortable, but we can't do that kind of op here and at the moment I'm just concerned with his arm. His spine needs review at a specialist centre, and I intend to refer him as soon as this arm is sorted to see if they can do something to improve the quality of his life. I just hope he's up to it but I'm afraid it might have been left too late.'

Libby studied the plates with a frown. She wasn't an expert on DMD by any means, but she'd been reading up on it recently, and she forced herself to recall the facts—not hard, under the circumstances, but hard to think clearly.

It was a progressive, inherited degenerative muscle disorder that affected boys almost exclusively, and girls carrying the defective gene were usually although not always unaffected. The deterioration, caused by a lack of dystrophin in the muscles, slowly but surely crippled the person until their body was unable to support itself. They usually died of heart or lung problems in their teens or twenties due to severe scoliosis compressing the chest cavity, but the spinal curvature was one of the things that could be improved. However, even she could see it didn't look good and the surgeons were going to have their work cut out to fix it—assuming the young lad got the chance. 'How old is…' she peered at the plates '…Craig?'

'Sixteen—so technically he's on the cusp of moving up to the adult ward, but as it's me who's dealing with him I wanted him on Paeds—it's more fun, and he's short on fun at the moment. Nice lad. You'll like him. Good sense of humour.'

She tried to smile. She'd met more than enough brave kids who made light of their situation with humour, and the worse it was, the funnier they could be. Till you caught them unawares and saw their true feelings. It wasn't so funny then. 'How long's he got?' she asked quietly, holding her breath for his answer.

Andrew shrugged. 'Who knows? His heart's enlarged, his body's very weak now—the muscles are packing up faster than I'd have expected. He's been in a wheelchair for five years already, so he's not going to make old bones, but he's still in full-time education, he's as bright as a button and he's amazingly gutsy. I just hope they can give him a while longer and make him more comfortable, but that all depends on the cardiac and pulmonary assessments—and first we have to sort this arm.'

She nodded slowly. 'OK. I'll arrange a bed for him. Do you want him in with the boys, or on his own?

'Oh, in with the boys. Joel's bored to death. They can entertain each other for the next few days. Right, I have to go, but I'll be back later with the MDT—can I leave this with you?'

'Yes, sure,' she said, her eyes fixed on the X-ray

plates, and he kissed her cheek and went out, leaving her standing there staring at the havoc wrought by this slow and insidious killer gene. A gene that was killing her cousin inch by inch.

A gene which, if she had inherited it from her mother's side of the family, would make her a carrier…

CHAPTER EIGHT

CRAIG was admitted an hour later, and she'd put him opposite Joel so they could see each other.

It was no good putting them side by side, since Joel couldn't turn his head with the halo splint, and as Craig was most likely to need nursing propped up in bed, it was the best way for them to be placed.

Luckily the boys' bay was quiet now. Christopher and Jonathan, the twins who'd fallen out of the tree and broken their legs, had gone home before the weekend, and the other beds had post-op fractures and ligament repairs, comparatively minor injuries which had needed surgery but didn't necessitate a long stay, so she was happy to shuffle them to make way for the boys who might well have longer to go.

Andrew was right—Craig was struggling. Every breath was a physical effort, every word took energy he didn't have, but his eyes were bright and alert and he was open and friendly. 'I've put you here,' she told him. 'This is Joel. I'll let him tell you why he's in here and what he's done to himself. Mr Langham-Jones said you'd got a good sense of humour!'

Craig chuckled and raised his hand to Joel. 'Hi, there. I'm Craig.'

'What happened to you?'

'I fell out of my wheelchair. It didn't like the kerb. What about you?'

'I fell through the roof of the conservatory.'

'What, glass?' Craig asked, looking suitably impressed.

'No. The wooden panel by the house. It's meant to be a fire escape, but it was rotten and I fell through it. Well, one leg did. The other one didn't, so I swivelled round and went off the edge head first and broke my neck. I was supposed to be going home but I've got an infection where the screws go into my skull.'

'Oh, gross!' Craig said, pulling a face. Libby chuckled and handed him the tubes so he could insert the soft prongs into his nose and link himself up to the oxygen. He did it without even looking at them, an indication of how much he'd had to do with hospitals and oxygen over the past few years, and she had to fight the twin urges to hug him and run away.

She did neither, the soft voice behind her murmuring her name jerking her out of her turbulent thoughts.

'Andrew!' She looked up, distracted, her head miles away on the other side of the country at a funeral, meeting her seventeen-year-old cousin, Edward, for the first—and probably last—time.

His brow pleated into a frown. 'Are you OK?' he murmured softly, and she nodded.

She wasn't. She was far from OK, she'd been slapped in the face by reality, forced to confront what her future might have been had she been born a boy. What the future might be for any potential son she bore.

'I'm fine,' she lied. 'I'll get the paperwork. When's the MDT meeting?'

'As soon as I tell them he's here,' he said quietly.

'We've gone through the notes, they want to meet him. I was just popping up to say hi and put him in the picture. Could you page them?'

'Sure, I'll go and do it now,' she said, and leaving the boy in Andrew's capable hands, she retreated to the relative sanctuary of her office.

He followed her in there a few moments later, shutting the door and giving her an odd look. 'Libby, is everything all right?'

'It's fine.'

'No, it's not. It's not fine. There's something the matter.'

'Andrew, I'm fine,' she insisted. 'I'm just busy.'

Busy, and unable to find the words to tell him, to bring the truth out into the open and give voice to it, because by doing so she'd be facing up to it and admitting that there was a possibility that she was a carrier of DMD.

'Good news. We can do Craig's arm under GA tomorrow,' he told her over the phone that night.

'That's great,' she said, trying to sound cheerful. 'So what's the bad news?'

'I'm tied up here and I won't get to you. I've had another look at Craig's X-rays and I want to go over the notes again, do a bit more research, and I'll be really late, so I might as well kip here. I'll see you here tomorrow.'

'I take it you're still at work, then?'

He gave a rusty chuckle. 'Yes, I'm still at work. I'm sorry. I thought—'

'What?'

He hesitated, then sighed. 'Nothing. I'll see you in the morning. Sleep well.'

'You, too. Try not to be up all night.'

'I won't. Take care.'

She stared at the phone. Damn. She'd geared herself up to talk to him, decided to tell him when he got to her house. And now he wasn't coming.

There was no way she could do it at work, so she'd have to tell him tomorrow night. Another twenty-four hours.

She went to bed, too troubled to sleep at first, but she was woken later by her phone. She struggled up on one elbow and picked it up, scraping the hair back out of her eyes with the other hand and peering at the clock. Two-thirty? 'Hello?' she murmured.

'It's me. I'm outside—can you let me in?'

Andrew. She slipped out of bed, ran down and opened the door, and he stepped inside and pulled her into his arms for a hug.

'I thought you weren't coming?' she mumbled into his shirtfront, and he eased her away and looked down into her sleep-glazed eyes.

'I wasn't, but—I don't know, there was something in your voice, and you keep telling me you're all right, but I know you're not. I know there's something wrong, and I just couldn't settle until I knew what it was.'

She turned her head away, but not before he saw the slight sheen of tears. 'You're right. I need to talk to you. There's something you don't know—something even I don't know yet.'

His heart pounded. He had no idea what it was, but his imagination was running riot and it wasn't coming up with anything good. 'OK. Let's go somewhere comfortable and talk about it.'

'Bed?' she suggested, and he nodded and shrugged off his jacket, hanging it over the end of the banisters as they went up the stairs to her room.

And as soon as they were settled in bed, with his arms around her cradling her against his shoulder, she carried on, 'I went to a funeral just over a year ago, of a great-great-aunt. And I met a young man there—a cousin. He was in a wheelchair.' She swallowed. 'He looked a lot like Craig.'

He felt a cold chill run over him. 'DMD?' he said, tilting her chin so he could see into her eyes.

She nodded, and he shook his head slowly. No wonder she'd been looking a little strange today, as if things weren't quite right with her world. Of all the cruel twists of fate, to have Craig on the ward. 'You didn't know about it?'

She shook her head. 'No. I had no idea. It's an X-linked recessive, so it doesn't show up in girls, and I've only got one sister, and my mother's an only child, and her mother was one of two girls. There's no evidence of it on our side of the family.'

'And this cousin?'

'He's on the other side, my great-aunt's side. We had no idea. We don't have any contact with them, really, because we're spread out all over the place. It was a complete bolt from the blue.'

'I'm sure. Oh, Libby, I'm so sorry,' he murmured, aching for her, this woman who was so good with children, a woman just made to be a mother, and the implications this could have for her. 'And you?' he asked, holding his breath for the answer. 'Are you a carrier?'

She shrugged, her face unhappy. 'I don't know. My sister Jenny and her husband were trying for another baby at the time, and they stopped immediately and went for genetic screening to find out, and discovered that she's a carrier. Luckily their first child's a girl, so they're having her screened, but they won't have any more.'

'Why? They can, with IVF.'

'I know, but apparently they just screen for sex rather than the gene, and implant female embryos, so you can still hand the gene on even if the carrier's unaffected, and Jenny says she couldn't do that. It's just handing the dilemma on to the next generation and, anyway, IVF's not exactly plain sailing, there's no guarantee it will work and there's still a chance of having a child with a disability because of the possibility of a damaged embryo. The embryo screening process isn't without risk, and it strikes me it's just swapping a known risk for an unknown one, and I'm not sure I'll want to do that, either.'

'You're getting ahead of yourself,' he pointed out gently. 'You don't even know yet if you *are* a carrier, do you? Are you waiting for results?'

She shook her head. 'No. I saw my GP about getting screened, but because I wasn't in a relationship and not seeking to become pregnant any time in the foreseeable future, there didn't seem to be any hurry.'

He let his breath out on a long, quiet sigh and drew her closer into his arms, deeply saddened for her. 'I'm so sorry. I had no idea you were going through all that.'

'Of course you didn't. Why should you? And I haven't really been going through it, I've been avoiding it, because it wasn't relevant and frankly I'd rather not know. Except now, seeing Craig today—well, I have to know, don't I? I have to find out. I can't just ignore it any longer. I can't afford to take the risk of bringing a child into the world to suffer like that. And he's so brave and so candid…'

Her voice broke, and he cradled her against his chest while she cried, not only for Craig, but for the uncertainty in her future, for the very real possibility that having children, at least naturally conceived children, might be denied her. It was something everyone took for granted, and he knew only too well how hard it was to come to terms with when it was taken away.

'Are you all right?'

Craig nodded sleepily, the pre-med taking effect. 'Yeah, I'm fine. Can't breathe very well, but that's par.'

She helped him shift, propped another pillow under his head and adjusted the flow of his oxygen. 'Better?'

'Yeah. Thanks.'

'My pleasure. The arm's a bit of a pain really, isn't it?' she added softly, and he gave her a tired smile.

'Yes. I could have done without it, but if I get through the GA, at least it'll prove I'm a good anaesthetic risk.'

She tipped her head on one side at his choice of words. 'Good working knowledge, too much practical experience or doctor in the family?' she asked, and he chuckled.

'All the above. I thought I'd want to train as a doctor if I stayed alive that long, but it's unlikely so I've adjusted my expectations. If they can straighten my scoliosis, or at least stop it getting worse, there's more chance, but I still think it's a long shot. Pity, really. I'd be good—lots of empathy!'

She laughed with him, touched by his straightforward acceptance of his condition, by the courage he showed in the face of an operation which, while routine in anyone else, could possibly cost him his life.

No. That was stretching it too far. Andrew wouldn't operate under GA if the team didn't feel it was feasible.

This time.

So what about next?

A shiver ran over her, and she was glad when the porter came to take him to Theatre. She walked up with him, not because his case meant more to her than any of the others but because of his courage, because despite it, she knew he had to be a little bit afraid.

'I'll see you later,' she said as the anaesthetist started the drugs, and he winked at her, his eyes glazing as the anaesthetic took effect.

'OK?'

Andrew was standing waiting, and she saw his eyes concerned above the mask.

'Fine. He's OK with it.'

His eyes studied hers for a second. They both knew he wasn't asking about Craig, but about her, and she smiled and nodded assurance.

His eyes creased in a smile. 'Good. We'll see you in a bit. It shouldn't take long. I'll let you know.'

Craig was due back on the ward later that afternoon, after a lengthy period in Recovery, but he'd done well, according to Andrew, it had all gone according to plan, he'd coped well with the anaesthetic and he would be fine. Nevertheless, she'd be glad to see him back in his bed.

So would his mother, who'd made herself scarce when he was going up to Theatre so she didn't embarrass him, but ever since had sat in silent vigil by his wheelchair, waiting for his return.

'He'll be back soon,' Libby told her. She'd made them both a cup of tea at the end of her shift, and they were sitting drinking it while they waited.

'It's funny. I've known for years we were going to

lose him, but this fracture has been a bit of an eye-opener. I mean, you expect him to die of cardiac problems or pneumonia, not a broken arm. And he could have done. If it had gone wrong—'

'But it didn't, and they wouldn't have operated like that if they'd felt it would. They would have done it with a local anaesthetic, but it wouldn't have been very nice for him.'

His mother laughed a little bitterly. 'None of it's very nice for him. We were really shocked when we learned what he'd got. There isn't any of it in the family anywhere that we can trace. It's just one of those things.'

'It happens like that sometimes,' she said. 'A freaky gene—a bit of damage. Things go wrong spontaneously from time to time.'

'I know. But why did it have to be my boy?' she asked, and Libby could see her eyes were filled with a sadness that ran too deep for tears.

'Change of plan,' Andrew told her on Thursday evening when he arrived at her house armed with the makings of supper.

'Change of what plan?'

'The weekend,' he said, buzzing her cheek with a kiss and grinning cheerfully. 'We're going to London tomorrow night and we won't be back till Sunday. Pack smart casual and something a bit dressier for going out for dinner—and bring a warm coat for walking by the river, and comfortable shoes for sightseeing.'

'Sightseeing?' she said, bemused, and he smiled.

'Don't tell me you've seen everything?' he asked. 'And even if you have, you haven't seen it with me, so just do as you're asked and go and pack while I get the supper.'

She felt a little fizzle of excitement, just at the thought of going away with him, but—London? It was so dreary in the winter, but of course with him it would be different. More fun. Everything was more fun with him. 'I'll have to get Amy or someone to feed the cat. I hope she can.'

'So do I. I'm tired. I want to get away.' He hesitated, frowning. 'Unless you really don't want to?'

'No, I'd love to, of course I would,' she said hastily, because he was tired, and he did need to get away. Away from his family, from the hospital, from all of it. And so did she. She desperately needed some downtime with him, and the idea of going away with him was suddenly wonderfully appealing.

'It sounds lovely,' she said with another smile, and ran upstairs to pack, thanking her lucky stars that she'd done the washing the night before and it was dry. She packed her best matching underwear, a nightdress and light dressing gown for the hotel, trousers, her little black dress, flat shoes, heels, pretty tops, and left out her decent black trousers and a pretty jumper for travelling down the next night.

'Done,' she said as she went back into the kitchen, and he smiled and held out his arms.

'Good girl. Now come and give me a hug, and then you can help me make the supper.'

'Make it?' she said, leaning back and laughing up at him. 'It's pizza and salad!'

'I told you not to expect too much of my culinary skills,' he grinned, releasing her and swatting her on the bottom. 'Come on, open the bag of salad and let's eat. I'm starving and the pizza's done.'

CHAPTER NINE

SHE rushed home after work on Friday, changed quickly into her decent black trousers, her favourite boots which were comfortable enough for sightseeing and decent enough for dinner when they arrived in London, and was ready and waiting when he pulled up at her door.

He came in, kissed her and then hesitated. 'Um—I lied to you,' he said softly, his eyes sparkling and an air of suppressed excitement about him. 'I hope you weren't fudging when you said you had a valid passport?'

She stared at him, her jaw dropping, and laughed in surprise. 'Passport?'

'Come on, we need to get a move-on. It is here, I take it?'

The look of panic on his face was comical, and she laughed again and opened the dresser drawer, waggling it under his nose. 'Here—all present and correct, valid for four and a half years. How long a trip were you planning?'

He laughed. 'Sadly only two nights. Come on.'

'Where are we going?' she asked, but he just tapped the side of his nose, helped her into her coat, pocketed her passport and put her case in the car while she locked the house.

'Andrew, where are we going?' she asked, butterflies having a field day in her stomach now, and he slid behind the wheel, shot her a grin and said,

'Paris.'

She felt her jaw drop. 'Paris?' she squeaked.

He shrugged. 'Well, when I asked you two weeks ago what you'd be doing over the weekend, that was what you said, and it sounded like a fantasy. So I thought I'd make it come true for you. Except we're not flying, we're going on the Eurostar from St Pancras.'

'That's fine,' she said a little weakly. 'I hate flying.'

They arrived at their hotel shortly before midnight, and when they went into the room, all she could see through the huge windows was the twinkle of a million lights. 'Oh, Andrew!' she breathed, crossing to the glass and staring out in awe.

They could see the bridges spanning the Seine, the arches illuminated in a rainbow of colours, and to their left the glittering Eiffel Tower soared skywards, with its flashing beam like a lighthouse sweeping across the night sky.

He slid his arms round her and eased her back against his chest. 'Enough lights for you?'

'Oh, yes!' She turned in his arms, lifting her face to his, and he lowered his head and touched his lips to hers.

'Good. Do you want anything from room service?'

'What, after that gorgeous meal on the train? I shouldn't think so.'

'Nothing to drink?'

'No. I'm happy drinking in the view. It's beautiful. Thank you so much for bringing me here.'

'My pleasure. It's lovely to get away.' He dropped a

kiss on her nose and smiled down at her. 'Time for bed? We've got a long day tomorrow.'

She smiled. 'Bed sounds lovely,' she said softly, and going up on tiptoe, she kissed him back.

He hadn't lied about the long day, he thought as they strolled along the Seine.

Breakfast in a patisserie, followed by sightseeing in the morning, a lunchtime river cruise from the quayside near the foot of the Eiffel Tower, returning them two hours later, then a good stretch to the Musée d'Orsay further along the Rive Gauche, where Libby gazed up, fascinated, at the curved glass roof of the old station building that now housed a fabulous collection of artworks by the Impressionists—sculptures and paintings that Libby showed a surprising knowledge of.

'I did art history at A level,' she told him, studying a picture by Manet before strolling on to the next one. And the next. And the next.

She had stamina, he thought with an inward smile as they left the exhibition. They'd walked miles already, and now they walked again, taking the metro to Montmartre and strolling round hand in hand, steeping themselves in more art and architecture and history before heading back to the hotel.

They showered and changed, him into his suit, Libby into her little black dress that did shocking things to his blood pressure, then headed out again.

'Where are we going?' she asked yet again, but he just smiled and kept her guessing.

'The Eiffel Tower?' she asked hopefully as they approached it. 'I was guessing wildly, you know—can you even go up it at night?'

'I don't know,' he lied, the fast-pass tickets burning a hole in his pocket, but as they arrived at the bottom and skipped the queue she laughed crossly and told him off for teasing, and he could see she was excited. They went to the top in the lift, changing at the second floor and soaring right up to level three for the most spectacular view, and then came down, stopping at level two to change lifts again—except instead of changing lifts, he led her to the restaurant.

'We're eating here?' she said, awed, as they were shown to a seat by the window. 'How on earth did you get a reservation?'

He chuckled. 'Sleight of hand and very fortuitous luck. They had a group cancellation, apparently. Normally you have to book weeks in advance, even in the off season.'

She tipped her head on one side and searched his eyes. 'Andrew, how long have you been planning this?' she asked, and he smiled.

'Two weeks?'

'Two weeks? But—that was your mother's birthday weekend. We weren't even—well—whatever we're doing.'

She floundered to a halt, her eyes troubled, and he reached out and took her hand. 'Seeing each other?' he suggested softly. 'Going out?'

'We weren't supposed to be,' she reminded him, looking confused and a little wary, and he smiled again, confused and a little wary himself, but it was too late for that, and if things had been different—but they weren't, he thought with an inward sigh.

'I know,' he murmured. 'But it sounded as if it was your dream weekend, and so I made some enquiries.'

'And craftily checked that I had a passport.'

He laughed. 'Only after I'd booked it. I had a moment of panic that yours might have expired like mine had the time I told you about, or that it wouldn't be at your house.'

'Where else?' she said, frowning in puzzlement.

'I don't know—your parents'?'

She shook her head. 'My father's dead, and my mother lives in Cork, in Ireland, with her new husband. And apart from that, there's only my sister Jenny and her husband and daughter in Cumbria.'

He realised he hadn't known any of that. Well, apart from the fact that she had a sister. Other than her recent revelation about the DMD, she'd shared very little of herself. Part of their unspoken agreement to keep things between them light—except he wasn't doing too well on that front.

Take this weekend, for instance. He'd squandered a fortune on it without a second thought, just to spoil her because he—

He stopped dead, his thoughts slamming into a brick wall. He what?

He *loved her*?

No.

Yes.

The waiter appeared to take their order, and he put the disturbing thought on the back burner. For now.

It wouldn't stay there, though. As they strolled back to the hotel after their meal—only two delicious courses because even Libby, with her taste for desserts, had been defeated after the generous lunch on the river—he threaded his fingers through hers and drew her to a halt, turning to stare out over the river. It was cool, and he slid his arm round her, holding her close against his side as the wind whipped across the water and swirled around them.

'Happy?' he asked her, and she nodded, her face alight.

'Very. That was a fabulous meal, thank you so much,' she said, snuggling into his side. 'I hate to think what this is costing you.'

'It's irrelevant. It's just lovely to get right away, and I haven't had so much fun for years. It's been wonderful,' he admitted, 'and it's all because you're here with me.'

She turned in his arms, lifting her face to his, her eyes luminous in the lamplight. 'Oh, Andrew…'

He cradled her cheek in his hand, stroking the pad of his thumb against the delicate skin. 'I think I'm falling in love with you, Libby,' he confessed softly, and her mouth opened on a soundless O.

She closed it and smiled, reaching up to touch his face, her hand cool against his jaw. 'I *know* I'm falling in love with you,' she replied, her voice quiet, sincere.

He swallowed hard, staring into her guileless eyes, suddenly swamped by sadness.

'Oh, Libby,' he murmured, tracing her lovely face with his fingertips. 'This wasn't meant to happen. It was all supposed to be strictly no strings—that was what I promised you, and now…'

'Now we're having a wonderful time together. That's all. And anyway,' she said, the shadow returning to her eyes, 'it may not be the problem you imagine.'

'How can it not be?' he asked sadly. 'I wish—you'll never know how much—that things could be different, but they aren't. I can't give you children, Libby, and I can't ask you to sacrifice your chances of being a mother for me.'

'I'm not asking you to. We've talked about this. You know how I feel about having children if I'm a carrier.'

'But we don't know if you are.'

'I know, but if I *am* a carrier, then I won't have children, not with all the risks, so the fact that you can't have them might not be an issue,' she said, tilting her head back again so she could meet his eyes. 'We'd both be in the same position, so we could let our relationship take its course.'

He frowned down at her, stunned at the implications of her words. 'But you wouldn't be in the same position as me,' he argued. 'You could still have children, Libby. IVF's not that risky.'

'I know, but it isn't risk free, and if I was with someone who desperately wanted children and could otherwise have had them, I might go for it for their sake—but I'm not. I'm with someone who can't have them, and so I wouldn't have to make that painful choice and potentially live with the consequences of it every day of my child's life.'

He felt hope swell in his chest, and crushed it ruthlessly. He wouldn't let himself think about it, wish a carrier status on her so that he didn't have to lose her. And he still wasn't convinced that, years down the line, she wouldn't regret her decision if she chose to be with him and pass up on the chance to be a mother.

'Get the test results and then we'll talk about it again,' he said, stopping his mind from getting carried away with planning the future—a future with Libby in it.

He let her go, slipping his hand down her arm and taking her chilly hand. It was too cold to stand and talk, and anyway he wanted to take her to bed and hold her, to tell her without words how he felt for her.

'Come on, you're freezing,' he said gently. 'Let's go back to the hotel.'

He was sleeping, sprawled on his front across the bed, one bare, hair-strewn leg sticking out of the duvet, his head turned towards her.

He loved her—or so he said, but she wasn't sure.

Libby sat on the chair by the window watching him sleep, happy to let him rest so she could think through his reaction to their conversation.

He hadn't seemed convinced about her electing not to have children if she was a carrier, or her suggestion that if she was they could let their relationship take its course. Rather, he'd seemed almost—wary. He'd brought her back to the hotel and made love to her with aching tenderness, but she'd felt there was a part of himself he was holding back. A part he always held back.

Habit? Because, of course, he'd spent years denying himself a meaningful, long-term relationship on the grounds that he wouldn't let it go anywhere—or so he said. But what if that was just an excuse? What if he just didn't want to get married, and used it as a justifiable reason to avoid a permanent entanglement?

She had no idea. They hardly knew each other, even though they'd worked in the same unit for months. And they'd been together now for just two weeks. Two ecstatic, delirious, blissful weeks.

Weeks in which she'd fallen in love with him, and he, apparently, with her. Or had he? Had he really?

Restless, she got to her feet and padded softly over

to the dresser unit to search for a magazine. Not that she could read it if it was in French. She was far from fluent, her schoolgirl French all but forgotten, but she could look at the pictures.

She drew a blank on the magazine front, but found a selection of tourist information leaflets, and flicked through them. Some were in several languages, including English, and she studied them while she waited for him to wake up.

Notre Dame, she thought. That looked interesting. Or perhaps the Louvre—

'Planning the day?'

She looked up, startled, and smiled at him. 'I didn't realise you were awake. I was just killing time.'

'You should have woken me.' He threw back the bedclothes and walked over to her, bending to brush his lips against her cheek. 'I need the bathroom. You could call room service and get breakfast sent up, and we can plan our day over a jug of coffee and a pile of hot, buttery croissants.'

'Consider it done,' she said with a smile, and put her doubts out of her mind.

They got back to Audley at eleven that night, exhausted, and went straight to her house to feed the cat.

'Oh, Kitty, did you miss me?' she asked, scooping her up, but Kitty's only interest was food, as usual, and Libby just rolled her eyes, put her down and fed her. 'Do you want a drink?' she asked Andrew, but he shook his head.

'No, I need to get home,' he said, disappointing her. 'I've got things to do before tomorrow, and I ought to check my messages and give Will a ring before I go to bed, and I've got a long day. We're on duty overnight tomorrow and it could be a bit hectic, and if I stay—well, you know what'll happen,' he said ruefully, hugging her. 'But I'll see you in the morning. We'll have coffee, or lunch, or something, anyway.'

She nodded, hugging him back. 'Thank you so much for this weekend,' she said, loath to let it end, knowing he was right and that he had to get some sleep before the busy week ahead. So did she, but somehow when she was in his arms that didn't seem to matter. 'Go on, go home while I'll still let you,' she told him, and, kissing him lightly on the lips, she eased out of his arms and opened the door. 'I'll see you tomorrow.'

He kissed her again, then slid behind the wheel and drove away. She watched his lights disappear, then closed the door and went to find the cat and check her phone for messages.

And discovered that Jenny had phoned, leaving a message for her to call her back. She put her mobile on charge, because of course she'd forgotten to take her charger with her and it had gone flat, and when she checked it she found two missed calls and a text, all from her sister.

RING ME!

Dreading the call, desperately hoping it was the news her sister had been praying for, she rang.

He hadn't wanted to leave.

It was true, he did have things to do, and he needed to get some uninterrupted sleep, but when he eventually got into it, he found the bed cold and empty and just plain wrong without her.

He was an idiot. He should have seen the way it was going, realised what was happening to him—to them—and called a halt, instead of letting himself drift along getting sucked in deeper and deeper with a woman who frankly deserved better than a life of barren frustration with a man who could never give her children—the children she would be so wonderful with.

His chest ached, and he rubbed it with the heel of his hand. Heart ache? Was it possible for a heart really to ache?

Stress, he told himself. Too much coffee, too little sleep, too much rich food—nothing to do with the yawning void beside him where Libby ought to be.

He turned over, thumped the pillow and shut his eyes. He needed to sleep. He had children tomorrow who needed his full attention, awake and alert and on the ball, not running on empty. So he rolled onto his back again, and tensed and relaxed all the muscle groups in his body in turn, a trick he'd learned years ago, and eventually his body shut down his mind and he slept.

'I had a message from my sister.'

Andrew stopped, his hand in mid-air, the coffee suspended as Libby stood smiling at him in his office doorway.

'And?'

Her eyes misted over. 'Her daughter's OK. She's not a carrier.'

Oh, hell, she was going to cry. He put the coffee down and hugged her. 'That's great news. I'm really pleased for her,' he said. He let her go, kissed her briefly and went back to the coffee machine to pour another cup. 'So what now?'

'Now? I'm going to contact my GP again, chase up this genetic screening referral. I have no idea how long it'll take.'

'Go private,' he said, shocking himself. 'I'll pay for it. I know the consultant here—Huw Parry. He'll sort it for you. I'll give him a ring.'

'I can't let you do that! Anyway, what are you going to tell him?'

'Nothing. Just that a friend of mine needs to see him urgently.'

'But it's not urgent!'

It felt urgent. It felt urgent to him, to know beyond doubt that she wasn't a carrier, to know if he was holding her in a relationship for his own selfish ends—a relationship she'd do better to move on from. And once he knew that, he could set her free, cut himself off from her and end their bitter-sweet affair.

'I think it's time you knew,' he said gently. Time they both knew, to put an end to this selfish and sickening hope that had arisen in him—and which disgusted him. Time to put a stop to it all before it destroyed him.

Libby stared at him, trying to read his eyes, and what she saw there didn't reassure her. Was he trying to find an excuse to get her out of his life? In which case, all he had to do was say so. Or was he seriously thinking about what she'd said, that if she was a carrier, she wouldn't have children?

'OK,' she said finally. 'Ring him—but I'll pay.'

He nodded, picked up the phone and left a message with Huw's secretary for him to call back, then replaced the phone in its cradle and drained his coffee—the fourth that morning. He was going to have a heart attack at this rate.

'I need to get on.'

'Me, too. How's Jacob?'

Reality. Thank God for reality. 'Good,' he replied. 'He's conscious and talking, and they're moving him to the high-dependency unit today. Looks like the brain injury may not be as serious as they'd feared, and his legs and pelvis are healing well, so hopefully he'll soon be up and about.'

Her smile lit up his world. 'I'm so pleased. Well done.'

'Thanks.' He didn't pretend false modesty. He knew he was a good surgeon, his high standards wouldn't allow him to be anything less, but her praise still warmed him, and he smiled back, stood up and pulled her into his arms and hugged her, unable to stop himself.

It felt so good to hold her. So right. And if Huw discovered that she *was* a carrier, then maybe…

'I have to go,' she murmured, snuggling closer and sighing.

He let her go and stepped back. 'Me, too.'

'Will I see you tonight?'

'Probably not. We're on take. I expect all hell will break loose. I'll give you a call when I hear from Huw—can I give him your mobile number?'

'Of course you can. I'll have it with me. And thank you.'

She reached up and kissed his cheek, then went back to the ward to check an IV line on a baby, and all the time she was working on him, then changing a dressing on another child, setting up an infusion in a child with Crohn's who was in for a few days to recover her strength before surgery to remove an obstruction in her bowel, doing the drugs round—through it all, she was waiting for Huw's call.

It came at lunchtime, after she'd done the discharge notes and said goodbye to Joel, who was going home to continue his convalescence, and as she went into the office to grab some lunch, her phone rang.

'Hi, it's Huw Parry. I gather you want to see me for DMD screening?'

'Yes, that's right,' she said, suddenly nervous as the reality of it hit her. 'I've been referred to you by the GP and I haven't heard anything, but it's not really urgent. I'm just getting a bit edgy, and Mr Langham-Jones suggested seeing you privately.'

'Are you busy now?'

'Now?' she squeaked, and swallowed. 'No, I'm not busy now. Nothing that can't wait, I'm on a break.'

'Can you come down? We can fill in a few forms, run through the questions and I can send off the bloods. Come to Medical Genetics and ask them to call me.'

'So how did it go?'

She pushed the cat off her lap and went to put the kettle on while she talked to him. She'd been waiting for him to ring for ages. 'Fine. He asked all sorts of questions, took a family history and about a gallon of blood and that was it, really. I already knew all the biology of inherited genes, the one in two chance of passing it on if I'm a carrier.'

'But only one in four of it affecting a child,' Andrew corrected.

'No. One in four that it's a boy with the disease, but also one in four that it's a girl who'll be a carrier, and as far as I'm concerned, that's affected, and pre-implantation genetic diagnosis wouldn't alter that. I'm not prepared to hand this bombshell on for my daughter to deal with when her time comes, any more than I want to give my son a life sentence. So, as far as I'm concerned, it's a one in two chance, even with screening, and that's crazy odds.'

She heard his good-natured sigh down the phone. 'OK, you win. One in two. So how long did he think it would take to get the results?'

'A couple of weeks. Maybe less, maybe more. There are several layers of testing. I feel sick now. I wish you were here.'

She heard him sigh. 'Me, too. I'm sorry, it's really busy. I've had a spate of little accidents—greenstick fractures, squashed fingers, a dislocated elbow. My registrar told me to go, but she's run off her feet and I don't like to make the children wait. I'll get over later if I can, just for a while.'

'Please do,' she said, suddenly realising how much she needed him there with her, how much she wanted to talk through what Huw Parry had told her.

Not that there was anything more to say, really, but somehow she just longed for the comfort of his presence, the warmth of his body hard up against hers, holding her while she waited.

Which was ridiculous, because it could be weeks, and he couldn't just be there and hold her for weeks, but so much hung in the balance. If she was a carrier, then she might—just might—be able to persuade him to give them a chance.

And perversely, having spent a year hoping she wasn't a carrier, she now found herself hoping that she was, because the thought of life without him was extraordinarily painful, far more painful than the loss of any theoretical family she might have in the future.

Besides, there was always adoption.

She hugged her arms around herself, needing him, wishing he was there, and when he came to her at ten she went into his arms without a word and just held on.

CHAPTER TEN

THE next two weeks were difficult, but as the days passed without a word from Huw Parry, Libby forced herself to put the results out of her mind and concentrate on the good things in her life.

Like Andrew, and her patients, who were fortunately keeping her busy. Jacob was doing well, up on his feet now and making slow, cautious progress with a frame—and of course Amy was up there, too, helping him walk again, his gait a little affected by the head injury but not so badly that he'd have any serious long-term issues.

And the trouble with Amy was that she saw too much.

'You look funny,' she said, getting straight to the point. 'What's going on, Libs?'

She looked away, her heart jerking against her ribs. 'Nothing. We've got some tricky patients at the moment. I'm just a bit distracted.'

Amy made a noncommittal noise, but Libby wasn't sharing her innermost fears and feelings with her friend. She was having enough trouble sharing them with Andrew, and he was involved.

Or possibly not, but she'd like him to be. He was still being cagey, though, a little distant, and she couldn't wait to get the results, but as the end of the second week came, she began to fret.

'Let's go away again,' Andrew said on Friday evening. 'Just for a night. There's a pub on the Thames, right down by the water. We could stay there—get right away.'

'Not Paris? Not a trick weekend like the last time you took me away?' she teased, and he chuckled.

'No. It's near Goring, on the Berkshire–Oxfordshire border. Why don't I ring them, see if they've got a room?'

They had, and she packed the next morning while Andrew went home and did the same, then he came back and picked her up and they set off, skirting London on the M25 and heading down into Berkshire.

'Good idea?' he said, locking the car and following her to the river bank at the edge of the car park.

'Lovely. It's so pretty—look, the weeping willows are trailing in the water, and there's a cherry flowering. Oh, and baby ducks! Oh, it's beautiful. Can we go for a walk?'

'Can we have lunch first?'

'I should think so,' she conceded with a smile, and they ordered sandwiches at the bar and ate them looking out over the river at the ducks and geese and moorhens, and then they went for a walk along the river's edge until they reached a fence and had to turn back.

She pulled a face. 'We can't get as far as I'd thought. Pity. I wanted to look at the houses.'

He chuckled. 'You want to snoop? We'll get a boat,' he said, and they went back to the pub and hired a little motor launch, and went upriver through the lock gates, gazing at all the houses—some modest, some outrageously ostentatious—whose gardens stretched down to the water's edge, and speculating laughingly on who lived in them. The ducks paddled hastily out of the way, and at one point they were joined by a swan which sailed majestically alongside, eyeing them with disdain.

And then at last, even wrapped up as warmly as they were, the chilly wind off the water got to them and they turned back, headed downstream to the pub and warmed up with a pot of tea and a slice of home-made gingerbread, snuggled together on a sofa by the fireside.

'This was a lovely idea,' she murmured, and he dropped a kiss on her hair and hugged her closer.

'Good. I'm glad you approve. It's a favourite haunt of Will and Sally's. They sneak down here every now and again for a bit of privacy, and apparently the restaurant's fabulous.'

'I'll need to work up a bit of an appetite if we're having dinner,' she said, staring at the empty plate in dismay. 'I only meant to eat a tiny piece of that. I'm getting fatter by the minute.'

He nuzzled her ear. 'Rubbish. You're gorgeous.'

'Andrew, you're feeding me constantly!' she protested. 'I swear my clothes are tighter.'

'Gorgeous,' he repeated, his eyes smouldering behind the smile. 'Are you finished with that tea? We need to dress for dinner,' he added, confusing her.

'Dinner? It's only five o'clock, and, anyway, it's a pub!'

'You're still going to need to dress for dinner,' he murmured. 'Unless you want to shock the other diners? You did say something about working up an appetite…'

'Andrew!' she whispered, scandalised and horribly tempted, a giggle bubbling in her throat as he got to his feet and held out his hand, a lazy, sensuous challenge in his eyes.

She took it.

* * *

Going away for the weekend was all very well, but on Sunday night reality came crashing back. She was alone again, Andrew as usual going home to attend to paper-work and catch up with his work, and the wait for the results was tearing her into little pieces.

She met him for coffee the next morning, after a sleepless and wretched night, and he frowned at her and touched the shadows under her eyes with a warm, blunt fingertip.

'You look tired.'

'I didn't sleep. Andrew, I don't think I can stand this waiting any longer, but I can't bring myself to ring Huw Parry and every time my phone rings I feel sick.'

He searched her eyes, pulled her gently into his arms and hugged her. 'Do you want me to ring?' he offered, holding his breath, because the truth was the wait was getting to him, too, and he wanted it over every bit as much as Libby clearly did.

'Would you?'

'Sure.'

He used his desk phone, switching it to hands-free, and called Huw's secretary.

'Hi, it's Andrew Langham-Jones here. Could you see if you've got the test results for Elizabeth Tate, please? She was having bloods and screening for DMD.'

'Yes, sure, of course.' They heard her flicking through files, the rustle of paper, and then the scrape as she picked up the phone again.

'Um, we haven't got the dystrophin gene result back, but the bloods are here: the creatine phosphokinase is normal and the pregnancy test was positive.'

His world ground to a halt, until even the clock

seemed to stop ticking, and he met Libby's stunned eyes in confusion. Pregnant? Libby was *pregnant*?

'No!' she mouthed, the blood draining from her face, and he felt sick. She couldn't be—not unless…

'Hello?'

'Um—hi. Yeah. Thanks. Um—tell Huw I'll call him, could you?'

'Sure. I'm going off now, but I'll leave a note for him, Mr Langham-Jones. Thank you.'

The dial tone buzzed loudly in the room, and he reached out an unsteady hand to press the 'off' button and met Libby's distraught eyes.

'Libby, I—'

'I can't be pregnant,' she said softly. 'Oh, Andrew, I can't be! How?'

'I have no idea. I can't—' he began, and Libby leapt to her feet, twisting her hands together, her mouth open, her breath jerking in and out of tortured lungs.

'Well, apparently you can. Oh, I can't believe I've been so *stupid*! I *knew* you hadn't had proper tests, I *knew* there was a risk—you even bought condoms, for goodness' sake! Why on earth didn't I let you use them? I must have been crazy! Oh, dear God, Andrew, what on earth are we going to do?'

He got to his feet, his legs shaking, and walked over to her, resting his hand gently on her shoulder. 'Libby, I'm so sorry. If I'd had the slightest idea—the merest *hint* that there was any possibility I could get you pregnant, do you imagine for a *moment* that I would have made love to you without using protection?'

She shook her head. 'It's not your fault, it's mine. I knew how important it was not to get pregnant with this hanging over me, but I did nothing about it, and I should have done. You *know* how I feel about it, about the prospect of conceiving a child who might be—'

She broke off, pressing her fists to her mouth, her eyes wild with grief and anger and despair, and the fleeting, momentary doubt that it could be his child was banished in that instant, replaced by the absolute certainty that he was the father.

He wasn't infertile. He had been, he was sure of that, but apparently not any longer. And now the woman he loved more than anyone else in the world was carrying his child.

And that child might have inherited a dreadful, life-limiting disease because he hadn't followed up his test results properly, just assumed that the situation hadn't changed.

'Libby, I'm so sorry,' he began again, but she drew herself up and away from him, her arms hugging her waist, her eyes tortured.

'Sorry isn't the point, Andrew. We're both sorry, but this is one thing that being sorry isn't going to change. I'm having a baby who may or may not be going to die after years of suffering, and it's my fault. Your fault, too, for not double-checking, but my fault for believing you, and only I knew the significance of an unplanned pregnancy. Why on earth did I do that?' she asked, a trifle hysterically. 'I'm not stupid, I know things can change. I should have insisted we used protection.'

He rammed his hands through his hair, his emotions knotting his stomach. 'Libby, I'm so sorry, but I really was so sure. I did the tests. Again and again.'

'But years ago, Andrew! And you said yourself you'd been ill. And when I asked if you'd had it checked by anyone recently, you said what's the point, either they're there swimming or they're not. And I didn't even question it, and I should have done.'

'I really believed it. It must have been a blip, but it went on so long—years. It was several years after I found out that I looked again, and, believe me, Libby, there was nothing.'

'Well, there obviously isn't nothing now, and you need to know that this is your child, so can I suggest that you go and get checked out?'

'Why? I have no intention of wriggling out of my responsibility,' he said quietly, tortured by guilt, reeling from the utterly unexpected news that he could have fathered a child. 'In fact, I have every intention of being there for our child on a daily basis, starting with marrying you.'

'Marrying me?' she said, her voice dropping to a shocked whisper. 'Why would you do that? You didn't sign up for this—for a disabled child.'

'You're getting ahead of yourself. It's only one in four.'

'That's pretty good odds if it was a lottery ticket,' she said. 'And, anyway, there's no way I'm marrying you. Not now you know you can have children with anyone you like. Maybe even Cousin Charlotte,' she added, and blinking back a fresh wave of tears, she yanked open the door and ran out, leaving him standing there, rooted to the spot, his thoughts in turmoil.

He wasn't sterile.

It had dominated his life, governed his every move, every relationship, every day that he spent with children. And it was no longer true.

He was going to be a father, and what should have

been the happiest day of his life was turning into a potential tragedy.

He closed the door softly, sat on the edge of the desk and stared blankly at the wall. Please, let it be a girl, he prayed. Don't let this child be stricken. Not my baby. Our baby. It's done nothing wrong.

There was a sharp rap on the door, and he swallowed hard. 'Yes?'

'It's only me. Hell, what on earth's happened?'

Andrew met his brother's shocked, searching eyes and swallowed hard.

'Libby's pregnant,' he managed.

'What?'

'Shut the door. There's a problem.'

'A problem?' He shut the door, his eyes piercing. 'What sort of problem, apart from her being pregnant? Don't tell me—she's demanding you marry her?'

'Actually, I asked her, and she turned me down. Suggested I ask Cousin Charlotte.'

Will's jaw dropped, and he sat down on the edge of the desk and frowned. 'Wow. Are you sure it's yours?'

He gave a startled laugh. 'Oh, yes. If you'd seen her face—you can't fake that kind of reaction. This is my child, I know it is, because I know she wouldn't expose herself to the risk of pregnancy at the moment and she didn't realise there was a risk, because I told her—oh, hell, you might as well know. I thought I was sterile.'

His brother's eyes widened. 'What? What on earth gave you that idea?'

So he told him, and Will stared at him in horror. 'And you never mentioned it? Hell, is this why you won't get involved with anyone?' He nodded, and Will scrubbed a hand through his hair. 'So—you thought you couldn't get her pregnant, so you didn't use anything?'

He nodded again. 'Only apparently I can, and did. And here's the problem. She's being screened for DMD—Duchenne muscular dystrophy. Her sister's a carrier.'

Will's jaw dropped, and he blew out his breath on a soft sigh. 'Oh, my God.'

'Yeah. So, the good news is I'm going to be a father. The bad new is—'

'Hey, stop. It's only a one in four.'

'Only?' he said drily. 'Or one in two, if you ask Libby. She doesn't want a daughter, either, if she's got the gene. She's adamant about not passing it on to a future generation.'

'She wouldn't…'

Pain sliced through him, and he had to force himself to breathe. 'I have no idea. I hope not, but she won't talk to me, and she said she wouldn't marry me.'

And suddenly it all got too much for him, and a choking sob rose in his throat. He pressed his fist to his mouth, but his chest heaved and he found himself wrapped hard in his brother's arms, held tight while the waves of pain and shock ripped through him, leaving him empty. Gutted.

'You need to go home,' Will said softly as he pulled away and dragged his hands over his face.

'I can't. I've got work to do.'

'Then have a coffee, and sit and talk this through with me for a while, because there's no way you're going anywhere in this state,' Will said firmly, and, pushing him down into his chair, he handed him a mug and then perched opposite, elbows propped on the desk, studying him.

'You need to talk to her, bro'.'

He shook his head. 'She walked out. She needs time, Will. I have to give her time—time to calm down, to think it through. And I need time, too. It's just so much to take in, and there's a bit of me that's trying to be happy because it means we can be together and raise a family, but the rest of me—'

He clamped his teeth together, fighting back another wave of grief for the child who might have been handed a life sentence by his careless assumptions. 'I'm a doctor, for God's sake! I should have known better. I should have checked, been properly investigated, not just assumed I knew enough to take that kind of risk. And now it's too late, and, as Libby said, this is one time when sorry isn't the point.'

'So what are you going to do?'

He scrubbed his hands through his hair and met Will's worried eyes.

'I have no idea. I really have no idea. But I'm not taking no for an answer.'

Libby didn't know how she found her way back to the ward.

She wouldn't have gone back there at all, but her bag was there with her car keys in it, and she had to hand over the ward to someone. And, of course, as luck would have it, the first person she saw was Amy.

Dear, sweet Amy, who took one look at her, shoved her into the office and shut the door.

'Libby? What's happened? Is it your sister? Your mother? Andrew?'

She shook her head, the tears she'd held back until now fighting their way to the surface, and Amy gave a soft cry and wrapped her in her arms, rocking her gently as she wept, one hand clamped over her mouth to stifle the great raw sobs tearing through her.

She couldn't tell Amy, couldn't share anything this personal, this agonising, because just to say the words out loud would make it real, and she was hoping, so desperately hoping that it would all go away.

Except, of course, it wouldn't.

'Oh, Libby!' Amy crooned softly. 'It's all right. It'll be all right.'

Oh, if only! Fresh tears scalded her cheeks, and she eased away, rummaging for a tissue with trembling fingers, blotting hopelessly at the tears which fell faster than she could catch them, as Amy steered her to a chair and sat her down, holding her still, stroking her face and murmuring softly to her.

'Is it Andrew? What's happened?'

She shook her head, pressing her fingers to her eyes until they ached, until everything went black, but she could still see his shocked face, the pain and confusion in his eyes as he came to terms with the fact that he was no longer sterile, and what that might now mean.

He wasn't the only one who was shocked and confused, though. She couldn't think clearly yet, needed time to let the news she'd never expected to hear sink in. Of all the random, cruel twists of fate, this was the one she might least have expected.

Of course it was, or she would have taken steps to ensure it could never have happened. Oh, how could she have been so stupid?

'I need to go home, Amy,' she said, battening down the tears and dragging out her self-control. 'Can you get someone to take over for me? There are some kids on the ward I was about to go and assess for discharge. Andr-Andrew's got the details.'

She got her bag out of the drawer and headed for the door, but Amy blocked her way.

'Libby, you can't drive like this.'

'I'll be fine.'

'At least tell me what's going on.'

She stared at her, her friend and yet not quite confidante, and shook her head. 'I can't. I will, but not now, please. Just let me go.'

Amy stepped out of the way, and Libby fled, running out to the car park, getting into her car and putting the key in the ignition with hands that were shaking so badly she could scarcely hold it.

Seat belt, she thought, clipping it, and drove home, blinking hard to keep the road in view. She shouldn't be driving. She knew that, but she had to get away, to get home, to crawl into bed and shut her eyes and wait for the pain to ease.

If it ever did…

'Libby's gone home.'

'Good. You should, too. Come back to mine.'

'No. I can't face the family.'

'Then I'll come to you, but you're not doing this alone,' Will said, and Andrew gave up. He'd been there for Will a thousand times, and they knew each other inside out.

'OK. I'll come to yours. Where are you now?'

'In the car park—I was just about to go. I'll wait for you.'

'Will, I'm fine.'

Will said something rude and to the point, and

Andrew dropped his phone on the desk and rang through to his secretary.

'I'm knocking off early—bit of a headache. Could you make sure the team knows? If there's an emergency, I'm sure Patrick Corrigan will cover me. He's on take today.'

'Sure, Andrew. Can I get you anything?'

A miracle? Or had they already had that?

Be careful what you wish for, he thought, and swallowed hard. 'No, I'm fine, Janet, thank you. I'll see you tomorrow.'

He grabbed his coat and headed out of the building, lifting a hand in acknowledgement as Will's Land Rover pulled up near his car and waited, engine running. His kid brother, crazy, reckless, always in trouble; he'd bailed him out so many times.

Maybe it was time to let him return the favour.

She cried for hours, curled up in her bed, rocking to comfort herself, her arms wrapped firmly over the still-flat abdomen that cradled her baby.

'Please, God, let my baby be all right,' she wept brokenly. 'Please be a girl. Please don't let me have passed this on!'

She couldn't lie there any longer, couldn't do nothing, but there was nothing to do, nothing to say, nowhere she could go to escape the agonising wait for an answer to her questions. She'd have to wait for the results to come back, for the examination of the dystrophin gene to be painstakingly completed. And in the meantime, she had to stop crying and try and rationalise her behaviour, so she got out of bed and went downstairs, made herself a cup of tea and curled up on the sofa with Kitty.

And then thought about the risk to a pregnancy from cat litter and began to cry again. Even her cat was out of bounds, she thought, tears cascading down her cheeks.

She needed Andrew. She'd never needed anyone so much, but she'd shut him out, implied that he'd let her down, but he hadn't. She knew—had always known—that he was a good man, that there wasn't a lying, deceitful bone in his body, that for all he might have been mistaken, he'd made an honest, genuine mistake, and he was every bit as shocked and distressed by it as she was.

She had to ring him.

She found her phone, checked for messages, then hesitated. Wouldn't he have rung her if he'd cared? Really cared, rather than being dutiful? Chris Turner had told her he would have given up everything to look after Will had it been necessary. He was that sort of man.

Did she want that?

No. No, of course not, but he'd told her in Paris that he loved her.

Only not today. Today, he'd just told her was going to marry her and be involved in their child's life, and she'd told him to go and marry Cousin Charlotte. So why would he call her? She had to call him, to apologise. Fingers shaking, she dialled his number and waited till it went to the answering-machine.

Then she rang his house phone, with the same result.

He might be in the shower, or still at work—that was it. He'd be at work.

She rang the switchboard, asked them to page him, and was told he'd left the hospital at four.

Four? He never left at four. It was rare for him to leave before six, and often it was later than that. But he had left, and he wasn't answering her calls. Which could well be because he was in the shower, she told herself, trying to be rational. He always showered when he got home from work.

She tried again later, both phones, and then at two in the morning she pulled on her coat and drove to his house, to find it deserted. No car, no lights.

Of course. He'd gone to Ashenden, gone to Will.

She had Will's number in her phone, and she hesitated, her finger hovering over the button, but then she threw it in her bag and drove home, a sick feeling in the pit of her stomach.

He'd asked her to marry him and she just walked out, refusing to discuss it. Why should he want to talk to her?

She went inside, threw her bag down on the sofa, went to bed and cried herself to sleep a little before dawn.

'I ought to ring her.'

'Really? You're drunk, Andrew.'

'I know. But I still ought to ring her—damn! Where's my mobile?'

'I don't know. When did you last have it?'

'In my office—oh, hell. She might have been trying me, and I don't know her number.'

'I've got her mobile number,' Will said, 'but it is three in the morning. She's probably asleep.'

'No. She'll be churning it over in her mind, and I ought to be with her. I should have been with her all the time.Give me the number, I'll ring her.'

Will threw his phone across to him, and he rang her. Three times.

Each time it rang and rang, then went to the answering-machine, but he didn't say anything, just hung up. He had no idea what to say; he needed to hear her voice, get some feedback, before he could launch in and say anything.

And she wasn't answering her phone to him.

He dropped the phone in despair and stared at Will. 'OK. You're the expert. What the hell do I do now?'

Will smiled a little crookedly. 'You go to bed, sleep off that brandy and I'll wake you up and take you to work. Got a clean shirt there?'

He nodded. He always had a full set of clean clothes at work, because you never knew when accidents might happen, especially working with children.

Children. He didn't want to think about children. Sick children, children with life-limiting conditions, children who were sick and going downhill and all you could do was slow the progress…

'I can drive myself.'

'No, you can't. You've been drinking, you'll probably be hovering on the limit.'

'So have you.'

'Not like you. And I hope you aren't operating?'

He shook his head. 'No. Clinics.' Clinics with children. Sick children…

Will eyed him thoughtfully. 'Actually, of course, there's only a one in eight chance,' Will said, reading his mind.

'What?'

'You don't know if Libby's a carrier. That's a one in two. That halves the odds. Or doubles them. Don't know which I mean, but it makes it one in eight, not one in four, that it's an affected boy.'

One in eight.

Better, but no way good enough to comfort him.

'I love her,' he said conversationally. 'And she loves me. Why aren't we together now, Will, talking this through?'

'Because it's three in the morning and she's upset? She'll calm down and think it through.'

'I don't think so. What the hell am I going to do if she won't listen to me?' He stood up and headed for the door. 'I'm going to bed. Wake me at six. Maybe it'll look better then.'

It was a forlorn hope.

Will dropped him at work at seven-thirty, and he went straight up to his office and found his phone lying there on the desk.

With two missed calls from Libby. He checked the time of her calls, late last night, and cursed the fact that he'd been stupid enough to leave his phone behind. Stupid enough to drink, so he couldn't just get in the car and drive round to her house and bang on the door and demand to talk to her.

Stupid enough to make assumptions, to rely on his clearly flawed judgement and make a colossal mistake with potentially massive consequences.

Hands shaking, he rang her, and got her answering-machine…

CHAPTER ELEVEN

SHE had missed calls on her mobile.

Three, from Will. Nothing from Andrew.

She didn't want to talk to Will, didn't know what to say to him. Did he know? Had Andrew spoken to him?

Or maybe, she thought as a chill ran over her, maybe something had happened to him. She checked the time of the calls. After three in the morning. Oh, lord. Was Andrew hurt? Sick? What if he'd had an accident?

She ran through the shower, slapped on some make-up to cover the ravages of the night and drove to work. She'd go and see if he was in his office, leave him a note. Check with the ED to see if he'd been brought in.

No. She wouldn't even let herself think about that until she'd checked his office, she thought, and hurried through the hospital, along the corridor to his office outside the paediatric ward. Her hand was raised to knock when the door swung inwards, and he stood there, looking like she felt, his eyes red-rimmed, his mouth set in a grim line, his cheeks sunken with exhaustion.

He was all right. Not in Emergency, or undergoing surgery, not in ITU linked up to a million machines. Just screening her calls. She felt sick, but she lifted her chin and met his eyes.

'Andrew, we need to talk,' she said, and he stepped back and let her in, then closed the door.

'I'm sorry.'

They spoke together, and then with a muffled groan he reached for her, hauling her into his arms and holding her close.

'I tried to ring you, but you didn't answer, and you weren't at home,' she mumbled into his shirt.

'Will took me home, and I forgot my phone. I tried to ring you on his.'

Will's phone. The missed calls. He *had* tried to ring her.

'I thought—I was so awful to you.'

'I deserved it,' he said quietly. 'I've behaved like an idiot. You were right, I should have checked. No wonder you hate me.'

'I don't hate you,' she cut in, tilting her head up so she could see his eyes. Tortured, tormented eyes. 'I just don't know if I want to marry you—not under these circumstances. You're a good man, Andrew, I know that. And I know you really thought you couldn't have children, but I'm scared and I just don't know—I don't know where to go from here.'

His hands gripped her arms reassuringly.

'Nor do I, but one thing I do know—we do it together. I love you, Libby, and you love me, and this is our baby. Whatever the outcome, whatever the consequences, this is our child, and we'll do this together. Marry me.'

Libby shook her head.

'Andrew, I can't! Not now, not like this! It's not a sound basis for a marriage.'

'Rubbish. We love each other, Libby. We have done right from the start. I've loved you since you told my brother he was a better dancer than me.'

She gave a strangled laugh. 'Maybe he is?'

'No, he's not. You were being generous—as usual. And I shouldn't have taken advantage of you that night."

'You didn't,' she corrected softly. 'I needed you so much. Needed to reach out with my hands, to touch you—I'd been falling for you for ages, but I didn't think you'd even noticed me until you asked me to go home with you for the weekend. So you didn't take advantage of me—if anything I took advantage of you. And it's not your fault I'm pregnant. I've known about this DMD for a year. I should have made sure I couldn't get pregnant, not just relied on my relentlessly single status.'

'That's my line.' He smiled, a little crookedly, then shook his head. 'I still don't see why you won't marry me.'

'Because it's not why you get married.'

'So why do you get married? If it's not because you're with the person you love, and you're having a baby together, and then you find out something might mean your child needs even more care, more love, and you'll need each other more than ever before—what better basis could there be, Libby?'

She shook her head. 'You didn't want to get married.'

'Of course I did! I've always wanted to get married and settle down, but I didn't want to trap a woman into a childless marriage and find out years down the line that loving me wasn't enough! You knew that. If it hadn't been for my infertility, I would have asked you to marry me in Paris.'

'And I would have said no, at least until I'd had the tests.'

'Why? Why do you imagine it would make any difference to me? I love you, Libby—you, not our children. If you'd decided not to have any, I would have been fine with that.'

'Would you? So why is it all right for you to decide to sacrifice your chance of being a parent, but not for me?'

He frowned. 'Because I'd know. I'd make the decision, stick to it, and know I could make it work for us.'

'But you couldn't have trusted me to do the same?'

He closed his eyes with a sigh. 'I couldn't have *asked* you to do that for me.'

'Well, it's not relevant now, anyway, is it? The fact is your fertility is not an issue. The issue is my carrier status, and I need to know the answer before I can give you one.'

'No. It won't make any difference to me, Libby. At the very least, we're having this one child, whatever the results of your test, and we love each other, and we'll love the child, and the greater that child's needs, the more important it is that we do this together. I can't cope with this without you, Libby. I need you. I'm not coming and spending time with my disabled son and then going home at night and leaving you to cope, if that's the way this turns out. No way. And if the baby's fine, if you're not a carrier or it's unaffected, then there's no reason not to be together. Not when we love each other so much. Is there?'

She searched his eyes, seeing only love and confusion and pain, but no doubt. Not a shred, not a trace of any doubt.

'No. No, there's no reason not to be together, and I can't do this without you, either,' she admitted softly.

'So you will marry me?'

She hesitated. This wasn't what she'd expected, what she'd dreamed of. That night in Paris, if he'd asked her then—or down in Berkshire on Saturday, maybe. But now? For expediency?

'I don't want to rush you,' he said softly. 'You obviously need to think about this.'

'No. I don't need to think about it. I love you, of course I do. I just wish…' She trailed off, and he sighed.

'So do I, but we don't have the luxury of choice. So is that a yes?'

She nodded. 'Yes, Andrew, it's a yes,' she said, and burst into tears.

He gathered her up against his heart, wishing he could make it different for her, for all of them, but he couldn't, so he just held her, unable to make any promises bar the one that he would love her for the rest of his life.

'Hey, come on,' he murmured. 'You're soaking me and I don't have another shirt here.'

She laughed, a strange, hiccuping little laugh, and let him go. 'You'd better phone Will, he'll be worried.'

'Yes. Look, I've got a lot to do today—will you be all right now?'

She nodded. 'I'll be fine. Can we talk tonight?'

'Sure. My car's at Ashenden. Will drove me in. I hit the brandy a bit—can you drive me out there and we'll tell my parents?'

Her eyes widened in what looked like panic. 'Really?'

'Really. And I want to marry you soon—as soon as I can. There's no going back on this for me, Libby, I want you to know that. I'll find out what the rules are and let you know. OK?'

She nodded, and went up on tiptoe and kissed his

freshly shaved and slightly nicked cheek. 'You've cut yourself,' she murmured, and he fingered the little slice in his jaw and smiled.

'Yeah. Must have been thinking about something else. I'll see you later—give me a call when you finish.'

Amy was waiting for her, and her face lit up with relief.

'Oh, Libby, I've been so worried! I was going to ring you, but—are you OK?'

'I'm fine,' she said, dredging up a rather weary smile for her friend. 'I'm sorry I worried you. I was just…' She trailed off, not knowing how to explain without giving all the details, the thought that she was to marry Andrew still filtering through to her exhausted and emotionally drained mind.

'What on earth happened?' Amy asked. 'You looked so awful—I thought someone had died.'

She shook her head. 'No. It was just...'

Amy waited, then smiled. 'It's OK. Tell me when you're ready, but if you need to talk, or a shoulder to cry on, just yell.'

'Actually, I do,' she said, her eyes welling up again. 'Can we do coffee later? I've got so much to tell you, and I don't really know where to start.'

'Better make it lunch, then,' Amy suggested with a wry smile. 'My treat.'

Amy sat in silence while Libby explained, and for once there wasn't the slightest hint of eager anticipation, just a quiet watchfulness that made Libby realise she'd underestimated Amy all along.

'So—how pregnant are you?' she asked eventually, when Libby ground to a halt.

'I don't know. It could have been anything up to four weeks ago.'

'Four—but that must have been the weekend of the birthday!'

She nodded. 'I didn't really know Andrew before the weekend, but I'd been so aware of him since I first met him, and suddenly there we were together, having an amazing time, and—well, it just happened. And we've been together ever since.'

'Wow. I thought you looked different, but I didn't realise how different. And then you decided to go for the test. Why? Why then?'

'Because we realised we were falling in love, and—you can't go into a relationship with that kind of uncertainty.'

'But you're going to marry him now?'

'Yes.'

'And not just for the baby?'

She shook her head and smiled. 'No, not just for the baby. I love him, Amy. He's a wonderful person, and he makes me laugh, and he makes me happy. But I'm so scared for the baby.'

Amy shook her head. 'Don't be. There are so many more treatments these days, and it's still possible to have a good and meaningful life with DMD. OK, it's progressive and there's nothing you can do about that, but there may be, in time. There might be some way of stopping the muscle wasting in the future, and with a paediatric nurse and an orthopaedic surgeon for parents, how could he do better? You'll be brilliant parents, whatever the future holds for your baby—and, anyway, you might not even be a carrier, so you could be worrying yourself sick for nothing.'

All of which she knew, but it still preyed at the

back of her mind all day, and when she picked Andrew up at five-thirty she was feeling sick with exhaustion and emotion.

'Do you really want to talk to your parents tonight?' she asked, and he nodded.

'We won't be long. I'll pick my car up and we'll go back to my house, OK, and talk it all through?'

She nodded. 'We need to feed Kitty now, then,' she said, and they did that on their way to Ashenden.

Will was crossing the stableyard as they pulled in, and he came over to them, smiling warily.

'Hi. Everything OK?' he asked, and Andrew gave a soft laugh and hugged her to his side.

'Yes. Everything's OK. I've asked Libby to marry me, and she's said yes.'

Will's eyes swivelled to hers, and his smile widened, lighting up his eyes as he reached for them and hugged them both, slapping Andrew on the back and laughing.

'Excellent. Go and tell the parents, they'll be overjoyed.'

'You haven't said anything?'

'What—and steal your thunder? I should think not. Go on, go and tell them the glad tidings, and I'll fetch Sally and we'll come and have a drink with you in a minute.'

'I'm not drinking,' Andrew said wryly, and with Will's chuckle echoing in their ears, they turned and went into the house.

'Andrew, Libby! How nice to see you! You should have said you were coming, I could have cooked for you.'

'It's fine. We'll eat later. Actually, we've got something to tell you. Can we sit down?'

His mother's eyes missed nothing, scanning them

both before returning to his face. 'Does this need the drawing room, or will the kitchen do?'

'I would have thought the kitchen would be fine,' he said with a smile, and beside him he felt Libby relax a little. 'Put the kettle on, Mum, and come and sit down.'

They settled round the table, and he told them, in edited terms, the good news and the bad news, in that order.

His mother's face crumpled briefly, and then she stood up and came to Libby and hugged her tenderly. 'Sweetheart, I'm so sorry, but we're here for you, whatever the result of this, and if there's anything we can do to help, in any way, at any time, then you must ask. Please, promise me you'll ask.'

'I promise,' she said, touched to her heart by this woman's compassionate kindness and warmth. 'And I'm sorry it's a little unconventional.'

Jane flapped her hand and smiled. 'Andrew was "early",' she said with a chuckle. 'You aren't the first and you won't be the last, and we couldn't have had a better, stronger, more loving marriage. So—when's the wedding?'

'As soon as possible,' Andrew said firmly. 'We haven't talked about the sort of wedding we want, but we do agree on that, don't we? Don't we?'

He shot her a questioning glance, and she nodded, suddenly sure that this was the right thing to do, even though the result was still hanging over them, because this was no longer about some theoretical question but about a real baby, and a real love.

'Yes, we do,' she said, just as firmly. 'I don't know what Andrew wants, but I'd like a quiet church wedding, if possible. My mother and her husband are in Ireland,

and my sister's in Cumbria with her husband and her little girl, but apart from them and Amy and a few others who I work with, there isn't really anyone much. A few old friends from when I was training, that's all.'

Jane was settling down with a notepad and pen.

'Right. The four of us, Libby, Sally, Libby's mother and stepfather, Libby's sister and husband and daughter, Amy, Chris and Louise Turner—you met them at the party, our GP.'

She nodded. 'Yes. I liked him. Isn't his wife the vicar?'

'Yes, which is really handy. Anyone else?'

'Not imperative, no,' Andrew said. 'Of course there's always Cousin Charlotte…'

The mischievous twinkle was back in his tired, red-rimmed eyes, and Libby chuckled.

'Poor Cousin Charlotte. She'll be heartbroken.'

'She will—you're unkind to her, Andrew,' his mother chided gently.

'She's fixated. She needs to get over herself. How many is that?'

'Fourteen.'

Libby nodded. 'That sounds OK—oh my neighbours. He's been really good to me and she's lovely. Oh, and there's a cousin, Edward,' she added, looking up at Andrew. 'I met him at the funeral. I don't know if he'll be able to come. He may not be well enough.'

'We'll ask him,' Andrew said gently.

'That's seventeen. I'm sure there will be a few more, but we'll keep it under twenty,' Jane promised. 'Leave it to me. I'll find out when the church is free—fifteen clear days, isn't it? Or three Sundays? Does it have to be a Saturday?'

'Any day suits me, I don't mind,' Andrew said. 'I'll

book it off as soon as we've agreed a date with the church.'

'I'll phone Louise now and find out the technicalities,' Tony said, getting to his feet. 'Andrew? Could we have a word?'

They left the room, and Jane looked up from her list and smiled. 'I'm so glad it's you. I really wondered if he'd ever settle down. I had no idea about the fertility issue. I wonder what made him check it?'

Libby had no intention of discussing that with his mother, but it was a rhetorical question, the woman who'd given birth to him and raised him much more concerned with the impact it had had on his life.

'You know, I always felt there was something wrong, but I couldn't put my finger on it,' she murmured. 'I mean, he's always been so strong on family, so loyal and dutiful, and I know he grumbles about this old place, but he loves it, really, and I know it'll be in safe hands when we're gone.' She met Libby's eyes.

'You do realise, I take it, that you'll be Lady Ashenden when that happens?' she said gently, and Libby felt her mouth open.

'Oh, good grief, I hadn't given it a moment's thought,' she said, panic washing over her. 'I can't possibly—'

'Can't possibly what? Love my son and raise your children here in this lovely, draughty old house? Of course you can, my dear. It's a wonderful place for children, just a great big adventure playground. And, anyway, we have no intention of handing over the reins for years, so relax and enjoy yourself and worry about it when we get carted off in a box.'

'Who's getting carted off in a box?' Tony asked, coming back in with Andrew, and Jane laughed.

'Nobody, yet. So what did Louise say?'

'We can be married here in the chapel so long as there's a registrar attending, because we don't have our own register, and we'll need a notice of marriage, so provided we do that first thing tomorrow, we can be married here two weeks on Friday.'

By which time, she thought, her heart pounding, she would know the answer. Even though it wouldn't change anything, she wanted Andrew to know what he was taking on—the fact, not the possibility. Suddenly, perhaps because she'd been reminded of Edward and his abrupt exit from her life, that had assumed a greater importance.

'Two weeks on Friday sounds fine.'

'Right. Libby, you may have your own ideas, but—I'd be so pleased if you'd let me do your flowers.'

Flowers? She hadn't even thought about flowers, but it suddenly came home to her in a rush that she was getting married, to a man she loved with all her heart, and his family were welcoming her with open arms.

'Thank you, that would be lovely,' she said, her eyes filling, and as she and Jane stood up and hugged, Will walked into the room with Sally, and they grinned.

'I take it you aren't being disinherited, then, bro'? Never mind,' Will said, and they all laughed, but Andrew's arm slid round her and hugged her close, and she knew that whatever happened, whatever fate had in store for them, it would be all right, because they'd have each other…

He eventually got her away from the family and back to his house.

'I'm exhausted,' she said. 'Don't cook, I only want a bit of toast.'

'OK. There's something I want to say to you first, though, and I know it's a bit cock-eyed and back to front, but…' He swallowed hard, feeling suddenly ridiculously uncertain, and, taking her hand, he knelt down in front of her on one knee and stared up into her bemused, strained, beautiful eyes.

'I want you to forget everything except us,' he began. 'Because this is about us, and about nothing and no one else. I love you, Libby. It started when you were dancing with Will and I was so jealous of him, and it hit me like a truck in Paris. I've tried to rationalise it, tried to talk myself out of it, and I can't. I love you, really love you, and it's a love that won't go away, won't fade, won't weary. I want to watch you grow old, I want to see you with grey hair and wrinkles, still smiling at me over breakfast, still loving me back the way you do now.

'I want to be with you for the rest of my life, for better, for worse, for richer, for poorer, in sickness and in health. I need you. You're my other half, and I know I said I was never going to marry, but I can't imagine how much it would have hurt me to let you go, or how I would have done it.

'I know I'm crabby sometimes, and I'll probably get a lot worse as I get older, and it means you'll end up living in a heap of dry rot some day, but I swear I will do everything I can to make you and our children happy, and to care for you, if you'll do me the honour of being my wife. Will you, Libby? Will you marry me?'

She stared down at him, her eyes filling until his dear, beloved face was just a blur, and then she knelt down in front of him and went into his arms.

'Oh, Andrew—of course I'll marry you! I can't think

of anything I want or need more than to be with you for ever. Of course I'll marry you. I'd be honoured.'

He hugged her, then released her gently and put his hand into his pocket, pulling out a ring.

A beautiful ring, three diamonds in a row in a simple, antique setting, which he slid onto her finger. 'It was my great-grandmother's ring,' he said softly. 'I didn't know if it would even fit you, but it can be altered if necessary.'

But it wasn't. It fitted perfectly, sparkling through her tears, and bringing fresh ones that welled up and spilled over. 'Oh, Andrew, it's beautiful!' she whispered. 'Oh, thank you!'

'You'll have to give it back one day,' he said with a wry smile, 'when our son's getting married.'

And then she remembered, remembered that if they had a son, he might not ever live to marry, and her tears fell again, mingling with his as they held each other tight and hung on.

'I can't zip my dress up—honestly, I can't believe how much my bust has grown!'

'Let me—there. You look fabulous,' Amy said, standing back and grinning broadly. 'Fantastic. You'll knock his socks off. Doesn't she look great?'

Libby's mother nodded, then her eyes filled with tears and she hugged her daughter gently. 'You look absolutely beautiful, darling. Gorgeous. He's a lucky man.'

Oh, lord, I hope so, she thought.

There was still no news. The clinic was open, she could ring Huw Parry, but she didn't want to, not now, not so close to the wedding.

The results were taking for ever, and she'd been so

sure they would have been back in time, but they weren't, and in an hour's time she was marrying Andrew with the uncertainty still hanging over them.

'Is that your mobile? I'll fetch it.'

Her heart crashed against her ribs, and she took the phone from Amy as she ran back upstairs with it, staring at the number in consternation.

It was Huw.

'Who's ringing you?'

'God knows.' He pulled his phone out of his pocket and stared at it. 'Libby.' He flipped it open. 'Hi, darling, what's up? Libby? Libby, for God's sake, talk to me.'

'I've got the results,' she said, and then started to cry again, incoherent.

He shut the phone and stared at Will. 'She's got the results. I'm going over there.'

'Not on your own, you're not. I'll drive you.'

For once he was glad that Will had no fear and that there was no traffic on the road—and apparently no police. They pulled up outside her house and he was out of the car before it stopped, running up her path and pounding on the door.

'Libby! Let me in!'

The door opened and she fell into his arms, her face awash with tears. 'Oh, Andrew!' she wailed, and sobbed into his shirt front.

'What?' he demanded, freeing himself and holding her at arm's length, desperately trying to work out what she was saying, but she was laughing and crying so hard he couldn't understand a word.

'I'm not a carrier,' she managed finally, but by then he'd worked it out from the laughter and the smiles of the women grouped around behind her, and Will slapping him on the back, and the huge ball of pain that had been lodged in his chest for the last few weeks dissolved, leaving nothing but a searing joy so great it threatened to overwhelm him.

'Oh, my love,' he said brokenly. Dragging her into his arms, they wrapped her hard against his heart and held her while he wept.

'Um, you're not supposed to see your wife on your wedding day until the ceremony,' Will pointed out, shoving a handkerchief in his hand when he eventually let her go. 'It's unlucky.'

'No way,' he said, shaking his head and smiling, but he backed away. 'I'll see you at the church. Um—your make-up might need a little attention.'

'And you need a clean shirt,' she pointed out, laughing a little unsteadily, then Amy pulled her back inside, pushed him out and closed the door.

They were married at twelve, in the little chapel at Ashenden, in a simple, joyful ceremony attended by their closest family and friends, and one year later, they were back there for the christening of their son.

They called him Edward, in memory of the cousin who had lost his fight against DMD just three weeks before, and William, for his uncle.

Amy and Will and Chris Turner were his godparents, and during the ceremony Sally rocked and shushed their baby Lucie—Lucie, whose birth had shocked Will into common sense, at last, and made him sell his horse and stop taking foolish risks.

It was a beautiful day, and afterwards they took a picnic down to the folly and drank champagne to celebrate.

There was so much to celebrate, so much to be thankful for, and as they strolled back to the house that would eventually be their home, their baby sleeping peacefully in his father's arms, Libby's heart was filled with joy.

'Happy?' Andrew asked, smiling down at her, and she smiled back, her love flowing over.

'Happy,' she murmured. 'Very, very happy.'

DR DI ANGELO'S BABY BOMBSHELL

BY

JANICE LYNN

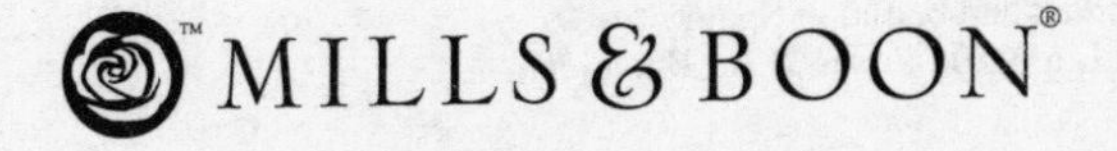

All the characters in this book have no existence outside the imagination of the author, and have no relation whatsoever to anyone bearing the same name or names. They are not even distantly inspired by any individual known or unknown to the author, and all the incidents are pure invention.

First published in Great Britain 2010
Harlequin Mills & Boon Limited,
Eton House, 18-24 Paradise Road, Richmond, Surrey TW9 1SR

ISBN: 978 0 263 87890 5

Harlequin Mills & Boon policy is to use papers that are natural, renewable and recyclable products and made from wood grown in sustainable forests. The logging and manufacturing process conform to the legal environmental regulations of the country of origin.

Printed and bound in Spain
by Litografia Rosés, S.A., Barcelona

Janice Lynn has a Masters in Nursing from Vanderbilt University, and works as a nurse practitioner in a family practice. She lives in the southern United States with her husband, their four children, their Jack Russell—appropriately named Trouble—and a lot of unnamed dust bunnies that have moved in since she started her writing career. To find out more about Janice and her writing, visit www.janicelynn.com

Recent titles by the same author:

PLAYBOY SURGEON, TOP-NOTCH DAD
THE PLAYBOY DOCTOR CLAIMS HIS BRIDE
SURGEON BOSS, SURPRISE DAD
THE NURSE'S BABY MIRACLE

To Anna Sugden—
true friends are precious treasures
and you're a jewel that sparkles brightly in my life.
Thank you for the years of laughter, shared tears,
and unfailing support. Love you!

CHAPTER ONE

"I NEED you to pretend to be madly in love with me."

Startled by the request, Dr. Blake Di Angelo tapped his thumbs against the sleek surface of his mahogany desk, thinking that perhaps the petite blonde pacing across his Knoxville medical office had already gone mad.

"You'll have to repeat that, Darby." He leaned against his leather chair's backrest, eyeing her with more than a little curiosity. "Because I don't think I heard you right."

His business partner paused long enough to bestow a glance on the bluest eyes that side of the Mississippi. Eyes that were usually sparkling with laughter. Not today. Today, her fingers clenched around a card of some sort, Dr. Darby Phillips' eyes were clouded with displeasure.

"You owe me." Her expression dared him to deny her claim. "Last weekend of the month. You're going with me to Alabama and you're going to pretend to be goo-goo-ga-ga, head-over-heels in love with me the entire time."

His brow arching at her determined expression, Blake grinned. God, she was bossy. He liked it. Had always liked Darby's assertiveness and self-assurance. From the time he'd met her four years ago, she'd been driven to be the best at everything she did.

"Why am I going to do this?" He couldn't resist teasing. Mostly because he knew how to push her buttons to have her going from zero to through the roof.

She started pacing again. "Because you owe me, and I'm collecting."

Blake's eyes traveled over her curvy little frame encased in a no-nonsense navy business suit, exposing shapely legs beneath her skirt hem. The shirt was tucked into a waist that his hands would probably fit around. Her breasts—well, he knew better than to let his thoughts go there. He valued their business relationship too much to acknowledge her as the desirable woman she so obviously was.

"And because of this." She tossed the embossed card onto his desk and shuddered. "Which I'd completely forgotten about."

She turned those big baby-blues on him again, stared with such beseeching that his insides shifted off axis enough to make his world wobble, to make him want to take her into his arms and promise he'd fix whatever had her so upset.

"How could I have forgotten that was this year? This month?" Panic brewing in the blue depths, her gaze bored into him. "I really don't need the headache of looking for a date who'll no doubt get the wrong idea by an invitation to something so personal. But I do need a man for that weekend." Taking a deep breath, she lifted her shoulders and took on the expression of a seasoned soldier, readying for battle. "Tag, you're it."

Blake picked up the card and studied the fancy maroon and gold embossing more closely. Armadillo Lake Ten-Year High School Reunion. "Don't they usually give folks more notice than two weeks for these kinds of things?"

Darby muttered something under her breath. "Usually."

"You could go without a date."

"Oh, no." Stray pale blonde tendrils loosened from her upswept hair danced at her almost violent head-shake. "I'd rather not go than go dateless."

"Then don't go. Problem solved. No one says you have to go to your high school reunion."

Although he had meant to, he hadn't gone to his. Darby had been sick with the flu and he'd covered for her at the hospital instead. No big deal, since he'd moved so often he'd never gotten particularly attached to any of the numerous private prep schools he'd attended.

She let out an exasperated sound. "It's not that simple. Besides, you owe—"

"Yes, I know," he conceded. "I owe you for bailing me out last month, when it was my turn to be on call and I wanted to go out of town." A weekend that had ended in disaster when his then girlfriend had got wedding bells on her brain. He liked his life as it was and had no intention of marrying. For one reason or another, marriages didn't seem to work in his family. Besides, he was enjoying bachelorhood too much for that.

"So you have to go to your reunion." He dropped the invitation back onto his desk. "Why the 'in love' stuff?"

"Mandy Coulson." Darby's agitation tripled. Quadrupled.

Blake's curiosity grew accordingly. Even when under intense pressure, Darby rarely lost her cool. God, he'd loved to watch her work when they'd been in residency—still did. Calm, cool, in control. Today she was hot under the collar, sweating like any normal person, and not because of his teasing. No, although Blake had thought he knew better than anyone how to get a rise out of his pretty little partner, apparently this Mandy person and a high school reunion had him beat.

He didn't see what the big deal was, but he was intrigued as to why Darby did.

"And Mandy is…?" He stretched his hand out in question. "Who?"

"Every shy kid's worst nightmare." The words hissed from Darby's pursed lips like air escaping a rapidly deflating balloon.

Interesting. He had a hard time imagining the confident young woman he knew as shy. Ever.

This trip might prove to be educational.

He tossed the invitation on his desk and waggled his eyebrows mischievously. "Okay, *darling*, I'll be your boy toy."

Boy toy? As if. Darby rolled her eyes before meeting her partner's black-as-sin gaze. As attractive as she found Blake, the man went through women as if he were competing for a world record. That didn't mean she wasn't crazy about him—just that she knew better than to feed his oversized ego.

"Keep that up and you'll leave me no choice but to call Rodney," she threatened, knowing Blake had never liked her recent attempt at dating. "If I pander to his ego a little—" a lot "—and tell him how rotten you are—" Rodney had been jealous of the "Italian Stallion", Rodney's label for Blake, not Darby's "—he's sure to go with me."

Although they'd only gone out for a couple of months, he was still calling her, trying to convince her they could make things work if only she'd have sex with him. Yeah, right. Not during this lifetime.

There was only one man she wanted to sleep with, and he had no clue that was how she felt.

"The hell you say," Blake growled. "He was the most suspicious man I've ever met—dropping by here all hours of the night." His strong jaw clenched, emphasizing the slight cleft in his chin. "What did he expect? To catch me with my pants down?"

For the first time since she'd stormed into his office her lips twitched. "Actually, that *is* what he expected."

And then some. She hadn't been able to convince Rodney that Blake was nothing more than her business partner. Maybe because from the time they'd met she'd hoped Blake would see her for more than her brain and medical skills. After four years of his treating her much as one of her brothers did, she'd decided she didn't register on Blake's female radar. Just as well. None of the women he was interested in ever lasted long. Blake's love-life consisted of a revolving door and multiple women. She wanted him forever, not just for a few weekends.

So she'd waited, hoped, become more and more frustrated.

"He thought you were getting lucky." Since Rodney hadn't been getting lucky, he'd automatically assumed Blake, being the only other man in her life, must be. *Men.*

Blake waggled his brows again. "Well, you can't blame the guy for thinking I'd get lucky. I am irresistible."

"And so modest, too." She snorted at his mock-innocent expression. "Luck has nothing to do with how you get women."

His lips twitched. "Enlighten me. How *do* I get women?"

Any way he wanted them.

"With that jet-black hair and those dark-as-midnight eyes you don't have to get women, they get you." The laughter in those black eyes had her feet wanting to shift—or run for the closest exit. How had the conversation even taken this turn? Her face grew hot and her skin clammy.

"At least, women *try* to get you," she rushed on, hoping he didn't notice how uncomfortable talking about his love-life made her. "You're oblivious to most, yet they keep chasing you. So, like I said, you don't have to get women, they get you."

"And, like I said—" he rocked back in his chair and blatantly eyed her with amusement "—I'm irresistible."

Dimples cut into his cheeks, making her think perhaps he was right. Certainly she'd always wanted him. Then again, with so little experience when it came to men, how could she be expected *not* to fall for someone so skilled in the ways of the opposite sex?

Because if Blake's love-life was a revolving door, Darby's was a vault that had rusted shut long ago from lack of use.

"For example," he continued, "I was recently propositioned to spend the weekend with a beautiful woman." His black eyes twinkled. "I even get to pretend to be in love with her. How much luckier can a guy get?"

Picking up a spongy ball—a stress-reliever advertising a pharmaceutical firm—she tossed it at him. "I wouldn't count on getting lucky that particular weekend if I were you. You're not that irresistible."

At least not that she'd ever admit. But if she thought

there was the slightest chance Blake could love her, she'd throw caution to the wind and make him notice she was a woman the weekend of the reunion.

He caught the stress ball with ease. "Come to think of it, my luck's never been *that* good. Just look at the last female who found me." He cringed with revulsion and gave an exaggerated shudder.

Darby bit back a smile.

So the foolish physical therapist he'd been dating on and off for a few months had thought Blake was taking her out of town to pop the question. Instead, the Yankees had been in Atlanta, and a friend had given him Braves tickets. Blake's proposal had consisted of, "Do you want mustard or ketchup on your hot dog?" When the game had ended, with no highlighted proposal on the scoreboard, Kristi had issued an ultimatum she'd regretted the moment Blake had waved goodbye.

He interrupted her thoughts. "But you have to admit I am better than Rodney."

True, but Rodney had been an okay boyfriend—a good start to her late-in-life attempt to develop dating skills. Well, an okay boyfriend except for his jealousy of Blake and how he'd pushed for sex. After Blake had dumped Kristi in Atlanta, Rodney's possessiveness had suffocated Darby. He would view going to her high school reunion as moving their relationship into another realm. A realm where she didn't want to go, as she had no intention of having sex with him. Ever.

Blake was right. He was the better choice in so many ways.

No one from her past would expect to see her with a man like Blake. With him at her side she could pretend she wasn't still the geeky girl who'd left Armadillo Lake with big dreams and stars in her eyes.

She picked up the invitation to return to Armadillo Lake, Alabama. Her hometown.

She had to go.

Had to prove Mandy Coulson wrong. Prove her entire class wrong. Prove to herself that she really was the confident young woman she looked at in the mirror each morning. She was, wasn't she?

Her hand clenched around the invitation Mandy had no doubt delayed in sending.

She'd go home with her head held high, with a gorgeous hunk attending to her every whim, and she'd show them all how wrong they were.

Or pretend to, at any rate.

And if along the way Blake discovered she was a girl behind her lab coat and high IQ—well, that would be icing on the cake, now, wouldn't it?

Blake stepped into Darby's office during the week of the reunion. "Can I get your opinion on Mr. Hill's leg?"

It was late Tuesday evening and Darby had already finished with her last patient for the day. She glanced up from the computer screen where she researched an unusual plethora of symptoms a patient had come in with that morning.

"Nathan Hill, from Strawberry Plains?"

"That's the one." He skimmed his fingers over the model of the heart on top of her bookshelf. It was a running joke that he had heart envy. Every time he came into her office he touched the plastic heart. Someday she'd give the darn thing to him.

"I just examined him," Blake continued, "but since you

were the last one to see the ulcer on his lower extremity, I wanted your opinion on whether you think it's improved."

"Sure thing." She bookmarked her page on the web and followed him into the exam room.

"Hi, Mr. Hill." She washed her hands and slid on a pair of disposable gloves. "Dr. Di Angelo has asked me to take a look at the place on your leg since I'd checked you a week or so ago." She smiled at the thin gentleman, patted his wrinkled hand. "How do you think it looks? Better? Worse? Or about the same?"

"Better," the seventy-year-old said. Unfortunately, Mr. Hill would say his leg was doing better even if his toes were black. Very simply, the man wouldn't complain. He'd just smile his toothless smile and tell her how he was doing just fine.

Squatting to examine his leg, Darby winced at the oozing ulcer that encompassed a good portion of his shin.

"Have you been taking the antibiotics I prescribed?" she asked, concerned that he'd gotten worse rather than better. "The culture I did on the area says the one prescribed should clear the infection, but obviously the medicine isn't working."

"I got the prescription filled." He scratched his mostly bald head with a thickened yellow nail that curved over the tip of his arthritic finger. "Only took a few. Figured I'd wait and see if I really needed them."

What was he waiting for? His foot to fall off? For the bacteria to build resistance to the antibiotics since he'd taken just enough to tease the infection?

Darby shook her head. "I stressed the importance of taking the antibiotics because they are vital to this area healing." She looked to where Blake stood. He'd entered the room with her, had been ready to assist if she needed anything, but was confident enough to stand back and let her do her job. She liked that about Blake. He trusted her, found her competent. Turning her gaze back to her patient, she gave him her most serious look. "I'd like to admit you to the hospital, give IV antibiotics for a few days, and keep a close eye on your leg."

Not liking Darby's assessment, Mr. Hill turned to Blake for another opinion. "Doc?"

"Admitting you to the hospital is what I was thinking, too, but you kept insisting you were better. Since I hadn't seen the way the area originally looked, I gave you the benefit of doubt." Blake raised a brow at Mr. Hill, who had the grace to blush. "Obviously you over-exaggerated."

Darby removed her gloves and tossed them into the appropriate disposal bin. She wrapped her arm around the older man and gave him a hug. "Obviously."

"It's not that bad," he insisted, giving Darby's hand a pat. "Definitely not bad enough to go to the hospital."

"You know I try to listen to my patients, Mr. Hill, and to take earnest consideration of their desires, but your leg is serious enough to warrant a hospital admission." Stepping back slightly, she took his hand into hers. "If the infection doesn't clear you could lose your foot. Do you understand? That isn't something I take lightly. Neither should you."

That got the older man's attention. She hadn't been meaning to scare him, but his ulceration was a big deal, and truly could result in amputation in someone with his poor circulation and diabetes. She spoke with him a few more minutes while Blake wrote admission orders to give to the man's daughter, who was waiting in the reception area.

Blake stuck the orders inside an envelope. "You give these to the lady at the admission desk. She'll register you."

They saw him out and spoke with his daughter, letting her know what was going on and stressing that even if her father changed his mind about going to the hospital, he really did need to go. When she'd brought the car around they saw him into the passenger seat, then made their way back toward the office.

"Do you want me to look in on him this evening and do the admission history and the physical?" Blake held the front door open for her to enter ahead of him. "Technically, I was the one to see him today."

"If it's all the same, I'll do the H and P when I check on Evie Mayo."

"Is she any better?"

Darby shook her head. "Unfortunately no. Her liver enzymes are through the roof and I can't find a reason why. Her hepatic ultrasound and her CT scan were both essentially normal. Only fatty streaks showed."

"Hepatitis profile okay?"

"All normal."

"You want me to take a look at her? See if I can come up with anything?"

Darby shrugged. "If you'd like. Maybe I'm missing something."

"I doubt that," he assured her, lightly punching her shoulder in a move her older brothers had often done when she'd been growing up. How long had it been since she'd seen Jim, John, Jerry and Ralph? Too long, since she'd opted to work last Christmas instead of making the six-hour drive to Armadillo Lake. She'd meant to go, but after Blake's mother had canceled plans last-minute to come to Knoxville for the holidays Darby hadn't been able to bear the thought of him alone at Christmas.

"But it never hurts to have a fresh eye give a second opinion," he continued. "Speaking of second opinions, what do I need to pack for this weekend?"

Dread filled her stomach. Was she really going to subject Blake to her humiliating high school experiences?

Of course, she was. Because she wasn't that shy, geeky girl who'd rather have had her nose stuck in a book than in a fashion magazine. She was a successful doctor with a fabulous life.

Okay, so she didn't have a real boyfriend, and was bringing her business partner instead, but no one had to know that the scrumptious man with her wasn't madly in love with her.

Her gaze landed on Blake. He *was* scrumptious to look at—the classic tall, dark and handsome—and she was half in lust with him, so that had to count for something, right?

No one would accuse her of being a virgin when she had a virile man like Blake making googly eyes at her. Which should be enough to ease the bile burning her throat, yet wasn't.

Why wasn't she eagerly anticipating the chance to prove to Armadillo Lake just how wrong they'd been about her? Surely she wasn't still intimidated by her classmates? By Mandy?

No way.

Or maybe she *was* intimidated, because at times she wondered if they'd been right about her. After all, she was a twenty-eight-year-old virgin. By choice, but still a virgin.

Maybe her nervousness stemmed from the man before her. Had she really asked Blake to pretend to be in love with her? To spend the weekend with her, share a hotel room with her?

"Saturday afternoon is a picnic at the town park, so something casual for that. The reunion itself is being held at the Armadillo Lake Lodge's ballroom and will be dressy. Not tuxedo formal, but you'll need a suit." She raked her gaze over him, imagining him at the party. He'd look good in a tux, but that would definitely be overkill. A tux would scream "trying too hard". She wanted their relationship to look real, not make-believe.

She wanted their relationship to be real, not make-believe.

She bit back a sigh. Their relationship *was* real. They had a great business relationship, were ideal partners. Anything beyond that would only make life complicated, because if she and Blake ever became involved that way she'd end up hurt and losing everything. But what if…?

"Picnic and dressy." Winking, he shot her with his finger. "Gotcha."

Fighting to look as if her mind wasn't racing in unwanted directions, she lifted her shoulders. "Wear that blue button-down you bought for the hospital Christmas party last year. I like how that looks on you."

His brow quirked. "Tell me, which part do you like?"

Darby winced. Had she really just said that she liked how his shirt fit him?

"The part that covers you up," she quipped, stepping into the back hallway leading to their private offices. No way would she admit to liking how the material emphasized his broad shoulders and narrow waist.

"Now, now," he chided, "that's not how you should be talking to the man you're madly in love with."

Certain her heart throbbed in her throat, despite knowing such a feat was physically impossible, Darby froze, rounded on him. "I'm not madly in love with you."

She might have feelings for Blake, but she didn't do love. At the young age of sweet sixteen she'd learned that love hurt way too much, and credited herself with being intelligent enough not to make the same mistake twice.

"Oh?" His brow lifted again, high enough that a lock of his inky hair hid the top of the arch. "Is this a one-sided love affair, then? I'm insane for you, but you're immune to my charms?" His lips twitched. "Or are you just using me for phenomenal sex?"

Trying not to think of phenomenal sex and Blake in the same context, Darby gulped. "You're crazy."

Perhaps she was crazy, too. Otherwise why would she have asked him to go to Armadillo Lake? Even forgetting how she'd deal with spending a weekend in a hotel room with him, he'd tease her mercilessly over the things he'd learn about the old Darby. She'd never live down the jokes, the puns.

"We really should get our story straight before this weekend." He took her elbow, led her into her office, pausing only long enough to caress the heart model as they passed by the shelf. "Maybe we should practice."

"Practice?" Darby's ears roared. Her heart thudded, pounding wildly against her ribcage and threatening to once again leap into her throat. Her gaze dropped to his lips and the desire to practice hit so hard she thought she might faint.

Then the most brilliant idea hit her. One in which she'd risk everything—but some risks were worth taking.

CHAPTER TWO

"DO YOU even like the people you went to school with?" Blake stuck a French fry in his mouth. Although he usually ate healthily, French fries were his Achilles' heel. The hotter and saltier the better. Thanks to the hospital cafeteria ladies knowing his vice, they always put on a fresh batch just for him.

"Of course I like them," Darby insisted, but color rose in her cheeks. "I went to high school with them."

"Doesn't mean you like them." He stuck another fry in his mouth, assuring himself the five miles he ran each morning would clear out the excessive cholesterol. "I've never heard you mention anyone you went to school with."

"That doesn't mean I don't like them. I had some good friends back in school."

"So good that you're bringing a fake date to impress them?"

She didn't meet his eyes, took a sip of her water. "You should be flattered, since you get to be the impressive fake date."

"There is that," he mused, studying her, trying to get a feel for whatever it was she was hiding.

And Darby *was* hiding something.

He couldn't put his finger on what, but something had her buzzing about the prospect of returning to Armadillo Lake.

"Tell me about your hometown."

Her face pinched into a scowl. "Not much to tell."

Right.

"I'm going to your reunion this weekend. Don't you think I should know a little about your past?"

"Not really." Her nose curled, as if she'd taken a sniff of something vile. "We've known each other for what—four years? What you don't already know, you don't need to know."

"I disagree." What did he know about her past? Not much. Just that she'd grown up in a small town in Alabama, gone to medical school in Knoxville, on full scholarship, and had decided to stay in Tennessee after he'd jokingly suggested opening a practice together. Surprisingly, since he hadn't made up his mind on where he'd end up, when Darby had said yes, he'd known practicing with her was exactly what he wanted to do. Not once had he regretted that decision, and for the first time since his grandfather's death he had roots.

"Oh?" She might have meant the word to be nonchalant, but the slight squeak gave away her anxiety.

A good person might have let the subject go, not put her on the spot, but Blake had never claimed to be good. Not in that sense, at any rate.

He zeroed in on the one name she'd let slip on the day the invitation had arrived. "I want to know more about Mandy Coulson."

Darby sighed, rolling her eyes toward the hospital cafeteria's ceiling. "You *would* want to know more about her, wouldn't you?"

He shrugged. "She's the only non-related person from your hometown I've ever heard you mention by name."

Her eyes flashed blue fire and her chin lifted. "Trey Nix."

Blake paused, fry midway to his mouth, dangling from his fingers. Trey Nix? "Who's he?"

Why did he instantly dislike him?

Face full-bloom pink, Darby pretended fascination with her chicken salad, raking her fork through the half-eaten entree. "No one."

Clearly she regretted having mentioned the name.

"No one?" He wasn't buying that. "Then why bring him up?"

"You insisted upon another name, and I knew you wouldn't quit until I gave you one."

"And Trey Nix—" what kind of name was Trey Nix, anyway? "—was the person who popped into your head?"

"It's just a name."

Uh-huh.

"Interesting."

Her gaze lifted to his. "What's so interesting?"

"That you mention a sworn enemy and then a guy." Pink blotches spread across her throat and Blake's suspicions rose. "Were you in a love triangle with Mandy and what's-his-name?"

"A *love triangle*?" She laughed. "You're crazy."

But the half-strangled way she said the words hinted that he'd hit the nail over the head.

"Besides I never said Mandy was my sworn enemy."

"No?" Good thing Darby had wanted to go into medicine and not acting. Not even the most gullible bloke would buy the bull she was attempting to feed him. Not liking how his fries weighed heavily in his stomach, he waited until her gaze met his. "Who was she?"

Better still, who was Trey Nix, and what had he meant to Darby?

Setting her fork next to her plate, she arranged the utensil on the tray. "For the first fifteen years of my life Mandy was my best friend."

Best friend? Now, there was a twist Blake hadn't seen coming.

The cafeteria wasn't crowded, or particularly noisy, but he had to strain to hear her next words.

"But that was before."

"Before what?"

She shook her head. "Let's change the subject. I've had enough of the past for one night, and no amount of poking or prodding from you is going to get me to say more, so let it go."

She dug into her salad with gusto. She'd been playing with her food all evening. He doubted she was even hungry. But apparently she didn't want to talk about Mandy and was sending a loud message for him to back off.

Her tone had switched to Darby bossy. The tone she used when he'd pushed as far as she would allow him to push.

Fine—he'd let the topic of Mandy go. For now.

"At least tell me what you expect of me this weekend."

She paused mid-bite. Startled eyes lifted to his. "What do you mean? I told you what I expected. Just pretend you're madly in love with me—as if I'm the greatest thing that's ever happened to you and you can't live without me."

"Okay," he said slowly, taking measure of the panic

in her eyes and wondering at his own rising panic at her words. "I can do that."

In many ways, meeting Darby *was* the best thing to ever happen to him.

"How long have we been dating?"

She blinked at him, as if he'd spoken in an alien tongue. "Pardon?"

"There are things inquiring minds will want to know. Questions that are usually asked when a person sees someone they haven't seen in a while." He gave her a pointed look. "How long have we been dating?"

"The simpler we make this, the better." Glancing down at her plate, Darby stared at her food. "We'll say we've known each other for years, but only recently became romantically involved. Let's stick to the truth as much as possible."

Why was she so nervous? Because she was going to see the man from her past she'd mentioned? What did it matter to Blake? He should be happy if she reconnected with some long-lost love.

Was Nix a long-lost love?

Blake's fries threatened to stage an uprising. "The truth works for me."

"Except that you're in love with me," she pointed out.

His irrational reaction to the idea of Darby having a long-lost love irritated Blake. "I got that."

Her gaze dropping to her plate, she nodded. "I just wanted to be clear."

"As crystal."

Her cellphone rang. She pulled out the phone and looked at the number. Grimacing, she shoved the phone into her pocket.

"Who was that?"

"Rodney."

Her ex? Why was he calling? "You didn't change your mind about getting back with him?"

He hoped not. Really hoped not.

He didn't like the idea of Darby with Rodney. She was way too good for the guy. Plus, crazy as it was, he wanted to go with her this weekend, wanted to meet Mandy. And maybe even Trey Nix, just so he could figure out what Darby's relationship had been with the man—although he had a pretty good idea.

An idea he didn't like any better than the idea of Rodney.

"No," she sighed, looking tired, as if this trip home weighed heavily upon her mind.

He knew she hadn't gone home last Christmas, but she had made the trip when her niece was born. During the four years he'd known her she'd gone home a few times a year, but never for more than a night.

"Part of me wonders if I should beg him to take me back rather than bring you to my hometown."

No, she shouldn't bring Rodney with her. Blake wanted to meet her family, see where she'd grown up, figure out what it was about her hometown that made a woman he admired for her confidence so unsure of herself.

Darby was his partner and she needed his help. More than she even realized. Whatever her issues were with her hometown, he'd help her. He owed her that for keeping him on task throughout his residency and the beginning of his medical career.

"I can behave myself. Even in a place named Armadillo Lake." He chuckled, letting the name roll off his tongue. "Sounds like a fun place to grow up. Is there really a lake?"

"Yes."

"And armadillos?"

"Yes."

"Your school team were the Armadillos?"

She gritted her teeth. "Yes."

"Let me guess—your school mascot was a giant armadillo?"

Gaze lowered to her plate, Darby nodded.

"Bet that went over great at football games." He chuckled. "An armadillo."

Darby had grown still. She looked as if she were praying he wouldn't put two and two together. Where Darby was concerned Blake always put two and two together. He grinned.

"You were the mascot, weren't you?"

The next morning Darby had barely climbed out of her car before Blake fell into step beside her in the clinic's employee parking lot. "I checked on Mr. Hill this morning. He's insisting on going home, and he's only been there one night."

She ignored him, just as she'd been ignoring him since he'd burst out laughing at her admission she'd once worn an armadillo suit to all major school sport events.

Not a cute little armadillo suit that showed off her legs—if such a suit even existed. No, she'd been in a full-bodied, hot-as-Hades, head-to-toe vinyl Armadillo suit that looked like something straight off a cheap Godzilla movie. And all to impress a guy—to prove that she was more than a brainy girl, that she had a sense of humor and could be fun. What had she been thinking?

"He's giving the nurses a hard time." With his usual persistence, Blake continued, following her down the clinic's hallway toward their offices. "The night nurse said he pulled out his IV line. She put the line back in, and threatened to strap his hands to the bedrails if he pulls it out again."

Darby already knew all this. She'd visited Mr. Hill, too. Blake had beaten her to the hospital, thanks to her sleeping late, but she had checked on her two patients this morning.

No wonder she'd overslept. Most of the night she'd lain in bed having nightmares about the upcoming weekend. Nightmares in which she'd shown up at the reunion not decked out to the nines as planned, in the new killer dress she'd bought, but wearing that awful armadillo suit. Trey hadn't been the one laughing at her. Blake had been the one shaking his head, pointing his finger, not understanding her desire to fit in. Not understanding how she desperately wanted him to notice that she was alive. The truth, she'd realized, was that this weekend was more about *him* than her class reunion.

She'd awakened in a cold sweat, certain she'd made a grave miscalculation—that thinking she could make Blake notice her as a woman was as foolish as wearing that armadillo suit had been.

Despite having sent in her RSVP, she didn't have to go. Most likely no one would even notice if she was there or not.

No, that wasn't true.

Mandy would know. Wasn't that why she'd sent Darby's invitation late?

If she didn't go, she was saying that she was okay with her and Blake's relationship never being more than what it was. And, although what they had was wonderful, Darby wanted more.

She was going.

Not only was she going, but she was going to have fun. And in the process of making Blake notice her she'd make Trey eat his heart out because he'd chosen the head cheerleader over the geeky, too-smart-to-be-understood school mascot. *What had he been thinking?*

She'd risen beyond her high school experiences and was a desirable woman who held the power over her life. Wasn't that what her wannabe-shrink roommate during her first four years at university had said—making Darby repeat the phrase while looking in the mirror each morning, insisting Darby go for formal self-confidence-boosting therapy?

She was in charge of her life. Dr. Darby Phillips, a woman worthy of respect and admiration. A woman who'd come a long way from wearing a dumpy armadillo suit and longing for a man she couldn't have.

Her gaze fell on the man keeping stride next to her.

Well, no one could accuse her classy navy pants and cream-colored blouse of looking like a scaly animal, at any rate.

"Ah, come on, Dilly, surely you aren't still mad at me?"

Why had she told him the mascot's name?

Blake being Blake, of *course* he'd tease her, call her by that name. She spun to where he'd followed her into her office.

Knocking his hand away from her plastic heart model, she straightened to her full five feet three inches and poked his thick chest. "Don't you ever make fun of my having been an armadillo again—do you hear?"

His eyes widened slightly at her outburst, but a smile curved his full lips. "Ah, Darby, come on. I'm sure you were a cute armadillo."

She glared. He was supposed to be groveling, shaking in fear, apologizing, not still laughing.

"Too bad I didn't go to your school." He tweaked her chin, his fingers sending shivers over her flesh. "I'd like to have seen you in that costume. Maybe you could wear it for me this weekend? I promise to show my school spirit."

Couldn't he be serious? Or at least pretend as if he felt threatened? Of course he couldn't. Blake was one of those annoying perpetually positive folks. As much as that did annoy her at times like these, his disposition was also one of the things she liked most about him. One of the things that had always drawn her to him.

He made her laugh. Had from the moment they'd met. She'd been so serious, so determined never to let a man make a fool of her again, so focused on getting her medical degree, she'd forgotten how to laugh until she and Blake had been assigned an emergency room rotation together. She might have been up to her eyeballs in work, but one wink from Blake could re-energize her sleep-deprived body and have her smiling from the inside out.

No one had ever been able to make her feel good the way he could.

Fighting to hang on to her angry bravado, she rolled her eyes. "The only costume you need to see me in is a white lab coat." She forced her brows into a scowl. "Isn't it time for us to get started seeing patients?"

He sighed with exaggerated effort. "You're in a foul mood this morning, Dilly."

She pursed her lips, crossed her arms and glared up at him. Way up. Why had she worn flats? "No more armadillo jokes."

She refused to back down. She didn't want Blake seeing her in the same light Trey had. After a moment of their facing off—her feigning anger, him grinning—he nodded.

"Fine, no more school mascot jokes." He put his fingers up in a Scout's Honor symbol. "If I get the urge to tease you, I'll just *dill* with it."

She looked heavenward. "This isn't funny."

He lifted one shoulder in a half-shrug. "From where I'm standing, it's pretty funny."

"Because you weren't the one wearing that horrible suit."

Perhaps she'd let too much of her past pain bleed through, because Blake stared at her a little too closely.

"Last I heard, folks aren't forced to be school mascots," he pointed out. "They volunteer for the job."

"Well, Mr. Know-it-all, sometimes there are extenuating circumstances that cause a girl to wear ugly suits and play a fool."

"What extenuating circumstances?" His dark eyes saw too much, and Darby fought from shifting her weight.

"It's complicated." Complicated? Yet another word for humiliating herself in an effort to get Trey's attention

Looking way too serious, Blake crossed his arms in a similar stance to her own. "I've got time."

There were some things that shouldn't be repeated. Her high school blunders were just a few of them. She glanced at her watch. "I don't. I need to see my morning patients. Bye."

She grabbed her stethoscope and rushed from the office. Without turning to check, she could feel his gaze burning into her, could feel the heat scorching her cheeks.

She also sensed his amusement. His curiosity.

"See you later, Dilly," he called from behind her, no doubt brushing his fingers over her heart model.

What had she been thinking when she'd told him about that wretched costume? About her nickname? Next thing she knew she'd tell him she'd been voted most likely to die a virgin and had yet to do anything to prove her classmates wrong. For a woman who prided herself on her intelligence, she sure was making a lot of stupid choices.

But there came a time when a woman had to either don an armadillo suit—or invite a man to spend a weekend in a hotel with her in hopes of being noticed or accept not registering on his radar.

As insane as her frustration was, Darby was tired of not making a bleep on Blake's radar.

She wanted his radar bleeping. For her.

Which just went to prove how little intelligence she really had.

Bleeping on Blake's radar would likely ruin everything she held dear, so why was she bleep, bleep, bleeping in her heart?

The closer Darby and Blake got to Armadillo Lake on Friday afternoon, the more Darby's stomach churned.

What was wrong with her?

She should be looking forward to the opportunity to return home and show her old schoolmates they'd been wrong about her on most accounts. And she should be excited at the prospect of maybe making Blake see her as a desirable woman…

After all, hadn't that been the idea behind her last-minute shopping trip to her favorite lingerie shop? She should be a lot of things, but she suspected if Blake wasn't the one behind the wheel she'd turn the SUV around and head back to Tennessee pronto. For so many reasons—not the least of which was that she was afraid of what the weekend might do to her and Blake's relationship.

But if she wanted more than what she had—and she did—she had to shake things up. Sleeping in the same bed should do that—had he even considered their sleeping arrangements when she'd invited him?

Darby stole a glance toward him and fought a very feminine sigh of appreciation. God, he was breathtaking. And, for the weekend, he was all hers.

"You've barely spoken the last thirty miles of our drive."

"You've talked enough for the both of us," she pointed out.

He had. Blake could carry on a conversation with a stump. His gift of the gab was a trait she envied. Although she'd taken classes to help her overcome her shyness, she'd been introverted for the earlier years of her life. She hadn't wanted to be shy, but when you preferred to have your nose stuck in a book than to drive into Pea Ridge to cruise the shopping mall—well, popularity wasn't your middle name.

"Didn't your mom tell you not to do that? Your face might get stuck like that."

Designer aviator glasses protected Blake's eyes from the blazing sunshine brightening their drive. If the manufacturer could hire him to model those shades, they'd sell billions. He made them look that good.

"Like what?" she asked, thinking life was unfair if one man could have been blessed with so many talents. Looks, intelligence, wit. Yet, Blake wasn't one of those men who walked around thinking he was a million bucks. Despite his teasing about his many charms, he was one of the most genuine persons she knew. Actually, he was *the* most genuine person she knew. What you saw was what you got.

She liked what she saw way too much.

"Like we just drove past another chicken barn with the windows down."

Darby bit the inside of her lip to keep from smiling. Not long after they'd crossed the Alabama state line Blake had rolled down the windows to experience some fresh country air. He'd gotten fresh country air, all right.

"Most likely we did pass another one."

This time it was his face that wrinkled—him who looked like he might need to pull the SUV over.

"I'll never eat chicken again."

Darby laughed out loud. "There are chicken barns in Tennessee. So don't tell me you'd never experienced a chicken barn up close and personal before."

"Apparently I'm still a city boy at heart," he admitted unashamedly. "From the car is as up close and personal as I want to get to a barn of any type. Especially one as foul as what we smelt earlier."

"Foul?" Shaking her head at his double entendre, Darby laughed again. Just as well she wasn't planning to take him with her when she dropped in on her folks tonight.

Her stomach jerked again. No doubt her brothers and their wives would start pushing for her to move home. They always did. Her family hadn't been able to understand why she'd been so driven to leave Armadillo Lake, to get her degree and make something of herself, to see the world. They especially hadn't understood when her plans to join a traveling medical program had taken a one-eighty turn and she'd stayed in Knoxville.

Then again, they'd never met Blake.

"What were you thinking about that made you scowl?"

She should have known he wouldn't let her change the subject. He rarely did.

"About the reunion."

He glanced away from the road just long enough for her gaze to meet the mirrored lenses that hid his eyes. He shook his head in confusion. "Most people look forward to high school reunions, to catching up with their old classmates, seeing who married who, who has the most kids, who gained forty pounds, who still has their hair."

"Yeah, well." She turned to stare out the window at the growing all too familiar landscape, her belly lurching. "I'm not most people, City Boy."

"That you're not." He chuckled, then surprised her by reaching across the gap between their seats and taking her hand into his.

Clasping their fingers together, he squeezed.

Her belly gave another jolt, a much larger one than before, and she faced him.

"No worries, Darby. Whatever it is that has you wound so tightly about this weekend, everything is going to be fine. You're going to dazzle all your old classmates with your intelligence, success, beauty, and especially with your impressive date." Smiling, he briefly dipped his head, glancing at her from above the rim of his shades. His black eyes bored into her. "I promise."

The warmth emanating from Blake's hand to hers almost made her believe everything would be all right concerning the reunion—that every fantasy she'd ever had of returning to Armadillo Lake and making everyone eat armadillo…er…crow, would come true.

Regarding the way every single cell in her body surged to life at how his hand still held hers, at how much she liked his hand holding hers, at how many hopes she had pinned to their spending the weekend together—well, that was another matter altogether.

CHAPTER THREE

FOR the dozenth time since they'd arrived at the Armadillo Lake Lodge, Darby stared at the queen-sized bed monopolizing the standard hotel room.

"Forget it," Blake warned, stepping next to her. His hands rested on his lean hips as he stared at the bed, too. "I'm not sleeping in a chair."

He thought she wanted him out of the bed? What would he say if she admitted to having been imagining the two of them there? To wondering what it would be like to spend the entire weekend in bed with him? Laughing, playing…something more…?

He'd probably laugh and tell her to be serious.

She sighed, shaking the bottle of fruity disinfectant she'd sprayed onto the top of the gaudy brown and orange comforter that likely had been in use since the lodge had first opened.

"I didn't say you had to sleep in a chair."

If they didn't share the bed, news would spread like wildfire. *This was Armadillo Lake*. Everyone knew everyone's business. After cleaning the room, Gertrude Johnson would no doubt spill the juicy tidbit to anyone who'd listen. The Johnsons had run the only hotel within a thirty-mile radius for as long as Darby could remember. If not for the tearoom that served as the town's only "nice" restaurant, and the large ballroom that hosted all major town events, the place would likely have gone out of business years ago. Armadillo Lake didn't attract many tourists.

Just unsuspecting women returning for their high school reunion while trying to convince the man of her dreams that she was the woman of his dreams. No biggie.

She turned to look at him. Despite their six-hour drive, he looked crisp. Not a wrinkle on the gorgeous man's khaki shorts that fell to just above his knees, nor on his expensive polo shirt. Just once she'd like to see him rumpled.

Her gaze shot back to the bed.

Okay, so she wanted to rumple him and rumple him thoroughly. More than once. A girl could dream, couldn't she?

She swallowed.

She had to quit this fantasy stuff. Blake was here to help her. If their near proximity helped him see her as a female, then so be it—but she didn't plan to throw herself at him. Either Blake wanted a relationship with her or he didn't.

Her gaze fell on the bed again.

"The bed's plenty big for the both of us. We'll share." She narrowed her eyes to what she hoped were menacing slits. "You stay on your side, and I'll stay on mine."

"Dibs on the top side."

"Fine, you can have that top side, and I'll take this top side." She pointed to the side of the bed closest to the bathroom for herself.

"That wasn't exactly what I meant." He laughed,

watching her lift the comforter and spray disinfectant between the sheets and on the underside of the comforter. "You're the only person I know who disinfects hotel room beds."

Darby shrugged. She wasn't exactly a germ-a-phobe. But she'd seen one too many television specials about what crawled around in hotel room beds not to come prepared, and she always brought her own pillow.

"Here." She tossed the spray bottle to him. "You're a big boy. Disinfect your own side."

Catching the bottle, he grinned. She turned to unpacking her clothes. Holding her breath, she pulled a black lacy number from her suitcase and dropped it into the drawer she'd also disinfected.

She glanced up in time to see Blake's gaze following her movements as she dropped another pair of tiny panties into the drawer.

His feet shifted. He swallowed. He tugged on the collar of his polo shirt.

When his gaze met hers, Darby had no doubts.

If this weekend accomplished nothing else, Blake had just realized she was a woman.

A woman who had a predilection for fancy undergarments.

In that moment, Blake wanted her.

She'd wanted him always.

Now what? Could her fantasies become realities, or would her hopes only lead to disaster?

Still fighting his reaction to the skimpy silk scraps Darby had pulled from her suitcase, Blake hung his clothes in the hotel room's tiny closet.

All these years he'd never known she had a penchant for sexy lingerie.

But why would he have known? They didn't have that type of relationship. Not one where they discussed boxers or briefs, granny whites or spidery webs of black silk. They were business partners—and he'd be a wise man to remember that instead of wondering how that tangled lace would look hugging her bottom.

The sound of something falling to the bathroom floor was followed by Darby mumbling something he couldn't make out through the closed door.

Pausing at the closet, he eyed his suit, hanging side-by-side next to Darby's brilliant blue dress. He reached out, ran his fingertips over the soft material of her dress.

Maybe he should pretend to sleep in the chair.

Pretend because even if the curved wooden chair that was designed more for looks than comfort was the most comfortable chair in the world there was no way he'd rest with Darby sleeping in the same room.

He hadn't thought doing this favor would be a big deal, but he'd never spent the weekend in a hotel with a beautiful woman he wasn't having sex with.

He sure hadn't ever slept in a bed with a woman he wasn't having sex with.

Especially when he wanted to be having sex with that woman.

But sex with Darby could never be just sex.

She was his business partner, his friend, someone he cared about.

All reasons why sex wasn't a good idea.

As much as he wanted to see Darby in those tiny bits of silk, sex between them would ruin everything. Darby didn't do casual sex, and Blake didn't do anything but.

The bathroom door opened. Blake faced the woman he'd just been imagining in her underwear. Again. Trapped steam from her recent shower kissed his skin—or maybe that was sweat from his thoughts of what she had on underneath her clothes. She'd changed into a pair of white shorts that showed off her toned legs and a trendy top that showcased her full breasts and made her waist look tiny. Dampness clung to the hair at the base of her neck. The rest of her blonde hair was clipped by a toothed hairpiece that could double as a torture device.

"I'll be back in a few hours." Her eyes didn't meet his. "Don't wait up."

Which of those silk numbers did she wear beneath her clothes?

He swallowed, trying to dislodge the brick stuck in his throat. *Granny panties, Blake. She's wearing big, ugly granny panties. Just keep telling yourself that and eventually you'll forget what you saw, what you want to see wrapped around Darby's curvy body.*

"Blake?" Her forehead wrinkled with concern. "You okay?"

Okay? No, he wasn't okay. His imagination was working overtime. What she'd said registered in his lingerie intoxicated mind.

"If you're going out, I'm going with you." Wherever she was going, she wasn't leaving him in the hotel room. With her underwear and his over-active imagination. Hell, no.

"No." Her tone held full Darby bossiness. "You're not."

"If you think I'm sitting in a hotel room alone while you go out, think again." He closed the closet door, for once not appreciating her bossy attitude. "Where are you going anyway?"

"To my parents', and you're not going. End of discussion."

Her parents? Of course. Darby's family lived here. Just because his mother made moving house a hobby that didn't mean normal families changed addresses on an annual rotation. Why hadn't he considered that she'd want to visit while in Armadillo Lake?

"I'm coming with you," he said matter-of-factly, knowing he'd win this argument, "and you should be grateful."

Bingo. She lifted confused eyes to his. "Huh?"

He gave a smug smile. "How will it look if the man who is madly in love with you doesn't go to meet your parents? Tsk, tsk, Darby," he scolded, crossing his arms. "You're the one who said you wanted this to appear real. Twiddling my thumbs in our hotel room while you visit with the family doesn't work."

He watched the unhappy realization that he was right wash over her heart-shaped face, watched as she searched for a feasible argument, summarily dismissing each one.

"I don't want you to go." She dropped onto the bed in an unladylike flounce that had visions of skimpy underwear flashing in his brain again. "My parents don't know you're with me. But they do know I'm here." Her voice had taken on an unfamiliar whiny tone. "I have to go, but you can't go with me."

"Did you plan to hide me away in the hotel while you snuck in the obligatory visit with the family?" The guilt on her face said that was exactly what she'd intended. "I'm an easygoing guy, Darby, you know that. But I'm not doing room service while you go to your parents." He frowned. "We've been partners for almost a year and I've never met your family. Why is that?"

She'd met his mother on the rare occasions Cecelia had dropped by Knoxville for a visit. But he hadn't met a single person from Darby's pre-Knoxville life. Not even at the grand opening of their clinic.

"Fine. You can come." She stood, eyed him as if she'd rather kiss a sewer rat than introduce him to her family. "But just remember you insisted upon going and that I was going to spare you the drama." Then her eyes took on a delighted spark. "Oh, and by the way, City Boy, there are chicken barns. Four of them. Hope you're real hungry for some of my momma's chicken and dumplings. Mmm, *chicken*."

Darby winced. No, her mother *hadn't* really just pulled up her shirt to ask Blake's opinion on the "bug bites" on her abdomen. Not at the dining room table. Not with the entire family present. Not while they were eating dinner.

Yep, Nellie Phillips had.

To his credit, Blake was taking her family—all twenty-two of them present and accounted for, and sitting at various places throughout the farmhouse—in his stride. Actually, he seemed amused by the chaos that was a permanent fixture at the Phillips home.

Standing there with her floral print shirt pulled up, her mother revealed a tiny sliver of thick white cotton and a wide expanse of pale white skin, marred only by the bright red vesicles clustered over her lower ribcage and wrapping around her trunk on her left side.

Concern replacing her mortification, Darby squinted at the "bug bites". "Are you sure something bit you?"

Blake examined the rash. "Looks more like Herpes Zoster."

Darby agreed. Those angry clusters were isolated to a single dermatome, and hadn't been caused by an insect.

"Herpes Zoster? Is that serious?" one of her brothers asked, leaning toward his mother for a closer look. "See, Mom, I told you to let me drive you into Pea Ridge to be checked."

Nellie gave Jim a silencing look. "Don't be silly. Herpes Zoster is a fancy term for shingles."

"Shingles?" Darby's dad spoke up from where he sat in his honored spot at the head of the table. He lowered his glass of iced tea and scratched his graying head. "Earl Johnson from down the road—you remember him, Darby? You used to clean house for him? He had shingles early in the spring. Had me kill my rooster for him."

Knowing Blake didn't want to hear about old wives' tale remedies for certain ailments, Darby scooted her chair closer to the table and reached for the bowl of fried potatoes. "Mom, how long have you had the rash? Are you taking anything to help dry it up?"

"Tell Darby about those spells you've been having."

Darby's gaze cut from her mother to her oldest brother and back again. "What spells?"

Her mother waved her hand. "No big deal. Just a few twinges of pain. I thought from the bug bites."

Concern sparked in Darby's chest. "What kind of pain? Haven't you been feeling well?"

"I'm fine. Fit as a fiddle." Darby's mother didn't meet her eyes, but instead passed a bowl full of greens to Blake. "I remember my mother having shingles. She had a lot of pain even after the rash disappeared, complained with her side hurting for months."

"Pain is normal with shingles." Blake accepted the bowl, staring at the contents with speculative eyes. He tentatively dipped out a small spoonful. "You should schedule an appointment with your doctor to get on an anti-viral and some pain medication."

"I don't like pills. Never have." Nellie smiled at Blake. "I'm like my mother that way."

Darby's niece came running into the kitchen, squealing that her brother had spilled his juice. Rosy jumped up to check on the spill, but Nellie placed her hand on her daughter-in-law's arm. "Let me."

Darby followed her mother into the living room and helped clean the juice puddle.

Watching her mother, Darby noticed the dark circles beneath her eyes. Dark circles she hadn't really noticed—probably because she'd been so distracted with worrying about Blake and his reaction to her family, worrying about her family's reaction to Blake. She also noticed the fatigue plaguing her mother's face, the deepening wrinkles, the slight tremble to her hand when she wiped the towel across the floor.

Her mother had shingles. Not the end of the world, but how long had she been suffering, ignoring the pain? Why hadn't she let Jim drive her to Pea Ridge to be checked? Why hadn't she mentioned the rash to Darby when they'd talked on the phone earlier in the week? Even if her mother didn't understand why she'd become a doctor, why she'd had to get away from Armadillo Lake, she knew she was a darn good one.

When they'd wiped up the last of the juice from the scuffed hardwood floor, Darby met her mother's gaze and felt as if she was five years old.

"Mom," she began, before they stepped back into the kitchen, "you didn't have to ask Blake about your rash. I would have checked it for you."

"Nonsense." Re-entering the kitchen, her mother waved her hand. "He's a *real* doctor." She shot an admiring glance toward where Blake sat talking with Darby's father. "No sense in you having to worry yourself over some little rash."

A real doctor. What was she? A pretend one?

Darby sighed.

Might as well be, since she was faking everything else this weekend.

Blake didn't have to be a rocket scientist to see that Darby was irritated with most of her family.

As the youngest of five children, and the only girl, her family treated her as if she were incapable of doing anything for herself. At each point Darby attempted to do something, even if it was only to refill her glass of tea, someone jumped in and did the task for her. Couldn't they see what a talented young woman she'd grown into? How much their attitude annoyed her?

Another part of him envied her the camaraderie, the loudness, the interactions that came with having a large family who so obviously adored her.

As a little boy he'd heard his grandfather talk about huge family gatherings back in Malta, but only Vic Di Angelo had come to the States to make his fortune. He'd met a lovely young New Yorker who'd died giving birth to their only child—Blake's mother. Victoria Di Angelo had gotten pregnant while a teenager and, although she'd married numerous times, she had never had more children, leaving Blake an only child. Since his grandfather's death family dinners had consisted of Blake and his mother in a nice restaurant in whatever city she currently lived in, making small talk while sipping on wine and pretending they had something in common other than memories of the gruff old man they'd both loved.

"More banana pudding, Dr. Di Angelo?" asked one of Darby's sisters-in-law. He couldn't recall which one of her brothers the tall redhead was married to, but she was obviously the mother of the three red-headed kids who ran in and out of the dining room every so often.

He was a tad jealous of the freedom the Phillips kids enjoyed. How exciting growing up in a place like this must be when compared to the fancy downtown apartments and condos he'd always lived in.

"Call me Blake—and no thanks on the pudding." He patted his flat stomach, thinking perhaps French fries had been knocked down a notch from the top of his food chain. "Wish I could, but I'm stuffed."

"Did he just say he's buff?" Another sister-in-law, giggled from across the table, fanning her face.

Blake grinned. Yeah, he liked Darby's family. A lot.

"I'd second that," another said, cradling her three-month-old daughter in her arms so she could nurse her.

When at the last minute she threw a baby blanket over her shoulder and soon-to-be-exposed breast, Blake felt Darby's relief much louder than he heard the soft sigh. Hoping to reassure her, he caught her eye, winked.

"I'm sorry," she whispered, leaning close to his ear.

Her warm breath tickled his ear, goosebumping his flesh, hyper-driving his heart rate.

"What for?" he asked, wondering if she'd apologized for making him so aware of her, for the fact that despite the table still being laden with delicious food all he could smell was her delicate floral scent. Or the fact that every time he looked at her he wanted to peel away her clothes to see what she wore beneath. And then he wanted to peel those away, too.

"For making you eat chicken, of course," she teased, but he read the truth in her eyes. Her worries centered around her assumption that he was enduring her family for her and was barely able to do so.

He would endure any unpleasantness for Darby—after all, they were business partners. But he was enjoying her family.

Well, except for the way her brothers kept glaring and asking leading questions about his intentions regarding their little sister.

That he could have lived without.

Then again, he'd never had a sister. If he had, he'd have been just as tough on any guy she brought home. Actually, knowing what he usually did with women, he'd have been tougher. If they knew what he wanted to do to Darby, her brothers should take him out behind one of those long barns.

"I think it's so romantic, you two working together and falling in love," the redheaded sister-in-law sighed dreamily, pulling a carrot-topped toddler into her lap.

"We worked together at the Co-Op during high school. I don't hear you calling *that* romantic," her husband pointed out, reminding Blake which brother she belonged with. Best as Blake could recall, Jim was Darby's oldest brother, and the only one to share his sister's deep blue eyes.

"'Cause folks fall in love down at the Co-Op all the time. I think it's the hormones they put in the feed. You just don't hear about two doctors falling in love." She sighed again, accepting wet kisses from the little boy who had his palms smashed against her cheeks. She laughed at her son's antics, then said to no one in particular, "It's like something you'd see on television."

"What she means," explained the brunette sister-in-law nursing her baby, "is that Armadillo Lake doesn't have a doctor, much less two. That's why they haven't heard of doctors falling in love except on T.V."

Blake blinked. "Armadillo Lake doesn't have a doctor?"

"Closest one is in Pea Ridge, a clear thirty miles away. That's the closest hospital, too." She gestured to the blanket covering her nursing baby. "I thought I was going to have to deliver this one here in the calfing barn."

The calfing barn? Did he really want to know? He turned to Darby, who conspicuously stared at her empty plate.

"I'm surprised you didn't set up a clinic here."

A wince crinkled Darby's forehead.

"We all hoped she'd settle down near Armadillo Lake—the actual lake and not just in town. She always loved that old plantation house down there," another sister-in-law explained. "Course that was before the mess with Trey."

Although she'd been sitting quietly, toying with her shirt hem, Darby's head shot up. She made a slashing motion across her throat to the pretty brunette who was ignoring her.

"He's single again, you know. That girl from up near Gadsden and him got divorced last fall," another added. "He moved back earlier this year and opened a plumbing repair shop. Business has been real good, I hear. He bought the old Jenson farm and is considered quite the catch."

"What mess?" Blake asked, wondering why a knot had formed in his stomach at the news Trey Nix was single and "quite the catch". Wondering why Darby's family waved Trey in front of Darby like a carrot. Was she supposed to be lured home?

She *had* a home. In Knoxville. With him.

"When Trey broke her heart, of course. High school quarterbacks are notorious for stealing girls' hearts around these parts." The brunette looked at her husband, who grinned back at her. Obviously Darby's youngest brother had been a quarterback who'd stolen *her* heart.

"Hello? I'm sitting right here," Darby reminded them, clanging her silverware against her plate. "Blake does not want to hear about Trey."

Actually, he did. But he took pity on the desperation in her eyes, knowing that before the weekend was over he'd learn what had transpired between his lovely partner and her high school quarterback.

But for now he'd play his role.

"Darby's right. I don't want to hear about men from her past, because they don't matter." He took her hand in his, laced their fingers for all to see. "She's mine now, and I plan to keep her."

Darby's mother beamed. A collective sigh came from the sisters-in-law. Her brothers exchanged looks. Her father shrugged.

Blake smothered a grin. He liked Darby's family. All of them. Why hadn't she introduced them in the past?

Next to him, she audibly caught her breath, and her eyes flashed with question. "Are you sure you don't want more dessert?"

He winked, letting her know he had this under

control. She could thank him later for rescuing her from conversations about old heartbreaks.

Turning to Darby's mother, he flashed his most brilliant smile. "What I'd really like is to see Darby's baby photos. Got any you'd just love to show me?"

Darby tried to ignore the fact that Blake's arm was around her, his hand pressing possessively into her lower back. She tried to ignore the fact that her sisters-in-law kept smiling at each other, that her brothers kept sizing Blake up, not quite sure what to make of him, that her parents were falling over themselves in hopes that he would save their baby girl from the follies of her youth by choosing medicine over marriage and children.

She was failing miserably, of course, and couldn't ignore any of those things, much less all of them.

No wonder. She and Blake sat squished next to each other on the same sofa she'd sat on when she'd still worn diapers. Her mother was on the opposite side of Blake, flipping through a family photo album and ecstatically pointing out various embarrassing pictures from Darby's youth.

She shook her head as Blake enthused over shot after shot—especially her "Dilly" photos.

Had he really asked to see her baby pictures? Had her family really not had an *aha!* moment and seen that this couldn't possibly be real? What man asked to see a woman's baby photos?

"The boys just hauled her with them wherever they went. She drove the tractor, helped haul hay—whatever they were doing, she was right in the middle. It's no wonder she was such a tomboy."

Dimples dug into Blake's cheeks, his eyes dancing with interest when he glanced toward Darby. "You were a tomboy?"

She shrugged. "For a while."

"Then she discovered books, and would hide in her room reading instead of doing her chores," Jim said.

"I think she read every book in the Armadillo Lake library. Never did see someone who liked to read so much." Darby's mother shook her head in confusion. "I kept telling her that reading books didn't put food on the table."

"Guess all that book-reading paid off in the long run. Look at her now—a doctor," Rosy said, smiling at Darby. "We're all so proud of her accomplishments, aren't we?"

"Sure thing," Jim grunted, at his wife's elbow jabbing his ribs.

Darby sent Rosy a grateful smile. Not that she bought her claim. Her parents would have been proud if she'd married a good ole boy straight out of school, had a half-dozen babies and farmed for a living. Becoming a doctor and living six hours away didn't even register on their "proud" radar.

They hadn't come to her graduation ceremony.

Or to the opening of her and Blake's clinic.

To give them credit, Rosy had given birth that same weekend—which she'd apologized for time and again. As if she'd had any control over when her son entered the world. But Darby had never been convinced her parents would have come regardless. To her knowledge, they'd never left sweet home Alabama.

"She is an amazing woman, isn't she?" Blake turned toward her, brushed her hair away from her face, and gave her a look that turned her to melted goo right then and there on her mother's sofa.

"I can't imagine not having her in my life," he continued, his voice low, seductive. He pulled her hand to his mouth and pressed the softest of kisses to her fingers.

Her breath hung in her throat, threatening to choke her. She couldn't pull her gaze from his dark one.

He'd been overdoing the lovey-dovey stuff all night, constantly touching her, smiling at her, looking at her as if he was visually stripping off her clothes and liking what he found.

Looking at her as if she was his whole world.

As he was doing at the moment.

Even though she knew he was role-playing, her body perked up to heights that made her mind feel a little numb and her body tingle in places she had no business to be tingling while sitting on her mother's sofa.

She'd wanted him to notice her, to be aware she was a woman, but was she really prepared to face the consequences of what she'd set into motion this weekend? Was she ready to lose what they had in hopes of winning love's jackpot?

CHAPTER FOUR

"HEY, sis, can I talk with you a moment?"

Darby turned toward her brother, alarmed at the concern in his voice. He knew, didn't he?

"What is it, Jim?"

If any of her brothers was going to realize her relationship with Blake was phony, she'd have guessed Jim. He'd always been able to see right through her.

"I'm worried about Mom."

Both relief and concern filled Darby. "What about her?"

"She's not been herself for the past few days."

"Because of her shingles, you mean?"

Jim scratched his blond head. "Maybe. I'm not a doctor, but I think something more is going on than her rash."

"What makes you think that?"

"She hasn't acted right."

"In what way?"

"I've seen her pressing her hand to her chest and wincing."

His words caused Darby to wince. Her mother was having chest pain? "What does she say?"

"That she's fine, and I should mind my own business."

Sounded just like Nellie Phillips.

"I'll talk to her and see if I can convince her to go in for a check-up on Monday."

"I'd appreciate it. Dad doesn't say much, but I can tell he's concerned, too. Yesterday she had to come inside and lay down for a while."

"Really?"

"Yep, and she's been snapping at him."

Her mother didn't snap. She gave orders, expected them to be obeyed, and tolerated no disobeying.

"I'll corner her before Blake and I leave and find out what's going on as best as I can."

"What's going on with you and this guy, sis? I like him, but there's something about him that doesn't sit well."

"It's probably just because he's dating your baby sister."

"Possibly." Jim glanced toward where Blake sat, surrounded by the Phillips womenfolk. "Are you serious about him?"

How did she answer? She couldn't lie to Jim. Not directly. "He's my business partner. Would I risk messing up our partnership if I wasn't serious about him?"

Her brother's mouth twisted and his gaze went back to Blake. "Possibly," he repeated. "With what happened with Trey, I don't want to see you hurt."

Darby swallowed. Her whole life wasn't measured by what had happened with Trey. Sure, she hadn't trusted a man until Blake, and that had taken years, but that was because she'd learned a valuable lesson, not because she'd been traumatized by Trey's betrayal. "That was over ten years ago."

"Ten years in which I've not seen you with another guy."

She'd dated. Rarely, and never for long enough to get close to any of them, but she had dated.

"We live in different states. You don't know how many guys I've been with." At Jim's scowl, she added, "Besides, Blake's a good guy. The best."

Her oldest brother shot another uneasy glance toward where Blake sat with the Phillips women. "He seems crazy about you."

Crazy being the key word.

Darby snapped her seatbelt and kept her smile pasted onto her face. No doubt lots of eyeballs stared out the front windows. She'd wait until they were out of sight before she tore into Blake, possibly dismembering him and tossing him into one of the chicken barns for what he'd done.

"That went well."

Darby inwardly scowled at the pleased-with-himself man pulling out of her parents' driveway. Was he insane?

Her entire family now expected her to announce that Blake was "the one", they were getting hitched, planned to buy the old Donahue place down near the lake, set up practice, and raise a family of their own.

She glanced into the side mirror to make sure her brothers hadn't jumped into a pick-up and followed them. Not only were there no headlights, but she could barely see the house or the four long barns off in the distance.

"I'm going to strangle you," she warned, curling her fingers into tight fists.

"I thought I did better than that."

"Better? There was no reason to put on a show in front of my parents, my family. You acted like a lovesick puppy. Now they think something's going on between us."

His brows knit together and he cast an odd look toward her. "Wasn't that the idea? For me to make them think I was crazy about you? To pretend that you were my whole world?"

"No. Yes. Oh, I don't know." Clearly she hadn't thought through the consequences of bringing Blake to Armadillo Lake for the weekend. She should have made peace with Rodney rather than hope to open Blake's eyes. Rodney was easy enough to explain away, and would have been bored to tears with her family. And would have bored her family to tears with his polished exterior.

Blake was not so easily explained away.

As her business partner, he was a part of her everyday life. After tonight's performance, her parents probably thought something had been going on between them for years.

No wonder. He'd been the perfect date—had he really been her date, that was. He'd been attentive, considerate, affectionate, had blatantly stared her brothers in the eyes, daring them to deny his right to date their sister, earned their grudging approval before the evening had ended, wooed her sisters-in-law, charmed her parents. He'd played his role too well. Way too well.

When he'd pulled her fingers to his lips and kissed them, in front of God and the entire Phillips clan, she'd had a momentary mental and physical lapse and wanted him to kiss more than just her fingers.

She'd wanted him to kiss her all over.

And she'd wanted to press her lips to his throat and kiss him. All over.

For real.

When she'd finally been able to drag her gaze from Blake's, her mother had been smiling. Not just smiling, but *smiling* smiling.

No doubt her mother was pulling out her grandmother's veil this very moment, envisioning how the simple pearl and gauzy netting would look on her daughter's head. "Finally," she'd be saying to her daughters-in-law.

Her mother would be heartbroken if she knew the truth.

"I'm definitely going to strangle you."

"You want to strangle me?" He checked for oncoming traffic prior to pulling onto the main highway that would take them the ten miles back into Armadillo Lake. "I'm disappointed. I was sure you'd be pleased and relinquish the entire top side of the bed as reward for my good behavior."

"Good behavior? Are you kidding? Do you have any idea what you've done?" How could she look at him and not long for what they'd pretended this weekend? Not want him to want her for real? Having tasted the sweetness of his affections—even knowing they were pretend—she just couldn't envision going back into the desolate wasteland that had made up her personal life. She covered her face with her hands. "This is horrible. They're expecting us to be married by Christmas, and are no doubt at this very moment discussing what they're going to wear to our wedding."

"Why? Do they try to marry you off to every man you bring home?" He chuckled. *Chuckled.* As if he hadn't turned her life upside down with his hot looks and incessant touches. As if he hadn't just waved her parents' fondest dream in front of them—Darby married and back in Armadillo Lake.

As if he hadn't just waved her fondest dream in front of her—*him*.

"If I gave them the opportunity." She wiped her face, knowing she'd pay for tonight's show for months to come. For years. She wouldn't live tonight down until she brought home a man for real. And how she'd live this down in her heart she had no idea. Regardless of the outcome, this weekend would forever haunt her heart, her dreams. "I've never brought a man home."

That got his attention, causing him to slow down the vehicle and glance toward her. "Never? Not even Trey Nix?"

Darby sucked in air. "Trey doesn't count."

"Why not?"

She shook her head. "He just doesn't."

Technically, neither Trey nor Blake counted.

After all, they'd both only been faking their feelings for her.

Darby had washed her face, moisturized, brushed her teeth, flossed, and combed her hair. She'd put on the modest pajamas the sales clerk had assured her were sexy without looking like she was trying to be sexy.

Time to face the music. Or, more aptly, Blake in a hotel room bed. Why was she acting so crazy? It wasn't as if he were lying there waiting for her to come to him like a virginal bride. It wasn't as if anything was going to happen between them just because he'd looked at her with desire earlier, then pretended to love her all evening.

It wasn't as if anything was going to happen between

them just because she hoped with all her heart that he'd someday really want her the way she wanted him.

She gulped back her nervousness and opened the bathroom door.

Light from the television illuminated the hotel room, casting shadows and short bursts of brightness across Blake's face. He sat in the bed, all the pillows, including hers from home, propped behind his bare back.

Where was his shirt?

Where had he gotten all those muscles?

She'd known he had a nice body, but, oh my, she hadn't known he'd been hiding all those beautifully sculpted lines and planes. If business ever got bad, they could run an ad of Blake wearing low-slung jeans, no shirt, and his stethoscope dangling from his neck. Business would be through the roof in no time.

Her pulse was already there.

Her gaze lowered. Pajama bottoms rode low on his narrow hips. The comforter bunched at his waist, hiding everything beneath the dark navy waistband.

"I thought you'd decided to sleep in the tub," he teased, thankfully unaware of her thoughts.

"Not likely." But if a functioning spine wasn't necessary for the following day, she might grab her pillow and give the tub a shot. How could she not have known what an awesome six-pack Blake sported?

No wonder women flocked to him, were devastated when he moved on to the next beauty who caught his eye. Four years and she'd never seen the man's naked torso. Now she'd never be able to forget—never be able to look at him and not know what he hid beneath those tailored shirts.

Lord help her.

Lord help him. Because she really wanted to just tell him how beautiful she thought his body was, how beautiful she found his heart and soul, his sense of humor, everything about him.

As if sleeping in the same bed with him was no big deal, she climbed in and tugged her pillow out from behind him. "Give me that."

As if sleeping with her were no big deal, he grinned at her. "I was warming it up for you. Say thanks"

"Thanks." What he'd done was make her pillow smell of his musky scent, all spice, sandalwood, and Blake.

"I turned the air down. That okay? I sleep better when the room is a little cool."

"Fine." She didn't need a play-by-play of his sleeping habits. Really. Just knowing they were going to be in the same bed, sharing the same blankets, that her pillow smelled of him, was already playing havoc with her imagination and her will power not to roll over and jump him.

Taking a deep breath, she reminded herself of mind over matter. She could do this. She *soooo* didn't want to run her fingers over those indentions on his stomach. She didn't want to trace each outline of that six-pack. With her hands. Her mouth. Nope, she was immune to Blake's charms if all he wanted from her was sex.

She was a mighty oak that couldn't be swayed by pin-up calendar abs and spicy musk that made a woman want to deeply inhale. Not her.

Right.

But maybe if she kept telling herself she didn't want him, she'd make it through the night without embarrassing herself.

Because she wanted so much more from Blake than just sex.

She wanted him. The whole package.

"I called the hospital and spoke with the night nurse. All of our patients are doing about the same. Dr. Kingston made a round on them this evening and introduced himself."

See, even lying there half-naked, with her on the opposite side of the bed, Blake was only thinking business. Just because she'd hoped this weekend would jumpstart their relationship into who knew what, that didn't mean he knew she'd asked him to Alabama innocently enough the afternoon the reunion invitation arrived, but quickly realized she hoped for much more.

"He plans to stop by the hospital in the morning."

"Thanks for letting me know." She'd meant to call and check on Mr. Hill and Mrs. Mayo after they'd first gotten back to the hotel room, but she'd been distracted by Blake pulling his acoustic guitar from its case. Somewhere between the country music classics she'd forgotten everything except soaking in Blake's hypnotic voice.

She tugged on the covers, tucking the material around her neck.

"You ready for the light to go out?"

Light? Oh, he meant the television. "Sure. We've got a long day tomorrow."

He clicked the remote, then put the device onto the nightstand next to his side of the bed. "Goodnight, Darby."

"Goodnight, Blake."

"Sweet dreams."

"You too.

They lay in the dark for a long time, with Darby acutely aware of each breath he took, of every movement of his body, of the fact his beautiful chest was bare beneath the sheet. All she'd have to do was reach out to feel those hard muscles bunched beneath his smooth skin.

She could accidentally brush against him. Just a quick brush of her fingertips against all that temptation.

"Why aren't you asleep?" he asked after a few minutes.

Because now that I've seen your chest I'm not sure I'll ever sleep again.

"Why aren't you?"

"I was thinking."

That you should put on a shirt, because you're the stuff fantasies are made of and I'm the last woman in the world you'd want to have those kind of fantasies about you?

"About?"

"What it must have been like growing up at your house."

Huh? She rolled onto her side, staring at his barely perceptible silhouette through the darkness. "Why would you think about that?"

She felt his shrug more than saw it.

"I liked your family."

He did? Why did that cause happy bubbles to dance in her belly? Until that moment she hadn't admitted to herself how much she'd hoped Blake had liked her family.

"They liked you, too. Even if my brothers didn't know quite what to think of me bringing home a city boy."

He shifted, and she expected him to roll over and go to sleep. Instead his hand clasped hers, lacing their fingers in a warm hold that she guessed was supposed to be friendly. *Friendly* didn't cover the excited tingles working their way through her body, starting somewhere in the pit of her belly and radiating outward, sensitizing every cell along the way.

"Tell me about them."

"My brothers?" She didn't move, just lay in the bed, acutely aware of his presence, acutely aware of the fact that for the dozenth time that day he held her hand and each time he'd thrown her heart into a tailspin of longing.

"Yes."

Her brothers. Where did she start? "John and I were always the closest when I lived at home. Probably because he's the youngest of the boys and only a year older than me," she began, tugging her pillow down a bit with her free hand. "But since Jim and Rosy married, I see them most often. They usually come up twice a year to go to a football game, and they never miss the Tennessee/Alabama game."

Long into the night, they talked. She told him about her family, life on the farm, about her favorite pets while growing up. At any point she grew silent he'd ask another question, and Darby would let more of her life spill into the darkness, thinking perhaps Blake had really hypnotized her with his music. Or maybe the darkness made her feel safe in sharing so much. Otherwise she'd never be lying in bed with the sexiest man she'd ever known, holding his hand and telling him all about her crazy but lovable family, and her rather ordinary childhood, growing up on a farm, that seemed to fascinate him.

Mmm, something smelled good. Still half-asleep, Blake breathed in a deeper inhalation.

Soft, flowery, elegant, feminine.

Something felt good, too.

He shifted slightly against the warm body curled spoon-fashion with his.

In the way one does when first awakening, he became aware of his body, of the way the soft body melted against him, her legs curled against his, of the way his arm snaked around her waist, her arm lying over his, of how his palm cupped her breast through too much material.

Her head was tucked beneath his chin and the alluring scent he'd smelled was a mixture of her shampoo and her own seductive fragrance.

She fit perfectly against him, his much larger body framing hers protectively, possessively.

Not opening his eyes, he kissed the top of her head, worked his way down to nuzzle her neck, her ears. Damn, she tasted good.

Better than French fries.

Better than Darby's mom's banana pudding.

Darby.

He was nibbling on Darby's earlobe.

He opened his eyes, expecting her to be awake, expecting her to lash into him and tell him exactly where he could go for taking advantage of her.

He couldn't see her face, but could tell she was still asleep by her even breathing.

But even in sleep she wasn't immune to what he'd been doing. When he stopped, she snuggled into him, tightened her buttocks against him, making him bite back a groan of pleasure and need, making him want to strip off her pajama bottoms and feel her silky skin glide against him, her female to his male in all the wonders of what made the world go round.

Which was all wrong.

He shouldn't want Darby.

Only he did, naked and beneath him, moaning his name in pleasure, wrapping her legs around his waist and meeting each thrust of his body into hers with an enthusiasm that matched his own.

He tried to tell himself that his desire was due purely to circumstances—that he'd want any attractive woman he woke up wrapped around, especially one who smelled so seductive.

He laid his head back on his pillow. A man's subconscious was hell. It caused him to ignore things he didn't want to acknowledge, like what he'd wanted to do since seeing her drop those naughty undies into the drawer. But it was more than sexy lingerie. It was the woman next to him. He liked her, enjoyed her company, her wit, her intelligence, her smile, the way she challenged him to be a better man, a better doctor.

All reasons why he wouldn't seduce her. Their relationship was more special to him than giving in to sexual need. Even sexual need as paramount as what currently ailed him.

Stirring, she turned, snuggled closer, tucking her head into the crook of his shoulder, wrapping her arm over his waist and running her fingers along his belly to settle just above the waistband of his boxers.

Ah, *hell*. He should get up, take a shower—a cold shower—anything to remove himself from the tempting lair he lay in.

But he didn't want to climb out of bed. Not yet.

Without moving his head, so as not to disturb her, he glanced toward the clock. It was still early. They'd talked way into the night and would have another late night with her reunion. He'd just let her sleep for a while longer—would pretend she wasn't who she was and that it was okay that he'd liked waking next to her more than he should have.

If not for his raging arousal that wouldn't—couldn't—be acted upon, waking next to Darby, lying with her like this, was nice.

Closing his eyes, breathing in her intoxicating fragrance, he lay next to her, willing his body under control and telling himself that any man who woke next to a beautiful woman would be reacting exactly the same way.

His mind and heart didn't race because the woman he held was Darby.

Without opening her eyes, Darby knew she was in trouble. She was wrapped around Blake like the candy shell coating on her favorite chocolate treat.

How had that happened? Obviously she'd gotten cold during the night and her body had gone in search of heat.

And Blake was heat of the hottest kind.

He was lying on his back with her cradled against him, and delicious heat radiated from the smooth skin of his chest.

And her hand.

Dear Lord, her hand was at his waist.

Not on *him*, but darn near close!

Hoping he was sound asleep, she lifted one eyelid and glanced into dark-as-sin eyes.

He was awake, and staring at her as if he wanted to see inside her head.

He *knew* she'd virtually attacked his body during the night.

"Um, sorry." Was that croaking noise really her voice? "Apparently I got cold." Trying not to appear as rattled as she was, she attempted to disentangle herself. "You make a good heater."

You make a good heater? What kind of stupid comment was that? Could she please just pull the covers over her head and never come out?

"Glad to be of service," he teased, sounding quite normal and as if nothing out of the ordinary had happened, that he hadn't just wakened with her body trying to be the icing on his cake.

He wasn't going to make a big deal out of her *faux pas*. Thank goodness. Then again, he probably woke with women wrapped around his fine body all the time.

Darby didn't. Hadn't ever. Despite the fact she'd had a few boyfriends, she didn't do sleepovers. Ever. Each time she got close, old doubts stopped her, making her question motives, making her lose all desire to risk her heart.

But who could blame her body for getting as close as possible to a six-foot-two hunk in the flesh? Especially when that flesh held the soul of a man she was willing to risk giving her heart to?

"Do you want the bathroom first?" she offered, hoping she sounded casual. She glanced toward the clock. Almost ten. They'd slept much later than she usually did. Much later than Blake slept too, since he usually went for a run in the mornings prior to his hospital rounds.

The picnic started at eleven.

In an hour she'd face her high school nemesis and the boy she'd once planned to give her virginity to. She'd be alongside a man pretending to love her and doing such a great job he'd thrown her internal circuits off kilter and was feeding her dreams of what it would be like to really be loved by him, both physically and emotionally.

Enough so that she'd almost throw caution to the wind and take whatever kind of relationship Blake would give.

A quickie relationship would cause everything between them to sour. But what if he really could fall in love with her? What if they could be both business partners and lovers?

"Let me go, real quick, then the bathroom is all yours."

Quick. Quickie. Heat burned her face. Had he really just said "quick"?

She tried not to look as he slid out from beneath the sheet. More and more of his flawless chest and abdomen were exposed. She tried to tear her eyes away from the arrow of dark hair that disappeared beneath his boxers.

Boxer briefs. She'd thought his waistband had been to pajama bottoms or shorts. "You wore underwear to bed?"

She'd slept with Blake. In his underwear. When she'd awakened she'd known there weren't many barriers between their bodies, had felt his hairy legs tangled with her smoothly shaven ones, but she'd thought he'd been wearing more than his underwear.

Stretching his arms over his head, drawing attention to the lean planes of his body, he lifted a dark brow. "Is that a problem?"

How dared he look so hot first thing in the morning? She'd wanted to see him ruffled, but she hadn't meant like this, with sleep softening his expression, his hair sexily tousled, his body barely covered with brief cotton boxers that left little to her imagination.

"Yes, it's a problem! You're not wearing underwear to bed tonight. Not if you expect me to be in that bed with you. Got it?"

His lips twitched with amusement. "Okay. If you insist. I wouldn't have last night if I'd known how you felt."

Scowling, Darby crossed her arms over her breasts, trying to hide her body's reaction to his stretch, to his near nakedness, to his comment that she knew was only his usual teasing.

"That's not what I meant, and you know it."

"Hey." He put his hands up in mock surrender. "I was just trying to follow orders. You know I like it when you're all Darby bossy."

"Fine, let's see how you do with *this* Darby bossy. Hurry up in the bathroom, because as you can tell—" she gestured to her make-up-free face and sleep-mussed hair "—I've a lot of work to do before we go to that picnic, and I don't want to be late."

Why miss a single moment of reminiscing over the most humiliating time of her life, with the man of her dreams there to watch?

CHAPTER FIVE

MANDY COULSON wasn't what Blake had expected.

She was petite, blonde, curvy, brown-eyed, and had a friendly smile that appeared genuine.

From the way Darby acted each time her name was mentioned, he'd been looking for horns and a pitchfork.

However, when she glanced toward Darby something did shift in her gaze. Something Blake couldn't completely read. Guilt? Regret? Anger? Resentment? Or maybe Mandy wasn't looking at Darby at all, but rather the man chatting with her.

Trey Nix.

Blake stood a little taller, held his head a little higher. And attempted not to spy on where Darby talked to the man whom she blushed at with every other word he said.

Damn it. *Blake* was the only man she blushed for. Didn't she know that?

He hadn't realized until that moment, but it was true. Darby didn't blush at any time except when he teased her as he had this morning.

She'd blushed like crazy when he'd climbed out of bed.

But she was also blushing right now, while smiling at something a man from her past said while he looked at her as if he'd like to take a big bite of her future.

Who was the guy, and what had their relationship been?

Based on what little Darby had said, on what her family had alluded to the night before, he'd guess they'd been romantically involved and Darby had been hurt.

"How long have you and Darby been together?" Mandy asked, glancing toward where Darby spoke with Trey. Her brown eyes narrowed at the talking couple.

No doubt about it. There had been a love triangle between the three of them.

Also glancing toward where the tall man flirted with Darby, Blake didn't like the direction his brain was taking him, nor the fact that looking at her blushing for another man made him feel caught up in a triangle of his own.

Which was crazy.

He and Darby didn't feel that way about each other. Even if going to sleep holding her hand and waking next to her had been unexpected pleasures.

"We met in medical school. The moment I saw her I wanted her."

He said the words as part of his madly-in-love-with-her role, but hearing the confession out loud sent cold chills over his body.

He *had* wanted Darby the moment he saw her.

He had been denying that want for years, because she wanted different things from life than he did, but the want was there all the same. It had definitely been front and center this morning, when he'd awakened holding her, wanting to do much more than that.

"She's a lucky girl."

Mandy's words had Blake's gaze returning to the woman, but only for a second. He didn't like how Nix had backed Darby against the widest tree Blake had ever seen, how his hand rested above her shoulder and he leaned in while talking to her.

More than that, he hated how Darby looked at the man, with rosy color high on her cheeks. Had she forgotten she'd arrived with him? That they were supposed to be together?

Pretending to be in love or not, no woman he arrived with was going to flirt with another man during their date. Hell, no.

"Excuse me."

Without waiting for Mandy's response, he went to interrupt Darby's tête-à-tête with the past.

Darby leaned back against the wide base of the oldest oak tree in Armadillo Lake. The rough bark digging through her clothing, she regarded the man who'd once devastated her teenaged heart.

"You grew up to be one fine-looking woman." Trey grinned at her, his green eyes twinkling just as they always had.

He hadn't gained fifty pounds, lost his sandy-blond hair, nor lost the good-looks that had won more hearts than just her naïve teenaged one. Other than the more pronounced crinkles at the corners of his eyes and mouth, he looked like the same old Trey, sounded like the same old Trey. The only thing that had changed was that he didn't elicit the same old heart-fluttering meltdown in her chest that he once had.

She didn't feel anything for him except anger that he'd treated her so shabbily all those years ago. Anger that burned her cheeks, made her curl her fingers into her palms to keep from slugging his grinning face.

His grin was all wrong, and it didn't reach his eyes—eyes that were the wrong color. His grin didn't lift his laugh lines just so, didn't make her want to smile back.

Not like the man she'd awakened with this morning—the man who did put her fluttering heart into meltdown in ways Trey never had, not even during the heyday of her high school crush.

Not like the man who was now chatting up Mandy. *How could he?*

She smiled up at Trey with more enthusiasm than she felt. "Um, thanks."

"Everyone was wondering if you'd be here." He rubbed his knuckles across her cheek.

"They were?" Nothing. He was touching her and nothing was happening. No flutters. No silly schoolgirl giggles in response to his attention. No desire to have him take her into his arms and kiss the fire out of her. No desire to hold his hand and talk long into the night. *What was Blake talking with Mandy about? Why was Mandy smiling?*

"Yeah." He grinned again. "They were taking bets down at the Piggly Wiggly."

Heat flooding her cheeks, Darby's gaze shot to Trey. She blinked. "Bets?"

"On whether or not you'd show. High school doesn't exactly have good memories for you."

He'd played the star role in those bad memories. For years she'd carried a crush for him, had dreamed of him noticing her, and when he had his attention had merely been to get back at Mandy.

"High school was a long time ago." Just look how

much smarter she was these days. Then again, considering who her heart pitter-pattered for these days, maybe she wasn't nearly as smart as she'd like to think. "Besides—" she forced a smile to her face "—the reunion was an excuse to bring Blake home to meet my parents."

His eyes momentarily darkening, Trey's grin kicked up a notch. "You could invite *me* to visit with your folks sometime. It's been a while since I've seen them. Your Mom still the best cook in town?"

"Yes, she is—and perhaps you've forgotten, but the last time I invited you it didn't go so well."

"I was young." He laughed, as if his explanation made everything okay. He reached out, cupped her jaw, and stared down at her. "If I'd been half as smart as you were, I'd have held on to you."

"Obviously you weren't that smart—but I am." Blake took Darby's hand. Unmindful of how close Trey stood, he pulled her to him, knocking the other man's arm away with the force of his tug.

Darby blinked at the menacing way Blake glared at Trey, at the possessiveness in his dark eyes when they shifted to her.

It took her a moment to recall he was just playing a role, that he was fulfilling his "crazy about her" part. That he wasn't really jealous.

With that, Blake's head lowered, his mouth brushing over hers in what could only be called a staking-his-claim kiss.

His kiss wasn't gentle, wasn't a caress.

His kiss was a branding of his mouth against hers—a kiss meant to say she belonged to him and none other.

Darby's heart pitter-pattered.

No, that wasn't a pitter-patter. That wild beat was a

thunderstorm, a horrendous onslaught on her senses, complete with lightning and thunder and raindrops that pierced her soul.

She let her fingers thread into his hair, tangle in the silky locks, pulling him closer, loving the solid strength of his body against hers. Her mouth opened and his tongue thrust inside, imprinting her with his kiss, stamping her as belonging to him.

Dear sweet heaven, she'd never been kissed so thoroughly and completely and all-consumingly. Blake kissed her as if she really was his, as if he really was ticked that another man had been making moves on her. As if he'd fight to keep her at his side. He was kissing her as if he wanted her, loved her.

The way she'd dreamed of being kissed by him.

Only he was faking.

She knew it, and so did he.

That knowledge gave her the power to pull away, the power to smile at Trey and give Blake an annoyed look.

"Blake, please, we're at a family picnic." Unsteady, she placed her palm against his chest, surprised to find his heart doing a rapid pitter-patter of its own. Still, she pushed against him, trying to establish space between their bodies.

His gaze narrowed, his thumb raked across his lips, removing the last trace of her lipstick. His eyes never left hers, never lost their steely possessiveness, never lost the dark swirls of desire that looked so real they took her breath away.

"Let's ditch the picnic and go back to the hotel, Darby."

"Just for the record," Trey drawled, leaning against the tree and watching them, "I'm a lot smarter these days."

Darby's gaze cut to him. She hadn't even remembered he was there. She blinked, sure she must still be asleep and having some weird dream.

Maybe when she woke up she wouldn't want to take up Blake's pretend offer to head back to the hotel. Because at this moment she wanted to. For real.

If she believed he was sincere, they'd be out of there.

Having followed Blake, Mandy stepped up beside them. "Good for you, Darby. I'm glad you've met such a great guy and won't die a virgin, after all."

Heat burning her cheeks, Darby rolled her eyes, sure Mandy meant the words as some type of dig, knowing Mandy had meant her to be embarrassed in front of Blake.

Blake's forehead wrinkled with a frown, his gaze going back and forth between Mandy and Darby. "What's she talking about? Dying a virgin?"

"Nothing, really." Mandy laughed, the sound sparkly. "Just one of those silly 'most likely' predictions kids make."

"Most likely?"

Mandy smiled. "Darby's was..."

Darby opened her mouth, tried to speak, tried to stop Mandy from saying it out loud, but words wouldn't come from Darby's mouth. Mandy's mouth had no such problems.

"Most likely to die a virgin."

Would the ground please open up and swallow her? Or lightning strike the tree and drop a branch onto Darby, knocking her senseless? Either would work. Just so long as she didn't have to look into Blake's eyes and see the pity there, see the realization that she'd been a loser in high school.

Blake's arm snaked around Darby's waist, keeping her close. "I can put that ridiculous prediction to rest."

"We noticed." Mandy giggled, fanning her tanned face. Her brown eyes twinkled at Blake. "If the thermometer wasn't reading over a hundred before, it is now. That was some kiss."

Mandy was right. The temperature must be triple digit, because Darby was melting from Blake's heat. His arm burned through her thin clothes, making her sweat.

"That kiss was nothing," he promised, making her wonder if he'd read her mind. "Not compared to what Darby and I share. She'll die a well-loved woman." He stared down at her, his eyes sparkling like gleaming black onyx. "As long as there's breath in my body, I'll see to that."

Darby stared at Blake in awe.

She could kiss him.

Not just because Mandy's jaw had dropped, not because Trey looked at him with something akin to envy, not because he'd just single-handedly saved her face over the past humiliations she'd suffered, but because in that moment, when he looked at her, she believed him.

Which was exactly why she needed to make sure she never kissed Blake again.

Because none of this was real.

Not his kiss, his looks, or his words.

Because Blake was faking and she was the idiot who'd asked him to. The idiot who had to keep reminding herself that none of this was real, no matter how much she wished it were.

She'd set a dangerous game into play, having Blake pretend to love her. A game she wasn't sure she could continue.

* * *

Thirty minutes later, Blake wondered if the people of Armadillo Lake were too blind to see the person Blake saw. Their lack of vision had damaged Darby's self-confidence in ways he hadn't realized.

But how could he have? She'd always come across as so together. So self-assured. So confident in who she was.

Only here, in a place that stripped her of the armor she'd so carefully shielded herself with, did he see the vulnerability in her eyes. The need to belong, to be accepted, to show that, despite whatever had happened in her past, she was somebody worthy, both then and now.

Darby had something to prove, and he couldn't help but wonder if that need went far beyond making a statement with an impressive "date".

He wanted her, caught glimpses of desire in her eyes, had felt her desire in their kiss, but did she really feel desire for him? Or just gratitude for his role this weekend?

"Blake, are you going to play softball with us?" she called, from where she stood with a couple of females who wore friendly faces and seemed to genuinely be glad to see Darby. He'd liked the women—their husbands, too.

"Maybe he doesn't want to get his city-boy butt whooped by a bunch of country boys."

Trey Nix he didn't like.

Had Darby really had a relationship with that strutting buffoon? Former high school star quarterback or not, the guy was a self-absorbed loser. One who'd taken a look at present-day Darby and decided to make up for lost time.

Over Blake's dead body.

He hadn't played softball ever, but he'd once been a

hell of a Little League baseball pitcher. Too bad they'd moved away near the end of the season, cheating him out of sure tournament victory. After his third unfinished season due to frequent moves Blake had opted not to play another organized sport, but he had played the occasional pick-up game at the fancy prep school he'd attended.

He wasn't sure that would keep him from getting his butt whooped, but even if he'd never gripped a bat before he wouldn't back down from the challenge in Nix's eyes.

Five innings later Blake was thinking perhaps he should have recruited a few of his old Little League teammates. His current team was losing by two runs, and he was up to bat with a runner on base. With the right hit, he could tie the game.

Before Blake's first pitch was thrown a loud wail had everyone's heads turning toward the playground near the park's pavilion.

"Bobby?" called a woman Blake had seen repeatedly with Mandy, while the other two women stared toward Darby, talking low. The woman abandoned her third base post to rush toward her crying son. "What's wrong?"

The game forgotten, the rest of the team made their way to where the boy lay on the ground, clutching his arm.

His broken arm.

"What happened?"

"He fell when he jumped from the swing," another boy informed them, his little face a mixture of curiosity and fear.

"Didn't we talk about not jumping from the swings?"

But even as she said the words the woman's face paled, tears clouded her eyes, and she hugged the boy to her.

Blake started to step forward to check the boy, but when Darby bent next to the mother and son he reached for his phone to call for an ambulance.

"Someone bring a bag of ice for Bobby's arm, pronto," she ordered. Smiling, she placed her hand on the boy's hand. "Hi, Bobby. My name is Darby Phillips, and I'm a doctor. Can I see your arm? I'll be gentle."

Obviously terrified, the boy shook his head, burying his face into his mother's chest.

"Bobby, honey, let her check your arm." Whatever differences were between them, the woman obviously had no problems with Darby examining her son. "She's an old friend of Mom's and Aunt Mandy's."

Nor with distorting the truth.

Although not happily, the boy let Darby check him.

While explaining to the ambulance service what had happened, Blake watched Darby assess the boy's arm, admiring the way she spoke with him, explaining what she was doing in that calm, controlled voice.

Trey handed Darby a plastic bread sack that had been filled with ice and knotted at the end. Darby shot him a quick look of thanks and placed the bag on Bobby's arm.

"Although the skin isn't damaged, both the radius and the ulnar bones are broken, just proximal to the wrist." Darby glanced at the woman. "I suspect the bones will need to be surgically pinned."

"I could drive you." Trey spoke up from where he stood next to her still, obviously eager to come to the rescue.

Blake opened his mouth to tell the guy to get lost, that he was on the phone with the emergency service and an ambulance should be on its way soon. But Darby took charge.

"Could you? That would be great. You drive us in Cindy's vehicle, so she'll have transportation at the hospital." Darby gave him a smile that had Blake's insides crawling. "Blake will follow us, and you can ride back with us."

Great. Just what Blake wanted—to chauffeur Darby and her ex. Why were they going to the hospital anyway? They couldn't do anything except keep the arm stable. An orthopedic surgeon would be required to correct the damage to the bones.

But if Darby wanted to accompany the boy to the hospital, he wouldn't argue. The whole weekend was about her, for her, and he'd agreed to play by her rules.

Even if he'd quickly realized he didn't like those rules.

"I'm going, too," Mandy piped up. "Cindy might need me."

Darby's expression tightened, but she didn't say anything, just turned her attention back to Bobby.

Listening to the emergency dispatcher, Blake whistled. Darby was right. The closest emergency service was thirty miles away and wouldn't arrive in Armadillo Lake anytime soon. They could get the boy to the hospital faster than waiting for the ambulance.

"Let's go."

CHAPTER SIX

FRESHLY showered, Blake sat on the hotel room bed. Humming to himself, recalling how Darby had clung to his every word the night before when he'd sung for her, he pulled on his black Italian shoes.

They'd gotten back from Pea Ridge about fifteen minutes earlier. They'd stayed at the hospital with Cindy, Mandy and Trey until Bobby had been admitted to a room on the surgery floor. He'd have surgery early the following day, to pin the broken pieces of his ulnar and radius bones.

As Darby had gone into the emergency room with Bobby and the boy's mother, Blake had been left in the waiting area with Mandy and Trey. That hour had been one hell of a long wait.

Making Blake happier than they could have possibly realized, Mandy and Trey had stayed at the hospital, rather than ride back with them.

On the drive home, Darby had looked spent and closed her eyes. He'd encouraged her to lie down on the bed to rest while he took his shower. When he'd come out of the bathroom she'd been on the phone, not surprisingly, and was firing question after question about what was going on at Knoxville Memorial Hospital regarding their patients.

When finished, she clicked her cellular phone closed. "I called and checked in with Dr. Kingston. He discharged Evie Mayo this morning, along with both of your patients."

His patients had been simple dehydration cases, so he wasn't surprised they'd been released to go home. He'd expected as much. Darby didn't sound sure about her patient.

"You don't think he should have discharged Evie?"

"We still don't know why her liver enzymes were so elevated. He says they've dropped to below a hundred and she was fine."

Blake had reviewed the woman's chart, examined her, and hadn't been able to offer Darby any suggestions other than perhaps the woman had an unusual virus. Her white blood cell differential had been slightly shifted, with an increased lymphocyte count, indicating the possibility of a virus.

"Evie was okay with the discharge?"

Darby shrugged. "He says she was ready to go home."

"He's a good doctor."

"Yes." Glancing at her watch, she nodded. "I should get ready. Thank goodness we only have to go downstairs."

She stood from the ornate chair, gathering her clothes to take into the bathroom with her.

"Darby?"

She turned, her gaze colliding with Blake's.

"Are you going to tell me what happened between you and Mandy before we go downstairs?"

She shook her head.

"How about what happened between you and Nix?"

"We're going to be late if I don't get my shower."

He sighed. He'd hoped she'd tell him last night, but she hadn't. She'd seemingly shared everything with him except whatever her connection was to Trey and Mandy. "When you're ready to talk, I'm here for you."

Before turning her back on him, she smiled, but it didn't reach her eyes.

"I know," Darby said. Blake had always been there for her. Not that she'd needed him often, but when she had he'd been there without hesitation. Like when she'd had the flu. He'd not only covered for her in the office and at the hospital, but he'd brought her a basket full of edible goodies and stayed with her in case she'd needed anything.

Her hand on the bathroom doorknob, she paused, spun to face him. "Why are you so good to me, Blake?"

His dark eyes clouded with confusion. "What do you mean?"

"Why are you here with me this weekend? Surely you had better things to do than go to my high school reunion?"

"You blackmailed me, remember?"

Her grip tightened on the doorknob. "Blackmailed?"

"Blackmailed might be a bit strong," he admitted, humor evident in his voice. "I owed you a favor so I'm here."

Pretending to be in love with her, so she wouldn't lose face with people from her past who didn't matter anymore. Why had she thought they had? Why had she given them such power over her life? Why had she let Trey's rejection impact her so much?

But somewhere along the way her reasons for keeping the opposite sex at bay had shifted from fear of rejection to waiting for Blake to notice that she was a woman, that they made a great team.

Only he never had, and she'd tired of waiting.

The kiss they'd shared flashed through her mind, lighting fires just at the memory of Blake's intensity. When she'd joined him in the waiting room his gaze had dropped to her lips. Had he been remembering their kiss? Or had he been pretending for Mandy and Trey's sakes?

"Oh, what a tangled web we weave when first we practice to deceive."

Biting into her lower lip, she sighed. She'd asked for this. Asked for him to pretend. What was that old saying about being careful what you asked for?

"I would have come anyway, Darby, if you needed me." His gaze searched hers. "Do you regret my being here?"

He'd seen more of her than any other man, had seen the real her, and he'd stood back and let her handle Bobby's injury this afternoon, knowing she'd needed to handle Bobby's care, to prove something to herself and to her hometown.

Inherently, Blake knew her. Sometimes he knew her more than she knew herself. He helped her see things more clearly. Helped her to feel more confident about herself, about the woman she was, and about who she wanted to be.

He helped her to trust the opposite sex, because Blake was the only man she trusted who wasn't blood kin.

"No, I don't regret you being here. Far from it," she admitted honestly. She trusted Blake more than any person she knew. With her business, her reputation, and with her past. "You're a nice man, Blake Di Angelo."

"Nice?" He coughed, sputtered, and snorted amidst laughter. "Don't you believe it, Dilly."

She rolled her eyes at the nickname he'd likely never let her live down. But, despite his antics and intentional teasing, she'd spoken the truth.

Nice? Darby thought he was *nice*?

Blake shook his head, picking up the remote to flip through the television stations, pausing to watch the world news, expecting any moment to see headlines flash: "Dr. Blake Di Angelo accused of being a nice guy. Truth soon to be revealed and partner to dump his sorry butt."

Because the last thing he was feeling in regard to Darby was *nice*.

He'd established that first thing that morning, and nothing had happened during the day to persuade him otherwise.

Darby was a wonderful woman, the best he knew, but their relationship was a strictly no-sex one. Not that they'd ever discussed sex—they hadn't. Not in regard to them having sex. There hadn't been a need.

He'd done his thing, she'd done hers, and the twain had never met.

But all his thoughts currently featured Darby, and no matter how many times he told himself to quit thinking of her in sexual terms his libido refused to cooperate.

Nice? She thought he was *nice*?

Surely after that scorching kiss they'd shared he rated more than "nice"? That kiss had practically had smoke curling from his fingers and toes and she called him a nice guy? What the—?

When the bathroom door opened, Blake was still

fuming. He wasn't a nice guy—didn't want Darby to think of him in that light. Which begged the question, how *did* he want her to think of him? Had he wanted that kiss to start fires inside Darby? Had he wanted her to see him as more than her business partner?

Glancing toward the door, he felt his body answer his question for him. He wanted Darby to want him, hoped his kiss had curled her toes and put stars in her eyes.

He wolf-whistled. Her hair was swept up in a fancy do, exposing the graceful lines of her neck. The blue dress clung in all the right places and sent his libido into hyper-drive.

And her shoes. Had he ever seen her in heels like those? Sexy black stilettos with a wide ankle strap that begged for a man's touch. He visually traced his way over her legs. His tongue stuck to the roof of his mouth. She was so tiny, but her legs went on and on. The heels pumped out the firm muscles of her calves, tightened the sliver of her quads that showed beneath the hem of her dress.

"You look amazing."

First turning, to give him the full effect of her outfit, unknowingly hardening him to mammoth proportions, she rewarded him with a smile. One that lit her eyes to sparkling blue gems and softened the fullness of her all too kissable pink lips.

"Thank you." Her gaze skimmed over his black pants, matching jacket, the blue shirt she'd suggested, and silver diamond-patterned tie. "You don't look too shabby yourself, City Boy."

Unable to drag his gaze from her, he drank in every delectable inch. "Let's forget the reunion and stay here, so I can prove to you how not nice I am."

Because her *nice* comment stung. What guy wanted to be described as nice?

Laughing, she rolled her eyes. "Be serious, Blake."

He was serious.

He wanted her. Enough that he was tempted to push her onto the bed, push up that silky hemline, remove whatever skimpy, groan-worthy scrap of silk she was wearing, and kiss her until she begged him to take her.

Which drew him up short.

This was Darby, not some flavor of the month. Despite the fact he'd been pretending to be in love with her all weekend, he wasn't. Acting on the sizzling attraction he was feeling toward her would ruin their business relationship, would ruin their friendship. A smart man would remember that.

Standing from the bed, he sighed with an exaggerated heave of his chest, determined to keep the mood light. She had enough on her plate tonight without having to deal with his unwanted sexual attraction. "If you refuse to stay here and let me see how few seconds it takes to get that dress off you, then let's go before I do my best to change your mind."

Her eyes gleaming with delight, she moved to the end of the bed. Her hips swayed, courtesy of her heels. "You're good for a girl's ego."

"That's me. *Nice*, and an ego booster."

"Don't make my compliment sound like a bad thing," she admonished, checking her appearance in the mirror. "It's not."

"Because that's how every man wants a beautiful woman to think of him. Nice, and her personal ego-fluffer."

She laughed nervously, smoothed her hands over her

skirt. "We're alone, Blake. You don't have to say things like that."

He eyed her curiously, wondering at her uneasiness. "Like what?"

"That I'm beautiful." She looked away, pink tingeing her cheeks. "Or that you want to get me out of my dress. You don't have to pretend when we're alone. Actually, I wish you wouldn't, because when you do I start believing things that aren't true."

Pretend? Was she kidding?

He walked around the bed, lifted her chin to force her gaze to his. Staring down into her blue eyes, he resisted the urge to kiss her until there was no doubt about what was pretense and what wasn't.

Instead, he stroked his finger along her jawbone, caressing her delicate features. He turned her toward the dresser, toward their reflection in the mirror. He stood directly behind her, close enough to feel her body heat, close enough to tease his senses with the brush of her dress against him. He was so hard he hurt, but this wasn't about him. This was about Darby.

Even with her high-rise shoes, she barely came up past his chin, but they looked good together—her blonde, blue-eyed perfection next to his dark Italian features.

"Look in the mirror, Darby," he urged, his gaze locked with hers. "See the woman I see. She's beautiful. Every red-blooded male is going to envy me tonight because they'll all know you'll be coming back here with me." He placed his hand on her bare shoulder, his fingers stroking over her soft skin, toying with the thin blue spaghetti strap of her dress. "You are a beautiful, intelligent, witty, desirable woman, and any man would count himself lucky to know you. I do."

Wordlessly, she stared at their reflection, her eyes big, blue, searching his. She swallowed, inhaled a quick breath, and her lips parted. "Blake, I—"

He couldn't breathe, thought he might suffocate at the heaviness that had come over his chest with his admission, with the way Darby was looking at him with a mixture of confusion and desire.

In that moment he knew he had to get out of the hotel, away from the queen-sized bed that called to him. He had to get air. Now.

Otherwise he'd forget thousands of years of human refinement, go Neanderthal, scoop Darby into his arms, and take what his every instinct dictated he possess.

"Come on, Dilly." He grabbed her wrist. "Let's go get this charade over with."

Before he forgot to be nice and was as bad as he wanted to be.

"We sure could use a doctor in town," the slightly overweight brunette intoned, giving Darby a dramatic look as they talked over the band playing Lynyrd Skynyrd in the background. "Just think what might have happened to poor Bobby's arm if you hadn't been here. Cindy said the doctor told her what a great job you did splinting his arm. Thank goodness you were here."

Darby smiled at Leah. They'd known each other since grammar school, but had never been close friends. The closest friend she'd ever had had stabbed her in the back. Over Trey.

"I second that," a tall, nice-looking man said, stepping up to where they talked. He shifted his beer to his other hand and stuck his hand out to her, then to Blake. "Mark Lytle—nice to meet you. Hey, Leah."

Darby shook his hand, trying to place him in her memory and coming up blank.

Seeing her confusion, he grinned. "I'm the local vet—moved here from Texas a few years back when Doc Tatum retired."

"Mark Lytle," she repeated, the name registering. She recalled her family mentioning him.

"I'm here with Debbie Earnhart. She's working the registration desk," he said, a friendly smile on his face. "Although it's definitely outside what I was trained to do, I'm forced to take care of minor human problems more often than you'd believe. Tell me how I can convince you to set up practice here."

Darby didn't say anything at first. Mostly because she didn't know what to say. She'd spent most of her teenage years wanting to get away from Armadillo Lake, yet in this moment she struggled to remember why, when her hometown really did need better access to healthcare. Her own mother would have to go out of town to have her shingles checked, and Carla had almost delivered in the back seat of John's truck because the closest doctor had been miles away.

"If I ever decide to relocate, I'll keep your offer in mind." Hopefully hiding her discomfort, she smiled. "Did you buy out old Doc Tatum's vet office?"

As she'd hoped, the conversation turned to Mark's animal health clinic. Several other couples joined them.

Blake stayed close to her side, attentive to her every need. His palm pressed low on her back in both possession and in reassurance that she could do this, had nothing to fear, and that he thought she was beautiful.

He didn't have to say the words again.

She could see the truth in his eyes when he looked

at her. Blake thought she was beautiful. On that, he wasn't pretending.

That alone kept a smile on her face, made her aware of his nearness at all times.

They made conversation with couples, ate buffet-style finger foods, and mingled—but all the while sexual tension sizzled between them, arcing higher and higher each time their gazes met, each time their fingers brushed against the other.

Tension that had been slowly building from the moment she'd asked him to pretend to be in love with her. Tension that had twisted her body into knots at waking curled against his body. Tension that had mounted during his possessive claim of her mouth under the oak tree. Tension that threatened to explode if he didn't quit looking at her as if he wanted to lick her from head to toe.

A commotion at the front of the room had Darby glancing that way. Mandy and Trey. Together. Homecoming Queen and King. Head cheerleader and star quarterback. Former best friend and former major crush.

For weeks she'd thought the sight of seeing them would be like taking a bullet to the heart. Surprisingly, she'd felt more regret over wasted time and heartache. During high school she'd lost her best friend—and over what? A guy. Okay, so when she'd been sixteen Trey had seemed like much more than just a guy, but what had she known back then? Not much.

Funny how time changed things.

Like her relationship with Blake.

Because this weekend *had* changed things between them.

When he'd kissed her earlier she'd burned right down

to her toes. She'd dreamed of him kissing her for years and now he really had. When she'd stared at her and Blake's reflections in the mirror she'd wanted him to kiss her again. She wanted him to kiss her now.

She wanted Blake in a way she'd never wanted anyone. She'd been attracted to him for years, but had always known he was a playboy at heart, had wanted more than what he gave to other woman. She'd settled to have him as her friend and partner, something he had reserved just for her. But this weekend, having his attention targeted on her, having him look at her with love in his eyes—well, she'd started believing the lies and wanting Blake's heart, wanting it badly enough that she wondered how she'd ever go back to the way things were if that was what Blake wanted.

"Darby?" He followed the direction of her gaze, cupped her elbow a bit too tight. "Are you okay?"

"I'm fine," she lied, knowing that if she ruined her relationship with Blake she'd never really be fine again. "I wasn't expecting to see them together."

Which was better than saying, *I wasn't expecting to want you even more than I already did—wasn't expecting to believe in your pretense of loving me since I know that's what it is—wasn't expecting to want to throw caution to the wind just because I can see you really do want to have sex with me.*

When Mandy's gaze connected with Darby's, she made a beeline toward them. Her glittery gold and brown dress hugged her trim figure as she smiled and waved. "I want to thank you for what you did for my cousin's little Bobby today."

Keeping a forced friendly expression plastered on her face, Darby nodded. "You're welcome. How is he?"

Mandy stood, looking gorgeous, but also equally awkward.

"Asleep." She sighed, giving a little shake of her beauty-salon-styled hair. "Cindy is with him. As part of the reunion committee she did a lot of work, trying to make this shindig a success. She shouldn't miss out on everything when Bobby is so sedated he won't know whether she's there or not."

Had it been *her* son lying in that hospital bed, Darby wouldn't have left him.

Her son?

Her blood pooled at her feet, leaving her light-headed. Where had that thought come from? Medicine had been her dream, the only one she'd ever given serious thought to after Trey. So why were there suddenly visions of dark-eyed, dark-haired toddlers dancing through her mind?

Mandy prattled on, looking almost as if she wasn't sure what to say next. She kept her smile in place, kept talking in her sweetest Southern twang. "But look at you." She motioned to Darby. "You always did want to be a doctor and now you are one, and you knew just the right thing to do when Bobby fell. You must be so proud."

Darby expected a "bless your heart" to hit her any moment. Why was Mandy being nice?

Unsure of her swirling emotions, Darby started to take a step back, but Blake's hand kept her in place, burned through the material of her dress, singeing her with reassurance that he was there if she needed him, that she needed to stand her ground.

Was she misreading the hope in Mandy's brown eyes?

"I only left the hospital a little while ago—had to get my hair done." She glanced at the blonde bangs hanging over her eyes. "The doctor said you did a fantastic job caring for Bobby. We were lucky you were here. You really should come home."

Armadillo Lake did need a doctor. Desperately.

But not her.

After a too-long silent stretch, Mandy gave a little wave of her fingers, and shot Blake an overly bright smile. "Well, I should mingle. After all, I was student body president and I am supposed to be the hostess."

Unsure what to think about the exchange, Darby watched Mandy blend into the crowd.

"Unbelievable," Blake breathed close to her ear. "She was trying to talk to you, and you cut her off. It's obvious she has regrets."

Turning toward him, Darby scowled. "Have you forgotten what she did to me?"

"No." His dark eyes cut into her. "I can't forget, because you won't tell me what she did. Why did you cut her down?"

Was he yet again taking Mandy's side? Were men so easily fooled by a pretty face? Was she forever to have her date defend Mandy? Would Blake leave the prom—the reunion—with Mandy, too?

Moisture pooled in her eyes, threatening to spill down her cheeks. She wouldn't cry. Not because of the past. Not because of whatever emotions ran through her, making her want to cling to Blake and beg him never to leave her, to never destroy her trust the way she'd been shattered at sixteen.

Which she would never do. Never again would she be so humiliated, so hurt by a man.

Not even Blake.

"Why don't you just butt out of things that aren't any

of your business?" she bit out, needing to put distance between them, needing to lash out at the sting she'd felt at his defense of Mandy. She spun to go in search of something to drink, and bumped into Trey near the bar.

"Hey, babe." He took a swig from the bottle of beer he held. "That was cool of you today with Bobby."

Still brewing over what Blake had said, she absently waved off Trey's praise. "It was no big deal—just what I do."

"Yeah, but not something most people can do—save someone's life. I'm impressed."

She blinked up at him. "I quit trying to impress you years ago." She hadn't really, she realized. Because every man she met, every man she dated, she saw through the pain she'd suffered at Trey's hands, saw without being able to trust in their words, their feelings for her.

"I've always felt bad about what happened." He glanced down at the drink in his hand, picked at the silver label with his fingernail. "But I didn't know how to tell you I was sorry. I wanted to, thought about it a million times, but finding the words to apologize for something like that wasn't something I seemed able to do."

"A simple 'I'm sorry' would have done."

"I'm sorry." He grinned, and she had a flash of remembrance of what she'd found so appealing about him. "Forgive me?"

Trey had only asked her out to get back with Mandy. It had worked. Whatever differences had split them up, when Mandy and another guy had pulled up to the lookout point, overlooking the lake, Trey, Darby's date—the guy she'd been making out with, planned to go all the way with—had jumped out of his car, punched Mandy's date and made up with her, leaving Darby to find her own way home.

"To be honest," he continued, "you scared the hell out of me. You were so smart, and knew exactly what you wanted out of life. I liked you, but felt like a goofy kid next to you." He sighed. "Then there was Mandy."

Yes, there had been Mandy—who had fallen for Trey at the same time Darby had. They'd idolized him from afar for years. When they'd been fifteen, Trey had fallen for Mandy. In the fallout, Mandy had dumped her friendship with Darby. It had only been when his relationship with Mandy had gone sour that he'd asked Darby out.

"I loved her, you know." He gave a self-deprecating shrug. "I admit what I did to you was wrong, was a sorry thing to do, but I never meant to hurt you that night."

No, he'd only meant to take everything she'd been willing to give—her virginity, her love, her wide-eyed trust—and then walk away the moment he and Mandy worked things out. Which they'd done.

Still, looking into Trey's sincere eyes, she did believe him. He'd been seventeen and a typical teenaged boy. Was it his fault she'd taken his loosely spoken words of affection to heart?

"Okay, I believe you didn't intentionally hurt me."

"Great. Let me buy you a drink. Friend to friend."

They weren't friends, and likely never would be. But her emotions were ragged from Mandy, Blake, and even from Trey. From the whole weekend. What would one drink hurt? It was what she'd come over here for, needing to escape the disapproval in Blake's eyes. He'd sided with Mandy. Didn't men always side with the Mandys of the world?

She shot a quick glance toward Blake. He sat at their table, his expression as dark as his eyes. He didn't have to crook his finger for her to know he wanted her back at their table, away from Trey. Not this time. This time her date would come to her, would claim her.

She lifted her chin and smiled at Trey. "Why not? I think you owe me a few."

"That I do." His gaze raked over her face and he grinned lazily. "And I intend to pay up in spades."

For the second time that day Blake interrupted Trey Nix making moves on his woman. "I'm cutting in."

"I don't want you to cut in," Darby argued, clinging to Nix's shoulders.

"Quit lying. The only reason you're on the dance floor is so I'd cut in."

Blake had stayed in the background, letting her stew on what had transpired between her and Mandy and come to realize she'd been the one to ask him to butt into her business by pretending to be in love with her in the first place.

Butt out of her business? Had she forgotten who'd invited whom?

He'd watched her down drink after drink with her first love, watched her glare defiantly, daring Blake to come get her, then flirt with Nix. He'd forced himself to wait for her to come to her senses, to be patient, but when she had gone into the other man's arms on the dance floor Blake had had enough, and butted into her life yet again.

Darby frowned.

Blake frowned right back, tugging her with enough force to unplaster her from Nix on the dance floor.

"Darby?" Trey said, lines creasing his forehead.

"Hold on a minute, Trey." She held up her fingers, then turned to Blake. "Maybe you should go find a friend to dance with and leave me alone."

"No more games, Darby. We both know who you came with tonight, and who you're leaving with. Me." He pulled her to him, holding her close so there was no doubt about who he meant.

"Are you so sure about that?" Her eyes flickered with annoyance, then softened, a smile curving her lips. "Did you just growl at me?"

He glanced into her happy eyes—eyes that made him want to dive into their unknown blue depths. "I growled. So sue me."

"You're a doctor—you should never say that," she warned, laughter spilling from her painted pink lips as she waved goodbye to Nix, where he still stood. Her gaze returned to Blake and she wrapped her arms around his neck. "Should never offer things you don't mean. Someone might take you up."

He inhaled her sweet scent. The fresh, light floral fragrance had been teasing him all night, making him want to lean in, making him hungry. Starved.

"You should never rub against a man who wants to kiss you, because he might take you up on your offer."

She stopped moving against him. The slightly dazed look in her eyes said she hadn't realized what she was doing, but then she smiled. "What took you so long, Blake? I thought you were never going to rescue me."

What had taken him so long? Rescue her? "You were the one who told me to butt out of your life," he reminded her, still more than a little irate at her blatant flirtation with Nix.

"I didn't mean it," she repented, without hesitation. Her eyes took on a serious hue, shone up at him with wide-eyed sincerity. "I want you in my life. Always, Blake. Just you."

His stomach somersaulted, making his insides churn. Just him. Noting the tremble in her lower lip, the fruit on her breath, he stared closer. Another growl rumbled from his throat. "How much liquor did that jerk ply you with?"

"Liquor?" She blinked, tightening her arms around his neck, laughter in her eyes as she toyed with the hair at his nape. "Trey didn't give me liquor. Just punch." She licked her lips. "Mmm, it was good. Best punch I ever had."

He might have laughed at her innocence if her pink tongue tracing over her lips hadn't put his entire body into a vice, hadn't grabbed hold of every nerve cell and demanded full attention.

"You're drunk, Darby. I should take you upstairs."

"I'm not drunk." She stared at his mouth. "But take me upstairs, please." Her long lashes brushed her cheeks. "What would you like to do to me first?"

Blake almost tripped over his feet. A million different items volleyed for first place in the "what he'd like to do to Darby" list. He wanted to do them all. He wanted to act on each and every vivid thought in his head. With Darby.

He gulped. "Maybe going back to our room isn't such a great idea."

Darby's lower lip pouted. "Why not?"

He tried to laugh off the way he felt, as if he didn't believe she was serious. "I might take advantage of you."

"Isn't that the idea?" Her fingers tightened in his

hair. She stood on her tiptoes and looked deep into his eyes, her expression inviting. "Let's go. Take advantage of me. Now."

There she went, getting Darby bossy again.

Didn't she know that turned him on? That *she* turned him on? More than any woman. Her earlier words seared through his mind. She'd told him to butt out of her life. Words that had cut deep. Words he should heed rather than the ones she currently shot at him. A smart man *would* butt out of her life.

"You don't know what you're doing."

"Yes, I do." She tugged on his hand, moving against him in a slow sway. "I want to make love with you. *Now*."

She spoke loud—loud enough that the couples around them heard and snickered.

"Guess we know for definite that Dilly didn't die a virgin."

Blake wanted to assure them Darby was the *least* likely woman to die a virgin. But, although Darby had occasionally dated, she'd managed to keep each of the boyfriends at arm's length, never really letting them close, finding faults in each that allowed her to remain in control.

He'd always admired her control. Now he wondered if her control had been a safety mechanism, a way of making men butt out of her life when they tried to get close.

He suspected he knew more about her, that he was closer to her than any man she'd dated, and until today he'd never so much as kissed her. *Was she a virgin?*

The idea was impossible for his brain to wrap around.

No way was the hottest woman he knew a virgin.

Still, the possibility struck him and he couldn't let it go—no matter how many times he tried to dismiss the notion as ridiculous.

"Are you?"

She rested her head against his shoulder, swaying in rhythm with him on the dance floor. "Am I what?"

"A virgin?"

Still punch-happy, she smiled up at him, her eyes starry, her lower lip pouty, begging to be kissed. "If I was, would you promise to save me from my 'most likely' curse?"

CHAPTER SEVEN

DEAR Lord, had she really just asked Blake to make love to her? To save her from her virginity?

Darby giggled to cover her nervousness.

She was nervous. For the first time she'd asked a man to make love to her. Not just any man, but Blake Di Angelo—the man she'd been waiting for her entire life.

Because she loved him.

Had always loved him.

"Is that what you want, Darby?" His hands brushed across her cheek, cupped her face so he could study her so intently she wondered what he saw. "For me to make love to you?"

More than her next breath.

Calling upon every ounce of courage she possessed, she stretched, tentatively touched her mouth to his, hoping to show him as words couldn't convey just how much she wanted him.

Would he push her away? Tell her she was crazy? That he couldn't want a woman who was more brains than beauty, who was so the opposite of the women he usually dated?

She tasted the soda on his tongue, tasted the masculinity that was pure Blake. Eyes wide, she deepened the kiss. He let her set the pace, but his rapidly hardening body was far from immune to her kisses.

He pushed her into a darkened corner of the ballroom, lifted her chin. "I want you, Darby. Tell me you want me to make love to you because you want me and not because you're drunk."

She barely registered when the music stopped, the lights brightened, and Mandy spoke into a microphone.

"I'm not drunk." She pulled back, smiled softly up at him, her fingers twisted in the hair at his nape. Lord, how she loved his hair. How she loved him. "I want you. Take me to our room and make love to me."

Blake's black eyes narrowed, his body tensed, and Darby wondered if she'd made a mistake. Had she lost him forever with her boldness? In admitting so much of her heart? He'd said he wanted her, too. Surely he wouldn't be frightened away by her honesty in telling him what she wanted? Namely him.

Or was Blake like Trey? Were his words loosely spoken during make-out sessions? Uncertainty flooded her. What if he didn't really want her? If he'd realized she could never be good enough? What if they made love and she couldn't please him? What if he decided he liked her better for her brains than her body? She wanted Blake to want both. The whole package. All of her.

Please, God, let him love her.

Because, no matter what the cost, no matter what the consequences, tonight she was laying her heart on the line. Because she didn't want to be just Blake's business partner or his friend. She wanted him. As her lover. As the man who wanted to share his life with her. Always.

If they weren't meant to be, she didn't want to go through life without knowing, without having taken that chance at grasping her dream.

Because in that moment her biggest fear was never taking that risk with Blake, never knowing *what if...?*

His jaw shifted. "You're sure?"

"More sure than I've ever been about anything." She was. She didn't want to continue pretending that she didn't love him when she did. She didn't want to pretend her heart didn't race when he walked into a room. She didn't want to pretend not to want to spend every moment of her life with him. Unable to guard her heart, she stared at him, willing him not to hurt her. "Please want me, too."

"I do. More than you'd believe." He cupped her face, kissed her so thoroughly she thought she might melt. He grabbed her hand. "Let's go, Dilly."

"About time, City Boy," she quipped back, practically running to keep up with his long strides out of the ballroom.

Nervous excitement fluttered in Darby's belly.

Tonight she was going to give herself to Blake and take whatever he was willing to give of himself.

The elevator door slid shut, locking out the world. He stared straight ahead, not looking at her.

"Blake?"

"Not now, Darby," he barked, startling her into taking a step back.

She wilted. This had all been a bit of a fantasy. One that she should have known better than to believe. "You've changed your mind?"

He turned, scorched her with his hot black eyes. "Unless you want me to wrap those long legs of yours around my waist and take you right here in the elevator, and the world be damned, I advise you to stand over there, look pretty, and be quiet."

Her lips rounded in a surprised "O". Why had she doubted him? Been so quick to think he'd changed his mind? That she'd be lacking in his eyes?

She wasn't sixteen anymore. She was a grown woman who knew the man she wanted and was wanted back by that man. She wouldn't doubt him again.

She took a step closer to him, displaying a smile on her face and a great deal of leg.

Blake shut the hotel room door, taking Darby in his arms immediately. She tasted good. Like a tall drink of water—and he was a man dying of thirst.

If the elevator hadn't dinged that they'd arrived at their floor the moment it had, they likely wouldn't have gotten out.

Her fingers curled into his hair, tugging him closer, urging him to kiss her more deeply. Her body squirmed against his, pushing him to the edge of sanity.

When her tongue slid between his lips and into the recesses of his mouth he fell. Deep. Hard. Swiftly. Fell into an abyss that was only him and Darby and the intense passion burning between them.

He wanted to be inside her. Had wanted to be inside her all evening. All day. Forever.

A warning rang in his head. A warning he would usually have listened to, but not tonight. Tonight he was going to have Darby. All night. Every way. She was going to be his.

Darby was his.

Tomorrow he'd worry about the consequences.

About the nagging voice that kept saying he shouldn't do this.

Tonight was his, to explore her body, to kiss every inch of her, to commit every nook and cranny of her body to memory.

Tonight he'd know what it felt like to drown in the blue of her eyes, to lose himself in her smile, to taste the sweetness of her skin, thread his fingers into the long tresses of her thick hair, and to know Darby belonged to him.

She stared up at him, her eyes hazy, her lips swollen from his kisses. "Love me, Blake."

With her demand, she reached for his belt, undid the catch with amazing speed and pulled the leather strap free from his pants. Her fingers curled around the belt.

He clasped her wrists, took the belt from her with ease. "Slow down, babe. We're not in a hurry."

Although he longed to reach the finish line, this was one race he planned to savor every step along the way.

With a clang, his belt landed on the bureau.

He turned back to the most beautiful woman he'd ever known, the most seductive. Slow and tender, he claimed her mouth, capturing her sigh of pleasure.

"Blake..." she murmured against his lips. She pushed at his jacket, dropping it off his shoulders and down his arms. He stepped back to let the jacket fall to the floor.

Her gaze locked with his, she undid the buttons of the blue shirt that matched the exact shade of her desire-filled eyes. A shirt he'd bought for that very reason—because the color reminded him of her. When she'd undone the last button, she tugged the material from his waistband, brushed her hands over his chest and removed his shirt.

Bare-chested, standing in his dress pants, he waited to see what she'd do next. He wasn't disappointed.

She ran her fingers along his abdomen. Sighing in appreciation, she bent, pressed her lips to his sternum, his collarbone, his throat. She rained kisses over his goose-pimpled flesh until he could stand no more.

"I want to taste you, Darby. Let me."

"All you had to do was ask." She turned, presenting her back for him to help remove her dress.

Inch by torturous inch he lowered the zipper, revealing more and more of her creamy skin, more and more of the black strapless bra. When he reached the indention of her low back, he pushed the blue spaghetti straps from her shoulders, slid the dress down her hips and let the material puddle at her feet.

She stood in the skimpy black underwear and garters he'd fantasized about only the night before, wearing heels that made her legs endless and his fantasies eternally grateful.

He swallowed, knowing her image was forever burned into his brain, knowing he never wanted to forget the way she looked or the desire for him in her eyes.

"You're beautiful." His voice rasped like that of a schoolboy, but he was thankful sound came forth at all, considering how thick his throat had grown.

"Thank you."

"I mean it, Darby." He ran his palms over her arms, laced his fingers with hers. "You are beautiful."

"So are you." Her gaze raked over him, reinforcing her praise, making him even harder.

She stepped into his embrace.

She tucked her head beneath his chin, wrapped her

arms around his neck, and swayed to a tune that only they could hear.

He moved with her, each sway of their bodies exciting him more, each kiss, each touch building the momentum of what was to come.

His hands moved lower, trailing along her spine, cupping her bottom through the black silk. He lifted her to him, hip to hip, his hardness pressing into her softness. The contact wasn't enough. He needed to be closer to her, needed to be inside her.

With him supporting her weight, and her arms wrapped around his neck, she raised her legs, pressing snugly against him, encircling his waist.

His legs turned to water and, not wanting to drop her, he moved forward, sitting her on the bureau. Her legs remained around him, the juncture of her body pressed enticingly against his groin. They kissed, over and over, touched, explored each other's bodies in hungry greed.

Blake undid the back clasp of her bra, freeing her breasts, taking a taut nipple into his mouth.

"Oh, Blake, that feels good. So good," she moaned, arching her spine toward him.

"It's going to feel better."

"Promise me you won't stop," she begged, her hands cupping his face, forcing him to look at her. "Ever."

"I'm not stopping, Darby. Not tonight. Not ever." Why would she think he'd stop? "Unless this isn't what you want?"

"*You* are what I want."

He'd never heard sweeter words. A rumble caught in his throat, emerging as a low growl. "As long as you want me, I'm yours."

* * *

Darby couldn't believe how bold she was. Blake might have been right when he'd said she was drunk. She certainly felt light-headed, intoxicated. Intoxicated, but amazingly powerfully feminine at the same time.

Blake's body responded to every caress of her fingers, to even the lightest touch of her mouth against his flesh.

Never had she imagined a man could be so in tune with her thoughts, her body, her desires. Never had she imagined she'd be so able to read how her touch made his skin burn, how her mouth triggered heat deep in his gut.

Knowing Blake wanted her as much as she wanted him was the most amazing feeling of her life.

He scooped her into his arms, carried her to the bed, and jerked the comforter back. He laid her down, kissed her, removed a condom packet from his wallet, and shed his pants with lightning speed.

She'd been right. He was beautiful.

"I want to make this good for you."

Didn't he know that as long as it was he who touched her, this would be good?

He unhooked her garters, slid her panties from her hips, pausing to kiss her thighs, her knees. Careful not to tangle the material on her heels, he pulled the scraps of black silk free from her body, then kissed her again. All over.

Holy smoke. How could a kiss light so many fires?

Fires that raged burning hot. How could his fingers trailing over the same places cause such tingling? Such liquid heat at her very center?

He was torturing her with his slow touches, his purposeful seduction of her senses. She wanted him. Inside her. Making her whole.

Pulling on his shoulders, she tugged him to her, locked her mouth with his, rotated her hips beneath him in a seductive rhythm. His body matched it, grinding against her, above her, pinning her beneath him, pressing her into the bed.

He slipped on a condom. Then he was filling her, breaking every barrier, stretching her body to accommodate his girth.

She muffled her cry of pain into the curve of his neck, dug her fingers into his shoulders, and prayed he didn't notice.

"Darby," he groaned, staring down at her with concern in his black eyes. "You weren't really a virgin, were you?"

"I'm not a virgin," she promised, not wanting him to stop, afraid he would. Afraid she wouldn't feel the ultimate pleasure his kisses, his fingers had promised would be hers with their consummation. She raised her hips, taking him deeper, moving her body against him, feeling pain give way to the pleasure she sought, welcoming the electricity spreading through her inner thighs.

She hadn't lied. She wasn't a virgin.

Not anymore.

Darby's head throbbed, her eyes burned, and her muscles screamed in protest at the night's activities. Her lips felt bruised, and she'd tossed her head back and forth to the point she'd never get the tangles from her hair.

Still, she smiled as she stretched.

What an amazing night. She ached in places she hadn't known she could ache. A good ache. Like when you'd run a marathon and won. Like when you'd been made love to over and over by a man who couldn't get enough of you.

She had.

Sweet and tender, hot and fast, Blake had claimed every inch of her body.

She'd done some claiming, too.

She smiled at the memories. Blake's groans of pleasure at her touch, his worshipping of her body and his teasing her awake with kisses when she'd thought she was too tired for more. She'd been wrong.

Not bad for a beginner.

With the way Blake had held on to her afterwards, she'd say not bad at all. They'd been good together. She didn't have to have experience to know they'd shared something special.

Was it because she loved everything about him? His eyes, his smile, his spicy scent, his pin-up abs that she'd licked every indention of, his intelligence, his…? Oh, she loved him. Enough said.

Rolling onto her side, she opened her eyes, ready to wake him and tell him every emotion in her heart. Instead she looked into black eyes.

Black eyes that were filled with regret. And guilt. And more regret.

Her elation fizzled like a deflating balloon that lay lifeless on the ground.

"Don't even say it," she warned, putting up her hand to shield herself from his recriminations. She didn't want to hear about how he regretted what they'd shared, didn't want him to make the most beautiful night of her life something cheap, shabby, wrong.

"Say what?"

As if he didn't know.

"What I see in your eyes."

"And that would be…?"

"That you think last night was a mistake." Maybe it had been a mistake, but, wow, on the scale of one to ten last night had been an eleven. An amazing *hallelujah* eleven.

He lay back on his pillow, stared at the ceiling, and ran his oh-so-talented fingers through his hair. "You were a virgin, weren't you?"

She couldn't tell him. Not with the angst already lacing his voice. Didn't he understand that she'd awakened wanting to love him forever, not face recriminations?

"I'm not a virgin, Blake, but until last night with you Trey was—" She stopped, knowing by the way Blake's head snapped toward her that she'd said the wrong thing.

"Trey?" Sitting straight up, he spat the name at her. "You slept with Nix? Is that what you meant to say? That he was the only man you'd slept with until last night?"

"No." She hadn't meant to say that. She'd meant to say that there hadn't been anyone she'd ever cared enough to have sex with except Trey, and Trey had been a silly schoolgirl crush.

"Don't lie to me, Darby."

She might have told him the truth—that, had he wanted her innocence, she'd have given her virginity to Trey on the night of her junior prom. But Trey had left her willing body to go to Mandy. She might have told him that every time she'd gotten sexually close to a man she'd backed away because she'd heard Mandy's voice telling her she'd die a virgin, and she'd wondered at her reasons for being with whatever man she'd been with since she hadn't loved any of them. The moment she had that thought she'd always stopped, and usually ended the relationship soon thereafter.

Last night she hadn't had any such thoughts. All she'd known, thought, *everything* had centered around the man lying next to her.

She'd been consumed one hundred percent by Blake.

But she bristled at his tone, bristled at the way his nostrils flared and the pulse hammered at his throat.

What right did he have to judge her if she *had* stupidly slept with Trey all those years ago? It wasn't as if Blake hadn't slept his way through enough beauties to fill a little black book—a big black book, for that matter.

"Just because we had sex it does not give you the right to suffocate me."

"Suffocate you?"

"Like Rodney," she accused, knowing Blake wasn't the only one who knew how to push buttons.

His nostrils flared. "Well, apparently you didn't sleep with Rodney, or any of the other guys you've dated during the time I've known you."

"No." Had the covers just shifted lower on his abdomen? How could she look at those flat planes and long to touch him during the middle of an argument? How could she want him so much after three times during the night?

"Why not?" He moved, and the sheets barely covered vital parts.

"Because I didn't want to." Please don't let the sheets slip lower. Not if she was to keep her sanity, her cool.

He punched his pillow, bunching the foam underneath him. He regarded her for several long seconds. "Why me?"

"Because…"

He stared at her, his expression as black as his eyes. "Was it was because of him?"

"I have no idea what you're talking about."

"Because Nix turned you on last night? Is that why you slept with me? Was sleeping with me some type of revenge?"

Was he crazy?

"Our having sex had nothing to do with Trey." Far, far from it.

"Right." He sounded angry. "We've known each other for a couple of years and nothing like this has happened. Throw loverboy into the picture and within twenty-four hours we're going at it. You can't tell me that's coincidence."

She could tell him lots of things. Like how hurt she was that he'd launched into an argument first thing that morning, when she'd been filled with such giddiness at what they'd shared.

"Believe what you want. I don't care." Okay, so she cared. Too much.

She had to get out of there now. Before she burst into tears. She swung her legs off the bed, hating that she was naked, but having no choice other than to pull the sheet around her toga-style. Somehow the thought of doing that made her feel more vulnerable than her nudity. To hide her body would be admitting she had something to hide.

How could she have thought of Trey when the man next to her consumed her every thought? The usual voices, the usual doubts—they hadn't come. Only she'd come. Time and again, in Blake's strong arms.

Shouldn't she be the one with regrets? Blake

should be an old pro at mornings after. This was her first. Surely there was something wrong with his being the one upset?

Of course she knew what the differences were. She'd been making love to him, and he'd been having sex with her.

Big difference.

This morning, first thing, he'd started a fight. Why? To put distance between them? To keep her from getting ideas that last night had meant something to him beyond sex?

Her back to him, she stood from the bed. Before she took a step, he grabbed her arm, pulled her back into the bed. "Where do you think you're going?"

Super-conscious of her nudity, she toppled onto him, her breasts squashing against his bare chest, making her even more aware of her lack of clothing. "Let me go."

His gaze locked with hers, he wrapped his arms around her, pinning her to him. He shook his head. His nose rubbed against hers more by accident than design. "Not until we finish this conversation."

"I don't want to talk to you." She wiggled against him, trying to free herself. After only a few seconds she realized all she was doing was turning them both on. He'd grown amazingly hard against her belly.

She'd grown amazingly hungry to feel him inside her.

Truth was, she'd awakened wanting him.

Had that been why he pulled her into bed? Because, despite whatever recriminations he had, he wanted her too? Had that been why she'd half-heartedly fought for her freedom, moving against his naked body with her own?

"Darby?" Her name came out on a low growl from deep in his throat. Desire shone in his eyes. Desire for her.

Her gaze lowered to his mouth. Soft, and full of the ability to give her pleasure. Maybe he was right. Maybe they did need to talk before this went further.

"Kiss me," he demanded.

"No." She wanted to, but somehow she held out. Somehow found the strength to pull away from him again. Probably from the hurt she felt at the regret she'd seen in his eyes. How could he look at her like that and then ask her to kiss him as if nothing had happened? They couldn't have sex again if he was only going to regret it afterwards.

"Yes." He lifted his head, straining to meet her lips, but Darby held just out of his reach.

In a quick roll, Blake pinned her beneath his long frame. His eyes dark, filled with fire, he lowered his mouth to hers, kissed her deeply. Kissed her until she was breathless and clinging to him, until she burned from the inside out.

"I want you, Darby."

"You said we needed to finish our conversation," she stubbornly reminded him, scared of how much she wanted him.

"Maybe we don't need words to communicate," he murmured against her mouth, his gaze locked with hers, waiting for her acquiescence. Why was she fighting him? Even if she never had anything beyond this day, she'd have this moment in time when Blake had wanted her. He must have seen the capitulation in her eyes, felt the softening of her body, because he claimed her mouth, body, and soul.

For the next half-hour, they didn't need anything but each other. Words would only have gotten in their way.

CHAPTER EIGHT

FRESHLY showered, and finished packing the last of her belongings from the hotel closet, Darby frowned at the number on the cellular phone in her hand.

Jim. Was he calling to invite her and Blake to her mother's Sunday lunch? Her mom always cooked big on Sundays, so the entire family could gather after church services. Darby had called and checked on her yesterday, but guilt slammed her. She should have gone by prior to the picnic.

Now, the last thing she wanted was her family witnessing whatever was happening between her and Blake. She hit the answer button on her phone anyway. "Hey, what's up?"

"I know you're probably already headed out of town, but I think you need to check on Mom."

The hotel room door opened and Blake stepped into the room. He'd carried his bag down to his SUV and come back for hers. His gaze met hers, but quickly glanced away. No smile. No wink. Just regrets. So far today, in bed, their bodies tangled together, was the only time he'd seemed comfortable with her.

"Why?" she asked her brother, watching Blake

move around the room, checking to make sure they hadn't forgotten anything. "Is her shingles bothering her more today?"

"Dad called to say she didn't feel well and could I feed the livestock. I stopped in to check her after finishing."

A cold chill of premonition ran down Darby's spine. "And?"

"She doesn't look right. Her skin is pale and she keeps clutching at her chest. She says she can't catch her breath, and when she stands she feels like she's going to pass out. She's barely been off the sofa all morning, but she refuses to let me take her to the hospital in Pea Ridge."

Darby's blood ran cold. "Call the emergency services. Give her an aspirin. I'll be right there."

Blake tossed Darby's bags into the back of the SUV.

"Since I know the way, I'm driving." She held out her hand. "We'll get there quicker."

Although he'd have preferred to drive, especially with Darby looking so shaken, he didn't argue, just handed over his keys and got into the passenger seat.

He understood she needed to be doing something. Anything. He'd felt similar emotions when he'd been six and his grandfather had died. Wasn't that when he'd decided to become a doctor? When he'd watched his mother, crying over his grandfather's body, neither of them knowing what to do?

Throughout his aimless, spoilt life that had been the one constant: his desire to become a doctor.

His mother hadn't understood. His grandfather had been a wealthy man, had left that wealth to his daughter and grandson. To his knowledge, his mother had never worked a day in her life, just flitted from city to city, from one social scene to the next.

Blake had hated the constant moving, never having roots. But for the first time in his life he'd awakened this morning understanding his mother's drive to move. He'd wanted to pack his bags and take off and not have to face what he'd done. What he'd ruined with Darby.

A night of sex—damn good sex—would lead them into troubled waters that were sure to prevent them from ever returning to their former relationship.

The fact he'd taken her virginity—and he knew he had, despite what she'd said and his momentary lapse of blinding jealousy over Nix—complicated things even more.

Darby had been a twenty-eight-year old-virgin and he'd taken that from her. What the hell had he been thinking? He should have stopped the moment he'd realized.

He shouldn't have been in a position of realizing.

She was his partner, his friend, his colleague. He'd had sex with her. Now what? What would she expect of him? She'd acted as if sex between them was no big deal, but he'd seen the hurt in her eyes, felt that hurt rip into his gut. What did that mean? What did he want it to mean?

What he wanted to do was go back to the point where she'd asked him to come with her this weekend and take his answer back. Surely he could have come up with a few thousand reasons why he couldn't go to Alabama this weekend?

Darby honked the horn at the car in front of them. Despite the solid yellow line, she swerved into the other lane to pass the car.

He braced himself by holding onto the dashboard. "You're not going to do anyone any good if you run off the road."

"I'm not going to run off the road." She didn't bother looking at him, just continued to fly down the highway.

He stared at her pale features, fighting the need to reach out and touch her, to offer comfort. "You're trembling."

"So?" she asked, leaving part of his tires on the pavement when she rounded the turn to take them up the long drive to her parents' farm.

So he wanted to comfort her. But knew he wouldn't. After last night, this morning, he needed to put distance between them, to steadfastly work on restoring their former relationship.

Maybe if they cooled things down, pretended nothing had happened, eventually they'd get back to where they'd been, back to what Blake knew had been the happiest time of his life. Why had he ruined everything by taking her to bed?

Last night had been amazing, the best sex of his life, but no sex was worth losing Darby. Deep in his gut, he knew he'd lose her before all was said and done, and he wanted to howl in frustration at his stupidity.

The SUV came to a jarring stop as Darby braked hard in front of the house. Without waiting for him, she jumped out of the vehicle and ran up the steps, across the wide porch, and into the house.

Blake got out, opened the rear of the SUV, and pulled a black doctor's bag from beneath the back seat.

What met him when he entered the house had his heart dropping to the soles of his shoes.

Nellie Phillips lay on the living room floor, her family

huddled around her. Darby was straddling her, doing CPR on her chest, tears streaming down her ashen cheeks.

Oh, hell.

Please don't die, Momma. Please don't die.

Darby begged over and over as she used all her strength to compress her mother's chest, as she blew life-saving breath into her mother's mouth.

Vaguely, she was aware of Blake dropping down next to her, rummaging in his bag, and withdrawing a syringe to inject her mother with adrenaline.

"Let me do the compressions."

Although her arms had turned to jelly she didn't stop, couldn't break her rhythm.

Don't die, Momma. I'm here.

She couldn't stop for even the briefest of seconds to let him take over. But when she bent to give her mother a breath Blake replaced her hands with his, compressing her mother's chest.

Wanting to collapse from the mental and physical strain, Darby gave her mother a breath every fifth compression Blake made.

As if in a dream, she heard her brothers talking, heard Rosy crying, heard her father's fearful voice. Her gaze went to Blake, watched him compress her mother's chest, his muscles flexing with each attempt to restart her mother's heart.

In a haze, she breathed into her mother's lifeless mouth. Praying. Wanting to cry. Wanting to be the daughter. Not the doctor trying to save a life.

Breathe, Momma, please breathe.

"See how far away the emergency services are,"

Blake ordered. "Tell them we need them here stat. We need a damned defibrillator."

"They've sent a helicopter," Jim said, holding a crying Rosy to his side even as he talked into his cellular phone.

But they didn't have a defibrillator.

Her mother's heart wasn't beating and they didn't have a defibrillator.

Darby's own heart hurt, wanted to burst from the pressure inside it.

No, her mother couldn't die.

Please, God, please don't take her. I need my Momma. I didn't know how much, but I need her in my life.

"I have a pulse, Darby. I have a pulse," Blake practically shouted, sounding almost as relieved as the feeling washing over Darby.

Her mother sputtered, sucked in a ragged breath.

Darby kissed her forehead. "Breathe, Momma, take another breath. I need you to take another breath."

Darby thanked God when she felt the light breath from her mother's nostril blow against her skin. "She's breathing. Oh, Blake, she's breathing."

He nodded, easing his compressions. She checked her mother's breathing while he checked her heart-rate.

"Respirations are ten."

"Pulse is fifty-six," he said, at almost the same time.

Too low, but a big improvement over not at all.

Please, Momma, hang in there. Just keep breathing.

The whir of a helicopter could be heard in the distance, and Darby's inner sigh of relief shook her entire body.

"Pulse is fifty-two," Blake said. "Thank God the helicopter is here."

Her mother's eyes fluttered open; she looked at her.

Her lips moved, softly speaking, but Darby couldn't make out what she said.

She leaned forward. "What is it, Momma? I'm here."

"Home." Was the only word Darby could make out. "Home."

The flight paramedic rushed into the house, took a quick history from Blake and Darby, while another paramedic put in an IV and administered medication.

"There's only room for one of you to ride in the copter with us."

Darby wanted to go with her mother, but glanced toward her father. He looked ill himself, as if little of his lifeblood pulsed through his pale body.

"Go with her," he said, his voice rumbling with emotion. "Go with her and take care of her for me."

Darby nodded, wanting to hug him, but knowing the paramedic wouldn't wait for her.

"I'll drive your father to the hospital, Darby," Blake said.

"Or he can ride with Rosy and I," Jim spoke up from where he stood next to their father.

Darby didn't wait to see how they worked out the logistics of who was riding with whom. She rushed out of the house, staying next to the stretcher that carried her mother, and with each step she took her prayers grew more and more fervent.

They'd gotten her mother's heart restarted, but had they been too late? Had she suffered brain damage from lack of oxygen? Would her heart be strong enough to keep beating?

Torn in a thousand directions, Blake laced his hands with Darby's, knowing she wouldn't stay seated on the waiting room sofa for long. She'd paced almost non-stop. But he wanted her to know that no matter what had happened between them the night before, this morning he was here for her. He hated what she was going through, and wished he could take away her worries. He gave her a gentle squeeze.

Her gaze dropped to their hands. Surprising him, she scooted closer and laid her head against his shoulder.

Fighting the panic rising in his chest, he wrapped his arm around her, pulling her close and taking her hand back in the opposite hand.

She needed him right now. In ways that had nothing to do with their having had sex. She needed him as her friend and colleague. It was okay if he held her, comforted her. It was no more than he'd have done even if they hadn't spent the night having sex.

"Thank you," she said softly. "I don't know what I'd have done if you hadn't been with me, Blake."

He understood. He had felt as if he was six years old again when he'd stepped into the room and seen Darby's mother lying on the floor. Only this time he'd known what to do. Just as Darby had.

"You'd have done everything that needed doing. Just as you always do," he assured her, knowing it was true. Darby was the most capable woman he'd ever known.

"I felt so helpless, so weak, as if nothing I was doing made any difference," she whispered, so low he barely heard her.

"You saved her life, Darby."

"We both did." She sucked in a deep breath. "I'm glad we were here."

"Me, too," he agreed, although the truth was he

wished he'd never stepped foot in Armadillo Lake, never crossed lines that shouldn't have been crossed. But now wasn't the time to deal with his recriminations. Not when Darby's mother fought for her life. Right now Darby needed him, and he'd be here for her. Once they were back in Knoxville he'd deal with straightening things out between them. "Armadillo Lake needs a doctor."

"She can't die, Blake. I couldn't bear it if she died." Darby's eyes closed, her body tensed, but she didn't say anything else.

He glanced up, his gaze meeting Darby's oldest brother's blue eyes. Jim didn't say anything, just took in how Darby leaned against Blake before nodding his approval.

Would her brother be nodding if he knew Blake had stolen his sister's virginity? That he'd taken something precious from her? Him, a man who used women for pleasure, gave pleasure in return, but never wanted anything more.

His stomach churned with guilt. Darby deserved better than what he offered women. She deserved roses, romance, and happily ever after. Things Blake had no reason to believe in, much less any desire to give.

Her entire family was in the waiting room now. Jim had called his brothers, and most had met them at the hospital. He'd driven his father and Rosy to the hospital. Blake had followed in his SUV.

"She's going to be okay, isn't she?" Darby spoke low, and Blake understood the reasons why. All day she'd been strong, had been the one fielding her family's questions. Only with him did she feel she could let her guard down enough to show the slightest weakness, the slightest fear.

Her raw pain caught him in the solar plexus.

"Yes," he answered, hoping he told the truth. Darby's mother had suffered a myocardial infarction and, according to the emergency room physician, was currently being examined by the cardiologist on staff. Blake stroked Darby's hair, kissed the top of her head. "She's going to be fine, sweetheart. You'll see."

Blake willed that to be the case, trying not to wince at his use of the endearment. In that moment he'd have done anything to keep her from hurting, anything to comfort her and give her happiness, and quite frankly that scared the hell out of him.

"Darby, we need to talk—"

"Oh, Darby, I just heard about your mother." Mandy Coulson and Trey Nix entered the waiting area. "Bobby had his surgery this morning," Mandy continued, before any of them could say a word. "Trey and I have been with Cindy, waiting in his hospital room. We stepped out to get a drink and ran into Carla. She told us everything."

Darby tensed in Blake's arms. Because of Mandy? Because of Nix? From desire? Hating the jealousy flowing through his green veins, Blake tightened his hold.

"I'm sorry to hear about your mother, Darby," Nix said, standing awkwardly near them.

Darby pulled loose from Blake's arms, straightened, smiled at the couple. "Thank you. That's sweet of you."

Sweet? Blake scowled.

"Is there anything we can do?" Mandy stepped closer.

Darby shook her head. "I don't think so."

Mandy's gaze lowered, then she nodded, as if in understanding of Darby's cool tone. "We'll keep her in our prayers."

Darby stared straight at Mandy, her expression unreadable. "Thank you."

The cardiologist stepped into the waiting room and all eyes turned to him.

"Mrs. Phillips has suffered an acute MI, but thus far isn't showing any major residual damage. She's going to be admitted for observation. I'm going to do an arteriogram in the morning, but overall she's a very lucky woman."

Everyone breathed a sigh of relief.

When the cardiologist left the waiting area, Darby couldn't resist looking to see if Blake had noticed the amount of tan flesh on display beneath Mandy's Daisy Dukes. Her gaze collided with his dark one.

He'd been looking at her. Why?

She couldn't read his thoughts—wished she could.

Had she really spent the night in his arms, opening her body and her heart to him? Feeling as if their souls were connected? Could one really share something so beautiful with a person and not know what to say mere hours later?

He leaned back in the uncomfortable waiting room chair, eyeing her as if she were an anomaly. No doubt she was. He dated a certain type of woman, and she wasn't it.

Her throat tightened. What was going to happen to them? Why did she even care? What was most important was that her mother was going to be okay. Still, she couldn't look away from Blake's dark eyes, couldn't help but wish he loved her.

She'd leaned on him, but she'd felt his tension, felt the awkwardness in the way he held her. Everything had changed between them and it made her sick. The entire day made her sick. First what had happened with Blake, and then her mother.

"I need some fresh air," she said, to no one in particular.

Blake stood as if to follow, maybe to confront her over what had happened between them, or maybe he'd seen the longing in her eyes and wanted to nip those thoughts in the bud.

Rising from where she sat with Trey, Mandy grabbed her hand. "I'll go with you."

Huh? Darby stared at her former friend, wondering why she could possibly want to go with her.

Darby didn't say anything, just left the waiting room.

"I'm glad your mother is going to be okay," Mandy said when they stood outside the emergency room entrance.

"Me, too."

"I'm sorry, Darby." Mandy stared at her hands, took a deep breath and continued. "I had no right to do what I did."

Darby didn't have to ask what she meant. "Why did you?"

"Trey."

"You were the one to dump him," Darby reminded her.

"Because I thought he had feelings for you, and then he asked you to the prom. I..." Mandy's concerned brown eyes lifted to Darby's. "I was wrong to do what I did, to interfere. All I can say in my defense is that I've always loved Trey."

"Yet you ended things with him a second time."

"Not because I didn't love him."

"Then why?"

"Because I couldn't stand that I'd destroyed our friendship over a guy."

Mandy's words sank in.

"What happened on prom night and the week after was poison to my relationship with Trey. I didn't think I deserved to be happy with him, so I refused to be happy." Mandy wrung her hands together, shrugged. "If I hadn't broken up with him when I did he'd have dumped me, which is what I deserved, but I beat him to the punch."

"I always thought you two would end up married," Darby mused. "When I heard he'd taken a job out of town and married someone else I was shocked."

"I cried myself to sleep for weeks." Mandy's hands twisted the thin material of her shirt. "I know it's wrong to be happy when someone's marriage falls apart, but when I heard Trey was divorcing I knew why I'd stayed single all these years." She let out a deep breath. "I was waiting for him. Not because I thought he'd get divorced, but because I didn't want anyone but him. Yet even with him single, I still can't have him."

"Why not?"

"My conscience won't let me."

"Because of what happened with me?" Darby asked in surprise, not quite believing what she was hearing. All these years she'd assumed Mandy hadn't cared how she'd hurt her.

"It wasn't until yesterday at the picnic, when I saw you with Blake, that I knew you and Trey weren't meant to be together."

Had it only been yesterday? The picnic seemed so long ago.

"You and Blake are perfect together."

Perfect?

They'd been perfect last night in bed.

They'd been perfect partners prior to this weekend.

Now? Darby wasn't sure *perfect* was the right adjective for what was happening between her and Blake.

"I envy you." Mandy grimaced. "I have another admission to make. Despite knowing I couldn't be with Trey, I couldn't bring myself to mail your invitation. I wanted you here for so many reasons, yet I was scared of what might happen when you came home." Mandy grasped her arm. "Can you ever forgive me?"

Surprised by all the emotional swings the weekend had brought, Darby glanced at the woman who'd once been her best friend, thought about all that had transpired, and tried to let go of past hurts. "I can forgive you, but I'm not sure I have it in me to do more than that. Too much has happened, too many hurts."

Tears shining in her eyes, Mandy nodded.

"Darby, is everything okay?"

Darby turned, stared at Trey, then beyond him to where Blake stood. Apparently both men had tired of waiting and come in search of them.

Seeing Trey's gaze go beyond her to Mandy, Darby nodded. "Everything's fine."

Except that her mother was lying in a hospital bed fighting for her life and she'd once again fallen for a man who didn't love her.

Darby and Blake watched Mandy and Trey leave. Mandy turned and waved. With a forced smile on her face, Darby waved back.

"What happened between you and Mandy?"

"We aired a few things." She turned to look at Blake, wondering how she could be so aware of him physically even when they stood outside the hospital. "I'm not going back to Knoxville tonight."

"I suspected as much. Do you want me to get us a hotel room here in Pea Ridge?"

Did she? Maybe if they were alone they could talk—could air things between them, too. Like the fact that she loved him and didn't want to go back to things being the way they were.

"That would be great."

"I'll call Dr. Kingston and ask him to cover for us. And I'll get in touch with our office manager and let her know what's going on, so she can reschedule our appointments for tomorrow."

She nodded. "You're sure you don't mind staying another night? You could go home tonight."

"I'm not leaving you to face this alone, Darby."

"Thank you." She didn't point out that she wouldn't be alone, that she'd have her family. Because when she closed her eyes tonight she wanted to be wrapped in his arms, with him purging the awful memories of the day, replacing them with new memories, memories full of hope for a better tomorrow.

But late that night, when they arrived at the hotel, Blake did leave her alone.

Alone in a hotel room, with him in a room across the hallway.

Darby cried herself to sleep.

Darby's mother's procedure went well the following day, and although she had mixed feelings about leaving, Darby knew she and Blake had to go home. If only long enough for her to pack a few things and drive back down by herself. Blake could cover at the office for however long was needed.

Jim walked them out to the parking lot.

Darby hugged her brother goodbye. "I'll keep my phone on me at all times. If anything changes, anything at all, you'll call?"

He nodded. "I don't know why you're asking me. If something changes you'll know before I do. I saw you give the doctor and nurses specific instructions on calling you."

"I don't feel right about leaving," she said for the dozenth time.

"I know." Jim put his arm around her. "But the doctor says she's going to be fine."

Her brother was right, of course.

She turned to Blake, found him watching her, and battled her conflicting desire to pound him with her fists and to lean against his broad shoulders.

They'd barely said two words to each other all day. He'd been with her all the time, but in the background, on the periphery of her life. Was he foreshadowing what to expect when they returned to Knoxville?

When she'd said her goodbyes to her brother, Darby rested her throbbing head against Blake's passenger seat.

"Hungry?"

She shook her head. Food was the last thing she wanted.

"You've not eaten anything since what little you nibbled at breakfast," he pointed out. "I'm starved."

"You can stop somewhere, but I'm not hungry."

"You need to eat, too."

Her stomach rumbled, reminding her that Blake was right. "Fine. I'll eat."

He pulled into a sandwich shop. They went in and ordered sandwiches, fruit, and drinks. Darby ate more than she'd thought she would, and felt better than she had when they'd arrived at the shop. Her headache had even eased.

If only her heartache would.

Blake stared straight ahead, as if the oncoming interstate traffic was the most fascinating view in the world.

As if he wasn't aware that Darby had given up trying to make conversation, had given up pretending to be asleep and instead had been intently watching him for the past thirty minutes. Her gaze hadn't budged.

Although he was acutely aware of her, he made no acknowledgement of her stare. To do that would open up more conversation attempts, and at the moment talking with Darby was the last thing he wanted.

What he wanted was to punch something.

He couldn't look at Darby and not want her.

He couldn't want her because then he'd want to act upon that want. And to do that would confuse things even more.

Which was why he'd gotten them separate hotel rooms the night before. Darby was vulnerable because of what had happened with her mother, what had happened between them. He'd had no right to take advantage of that vulnerability a second night.

He liked Knoxville. Having moved so many times during his youth, he hadn't really known what he was missing, but now, having been in the same place for several years, he liked the sense of belonging he'd found. Liked the feeling enough to want to protect the life he'd made for himself.

A home, a job, a partner he depended upon. The good life he'd made for himself had evolved around

Darby. They shared the same friends from medical school, shared colleagues, shared a clinic.

If he pursued her sexually, when it ended that life would fall down around him.

His best plan of action was to do as he'd done since yesterday. Act as if their making love had been no big deal, and hope that with time their relationship would smooth back out, that he and Darby could be friends again.

All he had to do was convince himself that sex with Darby had been no big deal.

CHAPTER NINE

"GOOD morning, Mr. Hill," Darby greeted the thin man lying in his hospital bed, a grumpy expression on his wrinkled face.

"It would be a good Tuesday morning if you'd tell me I can go home."

"Let me see how that leg is doing, then we'll talk."

Talk. As she and Blake hadn't done. The drive home last night had been almost unbearable.

Oh, they'd made occasional small talk, but that had been the extent of their conversation.

What had they done?

Better yet, what were they going to do?

How was she supposed to greet him this morning? As her business partner, or as the man she'd made love to repeatedly on Saturday evening and again on Sunday morning?

For Blake, sex was sex. She knew that. Knew that she had to pretend what had happened between them was no big deal because otherwise she'd lose him forever.

Only she wasn't sure she could.

Too much had happened over the weekend.

Too many old wounds opened. Too many questions raised. Too many new emotions that felt too right.

"Does that look mean I'm not going home?" Mr. Hill asked, pulling Darby back to the present.

"I'm afraid not," she admitted, replacing the wet dressing on his leg ulcer. "At least not for several more days. The good news is that your leg is healing, slowly but surely."

"I can't heal at home?"

Home.

Longing pierced her heart. *Home is where the heart is*. So where was home? Knoxville? Armadillo Lake?

"No, I'm sorry, you can't."

She spent a few more minutes talking to him, then left his hospital room. She'd barely taken two steps into the hallway when Blake came out of a patient's room.

Shock at seeing her registered in his eyes. "I wasn't expecting you to be here this early."

Obviously. Did that mean he'd purposely arrived early, in hopes of not bumping into her? Or was she being paranoid?

"After leaving the office on Friday I figured there's a lot to catch up." Why did her explanation feel stilted?

"Me, too." He glanced away, ran his fingers through his dark hair. "How's your mother?"

"Stronger this morning, according to her doctor. Apparently she's in as big a rush to go home as Mr. Hill."

"Glad to hear she's improving." Not meeting her eyes, he nodded. "Guess I'll see you at the office."

He turned and walked away.

Darby bit the inside of her cheek. After his pretending to love her all weekend, his can't-get-away-fast-enough attitude contrasted starkly.

It hurt.

Hurt that she suspected she'd forever lost the easy camaraderie she and Blake had always shared.

What did he expect? That if he acted normal she'd think the weekend had meant something? She knew it didn't. She knew he was a highly sexed man. After all, she'd benefited from all that experience. Repeatedly.

Then another thought hit her. Had she been so bad that he couldn't even meet her eyes? Surely not, or he wouldn't have made love to her again on Sunday morning? He had been right there with her, every kiss, every touch, and he had wanted her. He couldn't have faked the desperation with which he'd taken her. He'd been driven, wild, as if he were branding her as his own.

Or was that how all men were when a naked woman squirmed on top of them? Maybe it wouldn't have mattered who she was, or how good or bad she'd been, just that he got sexual relief?

She just didn't know, and Blake hadn't wanted to talk to her on the drive home or after they'd gotten to her apartment and he'd helped carry her things inside. He hadn't even come into her apartment—just set her suitcase inside the front door and skedaddled as if he was worried she'd knock him over the head and drag him to her bed if he lingered.

Why had that hurt so much? Why had she cried herself to sleep for a second night in a row?

When she got to the office, she found exactly what she'd expected to find. A desk piled with things for her to do.

Instead of starting the process of clearing the mountain of work she went to Blake's office, and found him diligently making his way through his own mountain.

"Are you upset with me because of what happened between us?"

"No." Clearly surprised by her candid question, he leaned back in his chair. "I'm upset with myself."

"Why?"

"Because we crossed lines we shouldn't have crossed."

Which said it all. Blake regretted what they'd done. Everything he'd done since Sunday morning had said that he did. Which left her with two options: pretend she regretted what had happened or tell him the truth—that she loved him.

"Fine." She shrugged. "We'll forget this weekend ever happened."

Blake's eyes narrowed. "Can we?"

"I already have." She lifted her chin, stared at him defiantly, her breaking heart well hidden beneath the professional veneer she'd perfected years ago. "Haven't you?"

It had been a hell of a morning and this afternoon was promising to be just as trying. Blake's schedule was packed, and he'd had one call after another from the hospital.

But the worst of it was that he couldn't keep his mind on his work. No, any lull and his mind went to wondering about Darby.

She'd forgotten what they'd done?

If only he believed her.

If only he could get the memories of her body arched into his out of his head.

He couldn't.

Last night he hadn't slept, thanks to missing her warm body snuggled next to his. The night before, lying in a strange hotel room, hadn't been any better. He'd never missed a woman before. Not in bed. He'd always preferred sleeping alone. Apparently that no longer held true.

He preferred Darby.

He'd missed the way she smelled—missed it so much he'd gone out to his car to retrieve the pillow she'd accidentally left in his SUV.

When he finally had gone to sleep it had been while holding her damn pillow, surrounded by her scent, dreaming of her eager kisses.

"Dr. Di Angelo?" His nurse caught him as he followed the patient he'd just finished seeing out of the exam room. "I put McKenzie Bartholomew into room four just then. She's having an allergic reaction."

Blake immediately stepped into the room, took one look at his patient's enormous lower lip, and agreed with his nurse's assessment. "What happened?"

"I've no idea. I was outside in our pool and my lips started tingling. A few minutes later my lip started swelling and we headed straight here."

Blake looked over her medication allergies, stuck his head out the door and ordered an injection to be administered.

Taking his stethoscope, he listened to the girl's heart and lungs. Although her heart-rate was slightly increased, at a hundred and four beats a minute, her breathing was normal, with no wheeze.

"My nurse will be in to give you some epinephrine, and I'll be back in to check on you in a few minutes."

He stepped out of the exam room, his gaze colliding with Darby's the second he did so.

"Everything okay?"

"Fine."

"Good."

"Thanks."

Having had enough of the monosyllabic dialogue, Blake took a deep breath and went into his next patient's room.

A month later, Darby was examining the right arm of an older man with a bad combover. "You're sure you didn't hit your arm?"

The man's hearing wasn't the best, and he stared at her, clearly not comprehending.

"Your arm—did you hit it?" she repeated louder.

He shook his head. "My fingers started hurting first, then the pain moved up my arm. When I took my shirt off last night, this is what I saw."

"This" being the dark purplish discoloration that ran from his shoulder to fade into his palm. The entire underside of his arm looked as if someone had beaten him.

"Have you accidentally taken extra of your blood thinner?"

Again he couldn't understand her, and she repeated her question.

His blood *had* to be overly thin. There could be little other explanation for his unusual symptoms. Still, under normal circumstances she'd have sought out Blake for a second opinion.

This was ridiculous. No matter what had happened last month, they were still partners. Partners who barely spoke, but partners. When they did speak, it was usually Blake asking about her mother, about her trips to Armadillo Lake over the weekends to stay with her family. Occasionally they spoke about patients, but never did they mention what had happened.

Darby kept hoping, kept praying that he'd relax, would realize that what they'd shared had been special. Instead they only seemed to be growing further apart. Each day felt more tense than the one before.

She was tired of it. Tired of walking on eggshells. Tired of his ignoring her. Tired of feeling like she'd lost her best friend.

She wanted his opinion on a patient, and by golly she was going to get it.

She excused herself and poked her head into the room where Blake had just finished with a patient. "Can I see you for a few minutes?"

She saw his hesitation, saw his eyes narrow before he answered. "What's up?"

"I'd like you to take a look at Clinton Rogers' arm. I suspect his blood is too thin but the results aren't back yet."

"What's going on?"

"No history of injury, but pain in his right arm eight on a scale of ten, that started at the base of his middle finger and moved up his arm. Started yesterday. When he undressed last night his arm was deep purple and felt cold to him."

"Why didn't he go to the emergency room?"

"You tell me." Mr. Rogers should have gone to the ER, but he hadn't. Now it was her job to decide if he needed to be admitted or if he could be treated at home, probably with vitamin K injections, pending his laboratory results.

Blake followed her into the room, examined Mr. Rogers' arm, then spoke loudly to the older man. "I'm going to drain this pocket of blood."

Darby nodded. She'd planned to do the same, but had opted to wait until the laboratory results were back prior to doing so.

Gathering the supplies he'd need out of the exam room drawer, Darby handed Blake a ten milliliter syringe with a large-gauge needle attached. Their fingers brushed, their eyes met. Her breath caught and held.

"Blake?" She couldn't hold back the emotion bubbling inside her. They hadn't touched since that weekend, and instantly Darby was filled with longing, filled with memories of their making love.

His gaze narrowed, grew cold. He turned his back to her, explaining quite loudly to Mr. Rogers what he planned to do.

He'd snubbed her, rejected her all over again.

Darby's hope that things would get better between them died a painful death.

She'd taken a chance the weekend of the reunion, and she'd lost. Lost not only the hope that Blake might someday love her, but lost him from her life completely—because she couldn't stand this hostile environment.

Couldn't stand to breathe the same air. Not when seeing him, smelling his spicy scent, hearing his voice, only served to remind her of what could have been had he only loved her.

She left the room, intending to check on Mr. Rogers' lab results. Instead she found herself dialing Mandy's number.

"Coulson Realty." Mandy had gone to work at her father's real estate company. "Mandy Coulson speaking."

"Mandy, this is Darby Phillips. Is Mack Donahue's place still for sale? I want to make an offer."

* * *

The following week, Darby stared at the blue lines on the test.

Pregnant.

How could she be pregnant? She and Blake had used protection. Maybe the test was wrong. Although most accurate with an early-morning sample, she hadn't waited. From the moment she'd realized her period hadn't arrived last week, not knowing had driven her crazy.

No doubt about it. Even with the time of day, and only being a week late, the positive had been strong and almost immediate. Hcg hormone was present in her urine.

The implications caused her head to spin.

Pregnant.

She was having a baby.

There was a baby growing inside her body this very minute.

Her, a mother.

She'd have to schedule an appointment with her gynecologist.

She'd have to tell Blake.

Blake.

They'd made a baby together.

How would he react?

Not well. With each day that passed they grew further apart, making her long for the days of his teasing, making her long for his touch.

She missed him, hadn't realized just how much time she'd spent with Blake until he'd blaringly exited her life.

Oh, he was still physically around. They worked in the same office, did rounds at the same hospital, but he went out of his way to avoid her and, unable to stand the regret in his dark eyes, the wince that often followed his seeing her, she'd taken to avoiding him, too.

Not only that, but she'd signed a contract on the house and five acres of the Mack Donahue estate in Armadillo Lake, and had been trying to decide just what that meant. She missed her family, was desperately needed in Armadillo Lake, but was she really planning to move home? Was she giving up on Blake?

She kept hoping they'd slip back into the easy relationship they'd always shared. After all, time healed all wounds.

Now she knew that was an impossibility.

They'd never go back.

When she told Blake she was pregnant, her news would forever destroy any hope of that.

She missed everything about him—his smile, his teasing, his wit, his friendship, his kisses. Everything.

Still, she had to think about the baby—a baby! His baby. She and Blake would have to talk, would have to figure out how they wanted to handle the future.

For her, abortion wasn't an option. If Blake wanted her to go that route he'd have to think again. He wouldn't suggest terminating her pregnancy, though.

Or maybe he would.

She just didn't know anymore.

Knowing she'd been in the private bathroom she and Blake shared too long already, she picked up the plastic pregnancy kit, clenched the test tightly in her sweaty palm. She couldn't leave the kit. Nor could she leave the wrapper.

Gathering up the test she'd taken from their small

lab, she stuffed it into her purse and zipped the oversized bag to hide all evidence.

Planning to lock her purse in her desk drawer, she stepped into the hallway separating her and Blake's offices.

They rarely shut their office doors, so as usual his was open. His voice carried out into the hallway.

"I'll swing by and do rounds before I go home tonight."

Darby's gaze was drawn to where he sat at his desk. His dark head was bent, studying a paper on his desk while he spoke on the phone. Would their baby have his dark eyes and hair? His superb bone structure? His quick wit and smile?

The depth of emotion swamping her stunned her. Never had she considered getting pregnant, but she wanted Blake's baby.

Unaware that she watched him, he initialed the paper, then flipped to the next. "Go ahead and draw another CBC. I'll check the results when I'm there later." He glanced up, saw her. His mouth tightened into a thin line of displeasure.

An intense longing for the days when he would wink or grin or motion for her to come into his office hit Darby.

She was pregnant.

With his baby.

Oh, Blake.

Of their own accord, her hands went to her belly.

His narrowed gaze lowered, widened, then rose to hers, full of wonder and question.

Darby's stomach lurched. He knew.

She had never been good at hiding her emotions.

Why would an unexpected pregnancy be the exception? She should have known Blake would take one look at her and know.

Whether or not she was ready to share her news, Blake knew.

They were going to be parents.

CHAPTER TEN

"I've got to go," Blake told the nurse he spoke with, his gaze never moving from Darby's guilty face. "I'll take care of anything else when I'm at the hospital."

An invisible hand kneading his insides, he hung up the phone and stared at the pale woman standing outside his office, watching him with mounting horror.

Was she?

Her mouth opened, almost as if she'd heard his silent question, but no words came out.

No denial. Only her hand lying protectively over her lower abdomen. Which was really the only answer needed.

Oh, hell.

Darby was pregnant.

His legs trembled at the implications of those three little words. Darby was pregnant.

His hands shook.

His stomach twisted.

His brain throbbed.

His heart squeezed.

Darby was pregnant.

Unsure if his legs would work, he pushed out from his desk, held on to the corner for support as he stood.

He was going to be a father.

Him.

He'd always thought that someday he'd marry, have children, pass on his grandfather's name—but now? Never had he had those thoughts in correlation with anytime soon.

"Darby?"

She shook her head, held up her hand to ward him off, almost as if she couldn't catch her breath. Her eyes had widened to tumultuous deep blue seas.

Did she think he'd be angry at her?

Never.

If anything, he was angry at himself. Clearly he'd been the one with the experience. He had no one to blame except himself for their mistake. His eyes dropped to her belly and he winced.

Mistake.

The idea that he'd thought of his child, his baby, as a mistake sucker-punched him.

His grandfather would roll with shame. Nothing was more precious than family.

If Darby was pregnant, he'd accept that fate and embrace the future, embrace the baby they'd made together, and somehow they'd make it work.

"We need to talk."

Her vocal cords apparently not working, she silently nodded, stepped into his office.

Blake shut the door behind her, not wanting their conversation to be overheard by any of their staff.

"You're pregnant." He didn't ask it as a question. Not when he could so clearly read the truth on her face.

Her eyes searching his, she nodded again.

He didn't ask if the baby was his. Didn't ask how far along. He didn't need to.

His thoughts reeling, he sank onto the corner of his desk. "How do you feel about that?"

Her face pinched and she found her voice. "What do you mean, how do I feel about that? I'm floored."

Blake stared at her, wondering if he'd said the wrong thing. Hell, what was the right thing in this situation? Was he supposed to say he'd be there every step of the way with her? That he'd go to Lamaze classes and be in the delivery room? That he'd be an active father in their child's life? Was he supposed to tell her that he was as floored as she was, but that this was their baby they were talking about and, floored or not, he'd be the kind of father he'd never had?

A million thoughts, a million questions, ran through his mind all at once. Questions he didn't have the answers to. The woman who did have those answers stood before him with pink tingeing her cheeks.

"What do you expect of me?" Did she want him to propose? To give their child legitimacy?

She blinked. "Expect of you?"

"What do you want me to do, Darby? Marry you? Agree to support you financially?" Blake's throat tightened, his hands sweated, his heart pounded. "Tell me what you expect of me and how all this makes you feel so I know what I need to do."

Was Blake kidding? Darby stared at the man leaning on his desk and wondered if she'd ever known him at all. Had he really just asked what she *expected* of him? How she felt about being pregnant?

"Nothing." She wished she had something to throw

at him. Something hard. And sharp. Her gaze landed on the stress relief ball. That soft little thing wouldn't begin to relieve the stress mounting inside her. Not even if the ball smacked him square between the eyes. "I don't expect anything from you."

"Every woman expects something from the man who's gotten her pregnant."

"You've already done more than enough."

"It's too late to point fingers, Darby. I take full responsibility. I know your baby's mine."

She hadn't even considered that he might think otherwise, so his comment stung even more.

She pressed her fingertip to her throbbing temple, hoping to calm the wild pulse hammering there. "You want to know how I feel? What I expect? I don't know, Blake. I only just did the test, and I don't know how I feel about any of this."

"You missed your period? That's why you did the test?"

Give Sherlock a cookie.

"I'm a week late." She glanced at him, tried not to wince at the tight lines of his face. How could he look so familiar, and yet so alien at the same time? "I kept telling myself stress was causing my missed cycle, but..."

"It wasn't."

She dug in her purse, pulled out the plastic kit from where she'd slid it inside the wrapper, and handed the confirmation of her suspicions to him.

"No."

Blake studied the plastic wand with eyes darker than she recalled ever seeing them. So dark they paled the night sky.

"You're pregnant."

Yes, they'd already established that.

Her legs growing weak beneath her, she sat down on the edge of his desk, next to him.

"I'm pregnant."

The rest of Blake's evening passed in a blur.

No wonder.

He was going to be a father.

How had that happened?

He knew *how* that had happened, just… Blake knocked on Darby's front door, wishing she'd hurry and let him into the apartment she'd lived in since they were in medical school.

An apartment that wouldn't be big enough for her and a baby.

She'd need more space—a place with a yard big enough for a swing and a sandbox.

When she opened the door, his heart lurched at her red-rimmed, swollen eyes. All day he'd been caught up in his own feelings about Darby's news. He'd asked how she felt, but truth was he'd asked in regard to how her feelings affected *him*.

How could he have been so callous?

"You've been crying."

Emitting a low sniffle, she rolled her puffy eyes at him. "So? Pregnant women cry."

He supposed they did.

"Are you going to invite me in?"

Sighing, she stepped back, waited for him to enter the apartment, then shut the door.

He sat down on her living room sofa, looking around for something to focus on besides the woman he wanted to take into his arms and promise it would all be all right. Somehow.

"You said you wanted to come by so we could talk," she reminded him. "I don't know what to say, Blake, so you're going to have to do the talking."

He didn't know where to start.

"I'm sorry I put you in this position."

She didn't glance at him, just sank onto an overstuffed chair at the far end of the sofa and curled her legs beneath her. "You weren't the only one in that hotel room. My getting pregnant took both of us."

That it had. Blake vividly recalled just what the two of them had done to get her pregnant, was haunted by the memories every time he closed his eyes, every time he saw her.

"We can't change the past."

"No," he agreed, wondering when talking to Darby had gotten so difficult, when he'd gotten self-conscious of each word. Of course he knew the precise moment. When they'd become lovers. He ached for his easy relationship with Darby, ached for what he'd lost in her friendship, her partnership. But she was right. They couldn't change the past. "Which leaves us trying to make the best of the future."

Her head lowered to her hands. "Agreed."

"I know you got upset when I asked this earlier, but my question was a legitimate one." He moved to the end of the sofa closest to her, reached for her hand, but she jerked away, shaking her head rapidly back and forth.

Trying to convince himself that Darby's rejection wasn't the cause of the sharp pain slashing across his chest, Blake sighed. "Tell me what you want, Darby?"

What *did* she want? Darby wondered.

"I want us to go back to the way we were," she

admitted, surprised at her candor, but figuring at this point she had nothing to lose. She'd already lost the best thing in her life, the thing she'd had for years yet hadn't had at all—him. "I miss my partner and friend."

He nodded as if he understood. "I've missed you, too."

He had? "Have you? I haven't gotten that impression these past few weeks."

"Our friendship and business relationship was special to me. I hate that we let sex come between that."

Friendship. Business relationship. Sex.

Darby winced.

"Our relationship won't ever be the same, Darby. No matter how hard we try, we can't go back to how things were."

Perhaps she'd said the wrong thing. Because she really didn't want what they'd had before. She wanted what she'd had in Alabama. She wanted Blake to be in love with her. For real.

She wanted to look into his eyes and see desire and love for her.

She wanted him to feel the same about her as she felt about him.

Because she was in love with Blake.

"I don't want to go back to how things were."

His brow arched. "You don't? But didn't you just say…?"

She shook her head. "I thought that was what I wanted, but I want more."

Eyes narrowed, Blake worked his throat, gulped. "More?"

So much had happened in the past few hours that it probably wasn't wise to make grand life decisions, but

Darby did. In her heart she knew she was making the right choice.

"I want to sell my half of the clinic to you, Blake. I'm going home."

"No." Steely determination shone in his eyes.

Darby frowned. "What do you mean, no? No, you don't want to buy my half of the clinic?" She shrugged. "Fine. I'll find another doctor to buy my half out. Our business contract reads that we have to offer each other first option, so that's what I was doing."

"I'm not buying your half of the clinic because you aren't selling." His tone brooked no argument.

Not quite believing his reaction, Darby stared at him, more determined than ever that she was making the right choice for her and the baby. "Actually, I am. I'm going home."

"Knoxville is your home."

"No," she sighed. "It's not. I belong in Armadillo Lake. They need a doctor."

"You don't belong there. You blackmailed me into going to your high school reunion so you wouldn't have to go there alone."

"I was an immature young girl who held on to her hurt way too long and let those hurts influence life decisions in ways I shouldn't have."

"What about me?"

He'd been the main reason she'd stayed in Knoxville. She'd wanted to be near him. Still, there was more to think about than her or Blake. She had to consider what was right for their baby.

"What about you?"

* * *

Good question. One Blake didn't have an answer to. He didn't have answers to anything. Just knew that he didn't want Darby to leave Knoxville.

Didn't want her to leave him.

She might not feel she belonged here, but Blake did. For the first time in his life he belonged somewhere, truly felt at home.

Darby couldn't just rip that feeling all to pieces.

He wouldn't let her.

"I have rights, too, you know."

Her forehead wrinkled. "Rights?"

"Regarding your pregnancy. Moving doesn't just affect you. Where you live affects me and my relationship with our child."

Darby's mouth dropped. "I wouldn't stop you from seeing our baby. You should know that, Blake."

"Should I?" Pain at the thought of his world being ripped apart clouded his judgement and he lashed out. "How do I know you aren't moving home to pick things up with Nix? That you aren't hoping he'll step in and play house with you and my baby? Is that what you've been doing in Alabama while I've covered your patients? Did you see him?"

Darby blinked. "You're kidding, right?"

"No."

"I have talked to Trey since that weekend, but not in the manner you're implying."

"Since the weekend you became pregnant with my baby, you mean?"

She gave him a stubborn look. "Yes, the weekend of the reunion."

"And Mandy? Have you talked to her?"

"Yes."

"And?"

"We've made our peace. You know that. You were at the hospital that afternoon, with her and Trey."

"Yes, I was," he snarled.

She stared at him. "What is wrong with you? Trey and Mandy are dating again. I'm happy for them. Their being together is how it should have been all along." She frowned. "If I didn't know better, I'd think you were jealous."

"Good thing you do know better."

"Yes, it is." She shook her head. "I don't want to argue with you, but I *am* going to sell my half of the clinic. If you want to buy me out, fine. If not, I'd love to say I'll just walk away, but I'll need the funds to start my life in Alabama."

Funds? She really had no idea as to his wealth, did she? Wealth any child of Blake's would be entitled to. Darby would never have to work another day if she chose not to.

"You're really going to leave me? On the day you discover you're pregnant with my baby, you're announcing you want me to buy your half of our life together so you can move six hours away?"

She didn't wince, didn't show the slightest remorse, just held his gaze. "I am."

"You believe that's fair to me?"

"I have to think about what's best for me and for our baby. My going home to Armadillo Lake is what's best."

"Why?"

"Because my family is there, and it's where I was meant to be. I'd forgotten that for a while, but a memory lapse doesn't make the truth any less true."

"You were meant to be with me."

At her surprised look, he added, "In Knoxville, at our clinic. We have a good thing, Darby. A good practice."

"It hasn't been good since we slept together, and you know it. You can barely tolerate looking at me."

"That's not true."

"It is," she accused, standing up from her chair and pacing across her living room. She spun toward him, her eyes as accusing as her tone. "You've been avoiding me ever since we slept together, and I can't stand it."

"That's why you want to move? To punish me for sleeping with you?"

"That's not what I said, Blake. I don't want to punish you. I just can't deal with the way things are between us now."

"Because we ruined everything when we had sex?"

"Apparently so." She folded her arms across her chest. "It certainly hasn't made things better between us."

No, that weekend had caused the foundation of their relationship to crumble, and now his world was crashing around him.

"What is it you want between us, Darby? What is it you expected after that weekend?"

"I told you, Blake, I don't expect anything from you."

"Apparently you do—or at least you did. Otherwise you wouldn't be leaving me." As he said the words out loud, their validity reverberated through him. She had expected something from him, something he'd failed to deliver.

"You're twisting my words. I'm not leaving *you*."

"How can you say that? You're walking away from everything we have together."

"Not everything, Blake." She placed her hand over

her belly. “There’s one thing we have together that I won’t ever walk away from. You can count on it.”

His gaze dropped to her belly and the blood drained from his face. Darby was going to have his baby, but she didn’t want him in her life, didn’t want to be a family with him.

And then it hit him. Darby had taken him to Armadillo Lake prepared to have sex. She’d had new lingerie, a full box of condoms. Perhaps she’d already gotten what she wanted from him? “Did you get pregnant on purpose?”

“What? How can you say that? We used condoms.”

“Some of them *you* bought. Did you tamper with them?”

Her eyes widened with a mixture of disbelief and anger. “Are you serious? Why would I do that?”

Hurt at her rejection of him egged him on. “No doubt a lot of women would like to reap the benefits of having my baby.”

Her eyes flashed with anger. “You arrogant son of a—”

“Fine. I know you didn’t get pregnant intentionally.” Blake had had enough. He’d known sleeping with Darby had been a mistake, but he hadn’t been able to stop himself. Now she wanted to cut him out of her life. “If you want to leave, I’ll make it simple. Have a contract drawn up for your half of the clinic and I’ll sign it. You want to take my baby far away from me—fine. I won’t stop you. But expect to hear from my lawyer, because I *will* play a role in my child’s life.”

CHAPTER ELEVEN

DARBY placed the last of her books into the packing crate. She couldn't believe how quickly the past month had gone by. Yet with the anger and hurt between her and Blake, each minute had also dragged by.

True to his word, he had signed the contract her lawyer had drawn up. She was no longer a partner in their clinic. She was no longer anything to him.

No, not true. She was the mother of his unborn child.

They'd always have that connection. Always.

A tear ran down her cheek.

Although moving home was the right thing for so many reasons, leaving Knoxville wasn't easy. When the movers had crated up the contents of her apartment that morning she'd burst into tears. She'd cried until her chest throbbed. She'd left to finish at the office, because she hadn't been able to watch them empty her apartment.

Because her heart had been breaking.

Home is where the heart is.

Her heart was with Blake.

If he'd loved her she would have stayed in Knoxville forever, would have gone wherever he was and been happy.

But he didn't love her.

As she had no choice, she accepted that. But if making him love her were possible, she'd fight for Blake's heart to her dying breath.

For all eternity.

"I can't believe you're really going."

Darby's gaze shot to the doorway. "Blake."

She swiped at her eyes, hoping he hadn't caught the waterworks. "How long have you been standing there?"

Had he come to start yet another fight with her? It seemed as if that was all they did on the few occasions they actually spoke.

God, he looked good, in his black pants and crisp white polo. Then again, when *didn't* he look good?

"Long enough to think you're not as confident about this move as you've let on. It's not too late to change your mind."

She took a deep breath, steeling herself for his verbal attack. "Being sad at saying goodbye doesn't make me any less confident that I've made the right decision."

He pushed off the doorframe, stepped into the office, and closed the door behind him.

Darby swallowed. She wasn't sure she was strong enough to deal with another fight between them. Not now, in her last minutes at the clinic.

"I don't want you to go, Darby."

If she'd thought she wasn't strong enough for an argument, she certainly wasn't strong enough to deal with his soft admission.

She took a step back. "We've been through this."

"But perhaps we haven't said the right things."

Hope lifted high in her chest. "What right things?"

If he asked her to stay, to be a family, told her he

loved her, she'd throw her arms around him and stay forever.

"You're a part of my life, Darby. A good part that I don't want to let go."

"Blake, two months have gone by and you've barely acknowledged my existence." Two months in which her heart had broken at every wayward glance, at every smile not returned.

"I've been aware of you every moment of every day. How could I not be?" he asked, moving closer. "You're carrying my child."

The baby. That was why he was here. Why he was looking at her with such longing. Question was, what motivated him? Actual concern for their child, or guilt that he was washing his hands of her and their baby?

"Regardless of where I am, I'll still be carrying your child, Blake. Location doesn't change that."

His lips pursed with displeasure. "Location changes everything."

Location wouldn't change her feelings for him, but perhaps not having to see him on a daily basis would make dealing with the shattered pieces of her heart slightly easier.

She doubted it, though.

"You know where to find me, Blake." She quit backing up, faced him. "You've always known where to find me. You've just never cared to look. Not at me. Not really."

Inches separated their bodies. He towered over her. "What's that supposed to mean?"

"I've always been right here, Blake."

"Just as I've always been here for you, Darby. Always. Every time you've needed me, I've been here for you."

"You have." She swallowed the knot in her throat. What was he doing?

"Yet you feel the need to leave? To just forget about us?"

She couldn't stand anymore. "Don't you get it, Blake? There has never been an us." She put her palms against his chest. "All we had was one weekend of pretense."

"Is that what you believe?"

"Tell me I'm wrong."

"You're wrong." As if to prove his point, he lowered his mouth to hers, kissed her so thoroughly her knees wobbled. "Tell me you don't feel that, Darby. Tell me you don't want me even now."

"That's only sexual attraction." *Tell me I'm wrong. Please, Blake, tell me you feel more for me than sexual attraction.*

"Don't knock chemistry. It's what makes the world go around."

"Not my world," she admitted softly.

Knowing she had to go while she still could, Darby pulled free from his loose hold.

She'd hoped he'd stop her, that he'd hold on to her and tell her what he felt for her was so much more than sexual attraction.

"If you stay, I'll marry you."

"Why?" *Tell me you love me. I'll go anywhere with you, Blake. Just love me.*

"For the baby."

A part of Darby died. The part that had been holding out hope that maybe, just maybe, he cared for her. But when push came to shove Blake wouldn't fight for her. Why would he? He didn't love her, and had never given her reason to think he did. In the long run, her leaving made things easier for him.

Darby touched his cheek, loving the feel of the light razor stubble that had popped up since he'd shaved that morning, wishing she could touch him forever.

"Don't make doing the right thing more difficult than it already is, Blake." She stood on her tiptoes, pressed a kiss to his lips, and stepped away. Her gaze landed on the one thing she hadn't yet packed. The one thing she hadn't been able to place inside a packing crate. Her heart.

Picking up the plastic model at its base, she felt memories assail her. Memories all made with Blake. She turned, smiled through her tears, and held out the heart.

"Here," she whispered. "Take this. It seems my heart won't be making the move with me. It's always belonged to you, anyway."

"What happened to that pretty female doctor?"

Blake frowned at Mr. Hill, and not because of the ulcer on his leg. Fortunately, the ulcer on Mr. Hill's leg now had pink granulation tissue forming and was slowly healing.

"She left."

The man cracked his arthritic neck, frowning right back at Blake. "To be a doctor, she wasn't too bad. Easy on the eye, too. Where'd she go?"

He didn't need a man in his seventies telling him Darby was easy on the eye. Blake knew she was easy on the eye. Good thing too, because whether his eyes were open or closed Darby was always what he saw.

"She moved back to where she came from." Did he sound bitter? Likely. He felt bitter. Darby had found out she was pregnant and immediately left him. Sure, he didn't know much about being a family, but she hadn't even given him a chance.

"Where's that?" Mr. Hill asked.

"Alabama." Blake answered.

Mr. Hill's bushy white brow quirked. "You don't like Alabama?"

"It's a state."

"And misery is a state of mind." Mr. Hill waved his hand in dismissal. "Why are you still here? You should go after her."

"No one asked for your opinion."

"You should have asked. I've been around awhile, learned from life experiences. You should try it sometime."

"I've learned from life experiences." He'd learned that he shouldn't rely on anyone except himself. He'd learned that he'd been a fool to stay in Knoxville following graduation. He should have left, joined a traveling medical group where he could change locales every few months. Wasn't that what he knew best? How not to get close to people because they came and went from your life?

"You ain't learned jack, or you'd be rubbing her leg instead of mine."

Blake dropped his hand away from Mr. Hill's calf. He'd say the older man had a point—except his rubbing had been covering the wet dressing with an elastic wrap to protect Mr. Hill's clothes from getting stained.

"You don't know what you're talking about."

"I know if I had a pretty young woman's heart I'd be with her."

He didn't have Darby's heart.

Well, actually, he did, but that was just plastic.

Blake froze. Darby's words hit him, pinging through his thick skull and sinking home.

Darby had given him her heart, had said her heart belonged to him.

After a lifetime of abstinence, she had given him her virginity.

She loved him.

He'd been too blind to realize.

Too blind to see.

But how could he have seen when he'd been too blind to even see his own feelings for Darby?

While in Alabama, pretending to love her, he'd realized he wanted her, that he'd always wanted her, but instead of acting upon that realization he'd run scared, wanting to hold on to the safe rather than risk getting hurt. To hang on to the tried and true rather than venture into unknown territories. In the process he'd lost her.

Blake set down his stethoscope, stared at Mr. Hill, and gave credit where credit was due. "You're a wise man, Nathan Hill."

The man smiled his toothless smile. "Looks like you're wisening up, too."

"That I am. Let's hope I'm not too late."

"I just can't believe you're really home." Rosy waved her paintbrush, droplets of paint splattering onto the plastic lining the floor. Her gaze lowered to the paint. "Oops."

Darby wiped the back of her hand across her sweaty brow, a smile on her paint-dappled face. Part of her couldn't believe she was home either.

"I can't believe you didn't bring that scrumptious doctor with you," Mandy said, glancing up from where she'd taped off a corner of the room they were painting.

The room where Darby would soon be seeing patients.

In Alabama.

In her own practice.

Far away from the scrumptious doctor in question.

"Blake is busy finding someone to replace me in Knoxville."

Mandy's gaze met Darby's, then lowered to the painter's tape. Darby hated her friend's sympathy. They'd all commiserated when she'd told them she and Blake had broken up. If not for her pregnancy, she would have told them the entire weekend had been nothing more than a pretense.

"In the office or in his bed?" Rosy eyed Darby curiously. "Because, as much as I want you home, I want you to be happy, too, and he made you happy." She gave a considering look. "Understandably so. Just looking at him made me happy, too."

"Whatever." Darby shook her head at Rosy. Her sister-in-law was as in love with her husband as the day they'd exchanged vows. Still, Rosy had a point. "I am happy."

Mandy glanced up at her, eyeing her even more curiously than Rosy had. "You're sure?"

Did her friends think she was depressed? Was that why they visited so often? Mandy had even fussed over Darby's lack of kempt hair and make-up that morning. What did her appearance matter for painting? But she appreciated their concern, so she forced a smile to her face. "I'm sure."

It was the truth. Mostly.

Sure, she cried herself to sleep at night, missing Blake, but she was happy, was confident she'd made the right decision to move home and raise her baby surrounded by her family's love.

She hadn't told anyone of her pregnancy yet. As she was only a little over three months along, she had a while before she had to tell anyone. She wasn't ready. She'd shared enough changes with her family over the past few weeks.

No doubt they would be disappointed that she'd be a single mother. But they'd love her and support her in the months leading up to and following the baby's arrival.

Other than missing Blake, her biggest concern regarding her pregnancy and the move was that the closest OB/GYN was thirty miles away. Still, that shouldn't present a problem, since most first deliveries didn't go quickly, and if it did there was always the calving barn.

As far as Blake replacing her, in the office and in his bed, well, she did her best not to think about that, as the thought of him with another woman hurt deeper than she wanted to admit.

So she'd focused on her new life. All she had to do was finish up the repairs and she'd be ready to open on October first, as planned.

She glanced out the window, catching sight of her brothers, Mark the vet, and Trey, down near the lake. Over the past few weeks, as their time had allowed, while she, Mandy and her sisters-in-law had worked on the inside of the house, the men had cleaned the yard, replaced the roof's shingles, and painted the outside of the house. Now they were building her a new dock.

Just as Darby and Mandy were slowly rebuilding their friendship, Mandy and Trey were rekindling old flames. Darby couldn't be happier for them.

"Hey, is that Blake with the guys?"

At Rosy's question, Darby's heart slammed into her throat and tried to pound its way out. Surely she was hallucinating. No way was Blake walking toward the house with Trey, Mark, and her brothers. No way.

But he was.

"Apparently, he's not so busy in Knoxville that he can't drop by for a visit," Rosy snickered, giving Darby a knowing smile. "After all, it's only six hours' drive out of his way."

Darby barely glanced her sister-in-law's way, barely took in Mandy's silence and inability to meet her eyes—had her friend *known* Blake was here? She reached up to check her appearance, realized she'd probably only managed to smear paint into her hair.

What was he doing here?

Why hadn't he called first? Surely he should have called prior to making that drive? What if she hadn't been home? What if she'd decided to go to Knoxville? Maybe Mandy really had known he'd be stopping by today.

Which would explain why her friend had fussed about her appearance earlier.

Darby felt light-headed and not from the non-toxic paint fumes or her pregnancy. All oxygen had disappeared the moment Blake stepped into the room.

His black gaze met hers, drank in the sight of her, and she had a flashback to how it had been between them the last time they'd been in Alabama. He'd held her, touched her, kissed her, loved her.

Only he'd been faking. So why was he here now?

Why was he looking at her as if he'd missed her?

As if he wanted to take her in his arms and kiss her until they were both breathless?

* * *

Blake wanted to take Darby into his arms and kiss her until they were both breathless, until they could only cling to each other and never let go.

Because he didn't want to let her go. Not ever.

He was probably a fool, but here he was all the same.

In Alabama. His new home.

Not that he technically had a home. Not anymore.

Land, yes—thanks to the real estate Mandy had helped him purchase. Home, no.

But, looking at Darby, he knew he was a hell of a lot closer to home than he'd be anywhere else in the world.

"Blake?" She stepped toward him, realized every eye in the room was watching them, and paused. "What are you doing here?"

"You told me I could visit any time I was in the neighborhood." Was she upset he was here?

"You were in the neighborhood?"

"Actually…" he began, wondering how she was going to react to his news, wondering if she'd think he'd overstepped. Maybe he *had* overstepped? His mother had certainly thought he was crazy when he'd told her of his plans. She'd also wished him luck and been excited at the prospect of being a grandmother, which had surprised him. "Actually, I'm your closest neighbor."

Darby's mouth opened, and she gawked at him as if he were crazy, too. "You are?"

The whole Phillips clan and her friends glared at him. Apparently Darby's less than enthusiastic greeting had clued them in that all was not well in paradise.

"I bought the place next to yours. The land was originally part of this place, but was subdivided into a separate parcel when you bought the house."

Why was he telling her that? Of course she knew the land had been subdivided. God, he was nervous.

"You bought the rest of my land?"

He nodded, noting she'd called the land hers, hoping before all was said and done she'd call *him* hers, too.

Her eyes shone blue as the cloudless sky, piercing him with regrets that he'd let her walk away from him. "Why?"

"Um, I think it's time for us to head home," Rosy said, linking her elbow with her husband's and giving the others in the room a look that said for them to leave, too.

Darby turned, stared blankly at her sister-in-law and the others in the room. Clearly she'd forgotten they weren't alone.

"Me, too," Mandy said, walking over and giving Darby a quick hug. "Call me later to let me know what time you want me to come over and help finish this up. Bye, Blake. Trey, you ready?"

Mandy and Trey left. But, despite their womenfolk tugging on their arms, Darby's brothers didn't budge—just glared at Blake.

Did they know Darby was pregnant with his baby?

They'd been friendly enough outside, but that had been before Darby's obvious surprise at seeing him. They'd thought she'd been expecting him. What had she told her family?

Did they all know what an idiot he'd been? That he'd let her leave Knoxville without telling her how he felt? That he'd let her leave without fighting for her—even after she'd given him her heart?

Literally.

Darby didn't move, and neither did her brothers.

Blake met each of her brothers' gazes, then hers. "Is there somewhere we can talk in private?"

Glaring, Jim crossed his arms. "Nothing you have to say to my sister that you can't say to us."

"It's okay, guys," Darby said, stepping forward and waving them off. "Y'all go on home. I'll be by Mom and Dad's later for dinner. I'll see you there."

"We finished the deck—was just coming in to get you to inspect it," Ralph said, his gaze not leaving Blake.

Darby nodded. "I'll walk out with you guys and take a quick look before y'all leave." She glanced toward Blake, her expression unreadable. "Blake can wait here."

He watched through the large window as she walked to the boat dock with her family, noting that her brothers glanced back toward the house repeatedly, and that Rosy kept a tight hold on her husband's arm.

When the group finally left, Darby didn't come back inside. Instead she sat down on the dock. With her arms wrapped around her legs, her chin resting on her knees, she stared out at the lake as if the weight of the world was upon her.

Blake figured he was that weight.

What was Blake doing here? What did it mean that he'd bought the rest of the Donahue estate? She'd known he had some family money, but surely not enough to afford all that property connected to the lake and her place? The price had been astronomical.

What did she want his buying the rest of her land to mean?

Ha, that was a trick question.

She wanted it to mean he loved her and had come to sweep her off her feet and marry her.

But if he proposed, did that really mean he loved her?

Or just that he'd been hit by a wave of guilt, or responsibility or whatever, and wanted to give their baby a home? A family?

Even if he looked at her with love, she wouldn't really know. After all, she'd seen what a great actor he was on the weekend of the reunion.

If Blake wanted her to believe he loved her, that was what she'd believe.

But would she really?

Did she really want to be with a man when she wasn't sure why he was with her? A man she loved whole-heartedly but who didn't love her in return? But what about their baby? Didn't she owe it to their baby to give him the benefit of the doubt?

Oh, this was crazy. If she wanted to know why Blake was here, what was she doing outside? Why wasn't she inside, *asking* him why he was here? Why he'd bought the rest of her dream property?

She started to push herself up from the dock, but realized Blake stood behind her. How long had he been there?

"You didn't come back inside," he said softly, moving onto the deck and sitting down beside her. He sat close enough that she felt his body heat, close enough that she could breathe in his musky scent. Close enough that she wanted to lean against his shoulder, feel his arms around her, and stay there forever.

Instead, she continued to look out at the lake, pretending to be mesmerized by the sunshine bouncing off the water.

"I needed a few minutes to digest that you're here." She could feel his gaze on her, wanted to turn and look at him, but refused.

"Is my being here a bad thing?" he asked.

"Just unexpected. You're always welcome, Blake. I told you that. I won't try to keep you away from the baby." Unable not to, she glanced toward him. "Is that why you bought the land next to mine? So you could build a place to stay when you come to visit our child?"

He blew out a long breath and shook his head. "I sold everything in Knoxville."

Her head jerked up. "You did what?"

"I sold the practice to Dr. Kingston, my house to an out-of-state couple. I'm moving to Armadillo Lake permanently."

"But...but what will you do?"

"I've applied for an Alabama medical license. I plan to practice here."

"But...but why?"

"Simple." His gaze met hers, held. "You're here."

"And the baby?"

"Yes, and our baby." He glanced toward her flat belly. "How are you feeling? Any morning sickness?"

"Mild nausea, but that's it." She studied him, wondering if she'd inhaled too many paint fumes and was imagining that he was really here. Maybe she'd fainted and was lying on the floor of her future examination room. "You really sold out in Knoxville?"

"I did."

"But you liked Knoxville."

"Not after you left."

Darby's heart came to a quick halt. What was he saying? Had he been struck by guilt that she'd taken off pregnant and alone? Had he felt responsible? Felt he had to come to Alabama to take care of her and their baby?

"Tell me you want me here, Darby. Tell me I'm welcome in your life still."

"I want you here." More than anything she wanted him with her. Always. But not because they were business partners. She wanted Blake in her life because he couldn't imagine his life without her. "You're welcome in my life."

His gaze searched hers. "Tell me you've missed me as much as I've missed you."

"Okay." She nodded, wondering where he was going with this, wondering why her heart shook like a motor sputtering to life. "I've missed you as much as you've missed me." More. Lots more, she silently added.

"This seems to be working pretty well." He took her hand into his, traced over the lines on her palm, then laced their fingers and gave a tight squeeze. "Let's try another. Tell me you love me as much as I love you."

Darby wanted to believe him. Really she did. After all, his eyes shone with sincerity. His palm felt clammy next to hers, as if he was nervous as he waited for her answer.

She sighed, pulled her hand from his. "You know how I feel about you, Blake."

"Do I?"

"I told you."

"What exactly did you tell me, Darby?"

"That my heart has always belonged to you."

"And then you gave me that plastic model heart." He shook his head. "I was stupid, Darby. Utterly stupid. I thought you meant the model, but you didn't, did you?"

Panic seized her, making her feel the need to protect herself. "I did give you the model, Blake."

"But you'd given me your heart a long time before that, hadn't you? That's why you stayed in Knoxville to begin with? Because I was there?"

She rolled her eyes at him, turned to look out over the lake. "You're so conceited."

"Tell me I'm wrong."

"You're wrong."

"You're lying."

Through her teeth.

"Maybe," she conceded.

"I stayed in Knoxville because of you, too, Darby. I stayed because I wanted to be with you even before I knew that was what I wanted."

Her head jerked toward him. "Huh?"

"Even though you and I weren't a couple, I felt closer to you than to any woman I'd ever known. When I was with you I felt as if I belonged, as if I'd come home. I wasn't ready to acknowledge the attraction I felt for you, because quite frankly you scared the hell out of me, but I wasn't ready to walk away from you either."

"You let me walk away."

"I was an idiot."

Emotions doing jumping jacks inside her chest, Darby leaned her head against her knees, stared out at the water, scared to believe him. "So where does this leave us?"

"It leaves me madly in love with the woman I've come to convince to give me a second chance."

"Blake, you don't have to say things like this just because I'm pregnant."

"I'm not saying anything I don't fully believe."

"You believe you're in love with me?"

"I am in love with you."

She shook her head, thinking this was too much to take in. "You're just in shock from the changes at work. From the fact that I walked away from our business.

From the fact that our weekend together resulted in my getting pregnant. That's all this is about, Blake. You miss practicing with me."

"I do miss practicing with you, but there are certainly things I miss more about you than our working together."

"Like?" she couldn't resist asking.

"Like how you smile at me when I walk into a room. How when something perplexes you, you ask my opinion and really listen to my answer. How when my lips touch yours my entire body catches on fire."

She liked all those same things about Blake. He'd always believed in her, always been confident in her abilities, and his confidence in her had given her strength.

"Your body catches on fire when we kiss?"

He studied her. "Yours doesn't?"

She nodded. "Yes, my body catches on fire when you kiss me, but that doesn't explain why you're here."

"To convince you to let me be your partner in Alabama, Darby. With the baby, you're going to need my help."

With the baby.

Was that why he was saying all the right things? Because he'd resigned himself to a life with her because he'd gotten her pregnant? "I'll get by."

"You'd get by easier with a partner," he pointed out. "I have references. I'm sure my last partner would be willing to put in a good word for me."

"Ha-ha, too funny."

"I'm being serious, Darby." He lifted her hand to his lips, pressed a kiss to her fingertips. "I want to be a part of your life. I've never considered living in Alabama, but I do know I belong wherever you are."

Darby's heart filled with love, filled with the knowledge that Blake loved her. Not because she was pregnant, but because he hadn't been pretending that weekend any more than she had. "How do you know?"

"Because home is where the heart is, and my heart is wherever you are."

EPILOGUE

WHEN Darby and Blake had added the fully equipped birthing room, they hadn't intentionally meant to be the first couple to make use of its facilities.

"You're sure you're okay?" Blake asked at the end of her latest contraction. He moved from where he'd been between her legs, pressed a kiss to her temple.

She smiled at her worried husband. Playing the role of both expectant father and doctor perhaps hadn't been their wisest choice. But Darby wouldn't have chosen any other way. Together they'd made their precious baby, and together they would bring him into the world. Just the two of them.

Of course the moment her family realized they weren't going to show for Sunday dinner, the entire crew would no doubt descend upon them.

"I'm fine."

At the moment she really was. If he asked her after the next contraction started she'd likely tell him otherwise, though. Not that he didn't know. Her last contraction had almost had her head spinning backwards and her cursing his manhood.

Which would be a real shame, since she'd developed quite an attachment to everything about her husband.

Each morning when she woke curled next to him, looked into his happy black eyes first thing, she wanted to pinch herself. Never had she imagined she could be so happy, so loved.

Blake loved her. With all his heart and soul.

When he'd slid the golden band on her ring finger last September, while standing on the dock with their family and friends on the bank, he'd said his vows to her. Love much brighter than the sunshine on the lake had shone in his eyes. Love real and wonderful and all-consuming.

The skin on her belly began pulling tight, warning the next contraction was starting. They were getting close. So very close to welcoming their baby into the world.

"Maybe we should have driven to Pea Ridge."

Darby shook her head. For as long as she could remember she'd loved this house, had dreamed of someday owning it. Over the past few months she and Blake had made the house their home, taking pride in each room, taking pleasure in decorating the nursery just off their bedroom. Giving birth to their son here would just ice the dream cake.

Or so she'd thought, since she'd wanted to deliver naturally anyway.

As the pressure low in her abdomen continued to build, she admitted she was now seeing the attraction of an epidural.

Her stomach clenched. Sweat beaded on her forehead.

Blake glanced from the monitor strip to Darby's gritted teeth. "Breathe."

Unable to speak, she nodded, the intense pain ripping her body almost unbearable.

"Push, Darby. He's almost here."

Surely she'd die any moment from the pain?

"One more push."

Darby pushed. And pushed.

Blake's cry of awe, followed by another cry, was her reward.

"He's beautiful, Darby."

Darby's gaze went to her red-faced son, lying on her belly. Blake cut and clamped the cord, wrapped their son in a soft cotton blanket, and handed him to Darby's waiting arms.

"He's perfect, Darby. Just like you."

Darby was too wowed by the precious bundle in her arms to laugh at Blake's "Just like you." Someday soon she'd remind him of her "perfection", but for the moment she could only stare at their baby. Jet-black hair covered his round little head. Ten fingers. Ten toes. The sweetest bow-shaped mouth. Perfect.

"Victor Charles Di Angelo." Darby said her son's name out loud, holding the baby where Blake could see him, too.

"It's not too late to name him Dillon."

"Never." She faked a shudder, knowing how pleased Blake had been at her suggestion of naming their son after his grandfather and her father.

"Don't say I didn't offer." He winked, love shining in his eyes.

"I won't," she promised. "You've been offering for the past six months, despite my repeatedly telling you we aren't naming our son after a high school mascot."

Her gaze dropped back to the yawning baby in her arms. She couldn't resist touching his cheek, running the pad of her fingertip over the smooth softness. His unfocused dark blue eyes stared at her, stealing her heart.

"Welcome to your new home, darling."

"He probably liked his old home better," Blake teased, bending to kiss Darby's cheek. "I know I certainly would."

Darby shook her head. "You're crazy, City Boy."

"About you. Maybe Victor needs a baby brother."

Meeting his gaze, she smiled, knowing where he was going with this. "Named Dillon?"

Grinning, he nodded.

Darby laughed, happier than she could ever remember being. Well, except for perhaps on her wedding day. Her wedding night. And quite a few days and nights since.

She laughed again. "I love you."

"I love you, too, Darby. With all my heart." He kissed her, then placed his hand over where the baby's fist wrapped around her finger. "Thank you."

She didn't have to ask what for. She knew. Knew, and was thankful to Blake for the same things. Remembering what he'd told her that afternoon on the dock, she couldn't agree more.

Home was where the heart was—and she'd come home to stay, for her own happily-ever-after.

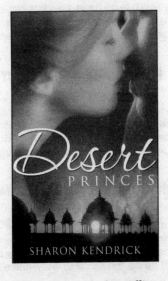

0510/03a

Coming next month

THE MIDWIFE AND THE MILLIONAIRE

by Fiona McArthur

Midwife Sophie Sullivan hates arrogant playboys like Levi Pearson! But when a helicopter crash leaves Levi and Sophie stranded together in the Australian outback, these two opposites find one thing in common – their attraction to each other!

FROM SINGLE MUM TO LADY

by Judy Campbell

Single mum Jandy Marshall wants nothing to do with high-flying city doc Patrick Sinclair. But Patrick has a big heart and a big secret... Could he be the Prince Charming this Cinderella nurse has been waiting for?

KNIGHT ON THE CHILDREN'S WARD

by Carol Marinelli

Heiress Annika Kolovsky is pursuing a career in nursing, but nothing prepares her for working alongside sexy paediatrician Ross Wyatt! Ross goes above and beyond for his tiny patients – but will he do the same to win Annika's heart?

CHILDREN'S DOCTOR, SHY NURSE

by Molly Evans

Determined to make the most of his new job, paediatrician Dr Mark Collins finds his new colleague, timid nurse Ellie Mackenzie, an unexpected attraction! As work forces their lives to intertwine, it's clear they hold the key to healing each other's heart...

On sale 4th June 2010

Available at WHSmith, Tesco, ASDA, Eason and all good bookshops.
For full Mills & Boon range including eBooks visit
www.millsandboon.co.uk

Single titles coming next month

HAWAIIAN SUNSET, DREAM PROPOSAL

by Joanna Neil

Dr Amber Shaw has come to Hawaii to recover from her past – but meeting her new patient's nephew, Dr Ethan Brookes, stirs up emotions she never thought she'd feel again. Guarded Ethan wants to keep his distance, yet he knows Amber is exactly what he needs – he'll do anything to give this doctor the happy-ever-after she deserves!

RESCUED: MOTHER AND BABY

by Anne Fraser

Daredevil doctor Logan Harris makes single mum and nurse Georgie McArthur's heart pound! But Logan will return to the army soon, determined to hide the scars no one can see – can he really be the family man Georgie craves?

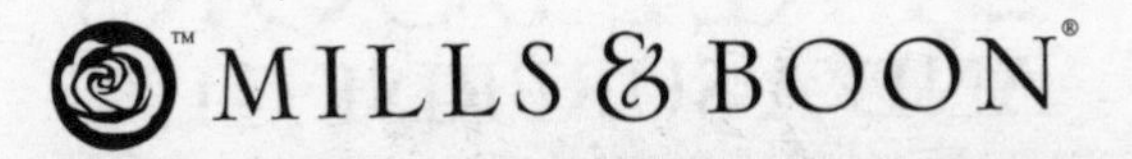
MILLS & BOON